Every Little Secret

SARAH CLARKE

ONE PLACE. MANY STORIES

HQ
An imprint of HarperCollins*Publishers* Ltd
1 London Bridge Street
London SE1 9GF

www.harpercollins.co.uk

HarperCollins*Publishers*
1st Floor, Watermarque Building, Ringsend Road
Dublin 4, Ireland

This paperback edition 2022

1
First published in Great Britain by
HQ, an imprint of HarperCollins*Publishers* Ltd 2022

ISBN: 9780008494919

MIX
Paper from
responsible sources
FSC™ C007454

SARAH CLARKE is a writer living in south-west London with her husband, children and stubbornly cheerful cockapoo. Over fifteen years, Sarah has built a successful career as a marketing copywriter, but her dream has always been to become a published author. When her youngest child started secondary school, she joined the Faber Academy Writing a Novel course to learn the craft of writing psychological thrillers. Sarah graduated in 2019. *Every Little Secret* is her second novel.

Also by Sarah Clarke

A Mother Never Lies

For Mum & Dad

Prologue

It's widely understood that unconditional love is reserved for a child.

Not for your brother or sister. Not your husband or wife. It's not even expected for your mother or father.

Unconditional love is one-way. And it can be a lonely journey.

If you're not sure that your child deserves it.

If they say hurtful things. Make selfish choices. Turn on the people who love them the most.

Can you push back against the forces of motherhood? Put your hand up and plead: *it's different for me – my child is not to be trusted anymore.*

I choose to give my unconditional love to someone else.

I don't know the answer to that question. Soon I will be tested, but not yet. Tonight I can look down at my sleeping child, so perfect and innocent in slumber, and still enjoy the miracle of motherhood. I can graze their forehead with my lips, tuck in the duvet, whisper that I love them. And mean it.

Then I can close their bedroom door behind me, walk downstairs and return to my husband.

Chapter 1

GRACE

2019

Grace gives Marcus an imploring stare, but he's immune to her plea. *Just do it*, his eyes say. No sympathy there. She stares around the room, but there's no option for escape either. She feels vulnerable, still in her pyjamas, sleepy dust lurking in the four corners of her eyes, her body trapped by their increasingly unnecessary winter duvet. She takes a deep breath and surrenders to the inevitable.

'Do you like it, Mummy?'

Grace swallows the tepid liquid and tries to ignore its pallid tone and the suspicious brown dots floating on the surface. 'It's delicious, honey. The best cup of tea I've ever tasted.'

Kaia smiles, relief etched into her face. She's always been like this, carrying the weight of an in-built urge to succeed. 'I made a card too.'

Grace takes the folded piece of cardboard from her daughter's proffered hand and sneaks a look at her husband, who's loitering behind the bed like a spare part. Perhaps that is his role today. This is the eighth Mother's Day that they've celebrated as a family, but even now, with Kaia's glittery *I love you, Mummy* sparkling from inside the card, it causes a lump to form in her throat. Theirs wasn't the smoothest route to parenthood, and Kaia still feels like a gift.

'Kaia has offered to make breakfast too,' Marcus offers, the tease in his voice apparent to everyone over the age of about 10.

'Gosh, what a treat,' Grace spars back. 'Perhaps you could make breakfast for Daddy as well. I'm sure he'd love that.' He's avoided the milky cup of tea; she doesn't see why he should miss out on burned toast or stodgy pancakes too.

'I'm not making Daddy's breakfast.'

Grace sits up straighter in bed. Kaia is usually such a Daddy's girl. 'Why not?' she asks.

'It's Mother's Day,' Kaia replies quickly, as though surprised Grace hasn't worked that out. 'It's not his turn.'

Grace relaxes back against the headboard and smiles. 'Yes, of course. Perhaps Daddy could help you make breakfast then?'

'I'm nearly 8. I can do it by myself,' Kaia announces.

'It appears that I'm redundant then,' Marcus says, holding up his hands with mock offence. 'In that case, I'll go for a shower instead.' Grace watches her husband walk into their en-suite bathroom, the muscles in his back expanding and sliding over bone as he stretches out his shoulders. His professional career ended seven years ago, but he still trains with the determination of an athlete. Then she turns back to Kaia, who's eyeing the bed with a longing expression. Grace smiles her approval, lifts up the duvet and lets Kaia wriggle inside until their heads are parallel. Kaia cups her small hand tightly over Grace's ear. 'But, Mummy,' she whispers, her warm breath crackling down the shadowy tunnel to Grace's brain. 'Will you make *my* breakfast? Because you're the best at that.'

*

4

Marcus offers to buy croissants from the local deli in the end. They sit at the breakfast table together, ripping apart the soft dough and smothering it with Grace's mother's famous damson jam, and Grace allows herself a moment of reflection. Life hasn't always been easy, and at times she's found it hard to stay optimistic, but here she is, eating delicious food in a home she loves, with her two favourite people in the world.

'Hey, Kaia, help me clear the table.' Marcus picks up the three plates dappled with crumbs, and gestures for Kaia to collect the rest of the crockery. As Grace watches Kaia walk between the table and the kitchen, she wonders what her daughter is thinking about. Usually she'd be giggling at Marcus's atrocious dad jokes by now, or calling shotgun on the washing up and barging him out of the way. But she seems miles away today. Perhaps this is just a sign of her growing up, claiming her independence one clandestine thought at a time.

Marcus looks at his watch. 'Time for rugby, Kaia. Race upstairs and get your kit on.' It was always Marcus's dream to have a child to share his biggest passion with, and he never allowed Kaia's gender to be a barrier. He signed her up with the local rugby club as soon as she was old enough, two years ago, and it's since become a Sunday morning ritual from September to April, the highlight of both their weeks.

'I don't want to go.'

Marcus looks up in surprise. 'Huh?'

'I want to stay at home with Mummy instead.'

'But you're the best player in the squad,' he reminds her, fatherly pride oozing out. 'Faster than all the boys. Awesome ball skills. You love it there. Why don't you want to go?'

Kaia shrugs and leans into Grace.

Marcus adds a bigger smile and tries a different tack. 'How about I promise to get you a hot chocolate at the end?' He winks. 'Marshmallows on top if you score a try.'

Grace watches her daughter weigh up his offer. Kaia has always loved rugby and comes home recounting stories of her achievements on the pitch. And she's a big fan of hot chocolate too. Perhaps Grace should give her one more push. 'And Grandad will love to hear all about it later,' she cajoles.

Kaia turns to looks at her. 'But what if someone kicks me in the eye?' Her expression is open and her tone innocent, but the question still causes Grace's croissant to rear up inside her stomach. She crouches down. 'It's non-contact rugby, Kaia. It's not the same game as Daddy used to play.'

Kaia stares at her, as though she's searching Grace's face for further reassurance. Silence sits between them for a while, but finally Kaia's eyeline drops and she sighs. 'Okay, Mummy.' Then she plods up the stairs and returns two minutes later in her Wimbledon Rugby Club strip.

'Thank you,' Marcus says, his low voice showing he hasn't fully recovered from Kaia's question, the arc of white skin next to his right eye a constant reminder of his own accident. He guides their daughter out of the front door and the house falls blissfully silent. The air feels looser with them gone, and Grace sucks it in.

She runs a bath, adds a generous dollop of bubble bath and climbs in. As always, her hand drops to the scar on her belly. She runs her finger along the slight ridge and wonders what it would have been like to have more children, multiple Mother's Day cards and unappetising cups of tea. But it wasn't to be. She sinks under the bubbles and listens to the gentle whoosh of water in her ears.

Chapter 2

'Darling, come in. So lovely to see you all!'

'Happy Mother's Day, Mum.' Grace pulls the older lady into a tight hug and enjoys the smell of her familiar perfume, a scent Faith has worn for as long as Grace can remember. It's one of the things she missed most during her time on the other side of the world. When they moved back from New Zealand, with a small baby and a shattered dream in tow, she knew she would need her mum's calm reassurance on standby, so they'd looked for a house as close to Wimbledon Village as they could afford. They'd ended up in Earlsfield, an area with a noisier, grimier vibe, but still only a ten-minute drive from this peaceful patch of faux countryside.

'I've cooked your favourite, roast salmon with baby tomatoes and asparagus. The daffs have all popped up in the garden and your father has got the rosé on ice. It seems we're dragging spring here, whether it's ready or not. Come through.'

Grace follows her mum down the grand hallway and into the wide kitchen and dining space at the back of the house. Her parents only moved to London when Grace and Josh left the family home; the big house in Devon with views of the sea wasn't so appealing without the energy of children to keep it alive. Henry was still working at the bank back then, so they'd decided to sell his two-bedroom flat in Pimlico and set up a permanent home in the capital. Wimbledon Village, with its thousand-acre common to explore, had been the perfect way to reacquaint themselves with city life gently.

'Is Uncle Josh coming for lunch, Granny?'

Faith's face clouds over for a moment before the smile returns. Grace can see that it's still not easy for her, the son she raised making a life for himself five thousand miles away.

'Not today I'm afraid.'

Josh had left for Stanford University in California as a fresh-faced 18-year-old undergraduate. No one expected him to stay in America, but his undergraduate degree grew into a doctorate in psychology, which then turned into a PhD and a career in academia, and he'd recently been made a professor there. Save for a few trips to Europe during the long summers of his first degree, he's hardly left America's west coast. Now the only time he comes home is at Christmas, and he only stays for a few days, always impatient to resume whatever study he's working on at the time.

'Oh.' Kaia's features sink a little, the corners of her mouth drooping with the weight of disappointment. She has always had a soft spot for her only uncle, but those feelings grew stronger on his last visit. It had snowed on Boxing Day and Josh had taken his niece sledging for the morning, with Faith joining them as official photographer. They'd returned, cheeks pink and mouths stained with hot chocolate residue, regaling her with stories of their near misses.

'Maybe one day we can go to stay with Uncle Josh in California?' Grace suggests. In truth, she knows that Marcus wouldn't approve, his dislike for her brother a rare cause of tension between them. But Kaia doesn't need to know that.

'He already invited me actually,' Kaia says with a disdain she's too young for. Grace turns to her mum to share a conspiratorial smile, but Faith is too busy putting the finishing touches to their meal.

'Well, if it isn't my second favourite mother.' A baritone voice sails across the room and Grace turns towards her father. While Faith is compact, like an expensive ornament neatly packaged away, Henry is a spreader, of whatever emotion he's feeling at that exact moment. Luckily today he's emanating respect for the matriarchy, so Grace folds into his broad chest and feels the weight of his – wholly undeserved – workman's hands on her back.

'Good to see you too, Marcus,' he continues, initiating the usual ritual: vigorous handshake, elbow grab, semi hug with hearty back slap. 'And last but not least, my little Kaia.'

'Hello, Grandad.'

Grace watches her father ruffle Kaia's hair until her attention is pulled away by her mum. 'Lunch is served!'

At Faith's instruction, they all move into the dining area. Weak sunlight is trying to edge its way through the large glass panels of the orangery and on to the long rustic oak table. As they eat, the conversation moves to Marcus's business and his upcoming pitch with Twickenham Stadium, the home of English rugby. Grace knows it would be the dream contract for his fledgling sports marketing agency, especially with his background, but it won't be an easy win. Ever since his snapped retina signalled the end of Marcus's rugby career – a mistimed kick that connected with his eye socket, as Kaia reminded him just that morning – he's struggled to find his place in the world. Grace hopes she won't have to pick up the pieces again when the results of this pitch are announced.

'What do you think, Grace, is he in with a chance?'

'Well, if anyone can persuade Twickenham to try out a new agency, it's my husband.' She catches eyes with Marcus and when he winks back at her, her belly flips. It's ridiculous that she still feels like this. They've been together for nearly fourteen years. Why does she still feel like the 16-year-old who happily accepted the bunch of flowers from him that hazy afternoon, along with his apology, and prayed he didn't notice her shaking hands?

The generous lunch leads to calls for a walk, so they don coats and scarfs against the cold wind (spring definitely hasn't arrived) and set out for the Common. The main pathways are busy – small children and exuberant puppies vying for space with the local, uniquely unflappable, horses – but Henry and Faith have mapped every trail in their heads over the past decade, so quickly guide them to a quieter area with narrow tracks and more tree cover. Grace weaves her arm through her mother's and enjoys the sound of their footsteps in sync.

'How's school?' Faith asks the routine question lightly.

'Well, fine, I think. But there was an incident.'

'Oh?'

'It was nothing really, but Kaia hit a girl in the face with a netball. Rebecca. It was an accident of course, but it gave her a nosebleed.'

'A risk you take when you play, I suppose.'

'Exactly! That's what I said. But Rebecca told her friends that Kaia had done it on purpose.'

'On purpose?' Faith's face twists in disapproval. 'That's not very kind of her.'

'No. But unfortunately Kaia didn't deny it, just walked away from the argument. And now none of her friends are talking to her.'

'Poor Kaia,' Faith murmurs. Then she purses her lips and falls silent again, her mind seemingly elsewhere.

They carry on like that for a while, and Grace turns her attention to her daughter. Kaia's walking slightly separately from them all, eyeing the undergrowth, delving in when she spots a good throwing stick for the imaginary dog that she's determined to make real one day. Grace smiles as she remembers the petition Kaia made to her and Marcus last autumn. She'd lined up all her soft toys – the dogs centre stage of course – and explained that the majority of the family voted in favour of a dog. Marcus had gone puppy-eyed too at that point. Grace had been the strong one, standing firm against the tide of Kaia's pleas, but it hadn't been easy, and her willpower is waning. Maybe a chocolate brown cocker spaniel, she muses.

A few moments later, her idyllic thoughts are interrupted by Kaia's voice filtering through the trees. She's walked deeper into the woods. 'Hey, Daddy, look what I've found!'

Marcus peers in her direction. 'What is it?'

'A perfect climbing tree!'

'Perfect, you say? I think I'll be the judge of that.' Marcus laughs and follows her into the woods. Grace's heart beats a bit faster. She knows that kids need to explore, but climbing is the one pursuit that Grace struggles with, tainted by a childhood fall of her own. She can barely see them now, just their shadows moving through the leaves. She turns back towards her parents and tries to shrug off the sense of foreboding that sits between her shoulders.

'It sounds like he's in with a good chance on this Twickenham pitch,' Henry observes, looking towards the blur of his son-in-law between the branches.

'He's worked really hard on it. I know he'd do a brilliant job.' Grace can see them in her peripheral vision, two dark shadows swaying upwards towards the sky. The dull sound of rustling leaves. She blinks a memory away.

'Well, we should all keep our fingers crossed. He deserves a break.'

Grace nods her head, takes a breath. They're high now, too high.

'Are you okay, darling?' Faith knows what Grace is thinking about, what's causing the sweat to form on her palms. 'She'll be fine, you know. Marcus won't let her fall.'

'I know,' Grace plans to say, but she doesn't have time.

Not before the scream that twists her neck round, allows her to see the shadow tumbling.

Not before the thud of a small body hitting the ground explodes in her ears.

11

Chapter 3

Grace stares at Kaia and wonders what the noise is, drilling into her head like an air raid siren. It's them of course, she realises, the ambulance cutting a path through the south-west London traffic. Kaia's hand is hanging limply off the side of the narrow bed, and Grace picks it up, lets it drop into her own palm. With Kaia's head strapped tightly to a neck collar and her body lying stiff against a spinal board, it's easiest to focus on her hand. The tiny tremors of wheels racing over tarmac rise up through them both. 'It's okay, baby. You're going to be fine,' Grace promises, smiling through the lie. Because she knows in her heart what the doctor at A&E will tell her. That Kaia has suffered a spinal fracture falling out of the tree, and that her life will never be the same again.

'I'm scared, Mummy,' Kaia murmurs. 'Everything hurts.'

Grace hears the rustle of a stiff jacket, then feels the press of an arm nudging against her. She can't remember the paramedic's name. She should do – he told her more than once. But it's gone now.

'Hey, Kaia,' he says, tilting his face to meet her eyes. 'You know, it's okay to be a bit scared. And I'm sure it feels weird being in that hard collar. But we're going to be at St George's in a couple of minutes and they have the best doctors in the world, so you're going to be very well looked after.'

'The best?' Kaia whispers, widening her eyes.

Grace feels tears smart again, but this time out of relief. Because this is the Kaia she knows, the child who values first place. Perhaps she's going to be fine, back on the rugby pitch next weekend. *You gave us such a fright, Kaia.*

'Absolutely,' the paramedic responds. Maybe he's called Lee, Grace thinks. 'And I'm going to help you with the pain right now. Do you know what a cannula is, Kaia?'

Kaia tries to shake her head but realises she can't. 'No.'

'It's a tiny tube that goes into the back of your hand. And once it's there, I can give you some pain relief through the tube that will make you feel loads better.' Lee smiles at Kaia then turns to look at Grace. 'May I?'

Grace knows she must let go of Kaia's hand. But she doesn't want to. She has a strange sense that if she breaks their connection now, with Kaia strapped down, in pain, it will be broken for good. Seven and a half years of construction knocked down in this one act. But that's crazy. All she's doing is hindering her daughter's path to pain relief. She drops Kaia hand onto the bed and backs away.

*

The metal wheels of the trolley clatter against the solid floor of the hospital corridor. Grace has been to this A&E twice before: when Kaia's temperature spiked at forty degrees as a baby, and again when she slipped off her friend's ancient swing and suffered a greenstick fracture in her wrist. But Grace doesn't recognise this entrance, or the triage nurse's swift instruction that rings in her ears. *Paediatric trauma, resus please.*

The nurse pushes against clear double doors with her back and Kaia is wheeled into a large, white room. Medical equipment hangs off every wall, gleaming under the severe strip lighting overhead. Grace blinks. Two beds are hidden behind a flimsy curtain, low voices slipping underneath, but the other six are empty. Pure starched sheets waiting patiently for carnage to arrive.

'This is Kaia Windsor; 7 years old,' Lee explains to the doctor who greets them, a slight woman in pale blue scrubs with black curls piled on top of her head and a sliver of a nose ring. 'Kaia fell approximately 2 metres from a tree,' he continues. 'Potential KO on impact but conscious when we arrived. Complaining of head, neck and back pain. Temporary loss of sensation in upper limbs but regained now; 360 milligrams of analgesia administered en route. On my count ...'

Grace feels like the distant cousin at a wedding. Etiquette demands that you're invited, but nobody cares if you're there. The feeling that started in the ambulance, the severing of their invisible umbilical cord, is getting stronger and she's almost over-whelmed by an urge to shove the medics out of the way and reclaim her daughter. She makes a fist with her hand and pushes it into her midriff.

'Hi, Kaia, nice to meet you. I'm Dr Gupta. Sorry about this.' The doctor wafts her hand towards the neck brace. 'I'm going to do a few quick checks now, then Seb here will take you for what's called a CT scan. It's basically a photo of your head and neck. Nothing scary. All being well, we'll have this off you within the hour. Does that sound good?'

Kaia smiles at the doctor and whispers 'yes'. As Grace watches the doctor at work, listening to Kaia's chest with a stethoscope, shining a pen light in her eyes, Grace can tell that Kaia already trusts her. But does she feel the same way? Is the doctor's gentle optimism enough to fend off bad news?

Her reverie is broken by a familiar voice from outside the room.

'I'm looking for Kaia Windsor. She was brought in by ambu-lance.' Grace can hear the panic in Marcus's tone and she feels torn. Part of her wants to go and comfort him, guide him to Kaia's side. But she can't leave her daughter.

'And you're Mr Windsor, Kaia's father?' a female voice responds, a passing nurse or the receptionist at the desk.

'Yes, I'm Kaia's father,' Marcus says irritably.

'Mrs Windsor?'

Grace's attention snaps back to the room.

'I'm happy for Kaia to be moved so my colleague will take her down to X-ray now. They'll do a CT scan first and then X-ray her spine.'

As the doctor steps back, a space emerges by the bed and Grace quickly shifts into it, reaching for her daughter's hand again. Kaia's eyelids are heavy, perhaps a mix of pain relief and the adrenalin finally wearing off, but she smiles, and Grace can feel her heart physically swelling.

'She won't be long. And the scans will give us a much clearer picture of what's going on,' Dr Gupta coaxes.

Grace sighs. 'Okay,' she whispers, and feels Kaia's hand slip away for a second time.

*

Grace leans back against the hard plastic chair and closes her eyes as Marcus's voice babbles like a brook after a rainstorm.

'I shouldn't have taken her so high. What the hell was I thinking? It seemed so sturdy, I just didn't think. What if there's permanent damage? I could never forgive myself.' He leans forward and drops his forehead into the heels of his hands. 'She just kept telling me to go higher,' he half whispers.

'Listen, Marcus, it's not your fault.' Grace drops her hand onto his back and realises that she means it. Yes, perhaps he did take Kaia too high, not think through the dangers. But hindsight is a wonderful thing. And she knows how dreadful he must be feeling right now. 'And she's going to be fine,' she adds forcefully. 'She's got feeling everywhere – that's a really good sign. She'll be back from X-ray soon; we just need to be patient.'

Marcus lifts his head and looks at her gratefully. His eyes shine with a film of tears, but Grace knows they won't grow any bigger. Marcus never cries. Not even when his lifelong dream was shattered, and his eyesight was in question. 'I love you, Grace Windsor.'

'I love you too.' She leans against his wide chest and stares at the double doors, counting the seconds until they open. Eventually Dr Gupta appears through them, but the easy optimism has gone from her face, replaced with a more serious expression. Grace's stomach lurches in response. She feels a crazy urge to run away, to twist out of her chair and slam through the fire escape.

'Mrs Windsor, could I have a word?'

Grace senses Marcus stand up next to her and reach down for her hand. She's glad he's here. They've always been stronger as a team.

'Actually, could I speak to Mrs Windsor alone? It will only take a moment.'

Grace looks across at Marcus, then back to the doctor. Is it bad news? Is she keeping it from Marcus to protect him, the father who let the accident happen?

'Oh, okay.' Marcus shrugs, pretending not to mind, not wanting to argue with the woman currently in charge of his daughter's health, but Grace can see the tension in his shoulders. 'Maybe I'll get us a coffee from the machine,' he says, but he doesn't move, and the three of them just stand there, staring at each other. 'Look, I just need to know,' he says eventually. 'How she is.'

Dr Gupta's expression softens slightly. 'Sorry, of course you do. All the scans came back clear. We've taken the brace off.'

The clamp that had been holding Grace's heart in its grip bursts open and she gasps with relief. 'Oh wow, thank God. So she's going to be okay? Can I see her?'

'There's no damage to her spine, and yes, she's going to be

okay. She's asleep at the moment. Of course you can see her, but it would be good if we could have a quick chat first?'

Marcus lifts his hands in acquiescence, a wide grin spreading across his face. 'I'll get those coffees. Now I know she's okay, I might even drink it.'

Grace watches her husband lumber down the corridor, then she turns to the doctor and looks at her quizzically. 'What did you want to talk to me about?'

'Mrs Windsor, Kaia has quite a large contusion on the side of her head, and she's been complaining of a headache.'

Grace's skin prickles. 'But she's okay. You said she's okay?'

'And she vomited in the X-ray bay.'

'What does that mean?' Grace whispers.

'Headache, vomiting, tiredness. These are all symptoms of concussion, and the contusion backs up that diagnosis.'

Grace's shoulders relax a notch. Marcus suffered concussion plenty of times when he was playing rugby. A few days' rest and he was back on the pitch. 'But concussion heals, right?' she asks, searching for eye contact with the doctor, impatient for the clinician to lighten her expression.

'It tends to have a more severe effect on children in the short term as their brains are still developing, but yes it heals.'

'That's good news then, isn't it?' Grace doesn't understand why Dr Gupta couldn't have said all this to Marcus too.

The doctor sighs and leans against the wall, obscuring a poster on what to do if you suspect a stroke. *Act FAST.* 'Concussion can cause confusion as well, and I'm trying to work out whether that's what's at play here.'

'She's confused? What about?'

'Kaia told Seb something on the way to X-ray. Then when I asked her about it, she repeated the story. She's showing clear signs of concussion, so she may well have just confused things in her mind. But her claim was very clear, and she sounded so sure.'

17

'Her claim?' Grace asks. 'What do you mean?'

Dr Gupta shifts round and looks straight into Grace's eyes. 'Kaia claims that her falling out of the tree wasn't an accident. She said her father pushed her.'

Chapter 4

MARCUS

2005

Marcus picks at the curling egg and cress sandwich and wishes the whole event was over. It's not like he's embarrassed by his parents; in certain circumstances they can even be impressive. But they just don't fit in here, among the stiff collars and glittering jewels of his friends' parents.

'Mate, this place is amazing. Gets me every time. I can't believe it's almost over; I'm still struggling to work out how you got a spot here in the first place.'

His dad's voice is loud, the New Zealand twang rising above the general hum of conversation. But his eyes dance with pride and Marcus can't remember the last time his grin stretched so wide. His mum isn't hiding her awe either, staring dumbstruck at the concert hall beyond the Headmaster's Lawn, the curved glass and brick structure where the awards ceremony will soon be taking place. He thinks back to when he felt like that, two years earlier when he started in the sixth form at Chilford School on a part scholarship, part bursary. How hard it was to pretend this way of life felt normal to him. He should give them a break. 'I guess you could take some credit.'

'For chucking a rugby ball at you before you learned to walk?'

'And taking me to the club on Sunday mornings.'

'You didn't exactly give him much choice there,' his mum interjects, her attention back with them. 'You'd be dressed in your strip before the two of us were even out of bed.' She laughs then, but it's more like a titter, her hand playing with the high collar of her halter-neck maxi-dress. His mum never wears dresses and Marcus can tell she feels uncomfortable in the one she's bought specially for today, its long skirt fluttering in the wind. He wants to tell her that it suits her, makes her look beautiful even. But she'd just laugh and slap the compliment away, unimpressed. Her philosophy has always been that life's too short to bother about your appearance, and she spends most of her time in some kind of soft denim.

'Mr and Mrs Stuart, good to see you again.'

Marcus watches the school's Director of Rugby shake hands with both his parents, his dad trying (and failing) to match the power behind Mr Morgan's gesture, his mum taking a more pliant approach. The ex-Welsh prop-forward weighs about eighteen stone and claims a one-hundred-inch chest, so his mother's seems like the more sensible choice.

'I'm going to miss your boy on the rugby field. He's been a great captain this past year,' he says, fondness for Marcus shining on his ruddy face. 'In fact, there's a rumour flying around that he's more talented than me.' Mr Morgan winks at him and Marcus tries not to let the euphoria show on his face. Everyone knows he wants to be a professional rugby player, as well as his ambition to play as an international for the All Blacks in New Zealand, the world's best rugby team.

But nobody can understand just how much he wants it, how fiercely the fire burns.

'Just as well – not sure he could do much else,' his dad responds, chuckling at his own joke. It riles Marcus, maybe because it's true. While he was thrilled to be awarded a fully funded place at Chilford, it was always assumed by everyone – himself included – that he'd study for a Sports BTEC rather than attempt more academic A levels. For all his rugby potential, he is a living, breathing one-trick pony.

'I don't know, he's not bad at ping pong either.'

His mum and dad both laugh in response and Marcus feels his mood sink lower. A gong sounds in the distance; it's time to go inside. As captain of the First XV, he'll be required on stage to pick up a trophy for the team, but there's an award for Sportsman of the Year as well, and he knows he's in with a chance of winning that. As he walks inside the vast building, butterflies form in his belly and his blazer suddenly feels tight across his shoulders. Like his mum craving her denim cut-offs, he wishes he was in his studs, kicking up turf on a rugby pitch rather than here, in his Next suit and house tie. As the crowd of guests compresses inside the hall, he herds his mum and dad away from the most glamorous sets of parents and manages to seat them without the threat of further chit-chat.

The academic awards come first, while the audience's attention is still fresh enough for a physics prize to sound interesting. Girls take the lion's share of course, and Marcus enjoys watching them climb the stairs to the stage, the hot weather giving them the perfect excuse to inch their skirts higher. He's never had a problem attracting girls when he wants to, and he wants to fairly regularly, but he's yet to meet anyone exciting enough to draw him away from his first love. Rugby.

'And the Morrisby Media Award – for his compelling documentary film about teamwork in sport – goes to Joshua Windsor.'

Marcus claps with a bit more enthusiasm as his Lower Sixth roommate, and best friend, walks onto the stage. Every sixth former is put in a shared room for their first year, and he'd arrived that first Sunday afternoon to find Josh already unpacked, lying on one of the beds in his allocated room. Marcus hadn't been looking forward to sharing with anyone; sixteen years with a fairly decent bedroom and a lock on the door meant that he'd got used to valuing his own space. But Josh and him connected pretty quickly. They must have been put together because of where they lived, adjacent villages on the south Devon coast, and it did give them some common ground initially. But they'd soon moved on to other subjects, including their mutual love of winning. When Josh suggested they challenge the other residents of their house to a table tennis tournament, and the pair of them came out on top, their friendship was sealed.

Marcus is pleased for Josh winning the media prize, especially as he had quite a starring role in Josh's film, but it still niggles a bit. Because Josh could just as easily have won the French prize (he spent a summer in Montpelier and came back pretty much fluent) or the racket sports prize (he beats everyone at tennis, including the teachers) or the science prize (he's predicted top grades in chemistry and biology A levels). Josh is the very opposite of a one-tricky pony. They catch eyes as Josh strolls back to his seat and Marcus forces himself to mouth 'congratulations'. But his friend just laughs in response, like the award means nothing to him, and Marcus wants to kick himself. He's been living in this world for two years, but he's still making basic mistakes.

The stage is finally cleared for Act Two, and the Head of Sport struts onto the stage, his tracksuit-clad entourage lining up behind him with a mix of trophies in their hands. Marcus sits through the cricket awards, the prizes for Chilford's best equestrians and then the rugby awards where he collects the trophy for his team. And then the crescendo moment. When Mr Morgan calls his name as Sportsman of the Year, his parents clap with unconstrained pride (luckily he'd remembered to ban whooping) and on the inside he does the same.

But Josh's flippant smile is still fresh in his mind. There's no way he's revealing what he actually feels. With all the restraint he can muster, he lopes coolly on to stage and accepts the award with a nonchalant wave.

Chapter 5

GRACE

2019

'Pushed her?' Grace repeats, incredulous. 'Kaia fell; it was an accident,' she blusters. Why does she feel guilty all of a sudden? Like she's covering for him? Marcus can't have caused Kaia's fall. She knows him; it's not possible.

'She said that she was asking to quit her rugby club, telling him that she doesn't like it anymore, and he got angry with her.'

A memory rears up unbidden, Marcus losing his temper. Grace runs a finger across her top lip, then blinks the image away. It was years ago, and only once. 'He wouldn't,' she says. 'He doesn't.' And it's true. Even when Kaia was a toddler and would scream because her toast was cut into squares not triangles, or she was given milk in the wrong beaker, Marcus never got cross with her. He would pause for moment to compose himself, and then that conciliatory smile always reappeared. Guaranteed. She forces herself to imagine them in the tree, Kaia losing her balance, her fingers sliding through the leaves. 'He would have reached for

24

Kaia when she fell,' Grace murmurs. 'The fear, the trauma – could that have distorted her memory?'

'Yes, it could have done,' Dr Gupta acknowledges. 'As I said, Kaia is showing other signs of concussion, so she may be confused about how she fell too. But I hope you understand that I need to be sure. The argument that preceded it, does that sound plausible to you?'

Grace's chest constricts and she wonders vaguely if she'll ever breathe again. Because of course it's plausible. She knows how excited Marcus was to introduce Kaia to rugby, and his pride every time she outperforms the other kids in her squad. He would be devastated if she wanted to give it up. But enough to push her, to risk her life? No. She thinks about how close they are, how upset he is, and shakes the idea out of her head. He wouldn't. Her chest releases and she inhales. 'They might have had a conversation about rugby, but nothing more. Marcus wouldn't start an argument halfway up a tree. He's not that stupid.'

Silence hangs between them for a while, the white noise of hospital machinery providing an ominous backing track, but Dr Gupta finally breaks it. 'Okay, fine.' Her voice scratches and Grace wonders if it's disapproval. 'I needed to check, but if you're certain that Kaia's mistaken, and that she's not at risk from her father, then I'm comfortable attributing it to confusion caused by her concussion.'

Something heavy drops onto Grace's shoulders and she almost buckles under its weight. Is she certain? The doctor said herself that Kaia's concussion offers a credible explanation, and Grace knows Marcus wouldn't hurt her. So why is she feeling like she's failed her daughter? She peers inside the double doors. 'Can I see Kaia now?'

The doctor's tone lightens a notch. 'Yes, of course you can. I'll take you in.' She pushes the right-hand door open and tilts her head towards the bed that Kaia was first transferred to, except it's now hidden behind a concertina curtain stretched around a metal frame. 'She was asleep a moment ago, which is good – it gives her body chance to recover – but you're welcome to go in.'

Grace smiles her thanks, but before she has chance to walk over, a hand slips inside her own.

'Just in time,' Marcus says, their matching clammy palms sliding over each other.

Grace looks up at her husband and gets a mild waft of coffee from his breath. 'Kaia's asleep apparently,' she says stiffly. She's spent the last few minutes defending her husband, but now that he's here, Grace feels a wave of animosity towards him. As though she suddenly *could* imagine him lashing out at Kaia for spoiling his dreams.

'I just want to see her without that horrible collar on,' he murmurs, his voice heavy with emotion. Grace's shoulders drop and she squeezes his hand.

'Me too.'

The curtain grinds on its rail as Dr Gupta pulls it round. Kaia is fast asleep and Grace instantly feels tears well in her eyes. Because her daughter looks normal again. Almost. There's a lump to the left of her forehead, and the cannula is still plastered to her wrist, but otherwise Kaia could be in her bed at home. A tiny smile floats at the corners of her mouth.

'And you've checked everything?' Marcus asks. 'She's definitely going to be okay?'

'The CT scan and X-rays came back clear. There are signs of concussion.' Dr Gupta pauses, gives Grace a look that she tries to ignore. 'So Kaia will need to rest, mentally and physically, for the next few days. But otherwise, yes. She's going to be okay.'

Marcus runs his hand over his head, the short spikes of his dark hair separating between his fingers. 'Thank f— I mean, thank you, doctor. Thank you so much. God, people like you. What you do. Amazing.' The relief in his voice is palpable, but a tiny voice in Grace's head wonders whether it's caused by love, or guilt. 'When can we take her home?' he continues.

'Well, I'd like to keep her in overnight, just for observation. Our bed manager is arranging for her to be moved to our children's neurology ward.'

'Neurology? I thought you said she was fine?' Marcus's voice quickens.

'Concussion has a number of side effects,' Dr Gupta starts. 'The ones Kaia is displaying suggest that her concussion might be quite significant. I'm still confident that she will make a full recovery, but I'd like to keep an eye on her for the next twenty-four hours. Just to be on the safe side.' She brushes her hand against Grace's arm. 'Anyway, I'll let you know when we're ready to move her.' Then she turns away from them both and disappears behind the curtain.

Marcus sighs, then leans against the bed and looks down at Kaia's sleeping form. 'So what did the doctor want with just you?'

Grace knew Marcus would ask this as soon as he got the chance – of course he'd want to know why Dr Gupta asked to speak to her alone – but she still hasn't prepared an answer to his question. Does she tell him what Kaia has been saying? Should she ask him if there is any truth in it? 'She wanted to tell me about the concussion,' she offers.

'That's hardly a mother-only conversation.' Marcus picks up Kaia's hand and strokes the curve of her fingers.

Grace walks around to the other side of the bed to avoid eye contact with him. Careful not to disturb her daughter, she perches on the side of the mattress. 'Kaia was showing signs of confusion, saying some strange things. Dr Gupta wanted to check whether they could be true.'

'Oh? What strange things?'

Grace hesitates. She knows that Marcus will be devastated at the thought of Kaia blaming him for her injuries. He feels guilty enough about her fall happening on his watch as it is. But she doesn't want to lie to him. And she needs to see how he'll react – she deserves that reassurance. 'Listen, this will sound crazy but …' A rustling from the bed distracts them both and Grace stops mid-sentence.

'Mummy?' Kaia's eyes are only half open and still a little dazed.

Grace shakes the sordid accusation out of her head and smiles at her daughter. 'Hi, baby. Look, Daddy's here too.' Kaia's eyes shift across the bed, then back again. Her expression is hard to read. 'How are you feeling?'

Kaia lifts her hand, runs her fingers tentatively across the mound of bruising. 'My head hurts.'

'It took quite a whack when you landed. But the doctor says you're going to be fine. My tough little warrior.' Marcus sinks onto the bed and Grace feels his weight pulling them all down. His eyes are dancing with happiness, but Kaia's remain still.

'Daddy?' she says eventually.

'Yes sweetheart?'

'I told the doctor that you pushed me.'

Marcus tilts his head, creases his brow. 'Pushed you when?'

'Out of the tree.' Her voice is louder now, clearer. 'That you pushed me and then I fell.'

Marcus lets out a small, nervous laugh. 'Why would you say that? Of course I didn't push you.' He turns towards Grace, realisation creeping onto his face. 'Hang on, is this what the doctor wanted to talk to you about? Does she think I caused this?' He stands up. 'Jeez, Kaia, I'm very sorry that I didn't stop you from falling, but that's a pretty low thing to do, blaming me.'

Grace looks down at her daughter, sees genuine fear in Kaia's eyes. Horror punches her in the chest. Could it actually be true? She whips her head around. 'Marcus, don't be cross with Kaia.' She tries to whisper but it comes out as a hiss. 'She's the one in pain, for Christ's sake.' She turns back to Kaia. 'Daddy loves you, baby. Do you think that maybe he was reaching for you as you fell and you got confused? Could that be it?'

'No.' Kaia crosses her arms.

'Come on, Kaia, please.' Marcus's voice is softer now, conciliatory.

'I'm not confused, Mummy. Daddy pushed me, I promise.'

Grace's head spins. What the hell is happening? Surely Marcus wouldn't lash out at Kaia? But Kaia wouldn't lie about something like this either. It must be a symptom of her concussion; it's the only explanation that makes sense. But she sounds so certain.

'And you should believe me, Mummy,' Kaia continues, her brow furrowing. 'Because I think he pushed you too?'

Chapter 6

Grace hangs her towel over the bright red wooden door of the changing cubicle and steels herself for what's coming. Brain freeze. Then she walks to the deep end, pulls on her swimming cap and goggles, and dives in. As she resurfaces, her lungs scream at her, furious that she would expose them to such icy cold water. And so early in the morning, before the weak spring sunshine has had chance to wake up. She sucks at the slightly warmer air, then dips her head back under, cutting a path through the ninety-metre outdoor pool with her fingertips.

Grace began swimming at Tooting Bec Lido during the summer after they moved to Earlsfield. She quickly fell in love with its generous size, stubbornly cold temperatures even when London sizzles in thirty-degree heat, and the uniquely cheerful art deco changing cubicles that line each side of the pool. When the pool closed to the public that autumn, she joined the South London Swimming Club so that she could visit all year round, and she still loves starting her day here. Although she's not as brave as some of the members – when there's snow on the ground, she gives it a miss.

By her third length her brain has thawed, and her mind wanders to the terrifying accusation that Kaia made in her hospital bed just over a week ago. Grace has to admit that, for a moment, she did start to think that Marcus had pushed Kaia. That it was an impulsive reaction to their daughter wanting to give up rugby mixed with the stress of his upcoming pitch. So when Kaia started talking about him pushing Grace as well, and she'd realised it was just the concussion talking after all, she'd felt terrible for even considering it a possibility.

Kaia had been moved up to the ward after that and had quickly fallen back to sleep. The atmosphere between Grace and Marcus had been a little awkward at first, both of them preferring to watch the air ambulance land on the roof opposite them rather than discuss what Kaia had said. But eventually Marcus had apologised for handling it badly, and Grace had brushed it off as understandable. And they'd slipped back into the familiar groove of their marriage. After a while, the nurse had quietly asked Marcus to leave, and Grace had settled into the chair-cum-bed beside Kaia for the night.

Kaia had woken up a bit brighter the next day and was discharged early afternoon with instructions to rest for a week. As her bruise moved from slate grey to purple, green and finally yellow, she'd slowly got her energy back. By Wednesday she'd stopped sleeping in the daytime, and on Saturday Grace had even caught her bouncing on the trampoline. Kaia had stopped talking about Marcus pushing her, and if Grace didn't dwell too long on what was missing, she could believe that her daughter had fully healed.

Grace checks her watch – a waterproof Apple Watch that Marcus gave her for Christmas – and calculates that she can fit in five more lengths before heading back home to drive Kaia to school. Her first day back after her fall. When they started thinking about Kaia's education, Grace had suggested the local state primary in Earlsfield – somewhere they could walk to – but Marcus had been adamant that their daughter should have a private education throughout. He explained that he didn't want

Kaia to ever feel like he did, the state-school kid gate-crashing a very exclusive party, and Grace hadn't wanted to argue the point. That it would be her income paying the fees was immaterial to both of them.

She powers through her final length and enjoys the thud of her heart against her chest as she pushes out of the water. The air temperature isn't much higher than the water's, and she shivers as she jogs back to the tiny changing cubicle, nodding and smiling at other hardy swimmers en route. She rough-dries herself, before pulling on her fleece trackies and trainers. Then she unlocks her bike from the railings, clicks her helmet tight and cycles the three miles back home.

*

Grace drops down one of the residential streets that links up with Webbs Road and parks at the bottom. 'Here we are.' She watches Kaia unclick her seatbelt and slip slowly out of her car seat. The bruise on the side of her head is now a weak yellow, like corn scorched by the sun, but it's still clear enough for Kaia to earn kudos points from her friends. As Grace climbs out of the black Land Rover (Marcus called it his one indulgence when his insurance finally paid out), that thought reminds her of the conversation she had with Kaia's teacher the week before the accident. It feels like a lifetime ago now, and Grace hopes that the friendship issues she mentioned have been forgotten. Kaia will need her friends today. They walk hand in hand towards the converted church where Kaia's school is situated.

With drop-off only moments away, Grace has a sudden urge to postpone it, to think of something vitally important to say that will keep her daughter close for a few moments more. 'We didn't have any cheese triangles, so I'm afraid you've got ham in your sandwich today.'

'That's okay.'

'And remember, no PE for another week.'

'I know.'

Grace pauses at the school gates. 'Will you be okay, Kaia? You're sure your head doesn't hurt anymore?'

'Can I go inside now?'

Grace sucks at the air. The truth is that while Kaia has healed physically, something has changed inside her, as though her mind took the scarring that her body managed to avoid. Nothing too obvious. But where once she was warm and malleable, now she's become a bit cooler. More brittle. And while both of them have witnessed this change in her, it's Marcus who's suffered the most from her new indifference. A wave of frustration washes over Grace. 'You know, Daddy has missed hanging out with you when you've been at home. How about you do something fun together later?' Kaia shrugs and look away. Grace clenches her jaw and guides Kaia towards her line. 'Great, that's settled then.'

Year 3 is the youngest in the Upper School and the two classes queue up either side of the main entrance. Kaia is in Miss West's class – a middle-aged woman with a short bob, perfect teeth, and possibly borderline OCD – and she's waiting at the top to chaperone the children inside. Grace has already spoken to her about Kaia's particular needs on her first day back at school, so she releases her daughter to the end of the line, and watches her walk inside.

*

Grace is at her desk by 9 a.m. with a large bowl of mango covered in granola and Greek yoghurt, and a pint-sized mug of piping-hot tea. When she was studying for her degree in English Literature, spending weeks dissecting medieval poetry and the Victorian classics, she didn't imagine that she'd end up writing children's phonics books for a living. Turning primitive sounds into stories enticing enough to keep 4-, 5- and 6-year-olds engaged. But she wrote one as a favour for a publishing friend when she was acting the rugby wife in New Zealand and was quickly commissioned to write ten more. Things really took off when her books were noticed by the US Department of Education in Washington, and now her *Just Imagine* book series is recognised by half the English-speaking families around the world.

With Kaia off school, she didn't get much chance to write last week, so she'd been looking forward to starting a new story today, crawling into the mind of a young reader and seeing what adventure her main character Quin might go on next (tackle the *kwu* sound early, the phonics expert had advised). But as she stares at her laptop, she realises that she can't settle to it. The only child she can picture in her head is Kaia, and she can't stop wondering where her warm and loving daughter has gone.

In the end, Grace manages to answer a few emails. There's one from her literary agent discussing new markets, and an invite to talk at a publishing event. There's also one from her accountant, a statement attached with her earnings for the last quarter. Grace knows how many authors struggle to make ends meet – authors who write exquisite, award-winning prose but still have to supplement their income – so she finds it strange how much money a few heavily illustrated pages can make her. She spends the rest of the day googling concussion. Reading horror stories about children feeling isolated, sad, angry, unable to concentrate. It's addictive though, so she's relieved when 2.45 p.m. arrives and she's finally forced to close her laptop.

But the feeling of relief is short-lived. As soon as she walks through the school gate, Miss West beckons her over, her perfect teeth hidden behind a stern-faced glare. Grace feels exposed as she crosses the playground, her heart thumping with each step.

'Kaia, go and play for a minute. I want to talk to your mummy about something.'

Kaia stares at her feet and twists on her toes. Grace wonders for a moment if she's going to resist, defy her teacher's instruction.

But then she clicks her tongue, a small protest perhaps, and walks towards the school play area. Grace watches her go, then turns back to face the teacher.

'Ms Windsor, Kaia did something today that we're taking very seriously.'

The thuds inside Grace's chest grow louder. 'Oh?'

'She grabbed the chair directly in front of her in tutor time and yanked it backwards. It was a miracle Lily didn't break her back.'

'Jesus,' slips out of Grace's mouth. Lily has been Kaia's best friend since Reception. She takes a breath and settles herself. 'Is she hurt? Will she be okay?'

'Luckily the chair scuffed the desk, which broke its fall,' Miss West explains, with the air of someone slightly disappointed that the outcome wasn't more dramatic. 'It gave Lily enough time to twist herself free. But that doesn't reduce the seriousness of the incident.'

'Of course not,' Grace agrees through gritted teeth. 'I assume they argued? That Lily did something to upset Kaia first?' She knows there's no excuse for such dangerous behaviour, but Kaia wouldn't have pulled Lily's chair without provocation. Surely?

'Absolutely nothing. I was talking to the children about online safety – you know stranger danger and so on. And the next thing I know, Kaia is lunging forward over her desk and grabbing Lily's chair.'

Grace's looks away. She can see Kaia now, staring through the fence that runs along the perimeter of the school. Like she's searching for an escape route.

'Now, I appreciate that Kaia has been through a traumatic incident, but that doesn't excuse this kind of behaviour.'

'Did she apologise?' Grace asks, her tone clipped. 'To Lily?'

'Unfortunately not. In fact, she didn't seem remorseful in the least. And when I asked for an explanation, she said something very strange.'

The skin on the back of Grace's neck tingles. She scratches it. 'Something strange?' she manages.

'She said that her father made her do it. And that he'd also caused her fall from the tree.'

'That's crazy,' Grace whispers.

'Ms Windsor, I'm not suggesting there's any truth to it. Just that it's an odd thing to say.'

'The doctor said that Kaia's concussion could affect her memory,' Grace offers weakly. 'And that she might do and say things out of character.'

'I understand that, I really do,' Miss West soothes. 'But I'm afraid I have a duty of care towards all the children in my class, not just Kaia.'

'I'll talk to her.'

'And there was the incident before her fall, when she hit Rebecca in the face with a netball.'

Grace draws in a breath. 'You said that was an accident.'

'I thought so at the time. But after today's incident, well, I don't know. And Rebecca was always adamant that Kaia did it on purpose.' Miss West pauses. 'Ms Windsor, I hope you don't mind me asking, but are there any issues at home?'

Of course she minds. Grace thinks about the rocky journey they've been on since Marcus's injury. Moving back to London, the jobs that didn't work out, the way he can't hold her gaze when the school invoice comes through, always addressed to her rather than him. And how her not taking his name when they got married still grates on him five years on, even though he says he understands why.

But there is so much fun too. Camping holidays with friends, the three of them heading off on cycling trips down the Thames, or visits to the Stoop to watch Kaia's favourite rugby team in action (which, much to Marcus's horror, is the local Harlequins and not his old team the Exeter Chiefs). And the simple things. Pancakes on a Sunday, hours spent in the park trying to throw an egg-shaped ball with some degree of accuracy, flip competitions on the trampoline. 'No, everything's fine at home.'

But the reassurance doesn't penetrate. 'I spoke with Mrs Armstrong this afternoon,' Miss West says. Grace tenses. The school head teacher. 'She suggested that Kaia talk to someone, a professional.'

'She just needs a bit more time to fully recover,' Grace splutters.

'It might help her, Ms Windsor.' The teacher's voice is softer now, sympathetic, and Grace half wishes the pious schoolmarm would come back. She looks across at Kaia, halfway up the fence now. Is therapy the answer? Grace imagines her daughter sat in a big armchair, feet dangling over the edge, a softly spoken woman asking questions designed to uncover her innermost anxieties. It feels dangerous for some reason, opening their family up to a stranger. But why? After all, what secrets could Kaia reveal? And if therapy could help Kaia recover from her trauma, perhaps it is a good idea.

'I'll think about it,' she says weakly, and turns to go. Then she retrieves Kaia from the playground and, feeling the sting of the teacher's stare on her back, walks out of the school gate.

Chapter 7

Grace smells the sweet spice of gingerbread before she walks into the kitchen. And the sight of Marcus and Kaia, heads over the work surface, icing pens in hand, gives her a warm feeling in the pit of her stomach.

She knows that she should have punished Kaia for the incident at school, stripped away her privileges and sent her to her room with a stern word. But she'd decided the last thing their family needed at the moment was more hostility. So she'd pushed her conversation with Kaia's teacher to the back of her mind and continued with her plans for the evening.

When Grace first reminded Kaia about doing something fun with Marcus, she'd tried to back out, claiming that she was too tired. But Grace had persevered and eventually Kaia had relented. Of course Marcus had behaved in the opposite way, jumping at Grace's request despite a busy day at work. She'd watched him don the family apron (their kitchen is only big enough for one head chef at a time) and challenge Kaia to a gingerbread man bake-off.

'Mummy, look, this is you.' Kaia holds one of her creations aloft, a dusting of flour shimmering on her face. Grace isn't sure the polka dot skirt and kipper tie are entirely representative of her wardrobe, but she takes it with a grateful smile.

'This is definitely the winner,' Grace says, unilaterally appointing herself the judge. 'Can I eat her?'

'Yes, but headfirst,' Kaia instructs. 'A quick death is better.'

Grace laughs awkwardly at Kaia's logic. 'Who else have you made?'

'This is Granny and Grandad. Daddy is making Harry Kane and Owen Farrell.'

'You can't eat Harry Kane – he's a national treasure,' Grace warns.

Marcus's head pops up. 'Good point. I'll make him Uncle Josh instead.' He winks and smiles, but it doesn't stop the hairs on Grace's neck rising as she watches him sink his teeth into her brother.

She turns to Kaia. 'Which one are you going to eat?'

'I'm going to eat Daddy,' she says solemnly, and yanks the brown-haired head off with her teeth.

'Ouch!' Marcus cries in mock pain, then tiptoes over towards Kaia, chuckling, his fingers aloft in full tickling mode. There's relief mixed with delight spreading across his face: bonding with his daughter again at last. He reaches for her midriff.

Kaia twists away from him and yelps.

Then she loses her balance and her little body slams into the fridge. 'No, Daddy!' she screams.

'What?' he calls in frustration. 'What do you think I'm going to do?'

'Hurt me.' Her eyes dart towards Grace. 'Again.'

'Kaia, what's going on?' Grace stutters with confusion. 'Daddy doesn't hurt you.'

'He does, Mummy. I promise.' Her voice is low now, almost spiteful. 'I got confused about the tree, you being there too. But he did push me.'

Grace shakes her head, whipping it left and right between the two people she loves most in the world. Kaia's eyes have narrowed and sizzle with anger, while Marcus looks shocked, as though he's the victim, wounded by her words. There's no way he can be abusing her. 'Kaia, I don't know where these crazy ideas have come from, but Daddy loves you.'

Kaia's eyes flicker around the room. Grace wonders whether she's avoiding their gaze, or searching for an escape, and her silent question is answered when Kaia darts for the door. She runs past the tiny cloakroom under the stairs and disappears into the hallway. Suddenly a loud crash emanates from the front of the house. Grace rushes out, but Marcus is faster. 'Oh shit, Kaia!' he groans.

Grace races into their front room and takes in the scene. Marcus's mood boards for his Twickenham pitch are strewn on the floor. A coffee cup lies next to them, its contents now sprayed out across two of the boards.

'It was an accident,' Kaia says, kicking at a sofa leg and staring at the floor.

The three of them stand in silence for a while. Grace wonders whether this will be one of those rare moments when Marcus loses his temper, the weight of his optimistic exterior proving just too heavy under the circumstances.

'It was your fault,' Kaia continues, almost like she's goading him. 'You were going to hit me.'

Marcus still doesn't speak, and his silence starts to feel oppressive.

'What time is your pitch tomorrow? Will you be able to print new boards?' Grace asks, trying to provoke some kind of reaction. She waits.

Then Marcus smiles, and Grace sighs with relief.

'Accidents happen – I'll sort something out,' he says. 'I spooked Kaia for some reason. My fault.' He holds his hands up, widens his smile. 'I think it's bedtime now,' he continues. 'Come on.'

Grace expects Kaia to bristle, to push him away and demand that Grace put her to bed instead. But she seems almost pleased that he's taking her. Is she regretting her outburst now? Has she realised how misplaced her antagonism is? As Grace watches Marcus usher Kaia out of the room, no sign of the annoyance he must be feeling, a wave of love flows over her. Because he is a great dad. And it could have turned out differently.

With his New Zealand roots, Marcus's dream from when he was six years old was to play rugby for the All Blacks, the country's national side. And when he was plucked from the Exeter Chiefs to join the Auckland Blues, and the local media began lauding his name as the country's future fly-half, he started to believe it might happen. But then he got kicked in the head and his injury forced him into retirement at just 25 years old. Kaia was only 6 months old when it happened, and Marcus was still adjusting to the sacrifices that parenthood demands. But instead of wallowing in self-pity, he focused on providing for his baby daughter, and has been trying just as hard ever since.

So as Grace listens to their faint footsteps on the floor above her, she says a silent prayer that Kaia's behaviour – and this new animosity towards her father – will improve soon.

*

Grace is cooking supper when Marcus reappears. He grabs two bottles of beer from the fridge, flicks the tops off, and hands one to Grace. Then he closes his eyes and takes a long, hungry swig. Grace can see tiny beads of sweat glinting on his temples.

'Are you okay?' she asks.

'What's going on with our daughter, Grace?'

She takes a sip. She knew this was coming. 'I read about post-concussion syndrome today,' she starts. 'It can cause outbursts of anger, rudeness, anxiety. I think Kaia's suffering from it. That, mixed with her confusion about what happened last Sunday.'

Marcus sighs. 'Does it also cause self-harm?'

'What?' Grace gasps.

'I've just caught her pinching her arm. Really hard, just above

41

her wrist. I told her to stop, and she did. But bruises were already forming. She wouldn't talk about it, but she had this weird smile on her face. Chilling, you know?' He takes another mouthful of beer, but lets it roll around his mouth before swallowing this time. Like he's cleansing his tongue, flushing out the words that have just slipped off it.

Grace remembers Miss West's words, her suggestion that Kaia see a therapist. 'I spoke to her teacher today,' she starts.

'Oh?'

'Kaia pulled Lily's chair over in class, for no reason at all.'

'Shit.' Marcus pushes the expletive out of his mouth with force. 'I suppose that's a symptom of post-concussion syndrome too?'

'Well, her teacher suggested it might even have started before. She brought up the netball incident, Rebeeca's nosebleed, questioned whether Kaia did it on purpose.'

'What are you saying, Grace?'

'She wants Kaia to talk to someone, a psychologist maybe.'

Marcus looks up. 'No,' he whispers.

'That was my first instinct too. But she's misbehaving at school. She's making up these accusations about you. And now she's hurting herself. We have to do something.'

'We can work things out between us.'

'This is serious, Marcus.' Grace watches him stare into the blackness of their garden beyond their glass doors.

'I get that,' he finally says. 'But what happens if she tells the therapist that I hurt her?'

A spider of disappointment creeps across Grace's shoulders. 'But isn't Kaia's wellbeing our first priority?' she asks. Seeing his conflicted expression, Grace softens her voice. 'And therapists are trained to work out the truth, so they'll realise that she's making it up.' She stares at her husband, looking for signs of discomfort or awkwardness, but there are none.

'I don't know, Grace. It still feels like too much of a risk.' He walks towards her, leans over until their eyes meet. 'We're good parents. We can fix her.'

Grace sighs. 'Kaia told her teacher that you pushed her out of the tree.'

Marcus runs his hand through the short spikes of his thick, dark hair.

'It was after she grabbed Lily's chair. Miss West doesn't believe her.'

'You know it's not true, right? That I would never harm her?'

Grace leans against him, breathes in his familiar smell. 'Of course I do,' she says, but as she closes her eyes, she can't stop the memory of a split lip seeping into her mind.

Chapter 8

MARCUS

2005

'You're sure you don't want to come back with us now?'

'Tania, leave the kid alone. Of course he doesn't. Grab that boot bag, will you. My hands are full.'

Marcus watches his mum balance his rugby boots on top of the pile she's already carrying. All three of them are weighed down with his belongings, the life of an 18-year-old rammed into rucksacks and sports bags. He pauses to look around the single bedroom. Save for the remnants of Blu-tack where he took down his Jonah Lomu poster – the All Blacks legend who defies the rules of physics on size versus speed – there's nothing to prove he's spent the last nine months living here.

'Are we set?' There's an impatience in his dad's voice now. The Devon summer season is in full swing, and Marcus knows he'll be keen to get back to their bed & breakfast, check the guests are behaving themselves and not overdoing it at the honesty bar.

'Thanks for taking my stuff home,' he says, pushing the door open and waiting for his parents to walk through. 'Josh can give me a lift home tomorrow, but he's got no space for my luggage.'

'You just behave yourself tonight. Pre-season training starts in four weeks, so don't go breaking anything. No drunken antics, okay?'

Marcus smiles. However close they are, his dad has always failed to notice that they're not the same. Shane was born on the west coast of Auckland, raised by the waves of Piha beach, and he approaches life like he surfs. If something big comes along, he doesn't hesitate, just rides the moment without any fear for what might happen. But when things are calmer, he's also happy to float around, enjoy doing nothing. Marcus has promised himself he'll be different. He's got big dreams, ones that require effort, and he's not going to let a night of drinking risk damaging that. 'I'm not as stupid as you, Dad.'

'He's got a point, love.'

'Don't disrespect me, woman,' Shane warns, putting on his best *Terminator* accent (which is terrible). But it still seems to work on Tania, because she giggles and drapes her arm around his shoulder.

'Never mind rugby training, we need you fit for the B&B,' she says, looking back towards Marcus. 'The place is booked up right through summer – you'll need to help out.'

'I thought this was supposed to be my holiday?'

'Just a few hours in the morning. It's not a lot to ask.'

Tension grows in the space between them. This is more than an argument about chores; the unspoken question is written across both their faces. *Are you too good for our B&B now? Too good for us?*

'Yeah, no problem, I can do that,' he says. The tight air releases, but the resentment inside him doesn't quite go away.

The three of them walk to the car, and Marcus hopes the ancient Land Rover looks cool rather than cheap as he tips his bags into the back seat. He gives each of them a quick hug goodbye and watches the 4x4 chug through the car park and, thankfully, out of the school gates. He lets out a long sigh, and wonders if he's been holding his breath this whole time.

As he walks back to his boarding house, he thinks about the prospect of working through the summer. His mates from his old school will be doing something similar, helping out on the family farm or picking up some kind of seasonal job. But his new friends won't be working; they'll be jetting off to second homes in Portugal or the south of France. A surge of jealousy rushes through him, but the emotion is quickly replaced by determination. He will build that lifestyle for himself.

Instead of going back to his room, he swings a left by the staircase and heads towards Josh's. As house captain, it's Josh's job to make sure their last night is a memorable one, and he's invited everyone over for a few drinks before heading to the pub in the village and then, who knows. Four weeks might not be long enough to fix a broken bone, but it's plenty of time to get over the mother of all hangovers. And he deserves one last night of rich-kid-don't-give-a-fuck-ness before the sheet folding and bed making begins.

He joined Chilford as the kid no one likes, half the people dubious of his West Country accent, the other half jealous of his skills on the pitch. Two years on, he's one of the boys. Yeah, he knows he'll never truly fit in. But playing the part is all that matters, and he's got that down to a fine art.

'Vodka and Coke?' Josh holds out a tumbler of beige liquid, the rookie barman clearly more generous with the spirit than the mixer.

'Thanks, mate,' he says and takes a long, satisfying gulp.

The drinking games start about an hour later. He's fine at first, keeping up with the different rules as they're brought in. But then he picks up his glass with the wrong hand, swears at his mistake, and then calls Johnnie by his actual name, and suddenly he's six fingers down and none of the rules are making sense anymore.

At some point, six of them, the hardcore group, head out into the village. The first pub, the one where the girls are, won't let them in. But they find a sympathetic landlord further down the High Street, and order pints of lager and shots of tequila.

'What shall we drink to now?' Josh asks, lifting up his shot glass.

'To me,' Johnnie pipes up, his mop of blonde hair now stuck against his sweaty forehead. 'A sympathy toast.'

'What for?' Marcus asks, not sure why he should feel sorry for the son of a hedge fund manager with his own helicopter.

'Tomorrow is going to be a hell day. Car's picking me up at five. All that airport shit. Flight to Boston. I won't get to the vineyard 'til … Well, I dunno 'cause fuck knows what time it will be there. But it'll be a long day.'

'Don't they have vineyards in France?' Marcus offers. He's trying to be funny, but still finds it weird that his mates laugh so hard at his joke.

'Martha's Vineyard, you fucking commoner!' Johnnie raises his glass in Marcus's direction, affection rather than antagonism shining in his eyes. But Marcus feels it. Hatred for these entitled cunts.

'Darts!' Josh shouts out, breaking the silence, pulling Marcus away from his dark thoughts. 'Anyone up for a game of winner takes all?' The two friends catch eyes, and Marcus wonders if his friend has read the situation, come to his aid. Josh comes from the same world as Johnnie, with his big manor house on the top of the hill, his dad some big banker dude in the City. But for some reason Josh seems to get it, to see the world from Marcus's perspective. He'll miss him when he heads to the States.

'Let's do it,' he says. And pushes back his chair.

Like sheep, they all decide to play then, no one willing to miss out on what might become a story worth recounting at a later date. They assemble around the faded dartboard and Josh explains the rules, the ones he's making up on the spot. 'It's quick-fire, winner takes all. Three darts, thirty seconds to throw them *and* shout out your score. Disqualified if you get it wrong, or run out of time. Okay?'

'Josh, how do you work out your score?' Hari looks confused. He's the most cultured in the group: Danish mother, Indian father, brought up in various expat communities around the world. But his cultural know-how clearly doesn't extend to the iconic British sport of darts.

Josh rolls his eyes and strolls over to the dartboard. 'See these numbers?' He circles his finger around the outer ring. 'That's your score if your dart lands in the main segment. If you hit this section, double it.' He points to the outer edge, then moves to the mid-section. 'Or this section, triple it. Easy, even for a linguist like you.' He winks at Hari. 'Oh, and the middle is bullseye, fifty points.' Then turns his attention back to the group. 'Who's first?'

One by one they pick up the set of darts and throw them at the board, some more recklessly than others. Matt and Dom both miss the rings completely with two of their darts, so score just seven and eleven respectively. Johnnie manages twenty-four and Hari benefits from beginner's luck with fifty-six. 'I'm in the lead!' he shouts with a mix of incredulity and glee.

'Ah, but the masters have yet to throw,' Josh says, aiming his first dart with precision, his drunkenness paused. He waits a moment, then thrusts the feathered metal arrow towards the board. Bullseye. Fifty points. He then turns his attention to the top sliver of the dartboard, the twenty-point segment. He hits a double and then just misses the triple section with his third dart. 'A hundred and ten!' he shouts, punching the air and following it up with a small whoop.

Marcus smiles at his friend's antics, but silently commits to beating his score. He also takes his time to prepare, letting his heart rate slow and eyes focus. He imagines he's on the rugby pitch, needing to convert a try to win the game, to find the sweet spot between the goal posts and kick the ball with enough distance to clear the crossbar. He launches the dart at the board and watches it fly.

'Fucker's scored a triple twenty!' Johnnie shouts out, not hiding his delight at Josh being knocked off his perch for once.

Marcus grins and releases his next dart.

'Triple eighteen! The boy's on fire.'

Marcus's third dart misses his target, only scoring him a five, but it doesn't matter. He's already won.

'Shout your number then, you idiot.'

'What?' Marcus pulls himself back to the present. What's his total? His brain won't fire. Shit. It's an easy sum – why can't he work it out?

'Sorry, mate, missed your time,' Josh says, pointing at his watch, then flipping his hands up in apology.

'Maths not your strong point, Marcus?' Johnnie smirks.

He looks around the room. The air is heavy, cigarette smoke hovers under the gloomy shine of dusty wall lights, and the floral wallpaper wilts under the tobacco stains. He doesn't feel drunk anymore, not the way he did anyway. He curls his hands into fists, feels the rage rise up.

'Pretty sure it's not yours either, is it, Johnnie?' Josh says, a new edge to his voice. 'Scraped a C, didn't you?'

Johnnie bursts out laughing. 'And that's with thousands of pounds in extra tutoring. I am truly shit at maths.'

The rest of them erupt too, loud guffaws spiralling around Marcus's head. How can he ever understand these people who parade their failings as proudly as their wins? Are they just trying to trick him with their fucked-up behaviour? Out him as some kind of poverty case? He squeezes his fists tighter and feels his heart bang against his lungs.

'Chill out, mate.' Johnnie nudges him, still laughing.

Marcus can't stand it. The posh bastard needs to shut the fuck up.

He surges forward, his arms swinging, his fists connecting

with soft jowls and a hard jawline. He loves the sound of his punches, Johnnie's pathetic cries, the horror of the rest of them trying to pull him off. He's so strong though, they can't touch him. Fucking losers.

The barman gets him in the end.

Slings him onto the street and tells him he's barred. Well fuck him. Fuck them all.

Marcus rubs at the grazes on his knuckles and starts the long dark stagger back to his room.

Chapter 9

GRACE

2019

'Mummy, did you hear me?'

Grace can't stop looking at Kaia's arm. The swirl of dark grey above her wrist, like angry thunder clouds. When Marcus told her what he'd caught Kaia doing, she hadn't wanted to think of it as self-harm. Kids experiment, with pain as well as pleasure. She remembers that from her own childhood, demanding friction burns from friends or being enticed by the farmer's electric fence. But now that she can see them, Grace knows that Kaia's bruises are more than that.

'I'm not wearing that top. I hate long sleeves,' she complains, flinging the blouse onto her bedroom floor.

Grace looks up and sighs. She loves Kaia's eyes. They're dark brown, similar to her own, but they have a distinctive shape. Almonds with tails. And they help, those unusual curves, at difficult moments like this. She crouches down and retrieves the rejected school blouse. Then she perches on the edge of the single bed and tries to soak up the bright optimism of the bumble bee duvet beneath her. Kaia's favourite cuddly toy, an evergreen tree with big red lips called Stan, is sitting proudly on the pillow. 'But you look so smart in your blouse,' she tries. 'And it will keep you nice and warm.'

'It's sunny today.' Kaia peers out of the window. Her bedroom overlooks the garden and the blossom on their small cherry tree is sparkling in the sunshine. 'I don't want long sleeves.' She crosses her arms and narrows her eyes.

Grace sighs. It is, frustratingly, a lovely day. And she doesn't blame Kaia for preferring her short-sleeved polo shirt, the soft cotton much more appealing to an active 7-year-old. But after Kaia's revelation to her teacher yesterday, she can't risk anyone seeing the bruises and reaching the wrong conclusion. Or the right one. A child harming herself isn't much better than an abusive father. 'Your arm looks sore,' she explains. 'Wearing long sleeves will protect it.' The lie sits heavy on her chest, but she takes a breath, and it lifts. If Marcus believes they can sort this out as a family, then she should give him room to try. The school doesn't need to be involved.

Kaia bites the edge of her bottom lip and looks down at her arm. The attitude has gone all of a sudden. 'It is sore.' She runs her finger along the wound.

'I'm sorry it hurts, but hopefully the pain will help you remember not to do it again.' Grace tries to sound encouraging, but Kaia just stares, her blank expression hard to make sense of. 'And if you get the urge to do it again,' Grace continues, 'you can use that memory to stop, and come find me instead.'

'I didn't do this to myself, Mummy.' Quiet, but resolute. 'Daddy did it.'

Grace takes a deep breath. Was she expecting this? Is this why she lay awake for hours last night both desperate for morning to come and dreading its inevitable appearance? Is this why the image of Kaia recoiling from Marcus's touch in the kitchen is still imprinted behind her eyelids? 'Please, Kaia, not that again,' she tries.

'He was angry with me for ruining his stupid boards.'

'No, he wasn't, he was very understanding.'

'Only downstairs. In my bedroom he got really mad, grabbed my arm and told me I did it on purpose. And that he wishes I wasn't his daughter.'

Grace's chest constricts and her eyes sting. How can Kaia say these things? She can't blame this on a confused memory. She pulls her daughter towards her and strokes her hair. Kaia was strawberry blonde as a toddler, but the colour has already darkened. The untrained eye might call it mousy, but Grace can see a dozen different shades from ash to auburn as she runs her fingertips through the soft strands. 'Daddy loves you.'

'I hate him.' Kaia pulls the blouse out of Grace's hands and takes a step backwards.

'Kaia, can you stop …' But the words trail off, because she's got nothing new to say. She's known Marcus since she was a teenager. He's never violent. Not since that one night, anyway. The reason for the bunch of flowers. The grovelling apology that turned into their first date. He's never lifted a finger against anyone since then, not even the man who finished his career with a misjudged kick. He would never hurt his daughter.

But Kaia sounds so certain.

And she did look petrified in the kitchen last night.

It had been easy to dismiss her accusations about Marcus when she was in the hospital bed, her head bruised, and tubes connecting her to various machines. Confusion caused by trauma. Especially when she labelled Grace a victim too. But now? Can a 7-year-old fake fear like that?

'Ah, my two favourite ladies.'

Grace jumps at the sound of Marcus's voice and turns to see his head arcing around the door.

'Sorry to interrupt the party, but don't you have a school to get to?'

Kaia goes quiet and starts pulling on the blouse. The sudden compliance is jarring, and her muteness stings the air. Grace feels an urge to fill the silence.

'Yes, we're almost done. Although we're going to have to race through breakfast to make it to school on time.'

'Shall I put some toast on for you? Peanut butter?'

Silence.

'Oh come on, Kaia. Can we please be friends?'

Grace can hear the hurt in Marcus's voice, but she can also see dark shadows pass across Kaia's face. The scene makes her heart break. How is she supposed to choose between her husband and her daughter? She squeezes her eyes shut, then opens them. She can't deal with this now; she needs time to get things straight in her head. She smiles at Marcus. 'You've got your Twickenham pitch today. You should focus on that; I'll sort Kaia out.'

He waits by the door for a moment, and Grace knows he's hoping the old Kaia might resurface if he stands there long enough. *Just kidding, Daddy! Please make my breakfast. I love you!* But she just stares out of the window and eventually he gives up. 'Okay then. Well, I'll see you both later.' He turns to go, his broad shoulders more sloped than usual.

'Good luck, honey,' Grace calls after him. But his response is too muffled for her to decipher what he says.

Chapter 10

'She's saying what?'

Grace's shoulders relax. It's good to see her own sense of shock reflected on her mum's face. She reaches across the work surface and takes a slice of banana bread, freshly baked and smelling delicious. She hadn't been able to stomach anything for breakfast, but here, in her mum's welcoming kitchen with its warm Aga and bright Le Creuset pans hanging on the wall, she suddenly feels ravenous. 'I just don't know what to think.'

'Well, it can't be true. Marcus would never hurt her.'

'I know.' Grace takes a bite of the soft cake and chews slowly.

'It must be fall-out from her accident. She's misbehaving at school too,' her mum reminds her.

Grace swallows, but a lump stays in her throat. 'There could be another explanation. That Marcus is being violent with her, and that's why she's acting up at school.'

Faith reaches for Grace's hands across the worktop. 'You need to trust your instincts. Do you think Marcus could abuse his own child?'

Grace looks directly into her mum's eyes. The only one in their family whose irises shimmer like the sea. 'No,' she whispers, and it's true. She can't imagine it.

'Good. Because neither can I,' Faith says firmly.

'Oh, Mum, I wish you'd been there when he tried to tickle her. Seen how she reacted.'

They both fall quiet and Grace pushes the plate away, her hunger gone again. She's been on an emotional rollercoaster all morning, swerving between horror that Marcus might be hurting Kaia, to fear for what would happen if he was, and then confusion for why, if none of it is true, Kaia would make it up. And all on about three hours' sleep. She's exhausted.

'What did the teacher say?' her mum asks, drawing Grace back to where the conversation started, the reason Kaia gave for pulling Lily's chair.

'She doesn't know about the bruises from last night, but she doesn't believe Marcus pushed Kaia out of the tree.'

'That's a relief.'

Grace nods. 'She wants Kaia to see a therapist.'

Faith is quiet for a moment, weighing up the possible consequences like ingredients for a cake. 'And how do you feel about that?' she asks gently.

'Scared, I suppose. Of what could unravel. But I can't do nothing, Mum. I'm sure Kaia is making it up. The Marcus I know would never be violent.' She shakes her head to stop the memory of her split lip resurfacing again. 'But why is she doing it? Lying on this scale can't be a symptom of post-concussion syndrome.'

'If you do take Kaia to a psychologist, there is a chance they'll believe her,' Faith warns. 'And involve social services.'

'I thought you're certain that Marcus is innocent?'

'Therapists are only human, Grace. And their focus is Kaia's wellbeing, not your family's.'

Grace pushes back the breakfast stool in frustration and walks towards the large glass panes overlooking the garden. The clouds have come over now, suffocating the earlier promise of summer with their bulging greyness. She watches two squirrels race across the neighbours' shed, their old tabby cat watching on, nonplussed by the interruption to her nap. Then Grace turns back to face her mum with a new resolve etched into her expression. 'She needs help. I have to do something.'

Faith picks up Grace's plate, then jumps slightly as the knife slips off and clatters to the floor. 'And what if you hear something you don't like?'

'If Marcus is hurting her? Well, I'd …' She pauses. What would she do? Leave him, of course. Take Kaia to safety. But would she report him? Open that can of worms?

'I don't mean that,' Faith interrupts. 'What if she tells you there's something wrong with Kaia?'

Grace looks at her mum quizzically. 'Do you think that's what a therapist would say?' she asks. Faith has always been a devoted granny.

'Of course I don't.' Faith opens the dishwasher and stacks the plate inside. 'I just mean that you don't know what conclusions a professional might draw.'

Grace sinks onto the small floral sofa and drops her head into her hands. When she feels Faith next to her, and then her cashmere-coated arms around her, the tears finally fall. It's always been this way. For all Grace's strength, her stubborn refusal to give up on a goal or wallow in self-pity if things don't go her way, she can never keep up that warrior demeanour in front of her mum. It was the same after her own accident, pretending to her friends that she was fine, then crawling into Faith's embrace after school and sobbing with the pain of it all. Josh was away at boarding school, so she had those warm soft arms all to herself.

She lifts her head up.

Josh.

How could she not have thought of her brainy older brother before now? Josh has spent the last five years teaching psychology at one of the best universities in the world. He must be better informed than most of the therapists in London.

'I should talk to Josh!'

'Your brother?' Faith sounds more surprised than enthusiastic.

'He's been studying the human psyche for over a decade. He must have some understanding of post-concussion syndrome, and if it could be to blame.'

'He's not a therapist though. I'm not sure academic study is quite the same?' The question sits on Faith's lips. 'And he's also very busy at the moment,' she adds, a smile of pride now creeping across them. 'His book comes out next month and apparently there's quite a buzz about it.' In a few weeks' time, Grace will no longer be the only author in the Windsor family and Josh's book – *Inside Out, a study on private personas* – is currently getting rave reviews on both sides of the Atlantic. 'Perhaps you shouldn't bother him at the moment,' she finishes.

That niggles. For all their closeness, Grace has always suspected that Josh is Faith's favourite child. Even though their relationship was more distant, Faith placed her son on a pedestal and glued him in place. Grace is her confidante, but Josh, with his many talents, is her idol. 'No problem,' Grace says, crossing her fingers behind her back like an idiot. 'I'll have another chat with Marcus instead.'

Her mum smiles. 'You've always been a good team. Now how about another cup of tea?' Then she gently rises off the sofa and retreats towards the kettle.

*

Once she'd thought of it, there was no way an impending book launch was going to stop Grace contacting her brother. Taking advantage of his expertise. She checks the time in San Francisco. She needs to leave for school in half an hour, so she hopes Josh is an early riser. After fourteen years on the West Coast, he'll probably be in the middle of a seaweed smoothie or a downward dog by 7 a.m. And sure enough, when he picks up on the second ring, he sounds wide awake.

'Gracie.' His public school accent is apparent in that one word;

it seems as though the longer he lives in the United States, the more British he becomes. 'Is everything okay with Mum and Dad?' he adds, concern for his parents filtering into his voice.

'Yes, yes, they're fine,' Grace rushes to reassure him. 'I just wondered how you are.'

'Really?' For all their mutual fondness, they don't keep in regular touch. Separate boarding schools – and Josh from just 8 years old when Grace was only 6 – meant they grew up as holiday pals rather than codependents.

'Well, maybe there is something.' Grace pauses but there's only silence on the other end of the line. She sighs. 'Kaia had an accident on Wimbledon Common. She fell from a tree.'

'Jesus, Grace. Is she okay?' The concern in his voice releases an arrow of guilt into Grace's chest. Why didn't she call him last weekend? Josh adores Kaia. She should have let him know.

'Yes, she's fine,' Grace says quickly. 'A bump on the head, but nothing broken. The hospital diagnosed concussion but she's much better now.'

'Thank God. You scared me for a moment. So how can I help?'

Grace leans into her desk chair and feels its rigid back dig into her shoulder blades. 'Well, her behaviour has changed since the accident. Deteriorated, I suppose you'd say. I thought, with your psychology background, you might know why.'

'I teach the subject; I'm not a shrink,' he warns, the Americanism sneaking out.

'I know. We're just not sure we want to try a therapist yet.'

A heartbeat of a pause, disapproval perhaps, and then he continues. 'So what's been happening?'

She takes a deep breath. There's no point keeping it from him, but it feels disloyal somehow. Josh and Marcus were best friends at school, but one spectacular falling-out proved to be fatal for their friendship. She's seen Josh attempting to thaw the icy atmosphere when he visits at Christmas, and how impossible Marcus makes it for him.

'She pulled a girl's chair from under her the other day.'

'Okay. Was it towards the end of the day?'

'Yes.'

'That could be tiredness. Concussion takes a while to fully recover from.' He pauses. 'How is she at home?'

'Distant, especially with Marcus,' Grace admits. 'She even accused him of pushing her out of the tree.'

'Trauma can do that, mess with your memory.'

'That's what the A&E doctor said,' Grace whispers, tears starting to prick at her eyes. 'But it's more complicated than that.'

'Oh?'

'Since her accident, she's got it in her head that he's dangerous.' Grace pauses. 'And she has some bruising on her wrist. Marcus said he found her pinching her skin, but she explains it differently. That he was angry and grabbed her …' Grace's voice trails off, and the line goes quiet for a while. In the silence her cheeks burn with a memory, and she wonders if Josh is thinking about the same thing. Last Christmas night. A sullen Marcus disappearing off to bed. She and Josh sharing the bottle of wine he'd brought with him from the Napa Valley. For years she hadn't said a word about her and Marcus's secret. The two of them had promised not to tell a soul beyond Grace's parents, and had crafted a narrative that made such secrecy possible.

But that night, oiled by red wine and festive joie de vivre, the story had tumbled out. Josh had listened without interrupting, given her the space to explain it all, and had joined the family pact to never mention it again.

Grace had been wondering if that secret could possibly offer some explanation for Kaia's behaviour, but when Josh speaks again, he makes no reference to it. 'Well, self-harming is rare in children as young as Kaia,' he says gently. 'But it does happen, and it's a growing problem.'

She sees an image of Kaia's face, her defiant expression when she blamed Marcus for the injuries. 'Could she be doing it for a different reason? So that she can make Marcus look guilty of something?'

The line goes quiet for a moment, save for Josh's gentle breathing as he processes her words. 'That's quite a claim,' he says eventually.

'But I've thought it through, Josh,' Grace needles; she's finally come up with an answer that makes sense and she needs his approval. 'Kaia believes that Marcus pushed her out of that tree. And the aftereffects of her concussion are making her feel angry. So perhaps she's mixing the two, creating an outlet for her anger and finding a way to punish him.' She tries to smother the desperation in her voice, but it seeps out, floats down the phone line.

'Listen, Gracie. When we're born, our world is so small that we're the only person in it. Then it gradually expands. By the time we leave home, the world has become full-sized.'

'I'm sorry, I don't understand.'

'Well, for example, the teenager world is multifaceted with influences coming from school, friends, partners, clubs, work and so on. Parents are still important, but less so. However, at 7 years old, your world is still mainly your nuclear family. Mum, dad, siblings if you have any. Life beyond that is more obscure, like the reference section of a book rather than the story itself.'

'And so?' Grace coaxes.

He sighs. 'Look, Kaia might be suffering with post-concussion syndrome, and she could be angry with Marcus about her fall. But setting him up as an abuser? Risking her nuclear family for no good reason? I'm sorry, Gracie, but from a child psychology point of view, that's very unlikely.'

'But if she's not trying to punish Marcus, why is she saying these things?'

'You've said that she's distant at home, and it sounds like she's attention-seeking at school. Gracie, have you considered the possibility that she's telling you the truth?'

Chapter 11

MARCUS

2005

Josh only dropped him at home fifteen minutes ago and Marcus is already feeling claustrophobic. He'd thought the atmosphere in the car would be tense after his falling-out with Johnnie, but the hour's drive south has proven to be the most relaxing part of the day. Marcus had started to apologise as soon as he got in the car, his head banging with alcohol and contrition, but Josh had just shrugged off the fight, even agreed the guy deserved it. Any atmosphere vanished and they nicely bantered the rest of the way home. Shame it didn't last beyond the front door of his house.

'I'm going to kill them,' he sighs to the empty space, then reverses out of his bedroom and clatters back down the narrow staircase. He's been lifting a lot of weights at school and he feels too big for their half of the cottage now. The property has eight bedrooms in total, but five of them are reserved for paying customers. The family has to make do with the smaller, dingier side of the house.

His mum wasn't home when he got back, but he can hear her in the kitchen now, emptying bags of grocery shopping. She'll have been to the Cash & Carry, stocking up on trays of eggs and giant bottles of tomato ketchup. He storms inside. 'Where the hell are my pain-in-the-arse sisters?'

Tania stops replenishing the fridge with packets of bacon and turns to face him. 'It's nice to see you too, Marcus. Welcome home.'

He huffs, then plants a kiss on his mum's cheek. 'My bedroom looks like a flipping Harry Potter shrine,' he moans. 'The bed's pushed against the wall, there's posters up everywhere, and loads of wizard shit all over the floor.'

'Sorry, love. Izzy and Karin are a bit excited. The sixth book is due out in a couple of weeks.'

'So? How does that explain my bedroom getting vandalised?'

'Apparently there's lots more dark magic. And there's a rumour that one of them is going to get killed off. But I can't see JK doing that, can you?'

Marcus raises then drops his eyebrows to show just how little he cares either way. 'Why can't they keep their stuff in their own bedroom? His twin sisters came along when Marcus was 7 years old, bringing his only-child status to an abrupt halt. He still remembers how put out he felt, the pair of them hijacking his parents' attention lock, stock and barrel for at least a year. He mellowed a bit when he discovered how much they adored him, and most of the time he tolerates them with something close to fondness. But he still has moments when he wishes they'd never showed up.

Tania rests her arms on the island unit and sighs. 'The girls share, and you've been away for three months. Our home isn't big enough to have empty rooms. Your bedroom has been commandeered as a kind of playroom.'

'You could have mentioned it,' Marcus grumbles, while silently cursing their small home. He can't imagine his school friends have to deal with siblings encroaching on their private spaces. 'Anyway, I'm back now. They need to clear it all out. Where are they?'

'They're at school, dimwit. State schools don't have the long holidays that you get, remember? Now you've got all this free time on your hands, maybe you could clear it out for them?'

'It's not my stuff.' He knows he sounds like a spoilt child, but he just wants to get his head down.

'Okay.' Tania draws out the last syllable, her set jaw showing her annoyance. 'Well in that case, you can help me unpack the shopping. There's a load more bags in the boot.'

Marcus flops down into a pine kitchen chair. It wobbles beneath his weight. 'But I just got back.'

'Oh sorry, Princess Marcus.'

Marcus knows his mum is only teasing, but it still annoys him. He has to deal with his school friends treating him like trailer trash, and now his mum's accusing him of being a snob. He can't win. 'Fine, I'll clear my bloody bedroom.' He pushes up to standing and plods out of the kitchen.

'It's good to have you back, love!' His mum's voice trails after him.

He tries to ignore the patches of threadbare carpet on the stairs and re-enters his bedroom. Harry Potter has taken over the whole place. There's a Lego display in one corner with various structures lined up. No Hogwarts castle or Hagrid's hut – those sets would have been too expensive for his parents' budget – but there's a carriage and a weird tree that looks vaguely familiar from the one Harry Potter movie he's seen. There are posters on two of the walls, Hermione clearly their favourite pin-up, and a dressing-up box overflowing with Harry Potter costumes. Marcus picks up a Gryffindor scarf and imagines strangling his sisters with it.

He's carrying a box of Lego into his sisters' room when he hears their footsteps on the stairs. He braces himself for what he knows comes next.

'Marcus! You're back!' Izzy squeals, launching herself at him. She lands on his back and wraps her spider legs around his waist.

'Did you miss us? Are you excited to see us?' Karin jumps on the spot, trying to reach the top of Marcus's head so she can ruffle his hair.

'Jesus, you two are so annoying,' Marcus mutters, but, despite his best efforts, a smile starts to form at the edges of his mouth. The relentless enthusiasm of his little sisters, identical in character as well as appearance, can be contagious.

'Mum says we're having fish and chips tonight, to celebrate your return.' Izzy rests her head against the crook of his neck, but kicks her legs in excitement, coming dangerously close to his groin with each back and forth.

'Oi, oi, Saveloy!' Karin shouts in her deepest voice, pumping her fist into the air. With their long blonde hair and enormous blue eyes, his sisters look like twin porcelain dolls, making them conclusive proof that looks can be deceiving.

'It doesn't take much to get you two excited, does it?'

'Oooh, Mr Sportsman of the Year, too good for fish and chips, is he?'

'Only lobster for him, darling.' Karin joins in, attempting her own posh accent.

'Or perhaps fillet steak, monsieur,' Izzy suggests, adding a French twist. 'Hang on, is that posh?'

The two girls dissolve into a fit of giggles, Izzy sliding off Marcus's back and onto the floor. Marcus looks at them in their faded gingham school dresses, white socks scrunched around their ankles, and a wave of envy washes over him. His sisters' dreams are so achievable. Fish and chips on a Friday night. A trip to Axminster to buy the latest Harry Potter book. For as long as Marcus can remember, he's had big dreams. Impossible, some might call them. His instinct is always to mock people who are willing to accept mediocrity. But maybe they're the clever ones? Able to feel content without a ladder of ever-bigger achievements to hang off. Maybe he should try it.

'Plaice and chips, mushy peas, and a pickled egg for me,' he says, counting the items on his fingers.

'Eurghh, pickled egg? You're gross.'

'And I'm going to breathe my eggy breath all over you.' Marcus laughs as both girls start screaming, then jump off the floor in sync. They push him out of their bedroom and slam the door shut behind him, their laughter still escaping around the edges. He returns to his own room and sinks down onto his bed. The village road under his window doesn't get much traffic, and he soaks up the peace and quiet. The duvet is soft underneath him, the sheets freshly laundered. He's still feeling the aftereffects of last night's heavy drinking session and his knuckles are sore from his run-in with Johnnie. Maybe it is good to be home after all. He closes his eyes and starts to drift off.

'Marcus!'

He opens one eye.

'Hey, Marcus, come downstairs a minute!' His mum has two volumes. Normal and head-banging.

'What do you want?!' he hollers in response. He would never be allowed to behave like this at school; if he shouted to a mate from his bedroom, the housemaster would march inside and coolly explain that only the rarest of circumstances permit raised voices.

But standards have always been lower in this house.

'Jesus, Marcus, get your arse down here.' His dad has joined the party, exasperation clear in his voice.

Marcus swears under his breath and stomps down the stairs. 'What do you want?'

'Phone call,' his mum says, holding out the receiver.

'Why didn't you just say that?' Marcus hisses, taking it from her.

'Why didn't you just come when I called?'

Marcus rolls his eyes and then turns his back on her, the telephone lead stretching around his shoulders. 'Hello?'

'Mate, it's Josh. Sounds like hell in your house.'

Marcus shifts between his feet. It is hell in his house, so why does his friend's comment annoy him?

'But don't worry because I'm going to rescue you.'

'Oh yeah?'

'Come over tomorrow. Bring your tennis racket.'

Marcus looks around the kitchen. Half the shopping is still lying on the work surface. His dad is leaning against the fridge, slurping at a bottle of beer, while his mum rummages through their odds and sods drawer, probably searching for the fish and chips takeaway menu. He pictures Josh's huge mansion, the garden rolling down to woodland. The tennis court nestled beyond. 'I'd love to,' he answers. 'What time?'

Chapter 12

GRACE

2019

The babysitter is due any minute and Grace is still reeling from her brother's words. If Josh thinks that Marcus could be harming Kaia, does that mean Grace has to believe it too? Josh said himself that he's not a therapist. He doesn't know Marcus like she does either, because he never gets to see what a brilliant dad he can be. On the rare occasions that Josh does visit, Marcus is always tense and distant; with him mainly, but it rubs off on everyone else too. It's easy to see why Josh could think he's not a good father. But it doesn't make it true.

When Marcus called to tell her that the Twickenham pitch had gone well, and how he knew in his heart that they'd won the account, she responded on autopilot. *That's great news, well done; yes, I'd love to celebrate with you; I'll book a babysitter and meet you in the Mudlark at London Bridge.* Of course, she's happy for him, and relieved that she won't have to pick up the pieces of another opportunity gone sour. But what difference does any of that make if Marcus is abusing their daughter? She flicks her newly straightened hair behind her shoulders and tries to settle the butterflies charging around her insides. Faith is certain Kaia's claims are false, and she's much closer to Kaia than Josh is.

Grace leans in towards the mirror and paints her lips a deep red, the final touch to her carefully applied make-up. She always makes an effort when she's out with Marcus's work colleagues. Not because she feels threatened by them. Yes, Marcus is good-looking and has one of those pin-up-style bodies, but he's never given her reason to question his fidelity. Not really. No, she makes the effort so that she can fit in. Marcus's colleagues spend their lunch break shopping on their phones, scrolling Instagram and Pinterest for the latest fashion tips, and ordering from ASOS or Pretty Little Thing with a couple of clicks. That level of commitment isn't for Grace, but she's happy to pretend on nights like this.

'Maisie is here,' Kaia shouts up the stairs, her newly acquired tone, somewhere between bored and hostile, filtering along the hallway and into the bedroom.

Grace swears under her breath. 'I thought I told you not to open the front door?' she calls back, picking her tan leather bomber jacket off the bed, and pulling the door behind her.

Kaia is standing at the bottom of the stairs. She shrugs at Grace. 'It's only Maisie.'

'But you didn't know that,' Grace continues, arriving next to her. 'It could have been someone dangerous.'

Kaia stares at her with a belligerent expression. 'Daddy's at work.'

Grace laughs nervously and drops her arms over Kaia's shoulders, with what she hopes looks like affection rather than constraint. Then she turns her attention to the 16-year-old girl with a Kanken rucksack hanging off one shoulder, hoping she wasn't listening too hard. 'Thanks for doing this at such short notice, Maisie. Marcus only suggested it a few hours ago.'

'No problem.' Maisie produces a polite smile, but it's forced;

her hearing must be good. Her eyes dart down towards Kaia, then back to Grace. 'Is Kaia okay?' she whispers.

Grace's chest constricts. Is this how it's going to be now? Explaining to everyone that Marcus isn't an abusive father while silently wondering if he is? She looks at Kaia and tries not to let annoyance leak into her tone. 'Kaia, go and watch some TV for a minute.' She inclines her head towards the living room. Kaia stares at her for a moment, then swivels on the wooden floorboards and disappears behind the living-room door. Grace turns to Maisie and tries to smile. 'Kaia has been acting up a little since her accident,' she admits. 'She might tell you some things about Marcus. They're not true,' she adds, her voice much clearer than the fog swirling around her head.

'That he's dangerous?' Maisie asks, her eyes wide. It reminds Grace that she's only a child herself really. Maisie lives five doors away and is in her final year of GCSEs at the local girls' school.

'It's to do with her concussion.' Grace forces her smile to stretch further. 'She probably won't say a thing, anyway. Now, we won't be late. You've got everything you need?'

Maisie looks a bit shellshocked, but luckily her manners take over. 'We'll be fine. You have a good night.'

Grace smiles her gratitude, pops into the living room to drop a kiss on Kaia's forehead, and slips out of the front door. But as she walks towards Earlsfield station, she starts thinking about seeing Marcus. Being in a busy bar with lots of distractions must be better than the two of them alone at home, but she's not sure she can look him in the eye anymore. Is that because she suspects him of abuse? Or because she feels guilty for considering it? Her head is so muddled.

There are dozens of trains to Waterloo every hour, so she only has to wait a couple of minutes for one to arrive. Grace was a newcomer to London when they moved there as a family seven years ago, and so her knowledge of the city centre mainly revolves around children's entertainment. The museums and theatres, parks with playgrounds. Evening venues are less familiar for her. Apparently the pub Marcus suggested they meet at is near Southwark Cathedral, which means the Jubilee line to London Bridge and a five-minute walk from there.

When she finished her degree, and her friends were venturing to the capital to start their careers, Grace headed straight to Exeter so that she could move in with Marcus at long last. They'd been together for five years by then, but never lived in the same city. After their first summer together, Marcus went to Exeter to join the academy of the local rugby team. She returned to Cheltenham to do her A levels and then two years later moved to Oxford for her degree. Three years on, she finally made it to Exeter, but as it turned out, they didn't spend long there either. Marcus got the offer from the Auckland Blues, and within six months they were on a plane to New Zealand, via a beach break in Thailand.

As Grace walks down Tooley Street, her mind wanders to that holiday. Their last one before Kaia came along and trips became altogether more family-focused. They spent their first ten days in Bangkok, dashing from one tourist hotspot to another, then retreating to their air-conditioned hotel as quickly as their traveller scruples permitted. Then they headed south to the beaches of Phuket in time to greet 2011. The capital Patong has a party reputation, and it didn't disappoint on that New Year's Eve, although Lady Luck also played her part in making it a night to remember. At least, the first few hours anyway. Things got a little messy after that, and Grace can still remember the rambling, red-faced apology she was forced to make at two different embassies before they could leave the country.

A shadow passes over her face for a moment. She takes a deep breath and shakes the feeling away. It's time to face her husband. She pulls open the heavy door of the Mudlark and walks inside.

Chapter 13

MARCUS

2005

Marcus looks at the impressive front door and wonders what to do next. There isn't a doorbell. Just a massive doorknocker that will probably sound like a bomb going off if he raps it. He's been to the house before, but only with Josh. And now he can't remember how they got inside. He bangs his tennis racket against the back of his heel and ponders.

'Well, hello, gorgeous.' A husky whisper drifts over Marcus's left shoulder. He looks up in surprise. A girl has appeared from around the side of the house, too young for the deep voice to be authentic. She reminds him of Medusa, which is weird because he doesn't usually use Greek mythology as a reference point. Maybe it's the green eyes. 'Sorry?'

'Impressive muscles, wide eyes. A little unsure.' Her tone has notched up a few levels, more soprano now. 'It's a sexy vibe.'

She sashays closer, only stopping when her face is a few centimetres away from his. He can see freckles now, faint dots across the bridge of her nose. And she smells good, like apples, or maybe grapefruit. He squirms, takes a step backwards.

'You must be Josh's friend,' she says, still inspecting him. She's slender, like a vine, and almost matches him in height.

'Yeah, do you know where he is?'

'Follow me,' she says, beckoning with a curled finger and swinging her hips as she walks away, her short summer dress wafting from side to side. Marcus doesn't move for a minute, nervous about following the exotic species anywhere, but also not sure how long he can languish on the driveway, even if it is big enough for twenty cars. And a small aircraft. But she soon bursts into laughter and turns back to face him. 'I'm just kidding with you. Josh is in the garden. Come on.' She turns around again, but this time drops the stylised walk, and Marcus decides it's safe enough to follow.

As he turns around the corner of the house, the only word that pops into his head is perfection. It helps that the sky is an indigo blue, and the sun is spreading its warmth. But it takes more than weather to re-create heaven. Josh is lying on a chaise longue in the centre of a sprawling stone terrace. Someone is swimming in the small pool beyond, going nowhere against a constant current set by some built-in technology. Music is playing in stereo through a set of outdoor speakers. And that's before he takes in the view of green hills and the distant shimmer of the sea.

Josh spots him, then swings his legs around and sits up. 'Mate! You've brought your racket. Awesome.' Josh looks at the Medusa girl for a moment, but then seems to change his mind, and turns towards the swimming pool. 'Hey, Gracie, fancy a game of doubles?'

Grace is Josh's sister. He doesn't talk about her much, like Marcus doesn't bring up Izzy or Karin if he can help it, but Marcus remembers that she goes to a girls' boarding school in Cheltenham and is a couple of years below them. He watches her stand up, jet streams of water now arcing around her tanned hips.

73

'Tennis? Now? With you and Marcus?'

They haven't met before, and he finds it quite flattering that she knows his name.

'No, with Roger and Rafa. They need a warm-up game before the Wimbledon finals tomorrow.'

'Ha ha, very funny.' She walks to the edge of the pool and hoists herself out, her triceps swelling with the effort. She's got a swimmer's physique, square shoulders and long, powerful thighs. Attractive, in an athletic kind of way.

'Tennis sounds fun,' Medusa pipes up from behind him. 'I'm Coco by the way, Grace's best friend.' She holds out her hand in greeting, and Marcus takes it. 'Sorry about the welcome.' She grins and her eyes sparkle. Her skin is incredibly soft, and Marcus fights the urge to let his thumb slide down the back of her hand. 'Shall we be partners?' she adds.

'Yeah fine,' he mumbles, avoiding full eye contact. There is something fascinating about her, and yet warning sirens are also blaring inside his head. Which is ridiculous. How dangerous can a 16-year-old girl be?

'Does that mean I need to play with my brother?' Grace calls out in mock horror, while pulling on a pair of white shorts over her swimming costume and leaning down to pick up her trainers.

'Who is also the best player here, remember,' Josh retorts, while glancing in Coco's direction, clearly his way of pointing out she's made a dud choice.

'Personally, I don't care about winning. It's the taking part that counts, isn't it, Marcus?' She takes his hand and intertwines her fingers in his. 'Shall we go and knock up?'

Marcus throws Josh a 'what the hell?' look but doesn't resist as Coco leads him down the garden towards the tennis court, his friend's expression somewhere between smirk and sympathy. They pass a small lake, dragonflies hovering over the giant lily pads, and then Coco guides him into a summer house next to

74

the tennis court. She opens one of the cupboards and picks out a selection of rackets.

'You know this place well,' he observes, as she picks up each racket in turn, carefully calculating its weight. Perhaps she's more proficient at tennis than she's letting on.

'I guess it's kind of my second home.' She decides on a black and yellow Babolat racket, then opens a drawer and pulls out two tubes of tennis balls, both seals still intact. 'My parents are away a lot, so I usually come here in the holidays.'

However much he moans about it, Marcus couldn't imagine being away from home during the holidays, missing that chance to totally relax. 'Do they work abroad?' It's the only explanation he can think of, but she seems to find his question funny.

'Oh, David and Martina don't lower themselves to working.' She giggles. 'We have houses. Lots of them. And my parents don't like staying in one place for long. In the summer you can usually find them in Marbella, or Saint-Tropez. Winters they split between skiing in Verbier and cruising around the Caribbean. Plus trips to New York and Dubai, of course. It's hard to keep up.' She turns to look out of the window.

'And you don't go with them?'

'I visit them most holidays. But it's awkward; I'm their only child and I cramp their style.' She turns back to face him and shakes her head, her long hair fanning out behind her. 'I prefer it here, with Faith and Henry. I love this family.'

'You and Grace must be close.'

'We're like sisters. We'd do anything for each other.' The gravity in her voice turns the air heavy and Marcus starts to feel uncomfortable. He wants the sassy temptress back.

'I hope that doesn't include throwing a tennis match,' he says, leaning in and using his flirtatious voice.

She giggles then, and Marcus enjoys the sensation of having lightened her mood. 'Oh, that's not going to happen. I've been having private lessons all term, just so that I can beat the masterful Josh Windsor.'

'Impressive commitment,' Marcus notes. 'Although now I'm worried that I'm going to let you down. Rugby is more my sport.'

'Well, it's good that I have a secret weapon.'

'Oh yeah?'

'You may have brawn and beauty, but I think you're naive in the ways of the Windsor family. Watch and learn.' She winks at him and strolls out of the summer house.

The siblings are already on court, Josh measuring the net height and Grace flipping the score cards to zero. Coco snaps open the balls, rolls four in their direction and hands two to Marcus. He walks to the back of the court, bouncing the balls as he goes, and tries to settle the nerves in his belly. He catches eyes with his best mate across the court, and attempts a smile, but the look between them is already adversarial. It's just a friendly game of tennis, he tells himself. Why does winning always mean so much to him? To both of them, of course.

Coco lives up to her promise of being excellent at tennis, but Grace isn't far behind, and they finish the set with six games apiece.

'Tie-break,' Coco announces, grinning at Marcus. It's like she's been waiting for this moment all along. 'You serve first, Josh.'

Coco is receiving, so Marcus moves forward, ready to volley. He is aware of her swaying gently behind him, her eyes wide, focused on Josh. Marcus watches him throw the ball high, then thwack it hard. It whizzes past Marcus and drops onto the line.

'Out!' Coco yells. 'Second serve.'

'Bollocks, it hit the line. Grace, you saw it didn't you?' Josh scowls across the net.

'Um, take two?' Grace suggests.

'No way, I was closest,' Coco declares. 'And the ball was definitely out. What do you think, Marcus?'

Marcus can hear the mischief in her voice. She's not lying about Josh's serve to win the point. She thinks it's funny, him feeling robbed, her knowing how it will affect the rest of his game. Marcus wonders if she understands how gutted Josh will be to lose. And whether he should right this wrong before it has chance to do any permanent damage.

'I think it was out too,' he says with as much conviction as he can muster, and smiles when Josh double faults on his second serve.

Chapter 14

GRACE

2019

'Hey, babe, thanks for coming. I love you.' Marcus's eyes aren't quite focused, and his grin is wider than usual, but for someone who's been in the pub for the last three hours, he's not in too bad shape.

'Hi, honey,' Grace says, smiling back. This is easier than it should be. Isn't she supposed to hate him? Or at least be suspicious, unable to hold his gaze? The problem is, now she's with him, she can only see the man she's loved for almost half her life. A man who would never harm Kaia, or risk their family happiness. Looking into his open face, his twinkling eyes, a sense of clarity descends. Kaia's accusations can't be true, she's clearly just struggling with her concussion. She needs help, and that's where Grace's focus should be. Not turning her husband into a monster.

Which means they need to find Kaia a therapist and stop fretting about the possible repercussions. They'll understand that Kaia's making the stories up. And it's crazy to worry about anything else.

'There's some prosecco in a bucket somewhere. Let me get you a glass.' Marcus looks towards the back section of the pub where five or six of his MGK Sports colleagues are chatting. 'Hey, Lauren, can you fill a glass for Grace?' he calls out.

Now that she's made the decision, Grace feels an urgency to talk to Marcus, to persuade him Kaia should see someone, and reassure him that nothing bad will come of it. But she knows this isn't the right moment, so she just nods her thanks and smiles.

A tall woman with a white-blonde pixie haircut and enormous blue eyes gives Marcus a thumbs up, finds a clean glass, and fills it to the brim. Then she wanders over and hands it to Grace.

'Thank you.' She takes a long gulp. 'Congratulations on the pitch. I hear it's in the bag.'

Lauren's title is client service director, but a more accurate description of her role would be fixer. While Marcus comes up with the ideas for helping sports venues improve their revenue streams, it's Lauren's job to make these things happen. Luckily, she enjoys a challenge. 'Well, nothing's certain until the ink is dry.' It's in her nature to be cautious, but Grace thinks she can detect a deeper apprehension and her skin starts to prickle.

'Have they said when they'll let you know?'

'They said soon. Maybe even tonight.' Lauren's long fingernails, shining with a bright blue marble effect, tap-tap against her gin and tonic. 'We were the last agency to pitch and with the Rugby World Cup coming in September, they want to get on with things.'

'I wish you'd been there, babe. Their head of events even asked me to sign his son's autograph book. They treated me like a celebrity!' Marcus sounds so excited, and it reminds Grace of the 23-year-old flying across the world to join his favourite team. But wanting to meet a former rugby great is not the same as entrusting them with your marketing budget.

Grace catches Lauren's eye; she's clearly not so convinced about their chances of winning. The urgency inside Grace steps up a gear. She needs to talk to Marcus about Kaia seeing a therapist before the decision comes from the client, while he's still in a good mood. 'Honey, can I talk to you about something?'

Lauren registers her tone instantly. 'You know, I think I can see Scott ordering shots. Now might be a good time for me to remove the company credit card from behind the bar.' She backs away and both Grace and Marcus throw her grateful smiles, albeit for different reasons.

'What's up?' Marcus runs his hand along the small of her back.

'It's about Kaia.'

'Oh.' His hand drops down by his side and his mood seems to sink with it. 'More trouble at school?'

'No, nothing like that. It's about the bruises on her arm.'

'Listen, I know it's worrying, her injuring herself like that. But kids do weird stuff sometimes. I remember thwacking an elastic band on my wrist for no good reason at all. Maybe we shouldn't read too much into it?'

'She said that you did it.'

'What?' Marcus's eyes widen, on full alert now. 'Not that again.' Then he drops his gaze to the floor and shakes his head. Grace can't help wondering if he's shocked at being accused, or just playing for time. Finally, he looks up. 'That's madness,' he says, his voice low and gravelly. 'I would never hurt her. You know that.'

Grace nods. She does know that, so why does she keep questioning it? 'I want Kaia to see a therapist, to find out why she's saying these things.'

'We talked about this last night, Grace.'

'But what if the school start to believe what she's saying about you and involve the authorities anyway? And tell them that we refused to let Kaia see a therapist? What happens then?'

'The school won't believe her.'

Out of the corner of her eye, Grace can see Lauren reaching for her phone, a look of concentration washing across her face.

Then the client service director walks into a corner of the pub, the quietest area, and starts speaking into it. A wave of panic grabs Grace. She knows the call is from the Twickenham client. She needs to get Marcus on side now. 'You're right – the school don't believe her.' She takes Marcus's hands in hers and looks directly into his face. 'But they do want her to see a therapist. Someone who can help her get over whatever's making her behave like this.'

'She just needs time,' he says, but Grace can tell his resolve is slipping.

'She needs support. We owe her that.'

Marcus looks exhausted all of a sudden and leans back against one of the square wooden tables dotted around the pub. 'I can't believe I have to make this choice.'

Grace's temper flares. 'You mean a choice between getting your daughter help, and protecting yourself?' The base from the pub's speakers thuds at her temples. 'Why are you so reluctant anyway?' she asks, hostility creeping into her voice. 'It's like you've got something to hide.'

'I have got something to hide though, haven't I? We both have.'

That. The secret that sits between them like heavy-duty glue. Strong, but constricting. 'We had no choice,' Grace hisses under her breath. Lauren has finished her call and is looking in their direction, her expression downcast. Grace wills her to stay away, to leave Marcus in blissful ignorance for a while longer.

'The truth could unravel,' he continues. 'What if the therapist gets hold of your medical records?'

Grace's hand drops to her belly and tears well in her eyes. She can't feel the scar beneath her black silk shirt, but she knows it's there. 'Marcus, you're either paranoid or being obstructive. Why would a therapist for Kaia want to know my medical history?'

'I don't know.' Marcus wipes his hand across his brow. 'There's just so much at stake.'

Lauren is moving towards them now. 'Look,' Grace says, lightening her tone. 'It will be maybe six sessions. They'll talk, draw, play with toys maybe. Her only aim will be to get Kaia to open up about how she's feeling. The school will be happy, and Kaia will have the space to work out why she's behaving like she is.'

'I still don't like it.'

'I promise it will be okay.'

'Marcus, could I have a word?' Grace has run out of time; Lauren has arrived by their side. The phone is still in her hand and the marble on her fingernails is wavering.

Marcus starts to say no, but as he turns towards her, he realises what it's about. He seems to have lost his earlier confidence, and his eyes just look questioning now. 'Did they call?'

Lauren nods. 'They loved you, and us as an agency. They said we'd definitely be on the pitch roster next time.'

'Next time?'

'I'm sorry, Marcus. We didn't get it. They said MGK is too small, not enough experience. You know the drill.'

Marcus pushes off the table and clenches both his fists, his face twisted into a scowl. 'How the fuck are we supposed to get experience if no one will give us a fucking chance? Arrogant fucking bastards.'

'I know, it's shit. But we'll get it next time.'

'You reckon? They'll probably come up with some other pathetic excuse. Failed rugby player, failure at everything. That's what those arseholes see.' He slams his glass on the table. Too hard. The stem cracks and the rim shatters. Lauren looks down, then back up again, her calm demeanour unaffected.

'We'll sign a Premiership club, and then they'll take notice. I promise,' she soothes.

Grace can't believe how easily Lauren accepts her husband's vitriol, how she can find a positive response without flinching at his behaviour. Is that because she's used to it? Is this foul-mouthed, angry person someone they're all familiar with in his office? Because this isn't the Marcus she sees at home, the generous dad who doesn't let things irritate him. Is that because he's happier with her and Kaia? Or is he just hiding his true self? A thought tries to force its way in but she doesn't let it.

'Maybe we should go,' she suggests, slipping her hand under his elbow. Whatever his colleagues are used to, she doesn't feel comfortable with them seeing him so incensed.

'Don't tell me what to do,' he hisses, pulling his arm free. 'I need some air.' He picks up his jacket from the table and stomps towards the front door.

Even though the pub is still busy, a quiet descends between her and Lauren, as though Marcus has taken the energy with him. 'I'm sorry about that,' Grace says eventually, even though she feels more rattled than Lauren looks. Married couples do that, apologise for each other. And she can still remember uttering those words, *for better for worse*, as Kaia sat on the step behind them, her eyes tracking the spider crawling up the vicar's cassock.

'Don't be silly. I can handle Marcus.' Lauren sounds so casual. Perhaps she is over-reacting. He has just lost out on the most exciting piece of work since retiring from rugby.

'I'll book a cab. Pick him up on my way out,' Grace says. She needs some space to work out what she's feeling.

'Good luck,' Lauren says with a wry smile. Grace tries to match her flippancy, then lifts her hand in a wave goodbye. As she works her way through to the front of the pub, she opens her Uber app and clicks on the closest driver. She can see Marcus through the window, leaning against the red-brick wall. He regularly tells her he doesn't smoke anymore, that he's given up for good this time. But she never believes him, so it's not a shock to see him sucking on a Marlborough Red.

'I've booked a cab.'

'Sorry for shouting at you.'

The anger has gone, and Grace feels her shoulders relax a little. 'It's one minute away.'

'Paul from the rugby club. His kid saw a psychologist – I can get the number.'

Grace's heart thuds faster. 'Does that mean …?'

'I remember the first time I saw Kaia. Looking into her tiny face, smelling the fuzz on her head. I loved her straight away.'

'I know; me too,' Grace whispers.

'But it was a shock; everything happening so quickly. And you were distraught. Part of me didn't want her.'

'Don't say that, please.' The memories start flooding back, however hard Grace tries to shut them away. The warmth of Kaia's tiny body; coupled with the fear and confusion racing through her own.

'I trusted you.'

'I know.'

'Kaia can see a therapist if you promise me one thing.'

'What's that?' she whispers.

'That whatever happens, you'll always trust me too.' He stands up and leans towards her. As he wraps his muscular arms around Grace, she nods, and wonders if it's a promise she can keep.

Chapter 15

COCO

31st December 2010

Coco curls up like a cat on her faded beach towel and burrows her shoulders into the sand. This is her favourite time of day. The sun has dipped low enough to give the sky centre stage, and from behind her (probably fake) Ray-Ban Aviators, she can stare into the endless blue without squinting. Wispy clouds hover over the languid waves of the Andaman Sea, while thicker ones collect over Kalim Hill to her right. She's been to dozens of beaches over the last five years, some exceptionally beautiful, others remote and peaceful. But despite the crowds, and the thud of dance music seeping out from the nearby Bangla Road, Patong Beach will always be her favourite. Perhaps because of that.

She rolls over onto her back and stretches out her legs, lifting one to inspect it, her gold anklet glistening in the late afternoon sun. Her complexion used to be pale, remnants of her father's Irish heritage. But her limbs are bronzed now, and the tan runs so deep that she can't imagine ever going back to her old colouring. There are other ways that she's been stained forever too.

Which is why her parents' letter is such bad news.

With an inward sigh, she reaches into her beach bag and retrieves the flimsy piece of light blue paper, its red and blue striped border signifying how it's travelled by air from their new manor house in Oxfordshire. They could have texted. Her parents know her phone has international coverage; they pay the bill after all. But of course they'd want some sort of written proof for summoning back their prodigal daughter.

The paper rustles in her fingers as she unfolds the letter for the hundredth time. She tips over onto her elbows, coils her back into cobra, and reads it again.

Dear Coco,

Happy birthday, darling – twenty-two already. Where did the time go? One day I'm buying babies' booties for you in Peter Jones, and the next you're a grown woman, walking your own path.

And what a fun journey you've had so far. Your father and I have loved your postcards, keeping up with your adventures. We thought you might stay in France when you got the job in that lovely bistro, but your appetite for high jinks got the better of you. No doubt you blame us for that.

Now that you're unquestionably an adult, we've decided it's time for you to return home. To take responsibility for your future. It's not right for you to wander the globe perpetually, chasing excitement. It will never be enough, darling, and then where will you end up?

Perhaps we should have forced you to accept that sixth form offer from Roedean after all, not let you disappear that summer with just a backpack and a wallet full of euros. We still don't understand why you went. Wanderlust or just lust, we were never really sure.

Or perhaps we should have been less generous with your monthly allowance ever since, forced you to stand on your own two feet.

But it's all water under the bridge now. We've transferred money for a first-class flight back to Heathrow, and expect to see you in time for Christmas.

And, Coco, there will be no more money, so don't do anything stupid.

We look forward to welcoming you home.

Mum and Dad

Coco refolds the letter and puts it back inside her bag. She's had it for more than a month. The message hasn't changed, but she's still five thousand miles from home.

Being stupid is her *raison d'être*, for fuck's sake.

The letter had reached her at a hostel in Tulum. The vibe had been chilled there, and she'd been enjoying spending her time smoking weed under a canopy of floating lanterns with a bunch of idle travellers. But it hadn't felt the same after the letter arrived, so she'd said her goodbyes, avoided the hippie from Tasmania who'd called her a prick-tease, and taken a bus to Cancun International Airport. She could have got a flight straight to the UK from there, turned up at her new family home in the Cotswolds in time for Christmas lunch. In fact, she'd sort of planned to. But then she had a better offer. And now it's New Year's Eve and she's in Phuket, having a blast of fun on her favourite party island.

Her very final blast, she's promised herself. Almost definitely.

There's a DJ playing a special set on the beach tonight and Coco watches four or five men, all dressed in black, put the finishing touches to the huge stage. She checks the time on her phone. It's nearly six, which means time for a beer before she heads back to the hotel to get changed. She doesn't know anyone here, and that might have caused her vague concern once upon a time. But not anymore. A few drinks, a pill or two. She knows she'll find her crowd pretty quickly tonight. She stands up, flicks the sand off her towel, and stuffs it into her bag. She pulls her denim cut-offs over her bikini bottoms, and slips her Havaiana flip-flops onto her feet.

*

'Bottle of Singha, please,' Coco asks, smiling at the bartender. He tips his head, then turns to the fridge behind him. When he hands her the drink, she gives him a hundred-baht note and waves the glass away. She turns to face the sea and takes a long draw on the cold glass lip. Delicious. She's going to miss this. The terrace is packed, but she's happy to stay by the bar, watch customers arrive empty-handed, and leave with jugs of lager and wider smiles. She stretches up onto a bar stool and lets her flip-flops drop to the floor.

'Excuse me, are you waiting to be served?'

She turns to face the girl speaking, shaking her head. 'No, I'm just … shit.'

'Coco?'

She's mute for a moment. Frozen. All she can do is stare.

'Oh my God, I've tried so hard to reach you! And now, what, I just bump into you in Thailand? This is too crazy.'

Coco smiles weakly, nods her head. 'Yeah, crazy.' How can this be happening? Grace should be in Devon, ironing rugby shirts, or whatever loved-up girlfriends do. Not on this party island, her fucking island. 'How've you been?'

'Good, I guess.' Grace walks closer.

Even with the pungency of salt water and coconut sun cream, Coco can detect her old friend's unique family scent, and it's enough to bring tears to her eyes.

'But I've missed you. Why did you leave like that? One text and gone.' Grace's shoulders lift and drop.

'I went to stay with my parents in Saint-Tropez,' Coco says, her voice guarded. 'I met this guy, I told you about him.'

'I know, some hot French guy. But you didn't say you'd be gone forever, or that you wouldn't keep in touch. Did you go travelling together?'

Coco smiles at a memory. She's only got one photo of their time together, but she's kept it with her ever since. Dog-eared and faded. 'Something like that.'

'You know, I wondered if I'd done something,' Grace admits. 'We were having a fun summer and then you just disappeared.'

'You didn't do anything!' She's genuinely shocked that Grace might think she did. 'No one did anything. I went to see my parents, then took a trip from there, and it was cool. So I kept, you know, tripping.' Coco grins, relieved to see that she's got her mojo back, at least enough to disguise her hammering heart. 'Anyway, what the hell are you doing on Patong Beach at New Year? Shit's gonna get crazy, you know,' she warns, with a wry smile.

'Jesus, Coco, I'm not Mother bloody Teresa. We've been here a few days, head back to Bangkok tomorrow.'

'We?'

'Me and Marcus. Oh, I guess you don't know, we got together. After you left.'

Coco shifts on the bar stool. There's no reason to tell Grace that she does know, or that she's kept track of their budding romance from a distance. 'That's nice,' she says, sounding deliberately vanilla. 'And holidaying together,' she muses.

'Well, this is more of a stopover than a holiday.' Grace pauses. 'We're moving to New Zealand.'

'Wow. That's, like, a million miles from everywhere.'

'Marcus signed a contract with the Auckland Blues. They're a rugby team,' she adds helpfully. 'Best chance he'll get of playing for the All Blacks, so here we are.' She shrugs in an apologetic manner, as though she realises that following her man halfway around the world isn't very twenty-first century.

'Love can be very life-limiting, can't it?'

'I'm going to take up surfing.'

'Yeah, that'll show him.'

Grace bursts into a fit of giggles and Coco can't help joining her. She puts her arm around the only best friend she's ever had, and breathes her in. 'I've missed you too.' They smile at each other and Coco has the sensation of her life rewinding. The aeroplane rides, the cheap hotels, the drug-fuelled parties and brutal hangovers. They flood past at breakneck speed until she's back, in the Windsors' garden, lying next to Grace in the hammock strung between two old oak trees, staring at the stars.

'We have tonight,' she says. 'We could see in 2011 together?'

'I'd love that,' Grace whispers, and kisses her friend's hair. Then she takes Coco's hand. 'Come and see Marcus, he'll be blown away that you're here.'

Coco stares out at the terrace; she thinks she can see him now, leaning back against the wooden chair, muscular legs stretched out, crossed at the ankles. It brings back memories. 'Are you sure?'

Grace pauses, lowers her voice. 'Of course, I'm sure. Why wouldn't he be?'

Coco looks into Grace's trusting face. Then she takes a breath and lets herself be led through the mass of tables until they reach the edge of the terrace, and Marcus, looking out to sea.

'Look who I just bumped into! It's mad, isn't it? Small world proof, right here.'

Coco watches Marcus unfurl his broad frame and turn to stand up. 'Hello, Marcus.'

He lifts his eyeline, then takes a step backwards. 'Wow, you.'

'It's been five years, Marcus, not five centuries,' Grace remonstrates. 'You look like you've seen a ghost!' She swats him on the arm, then slips her hand down to his waist. Perhaps she senses something.

'Just um … Just a surprise, I guess.' He stumbles over his words. 'We should have a drink. To celebrate our reunion; your reunion, I mean. I'll get them.' He spins around and manoeuvres his way to the bar, his athletic body moving fluidly between the tables.

Chapter 16

Coco applies the (probably fake) Burberry matte rose and rubs her lips together. It's the only shade she's got, but she knows it brings out her eyes. It's a combination that's proved successful enough over the years. She slips her flip-flops back on – only a fool would wear proper shoes at a beach party – and pulls the door of her hotel room closed behind her. She knows she looks hot tonight. The black teddy suit clings to her subtle curves, and the sheer white mini dress doesn't leave much to the imagination, slashed in two by the black crossbody strap of her tiny handbag. If this is going to be her last night of proper fun, she's going to make it count.

Bangla Road is heaving. Every bar is pumping out music, and hundreds of people wander the street. Touts confront tourists with wide smiles and twinkling eyes, encourage them into the go-go bars or nightclubs with promises they'll never keep. The odd moped drowns out the music for a moment, its engine revving then quietening as it disappears along the main beach road. Coco soaks it up. The noise, the stench of illicit sex and tomorrow's regrets. She belongs here, not in some stiff Cotswolds village. She once thought she belonged in an east Devon village close to the sea, but that feels like a lifetime ago now. She walks inside the

Smiley Bar and spots them straight away. As she slips onto the blue bar stool next to Grace, a waitress appears by her side.

'Three Thai sabais please,' she shouts above the music. 'If we're going to make this a night to remember,' she continues, turning to Grace and Marcus, 'it needs to include the local rum.'

'I'm up for it,' Grace shouts back grinning. 'It's like fate telling us to get smashed.'

The waitress arrives with three cocktails, slices of lime and Thai basil leaves decorating the rim of each glass.

'Cheers!' Coco calls out, and the three of them clink glasses. Marcus still looks a bit uncomfortable, as well he might, but hopefully a couple of drinks will loosen him up. Not enough to talk about that night, but she's confident he wouldn't do that. Not with Grace around. And anyway, tonight isn't about raking up the past. She just wants to hang out with Grace for one evening. Then the lovebirds will fuck off to New Zealand, and she'll crawl back to her hell life with Mummy and Daddy, and there will be no ugly consequences.

The drink is fresh and cold, and sweet enough to slip down like fruit juice. The first one disappears inside ten minutes and the second doesn't take much longer. By the time Coco has finished her third cocktail, she can feel the release that alcohol brings. She checks her watch. 'Guys, it's half ten. We should go to the beach.' She can hear the DJ ramping up the tunes now, Rihanna's voice flooding over the top of the buildings. She stands up and starts swaying with the music.

'Yes, let's do it. There's a bar on the beach, I guess?' Grace asks, her words already slurring.

'I can do better than that, come on.' Coco reaches for Grace's hand and the three of them leave the Smiley Bar and walk down Bangla Road towards the beach. When they get to the edge, Coco pulls Grace under a palm tree and, in the relative darkness, pulls a tiny plastic packet from inside her handbag. 'I scored some ecstasy earlier. There's one for each of us.'

Grace stares at the three little pills inside the bag. 'I've never done Class As before.'

'Coco, we're not doing that. Grace and I don't do drugs, okay?'

Coco watches her friend bristle at Marcus's words. Grace was always so independent at school, choosing how to pass her time on her own terms. Making her own decisions. They were generally right too. While she didn't win a multitude of prizes like her brother, she quietly got on with things, and made a success of every single one.

'I'm 21, Marcus. Just because I haven't done drugs, doesn't mean I don't do drugs.'

'Doesn't it?'

Coco can't tell whether he's threatening Grace, or her explanation has genuinely confused his rum-addled brain.

'But tonight …' Grace pauses, the suspense causing Marcus to hold his breath. 'I don't want one. Thanks for the offer though.'

Marcus sighs with relief and Coco can see his shoulders drop. She wonders, if things had panned out differently, whether he'd have ever felt the same level of concern for her. She pushes the thought away, then takes a pill out of the bag, shrugging at the pair of them. She places it at the back of her tongue, and a fizz of excitement squirms in her belly. She knows what comes next. The surge of euphoria, the endless energy. Fuck Grace and Marcus with their boring lives and pathetic morals. She feels sorry for them.

'I'm going to the bar,' Marcus informs them, and heads to the makeshift beer hut erected for the night, his hands stuffed into the pockets of his navy cargo shorts.

'He's pissed off with you,' Grace observes. 'He thinks you'll lead me astray.'

A wave of sadness washes over Coco before she can stop it. Even before she left for Europe, she carried the label of perpetrator, never victim or even bystander. She brought it on herself. Slipping out of her dorm to meet a boy when she was 14. Dealing hash a year later. It was only among her friends, but the school

93

still threatened her with the police. Until her dad stepped in, and the new drama studio finally got built. And here she is, still the naughtiest kid in the room. The pill clearly hasn't kicked in yet, because Coco feels an overwhelming urge to sit down.

'Are you okay? I didn't mean to upset you.'

Coco smiles and lets the music seep through her pores. As the chemicals finally start to unleash their power, nostalgia swells inside her and releases a burst of affection. She takes out her phone. 'Come on, let's have a selfie.' She likes to record special moments with a photo, and this one deserves at least that.

'A what?'

'Wow, Britain is so behind Asia.' She puts her arm around Grace's neck and draws her in. Arm outstretched, she taps her phone, then checks the picture and smiles, satisfied. 'Come on, let's find Marcus. If I can't lure you with class As, then I'm going to make damn sure you're wasted by the end of the night.'

The closer they get to the stage, the more the music pumps inside Coco's chest. As the ecstasy rears inside her, she finds a spot to dance and closes her eyes. Her body feels like water, fluid and weightless, with an electric current of dance music pulsing through her. Grace is dancing with her now, beer spilling down her black dress, her sparkling clutch bag spinning around her head. Marcus is there too, a shadow in the strobe lighting, holding Grace up when she stumbles. The countdown begins and in three, two, one, it's 2011. Fireworks erupt in the night sky, Katy Perry screams through the giant speakers. Coco floats her arms above her head and tries to forget what the year ahead has in store for her.

A minute later, or maybe an hour or two, who cares, someone grabs her by the shoulder and turns her around. It's Marcus.

'Listen, I need to take Grace back to the hotel. She's too drunk.'

Coco looks through the crowd. Grace is sat on the beach, head in her hands, an untouched bottle of water beside her bag.

'What will you do?' he asks.

94

Coco turns to face him. His tone has changed. It's softer, more vulnerable, and a worm of affection wriggles in her chest. 'I can help you get her back, if you'd like?'

'Thank you,' he says, and Coco can hear the same relief he showed when Grace declined the pill. Is she the sensible one now? Will she be Grace's saviour for once?

Together they walk back up the beach, both silent as they concentrate on navigating through the army of revellers. The DJ set won't finish until morning and the sky is still black; a sign that the party is far from over. Marcus lifts Grace off the sand and wraps her arm around his neck. She's almost comatose now, and just groans some kind of greeting that neither of them understands. Coco takes her other arm and picks up her bag. Together, they drag her up the beach, the artificial source of energy giving Coco the extra strength she needs.

Luckily their hotel is just one street over from Bangla Road, and they make the journey in less than ten minutes. There are a few guests sitting around tables in the open-air bar, but the music has finished, and no one shows any interest as the three of them stagger past. Eventually they reach a corner room on the ground floor and Marcus pauses. He pulls a credit-card-style key from his pocket and buzzes them inside. The first thing Coco notices is how clean the room is. She's stayed in many beautiful places during her travels, seen views that have taken her breath away, slept in handcrafted beds, enjoyed open-air showers. But this room, with its polished stone floor, king-sized bed, and oak-panelled snug scattered with scarlet silk cushions, offers something else. Comfort.

'I might give her a quick shower. She's covered in sand.'

Coco nods and watches Marcus guide Grace into the bathroom. A moment later, she hears the rush of water. Her body is aching to move, to dance, but there's nowhere to go. She flops down on the bed, but her body keeps swaying, picking up the faraway sounds of music from the beach. She spots Grace's bag where she dropped it, and curiosity takes over. She clicks it open. Lipstick, biro, Thai notes and Grace's passport. Coco flicks to the photo and gently runs her fingers over the laminated image. She remembers Grace having that taken; sliding into the booth, pulling the cheap curtain across, trying to keep a straight face as Coco tickled her ankles. Those were good times.

Eventually Marcus appears with Grace wrapped in a towel. He pulls back the covers and lays her onto the bed. She's fast asleep in seconds.

'Drink on the terrace?' he offers, then smiles when Coco nods her head.

Chapter 17

GRACE

2019

Grace looks at her watch. As soon as Marcus gave his blessing, she'd phoned Dr Harriet Gray, the psychologist Marcus had mentioned. She didn't want to risk either of them changing their mind. The secretary she spoke to had explained that Harriet's diary was very booked up, that there was a supply and demand issue with children's mental health these days, but had eventually offered her an appointment at 11 a.m. on Wednesday 17th April.

And if they're not careful, after waiting a week, they're going to be late.

'Kaia, where have you disappeared to? We need to leave in a minute.' With a mid-morning appointment, Kaia could have gone to school for the first period, but Grace couldn't face picking her up in the middle of the school day, having to see Miss West up close again. Over the last few days, the teacher's demeanour has mutated from sympathetic to hostile, as though she's decided the whole family are rotten. At least school is breaking up for the Easter holidays tomorrow, and Kaia will be away from suspicious eyes for three weeks.

'I'm coming.' Kaia plods in through the sliding doors at the back of the house, trailing muddy footprints behind her. 'Where are we going again?' She looks up at Grace. Her expression is more open than Grace has become used to lately, but it's apprehension rather than warmth that's woken up her face.

'To see a lady called Harriet, remember?' she says gently.

Kaia lowers her eyeline and nods. 'Why am I going?'

Grace and Marcus have been purposefully vague about today's appointment, but she knows she needs to give her daughter a bit more information now that the day has arrived. She tries to sound upbeat and nonchalant at the same time. 'Harriet is a really nice lady who you can talk to about stuff.' She picks up her bag from the side, and two freshly filled water bottles. 'Does that sound okay? Shall we go?' she coaxes.

'What stuff?'

Grace pauses for a moment. 'It will just be you and Harriet for most of the session. What do you think you might want to talk about?' She waits, poised for some comment about Marcus. Over the last week, Grace has tried to get Kaia to explain what's wrong, why she's shutting Grace out and demonising Marcus, but Kaia refuses to answer Grace's questions. She spends most of her time in the garden, throwing a ball against the fence or lying on the trampoline staring at the sky. The only time that she initiates conversation is at bedtime, when Grace kisses her goodnight and she responds by whispering in Grace's ear. *He did push me, Mummy.* The mantra has spiralled around Grace's head constantly, when she's supposed to be working, or sleeping, or listening to the woes of her husband still coming to terms with the lost Twickenham pitch.

He did push me, Mummy.

There have been no more injuries, thank goodness. But Kaia did accuse Marcus of getting angry with her when Grace went swimming on Saturday morning. And she announced that he ran the bath too hot for her on purpose that night. Marcus denied both these claims as vehemently as Kaia made them, and Grace hasn't felt any closer to working out the truth.

'I know what I'm going to talk to her about,' Kaia says, crouching down to pull on her trainers. Grace sucks in some air and feels her resolve slip. Is she doing the right thing? Or is she throwing Marcus to the wolves by involving a professional in their complicated family life?

But could she live with herself if she didn't give Kaia this opportunity?

She purses her lips, reaches for Kaia's hand, and they walk out of the house together.

The car is parked on the road just opposite the front door, which is a relief because the strong wind that brought sunshine half an hour ago, has now dragged a rain cloud over their heads. Luckily Kaia is protected from the heavy droplets by the Stanford Cardinals baseball cap that turned up in the post last week. Gifts have always been Josh's way of showing his affection. Like the iPad he bestowed on Kaia at Christmas time; Grace can still remember the look of thunder on Marcus's face when their daughter opened that leaving gift. Luckily for them, Kaia mainly prefers staring at the sky to a screen, and the twenty minutes' iPad time that she requests before bed feels reasonable enough. Of course, the burgundy cap with the distinct Stanford tree is much more restrained than an iPad, but it's also a constant reminder of her brother's warning, and Grace can't help wishing he hadn't been so thoughtful.

Grace guides the Land Rover across the busy A3 and heads towards Putney. Harriet works in a therapy room above a yoga studio on the Upper Richmond Road, and Grace easily finds a parking space on a side street close by. She pays for two hours via the app even though Kaia's session is only meant to last for fifty minutes. There's no point adding parking anxiety to her

99

already stressful morning. As she opens the rear door to let Kaia out, she looks into her daughter's eyes. 'What's most important,' she says carefully, 'is to be honest with Harriet.'

Kaia stares back. 'I will be,' she promises, but a crease appears in her forehead and she bites her lip. Fear and determination sparring.

Grace draws a breath. She knows she should leave this to Harriet, the professional, but the risks feel too high now, and the words just tumble out. 'Kaia, why are you saying these things about Daddy? It's really upsetting me.'

The corners of Kaia's mouth drop and she looks away. 'I don't want to upset you.'

'These stories about Daddy hurting you, I don't think you understand where they might lead. And that's okay, because you're only 7, but now would be a really good time to stop.'

'Do you want it to be our secret?' she asks. 'Because I can keep secrets.'

'No!' Grace checks her voice. 'Of course not. Kaia, I want you to feel like you can tell Harriet anything. But she's really experienced at spotting the truth, so please think carefully about what's real and what – for whatever reason – you're making up.'

Kaia blinks, then narrows her eyes. 'I don't want to see Harriet anymore. Can we go home now?'

Grace feels her chest constrict. This was exactly what she was trying to avoid. 'I'm sorry, honey, I shouldn't have said that. I don't want to scare you. Harriet will be lovely, I'm sure of it.'

'But she can read my mind? Like a witch?'

'No, Kaia. She's just a plain old human, like me. Not magic at all.' Grace gives Kaia the biggest smile she can muster. 'It will be fine, I promise.' Then she turns towards the door and presses the buzzer labelled Dr Harriet Gray.

Chapter 18

'Hello, Kaia.'

Kaia stares, as though she's mapping out the psychologist in front of her. Straight brown hair, blunt fringe. Long nose and big white teeth. Grace wonders if her daughter is seeing a horse too.

'Hello,' Kaia whispers back, polite but wary.

'Why don't you jump on that chair? It's really comfy.' Harriet uses just the right tone, encouraging but not patronising, and Grace watches Kaia's shoulders relax a little. Another pause, and then Kaia clambers onto the leather lounge chair opposite Harriet's small mahogany desk. The traditional furniture seems out of kilter with the white walls and laminate floorboards to Grace, but Kaia is oblivious to the decor. She shuffles backwards in the chair, and stares at her feet bobbing in the air.

'That's perfect, Kaia. Well done. Are you happy for your mum to wait outside while we talk?'

Kaia doesn't speak, but she grabs the brim of her cap and pulls it up and down, forcing her head into a reluctant nod.

'I'll just show her where to sit – I won't be long.' Then, for the first time since they were ushered into the room, Harriet turns towards Grace. 'Shall we have a quick chat outside?'

Grace nods and tries to smile as the psychologist guides her back to the reception area. Harriet gestures to a chair, and they sit down in unison.

'Thank you for seeing Kaia,' Grace starts.

'Well, thank you for letting me talk to her alone. Some parents are nervous about losing that control, but it means I can build a rapport much more quickly.'

Grace feels a sudden urge to change the rules. She didn't realise that she could sit in on Kaia's session, help mitigate any disasters. But now Harriet's praising her trust, she feels hemmed into a corner. She sighs. 'Kaia had a fall, from a tree on the Common, and got concussion. It was a few weeks ago now, but she's not been herself since. Misbehaving at school, struggling with friends.'

'Thanks for explaining that, Grace. I've had some experience with concussion in children. It can take its toll on their behaviour. And at home?'

Grace thinks about the hours Kaia spends by herself in the garden, her closed expression. The whispered words at bedtime. 'Quiet. Distant. And angry, especially with her father,' she admits.

'Oh? How does that present itself?'

Grace scratches nervously at her neck. She and Marcus had agreed not to mention Kaia's accusations unless she brought them up with Harriet herself. But they're banging at her temples now. She's not sure she can talk to Harriet without them slipping out. 'She won't do anything with him anymore, or let him get close to her,' Grace offers.

'Has she explained why not? Has he done something to upset her?'

Grace suddenly feels defeated by this woman with her long face and soulful eyes. Perhaps it's better to forewarn her, provide some context; Kaia is bound to tell her anyway. 'She's got it in her head that Marcus pushed her out of the tree. We don't know why. And she's made other accusations too …' Grace's voice peters out. 'Obviously, none of them are true,' she adds.

Harriet is the first person to not seem shocked, but she does change her body language. Like Kaia's case has become more interesting and she's keen to get back to her. She sits up tall and slides to the edge of the seat. 'That must be upsetting for you,' she observes with a weight of sympathy and a streak of curiosity. 'But you're doing the right thing, bringing Kaia here, giving her a chance to explain. I'm sure together we can resolve this.' Then she rises out of the chair, walks back to her office, and with just a brief look back towards Grace, pulls the door closed behind her.

The rest of the session crawls past, minute by minute, and Grace tries to distract herself by scrolling through Instagram. As usual, she wishes she followed more interesting people. As well as the requisite clothes adverts, it's a constant stream of toddlers feeding ducks, groups of women in bars with big sunglasses and flushed cheeks, and grinning sweaty faces next to red squiggles on Strava maps. Finally the clock hits the fifty-minute mark and the door to Harriet's office opens. The psychologist guides Kaia into the waiting room.

'Kaia, now it's your turn to hang out here while I talk to Mummy. Is that okay?'

Kaia doesn't say anything, but she nods and drops onto the chair Grace has just vacated. She sits on her hands and kicks her legs back and forth.

'You have an interesting daughter,' Harriet says once her office door is closed. She gestures to the chair that Kaia was sitting on moments before.

Grace lowers herself down, her legs shaking with the effort. She feels like a criminal awaiting sentence, Harriet the judge, Kaia an unpredictable witness.

'Kaia was happy to open up about certain subjects,' Harriet continues, sinking into the chocolate brown office chair on the other side of the desk. 'Her grandparents, the rugby team she supports.'

Grace nods, unsure where this is heading.

'But she was wary too. And she paused after each one of my questions, like she was assessing whether it was safe to answer.'

Grace crosses one knee over the other, interlocks her fingers. 'And does that mean anything?' she asks.

'It could suggest Kaia struggles to trust people,' Harriet muses.

'Because someone is letting her down,' Grace whispers, more to herself than the psychologist.

'Or it could be a sign that she's hiding something. Perhaps the fact that she's making up these stories about her father. Deception requires more thinking time than truth.' Harriet rotates a pencil between her fingers, then places it on the desk and smiles at Grace. 'It's early days, I'll need to spend a bit more time with Kaia to build a more accurate picture.'

Grace catches Harriet's eye and steels herself for the question she knows she needs to ask. 'And did Kaia talk about her accident at all?'

'In part. She told me about Dr Gupta, what a brilliant doctor she was. And the helipad that she could see from her bed.'

'And her father?' Grace whispers.

Harriet takes a sip of water then carefully places the glass back on her desk. The water line dips slightly, then levels. 'When you told me that Kaia blames her injuries on Marcus, you seemed very sure that she's making it up. That Marcus is the innocent one. Why is that?'

Grace's heart quickens its pace. 'I've been with Marcus since I was 16.' She tries to sound authoritative. 'I know him. He's not the violent type.'

'And you're absolutely certain? You've never seen him act aggressively?'

'Not once.' The lie sits heavy in the air between them but Grace forces herself to keep eye contact. She waits for the psychologist to say something, but she doesn't. Grace needs to fill the silence. 'So did Kaia say something about Marcus? Is that why you're asking me this?'

'Kaia clammed up when I asked her how she got her injuries. And she didn't accuse her father of anything.' She pauses. 'But she did say something that concerned me.'

Grace holds her breath.

'She said that you're being forced to do it.'

'Do what?' Grace whispers.

'That's all she said, so I'm afraid I don't know.'

*

Grace doesn't really remember leaving. She managed to shuffle backwards without her smile disintegrating and move through the doorway of Harriet's office without yanking it open, or slamming it closed. But that's as much as her numb brain could achieve. There's a vague recollection of reaching for Kaia's hand in the waiting room, roughly she thinks, and booking another session with the receptionist. But nothing more.

Forced to do what? Does Kaia think Marcus is forcing Grace to deny his abuse? Is that how her 7-year-old brain is reconciling Grace's unwillingness to accept her claims? A wave of nausea rises through her chest and she stops walking to let it pass.

Because of course she did deny a truth, telling Harriet that she's never seen Marcus act aggressively.

It was only once. But how much proof does she need? How many times does someone need to display raw violence to be considered capable of it?

'Are you okay, Mummy?'

Grace looks down at her daughter. She can see the old Kaia now, the warmth of concern shimmering on her face. She squeezes her hand and smiles.

'Don't worry, I kept your secret,' Kaia whispers.

Grace stifles a gasp. Is this what she's doing? Coercing her child into staying silent? Siding with a violent husband over an innocent child? She takes a deep breath and forces herself to think about that night. Fourteen years ago, when Marcus hit her. He apologised a few days later, desperately, and she forgave him. And that was that. Was she wrong to let him off so lightly? Should she have walked away? Or at least pushed harder to find out what drove him to it?

There were other people in the room too. Josh. Coco. They witnessed what ignited Marcus's fury. Josh has never been willing to explain it to Grace either. And Coco isn't there to ask.

Tears sting in Grace's eyes as she thinks about Coco. How much she still misses her childhood friend. She hasn't seen her for years, but Coco was by her side through all the big moments. The many milestones of growing up. That summer when she first met Marcus, including the night when his rage flared. Then fate brought them together again on that crazy New Year's Eve in Phuket when she got so drunk that Coco and Marcus had to carry her to bed.

And Coco also knows the truth about Kaia's start in life.

With a wave of desperation, Graces wishes her friend was with her now.

She unlocks the car with a click and pulls opens the heavy door. She helps Kaia climb into her seat and lets it fall closed again. Released from her daughter's watchful stare, Grace leans against the shiny black metal and lets the freshness of the wind wash across her skin. But the tears are too heavy now and they start to weave a path down her face anyway.

Either Marcus is hurting Kaia, or Kaia is turning her father into a monster inside her head. Neither explanation seems possible to Grace. And Grace's mother and brother are giving her conflicting advice. How can she solve this by herself?

She thinks again about Coco, and the fragility that hides behind her party girl image.

She's been to places that Grace can only guess at, physically and mentally. Is that what Grace needs? A damaged mind to see things she can't? But that's not the only reason she wants Coco by her side. She knows there are other insights that her best friend could provide.

With that thought, a sense of certainty settles on her shoulders.

Coco will know what to do.

Now Grace just needs to find her.

Chapter 19

MARCUS

2005

Marcus tries to concentrate on the task. He flicks the white sheet, and it hangs in the air for a second before floating down onto the double bed. He tucks in the corners, swears with the effort required for the final one, and starts on the seashell-dotted duvet cover.

But it's not working.

He can't get her out of his mind.

He picks up the can of Pledge and sprays it haphazardly along the various surfaces in the room. Two bedside tables, a chest of drawers, windowsill. Then he finds a clean corner of the duster and flings it from left to right, smearing the white splodges along the woodwork until they finally disappear, replaced with a shine just about good enough for his mum to sign off.

He's never felt like this before.

He's had a couple of girlfriends since he started at Chilford. There was Bex in the summer term of Year 12, after the rugby season finished and he'd got some spare time on his hands. But *out of sight, out of mind* ruled that relationship and they broke up early into the summer holidays. Then there'd been Bronwen, a girl he'd met on a Christmas rugby tour to Wales. She shared his passion for the sport, but that didn't help much in the long run and their fling had fizzled out by New Year.

So he doesn't understand why he's spent the last six days obsessing over Coco. When Josh phoned last night to suggest a day out to the beach, he hadn't dared ask whether the girls were part of the plan, but he'd found himself making a silent wish that they were. And that's what forced him to admit that he's fallen for a sassy 16-year-old with more family issues than the Osbournes.

He throws the Hoover around the bits of carpet he can see, then packs up the cleaning stuff and takes it downstairs, shoving it back inside the utility room. He's due at Josh's house at 11 a.m., which means he's got just enough time to shower off the smell of bleach and transform back from a domestic skivvy into a desirable future rugby star.

'Have you finished all three rooms already?' Tania looks at her watch, then eyes him suspiciously. It's true that he doesn't normally start his list of chores until at least midday, but he hasn't had much reason to get on with it before today. Other than his daily training session – sprints in the park plus a full-body-weights workout at home – he's spent all his free time since Saturday either sleeping, playing FIFA or moping around the house. He'd thought about catching up with mates from his old school, but had decided he couldn't face it, the piss-taking he knew they'd subject him to. So he'd stuck his headphones on, played Arctic Monkeys on loop, and tried to get the image of Coco out of his mind.

'I'm going out today, so I started early.'

'Somewhere nice?' She peers at him.

'Just out with Josh, Lyme Regis probably.'

'You're spending a lot of time with him,' she observes. 'Don't you want to catch up with mates from your old school now you're back? They miss you.'

Marcus looks at the doorway and wonders how soon he'll be able to escape. 'Yeah, maybe.'

'Don't forget your roots, love.'

A spark of anger sizzles on his skin. Why is having big dreams such a problem in this house? 'Why send me to Chilford then? If you don't want me to move on?'

'Chilford was for your rugby career, not a personality transplant.'

'Why the fuck can't you just be happy that I've got ambition?' He juts his jaw forward and stares at her. But she holds his gaze.

'Because you swear at the woman who raised you.' Then she twists on her heel and walks out of the room.

*

Fifteen minutes later, the shower has done its job and his mood has improved. He packs a few essentials in his Canterbury rucksack and kisses his mum goodbye, an apology of sorts. Then he pulls his mountain bike out from the shed. Josh's house is three miles away as the crow flies, and Marcus takes the direct route through wheat fields, where combine harvesters have already started the annual cull. He listens to the gentle hum of machines and lets his mind wander to Coco again. He can't work out whether the attraction is mutual. Yeah, she flirted like a flamingo on heat, but he gets the impression that's standard behaviour for her. His instinct tells him it was more than that, but is that just wishful thinking?

He arrives at the corner gate of the field and turns onto the main road that runs through Josh's village. It's more country lane than highway, and he only passes a couple of cars on the final leg of his journey up the hill. When he reaches Northcross House, he's once again awed by the stature of his best friend's home, but at least this time he knows how to get in.

Except he doesn't need to.

The garage door opens and a silver BMW Z4 backs out, its roof down and exhaust rumbling. Josh is at the wheel with Coco in the passenger seat. Grace is sitting in the back, a long, tanned arm draped over the side of the car. So the girls *are* coming. A frisson of excitement flames in Marcus's belly, and he takes a deep breath to calm it down.

'Jump in,' Josh calls, eyes hidden by Oakley sunglasses, mouth grinning like he's won the lottery. As it turns out, that's not far off. 'I won a bet with my dad and now we've got this badass beauty for the day.' He revs the engine to make his point.

Marcus leans his bike against the outer fence and leapfrogs into the back seat. 'What would have happened if you'd lost?'

'A month of mowing the lawn.'

'Ouch. I thought you had a gardener?'

'Irrelevant, my friend. This is Henry's way of teaching me about risk and reward.'

Marcus nods to Grace sitting next to him, and she smiles back, her white teeth sparkling in the sunlight. He hadn't noticed how generous her smile was before. He leans back against the plush headrest and feels the increasing wind on his face as Josh accelerates down the hill. 'He lost the bet though. Maybe your dad needs his own lesson in risk and reward?'

'Don't you dare insult the great Henry Windsor,' Coco pipes up. 'This is all part of his master plan.'

'Oh yeah?' Josh asks, sounding like he's genuinely interested in Coco's observation about his father.

'Think about it. This thing does nought to sixty in maybe three or four seconds?'

'Probably. How did you know that?'

'Wandering around the paddock at Monaco Grand Prix every year while your parents quaff champagne, you pick stuff up. Anyway, driving this car is the real game of risk versus reward. Do you push it to its limit, take the thrill but risk smashing the fuck out of it? And later, when I whip out my stash of vodka, do you enjoy the pleasure of drinking with me but risk getting stopped by the police? It's mind games, Joshua; Henry is still the master.'

Josh laughs, seemingly unbothered by her warning. Marcus feels impotent in the back seat. Coco is flirting with Josh just like she did with him last week, and there's nothing he can do about it, not while he's stuck in the back like a child. He turns round to look at Grace again. She's tied her hair back now, a more sensible approach than the one Coco has chosen, whose long red tresses are currently whipping around her headrest.

Marcus leans forward, between the two front seats. 'Have you had any thoughts about what we should do in Lyme Regis?' They've reached the main road and Marcus has to shout to drown out the roar from the wind.

'Yes, mate. I booked water skiing for us all. It's thirty quid each, okay?'

Marcus grits his teeth, nods and forces a smile. A bloody fortune for a sport he's never managed to conquer. While his parents have never approved of motorised water sports – why pollute the planet when you can harness the energy of a wave? – he has tried it a few times with friends and never managed to even get out of the water. It's his stature, he's always claimed. Too heavy for those stupid skinny planks.

'Ooh I love water skiing! Great idea, Josh.'

Marcus watches Coco rest her hand on Josh's arm, then let it slowly slip away, stroking his triceps with her fingertips as they fall. Jesus, what a prick-tease she is. She was all over him on Saturday; now it seems to be Josh's turn. He can't believe he's wasted a week thinking about her. He turns to Grace. 'Are you a fan of water skiing too?'

She gives him a small smile and shrugs. 'Swimming is more my thing, but I guess hanging out in the water is always fun?'

Marcus likes that she says it as a question, not willing to make it fact until he concurs. He returns her smile and leans back again. The sun is warm on his face, and the wind flooding past him feels good. Grace is right. Taking a speedboat far out into the sea will be fun. And who knows, he may even get out of the water this time.

Chapter 20

'Come on, man. Think PMA and you've got this.'

Marcus bobs in the water, trying to ignore the welts already forming on the underside of his knuckles. 'Fuck your positive mental attitude,' he mumbles under his breath. This is his fifth attempt at getting up and positive thinking has done fuck all to help him so far.

'You can do it, Marcus!' Coco giggles, her legs moving fluidly with the sway of the boat while her upper body stays balanced. She's wearing an emerald-green bikini and there's the hint of a tattoo snaking down one side of her midriff. He'll have his own tattoo one day soon, he thinks to himself, as the water laps at his chin. A Maori symbol to mark his first cap for the All Blacks.

He swears again, then drags his legs in front of him, no easy task with two inflexible planks attached to each foot. He pulls his knees into his chest and straightens out his arms, just like he's been taught, gripping the handle as tightly as he can bear. This time he's going to get the fuck up, he promises himself. The engine of the speedboat builds to a roar and he can feel the familiar resistance in his arms. He stays curled and waits. Then out of nowhere, the boat pulls him up. He's upright and his feet are still attached to his skis!

Suddenly he's flying through the water. He wills himself to keep leaning back and let the judder of tiny waves ripple through his knees. Josh waves from behind his video camera, Coco whoops, and Grace claps her congratulations. He beams at them all, like he's just climbed Everest. Then he eyes the wake building either side of him. Fuck it, he can't just hang behind the boat all day. He takes a deep breath and leans to the right. His skis read the situation instantly and turn to face the mound of white water. Then he hits it. Boom! But the skis don't cut through like they should. They stop dead, the rope spins out of his hand and he plummets headfirst into the water.

'Marcus, are you okay?' Grace is the first to lean over the side of the boat as it circles round to pick him up.

'Yeah, fine.' He grimaces, shaking the water out of his ears and trying to ignore the throbbing sensation where his head smacked the water. Luckily his skis came off in the crash, so he doesn't have the embarrassment of manhandling them off his feet in front of everyone. He holds them aloft and Josh reaches down to grab them. Then he pushes down on the back of the boat and swivels round to sitting. At least he has impressive upper body strength.

'Trying the wake on your first ski, brave move, mate.' Josh pats him on the shoulder like a stray dog. 'Right, me next, I guess.' He dives into the water and gestures for Marcus to throw him the mono ski. Of course he's too good for two skis, just like the girls had been on their turns. Josh slips it on, gives the driver a thumbs up, and rises out of the water like some modern-day Jesus. After a minute or two, he lifts his thumb again, and the boat goes faster. Suddenly Josh leans hard left, and whips across the wake. He takes one hand off the handle and lets it trail in the water, before moving back across the wake, still at breakneck speed, and out to the far right of the boat.

'My, your brother is quite the skier,' Coco purrs, dropping her sunglasses and peering out to sea.

'Especially when he's got an audience,' Grace notes with a smirk.

'When the reward outweighs the risk,' Coco muses. 'I must say, I find it a very attractive trait.'

Marcus lets out a disgruntled sigh and hopes neither of the girls notice. Luckily they don't.

'Eurgh that's gross,' Grace sniffs. 'He's my brother, remember?'

Coco erupts into laughter. 'I'm only joking, you idiot. Josh is practically my brother too. And there are many other gorgeous fish in the sea, aren't there, Marcus?'

'What?' This girl is messed up – he can hardly keep up.

'Gorgeous fish in the sea. I wondered whether you might have swallowed one?'

Grace snorts with laughter, then sucks it back in. 'Sorry, Marcus.' But her face creases again, and despite himself, Marcus can't help joining in. By the time Josh signals for the boat to pick him up, and they loop round to meet him, the three of them are laughing so much that they can't even catch their breath to explain the joke, and he looks a bit put out as he climbs on board.

Ten minutes later the driver drops them at the edge of the Cobb, a long stone jetty that doubles as the border for Lyme Regis harbour. Coco hands him a sizeable tip, then kisses his cheek and tells him it was the smoothest water ski she's ever had. Marcus watches the driver smile his gratitude and help her out of the boat like she's a Victorian-era aristocrat. There are a hundred or so boats lined up within the harbour walls, their noses pointing out to sea, and as the four of them curl around the Cobb and make their way onto the beach, Marcus imagines owning one of the shinier powerboats one day.

*

Marcus lifts up onto his elbows and stares out to sea. Then he shifts his eyeline to Coco's bum. It's pale and smooth, moulded into a perfect curve. She's lying on her front, her head resting on the back of her hands. Asleep, he thinks.

'Caught you looking.' Coco lets out a low chuckle, then unfolds one arm and rests her hand on Marcus's knee.

'No, I wasn't,' he spurts out, horrified that she might think him a perv.

'I don't mind, you know. It's a compliment.' With her other hand she reaches into her bag and brings out a plastic water bottle. 'You want some?' she offers.

Marcus is about to shake his head when he notices the glint in her eye. 'Your stash of vodka?' Her smile grows and he takes the bottle from her. Josh has got his headphones on, oblivious, and Grace is pounding some lengths out at sea. He takes a few swigs, the alcohol scorching a path to his belly, then passes the bottle back to Coco. She sits up, huddles close to him, and takes a few mouthfuls.

'This rugby thing,' she starts.

'Yeah?'

'Are all your muscles as big as your biceps?' She flutters her eyelids and her cat's eyes twinkle in the fading sun. Slowly one corner of her mouth curls upwards.

'Can I ask you something?' Marcus isn't immune of course, he can already feel himself hardening, but he's not giving in so easily this time.

'Anything,' she offers, and makes it sound like a promise.

'Why do you flirt all the time? With everyone?' She doesn't answer straight away, and he wonders if it's sadness that washes over her face. But it's gone in an instant, and quickly followed by a smile more suggestive than the last.

'Because it's fun. And I love to have fun, Marcus.' She shuffles a bit closer, until their lips are almost touching.

He can smell that scent again. The freshness of fruit, but this time mixed with salt and sun cream. He pushes a few strands of red hair away from her face and feels his heart rate slow. Should

117

he do this? Lean in for a kiss and pray he doesn't make an idiot of himself? Or is that a stupid idea? Coco was all over Josh on the way here, then giving that ski boat driver the eye. Is the whole thing just one big game to her?

Fuck it.

'Do you want to have fun with me?' His voice is lower than he planned, and gravelly, like he thinks he's a Hollywood movie star. He steals himself for the inevitable smirk, the chime of her laugh. But she stays silent, just looking at him, as though for the first time. And then eventually she speaks. 'Maybe I do.' She sounds surprised, like she's only just realised it, and it makes him smile. He slowly leans forward.

'Jesus, it's freezing in there! Coco, hand me a towel will you.'

Marcus's head whips round. Grace is stood over them, water droplets trickling down her arms.

Coco jerks back too, and gives him a hard *don't say anything* stare. Then she smiles at Grace. 'Darling, you need something stronger to warm you up, you crazy ice-water maiden.' Coco holds up the illicit water bottle. The old Coco is back now, giggling like a toddler with a bagful of sweets.

Grace rolls her eyes but takes the bottle anyway, its plastic rim banging against her chattering teeth.

Marcus takes pity on her and throws her a towel. He watches her dry off, then pull her long hair free of its ponytail.

'What's going on?' Josh sits up on his elbows and pulls the headphones off.

'We're having a vodka party, and you're not invited, Mr Designated Driver.' Coco wiggles her finger at him.

'Well, in that case …' Josh stands up, flicks sand off his towel. 'I think it's time to go.'

And as Marcus tries to shove his towel into his bag, he can't help wondering whether that moment with Coco – that fleeting moment – actually happened at all.

Chapter 21

GRACE

2019

A grey light washes over the kitchen as Grace steps inside and nudges the door closed behind her. The heating hasn't come on yet, and she wishes she'd thought to grab a jumper before coming downstairs. She's rusty at this now, getting up in the dark when her body is still craving rest. Kaia was quick to sleep through the night as a baby. Other new mums put it down to her being bottle fed. They'd say it in a tone that implied disapproval, but Grace knew they were just trying to hide their envy.

It wasn't Kaia who had woken Grace at 3 a.m. last night though, at least not directly. Grace had tried to get back to sleep, forced her body to stay motionless in the hope that it would stem the flood of thoughts racing around her mind. But it hadn't worked. And when her phone reached 5 a.m. she finally gave up trying and slipped out of bed, careful not to wake Marcus quietly snoring beside her.

She flips down the kettle switch and drops a teabag into her favourite mug, hand-painted by Kaia at a local pottery studio when she was 2. While Grace waits for the water to boil, she traces the rose-pink shapes with her fingertip, Kaia's tiny hand-prints splayed out both sides of the ceramic surface. It had been a special afternoon, the two of them with their heads together creating unique pieces of crockery, a handful for their kitchen and then Christmas gifts for the family. They'd gone to Devon that year to spend Christmas with Tania and Shane, who'd been delighted with their Granny and Grandpa cereal bowls. The twins were 19 by then and had been brilliant with Kaia, crawling in and out of her new jungle gym, narrating their favourite Santa stories. Marcus hadn't been able to relax though; the secret that created an invisible wall between him and his family made that impossible.

She catches the kettle before it rumbles to a crescendo, then pours water over her teabag and squeezes it hard against the side. She needs builder's tea this morning. She slides onto a stool and takes a long sip. That's better. Her laptop is sat on the breakfast bar and she thinks about leaning over, dragging it towards her. But what would be the point? She's already searched online for Coco every way she can think of. Once she'd realised how much she needed to see her best friend again, she hadn't been able to let it rest. She'd started looking as soon as she got back from Harriet's office on Wednesday, and then again yesterday when she was supposed to be using Kaia's final day of school before the Easter holidays to catch up on work.

She tried the obvious websites first. Google, then Facebook, Instagram and Twitter. While she searched frantically for her best friend in the aftermath of their last reunion, she hadn't tried for over seven years, so it made sense to start at the beginning. But she found nothing. There were a few name matches, but the profiles had quickly shown those accounts belonged to different Coco Byrnes. Then she'd ventured a bit further, tried YouTube and TikTok. She'd even checked out LinkedIn in case Coco had defied her teachers' predictions and built some sort of career. But no luck there either.

She knew Coco could be married by now, and have a new surname. That thought had taken her down a few winding rabbit holes on Thursday morning, but after checking hundreds of profiles where Coco was the first name, she'd still come up blank.

Grace steeples her fingers and drops her chin on top. It's doesn't really make sense. The Coco she knows – new surname or not – would be super active on these sites, even trending on her good days. It was like Coco was practising for social media before it even became a thing. She loved to dance in front of the mirror in the bedroom they shared at school, pretend to be Christina Aguilera or Britney Spears and copy their famous moves. She'd get Grace to film the performance with her video camera, and another girl in their house would put the footage to music and somehow link it to the TV in their common room. Coco could probably have invented TikTok if she'd put her mind to it. Except applying herself wasn't really Coco's style.

Grace doesn't want to think of the one glaring reason why Coco might not be online. The possible ending for a girl who spends her life wandering the globe alone, finding drugs and parties wherever she can. Someone who puts herself in risky situations without caring about her safety. And Coco can't have been thinking straight after their last time together. She just upped and left one morning before Grace woke up. She'd left a note. *Thank you; don't worry; I'm sorry.* But nothing helpful like a forwarding address. Grace loads up Google and types 'Coco Byrne' again but this time, after a pause, she adds 'death'. A British woman killed overseas would always get at least a mention in the press, so if nothing comes up, there's a high chance she's still alive. She scans the page, then lets out a long sigh of relief. Nothing.

But what next? Believing Coco's alive doesn't bring Grace any closer to finding her.

'You're up early.'

Grace jumps, sucks in some air.

'What are you doing?' Marcus peers over her shoulder.

'Nothing.' She taps the lid closed, and turns back towards him, plastering on a smile. 'Cup of tea?' she asks.

'I'll make it.' He wanders over to the kettle, unaware of her quickening heartbeat. He wouldn't approve of her looking for Coco now. Marcus made her promise to put the events of those few weeks after Kaia was born behind them, to scrub them out of their past and pretend life was normal. 'Why couldn't you sleep?' he adds, not looking up.

'Things on my mind, I guess,' she improvises. 'Work stuff, school holidays.'

'Not Kaia then? You still haven't told me what the psychologist said on Wednesday.'

Grace pauses, unsure how much to tell him. That Harriet is suspicious of him? And that Grace lied to protect Marcus and now that lie is sitting on her chest like a heavy anchor? 'She said Kaia seemed quite wary at times,' she chooses. 'Hesitated before answering each of her questions.'

'That's understandable. A stranger in an unfamiliar setting.' His voice sounds strained. 'I hate that we're putting her through that.'

Grace looks at the man she's loved for fourteen years. His shoulders are broader than most and his biceps swell beneath his T-shirt. The traditional Maori tattoo that runs the length of one arm could appear intimidating to some, but she knows it's a symbol of his loyalty and commitment. The same attributes that he's always shown towards Kaia. He can't be hurting her; it's impossible. 'Harriet's lovely,' she says, trying to pacify him. 'And Kaia likes her.'

'I suppose she blames me,' he says, bitterness creeping in. 'I assume Kaia told Harriet that I pushed her out of the tree?'

Grace looks at her hands. 'No, she didn't mention it,' she mumbles, not willing to admit the part she played in that revelation.

'Really? Well, I suppose that's something.'

He sounds so surprised that distrust starts to bubble again. Grace doesn't want to catch his gaze, so she hides behind her cup of tea and pours the cold dregs down her throat. She senses him place his mug on the breakfast bar and move behind her. His hands land on her shoulders. She tenses at his touch, but he takes that as his cue to rub them. 'Whoa, you're tight.'

His thumbs push against her neck, and suddenly she can't bear it. There are so many questions swirling around her head, that she needs space. Time to find the answers. She squirms away from him, and Marcus drops his hands, a dark look flitting across his face.

'Anyway, I thought I would take Kaia to the aquarium today,' he says. 'Just the two of us. A special Good Friday treat.'

Grace imagines them leaving for the day, Kaia's safety entirely in his hands. She can't do it. 'Sounds great. I think I'll come too.'

'Really? I thought you'd relish the chance to go to the lido for a swim.' He pauses for a moment, and Grace watches his expression change. He fires out an acidic chuckle. 'You don't trust me, do you?'

'Of course I do.'

'You think Kaia needs protecting from me.'

'I just want to spend the day with my family.' She steels herself to look at him, then searches his eyes for clues: guilt, discomfort, annoyance at her ruining his plans to have Kaia to himself. But there's only sadness and disappointment there.

'Whatever, Grace,' he says, and disappears out of the room.

Chapter 22

Kaia dips underneath the glass display unit and her head disappears into the pop-up viewing area. So Grace focuses on her daughter's feet instead. Kaia is pivoting on the toes of her Nike trainers, her purple-edged heels swaying left and right. It's something she's done since she could walk. A sign that she's either excited or nervous. And it's such a relief to know that today – finally – it's excitement that's fuelling her endearing little tic.

'What can you see up there?' she calls out.

'A huge, hairy spider,' Kaia exclaims with awe. 'And his legs are bright blue. I want to stroke him.'

A grin spreads across Grace's face as she absorbs Kaia's enthusiasm. It's been too long. But she's read the plaque next to the display and the blue baboon tarantula doesn't sound like the most endearing companion. 'I'm not sure that's a good idea.'

'Shall we go and see the fish now?' Marcus suggests. 'They've added a new section to Coral Kingdom apparently; it sounds really cool, Kaia.' He's trying to appear upbeat too, but Grace can hear the growing impatience rumbling under the surface. He'd suggested Coral Kingdom when they first arrived at the London Aquarium, and Kaia had responded by asking to visit the Rainforest Adventure instead. Marcus had tried to convince her otherwise, reminded her about the stingrays splashing in the open pool and the sharks prowling around the three-storey central tank, but she'd claimed that the poisonous spiders and red-bellied piranhas were more fun. Grace had solved the impasse by suggesting a half an hour time limit in the rainforest and then moving on. They've now been there almost an hour and Marcus is getting restless.

'Daddy's mad with me,' Kaia announces as she ducks back from underneath the display.

'No, I'm not,' Marcus responds, although his tone suggests otherwise.

'Are you going to hit me again?'

Marcus's eyes dart around the room. Small groups of people wander around, but they're just silhouettes. The lights are so low that they're almost in darkness, save for the glow from the displays. He grabs Kaia by the shoulders and pulls her towards him. 'Stop saying that,' he growls.

'Why?'

'I would never hurt you.'

'You're hurting me now.'

Grace looks at Marcus's hands. Even in the gloom she can see his knuckles whitening with the effort of holding on. 'Let go of her,' she whispers.

Marcus looks down at his hands as though they belong to someone else, then releases his grip and pushes them in his pockets. Like he's neutralising a weapon, Grace can't help thinking. Kaia takes a couple of steps backwards, but not towards her, Grace notices. Is this the price she's paying for not believing her daughter?

Marcus turns to Grace next, his jaw set with anger. 'Jesus, Grace, *you're* making out like I'm an abusive father now.'

'Well, are you?' The words just tumble out. She regrets them instantly; she doesn't want to have this conversation in here. But it's too late. He's staring at her, the few lighter flecks in his brown eyes flickering in the darkness.

'No, I'm fucking not, Grace.' It's a whisper, but he spits it out with venom. 'I can't believe you'd ask me that. After everything I've done for you and Kaia.'

Grace looks around the room. There are a couple of other families in here, but they seem captivated by the creatures on display, not interested in a domestic dispute between a family they don't know. 'It's not me saying it though, is it? It's Kaia. So either she's a liar, or you're hurting her.'

Marcus turns away and rests his forehead on the thick glass pane of a display. A colony of ants scurry along the mock rainforest floor, each carrying a tiny section of leaf, seemingly oblivious to its enormous weight on their shoulders. Grace thinks about the weight she and Marcus carry – have carried for so long – and wonder if its enormity has proven too much for her husband.

'I don't know why she's saying it,' he admits, his voice muffled against the glass. 'Why her concussion has translated into hating me. But I can't lose your trust. You promised me.' He pulls away from the display and turns to face her. 'Think of everything I've done for you, and Kaia. We can't let her behaviour come between us.'

His words make Grace feel sick. Surely a child should always come first? It's their job to protect Kaia, not each other. She turns to look at their daughter, now staring intently at the dwarf crocodile display, searching for their bulging eyes in the murky water. 'She's our daughter,' she growls, a warning shot.

Marcus looks angry for a moment but then his face drops, a hint of shame spreading across it. He turns back towards the display. 'I know you're looking for Coco again.'

'What?' His accusation has knocked her off guard.

'I saw it in your search history. I wasn't spying on you,' he adds. 'I borrowed your laptop to look at the opening times for the aquarium and came across it.'

Grace doesn't know what to say. She takes a hairband off her wrist and twists her hair inside it. Maybe she would have told Marcus about her search eventually, explained it calmly, why she needs Coco by her side. Why they both do. But not now, not here.

'Why are you looking for her, Grace?'

It's stuffy in the dark, windowless room and it makes Grace feel claustrophobic. She wants to walk away. From him, from everything. But that's not what Grace Windsor does. She toughs it out. So instead, she flicks her head and turns to face him. 'I know Coco is a stranger to us now,' she starts. 'And Kaia is a stranger to her.'

'Exactly, I don't think it's a good idea to try and find her after all this time.'

'But she was my best friend Marcus, more like a sister really. I've never been that close to anyone since Coco, except you.'

'And you trust her more than me now?'

'There are so many people giving me their opinion: you, Kaia's teacher, my mum, Harriet ...' Grace pauses. She can't let Marcus know she's spoken to Josh. 'And Kaia, of course. I want to talk to someone who's known me forever; and who knows you too,' she adds cautiously.

'You think Coco's going to have the answer? What will she say? Sure, Grace, Kaia's bound to be fucked up after her start in life, or yes, I always suspected Marcus was a child beater. Jesus, Grace, she hasn't seen us for over seven years, Kaia was a tiny baby for Chrissakes. How the hell is she going to make that kind of judgement?'

'She was there,' Grace whispers. 'That night you hit me.'

Marcus swivels away from her, pushes his hand through his hair. 'Shit, Grace, that again? How many times do I have to apologise? Promise it will never happen again?'

'You split my lip.'

'You took the flowers, accepted my apology. You agreed to go on a fucking date with me. Why are you bringing it up now?'

'Why do you think?' Grace spits out. 'If you're hurting Kaia—'

'I'm not.'

'—and social services come for you—'

'They won't.'

'—then they'll come for me too, won't they? Everything we've done to protect our family, every lie we've told. It will all be for nothing. Because they'll ransack our life until they find out the truth.'

'God, Grace. Kaia is making it all up! I don't know why, maybe it's just her concussion talking. You have to trust me!'

'How can I though? When I know first-hand how good a liar you are?'

He freezes. Stares at her like she's betraying him. Perhaps she is. She bites her lip and looks away.

'You think finding Coco will help?'

'I need her, Marcus.'

'You'll be opening a can of worms,' he whispers.

'I don't care.'

Marcus turns to look at Kaia, then back at Grace. 'Don't let Coco come between us, Grace.'

Grace manages a tiny smile, then walks over to Kaia, wondering who Marcus means by 'us'.

Chapter 23

COCO

2011

Coco wonders whether it would be appropriate to have a cigarette. Not here, obviously. But out there, on the balcony. Make her little contribution to the pollution party. She's just not sure if she can walk. She sighs, stretches out her arms, then wriggles down the bed. Time for a status check. Toes work, calves and thighs clench and relax well enough. There's a whole load of pain burning between her legs, but that's to be expected, under the circumstances.

Satisfied that she can make it to standing, she pushes back the cover and drops her legs over one side. Hospital beds always sit a bit higher than regular ones, saving nurses' backs probably, but she finds solid ground eventually. With the soles of her feet firmly planted on the cool tiled floor, she twists her upper body and drags it into a sitting position. A wave of nausea rises, but quickly settles. This is going better than expected. She takes a deep breath, and pushes off. She staggers more than walks, but manages to retrieve the packet of Marlboro Lights she stashed in her overnight bag en route, and slides open the door. She breathes in the warm, stagnant air.

The balcony is tiny, less than two metres square, but there's just enough room for a small table and one chair. She lowers her battered body until it reaches hard plastic and stares out across the body of water cantering along in the breeze. The Chao Phraya River is a deep chasm that runs from the centre of the country through Bangkok and out into the Gulf of Thailand. It's not a peaceful view. Ferries, river buses and long-tail boats chug up and down; motors drone, tourists snap pictures, drivers shout out to one another. But at least it takes her mind off things, like what the fuck she's going to do next. She pulls a cigarette out of the packet, flicks down the lighter, and takes a long, satisfying draw.

She's been in Bangkok for over four months now and has gradually discovered that the only way to find tranquillity in the city is inside one of the Buddhist temples. Not the well-known ones, like the Temple of the Emerald Buddha at the Grand Palace, where tourists congregate and guides try to herd them around with interesting facts and warnings not to touch, take photos of, or turn your back on Buddha's image too soon. But there are others tucked away, still glorious in gold and marble, but without the crowds. Coco has spent more time wandering temples over the last few months than she would ever have imagined at the start of the year, hoping some higher power would have the solution that she – a mere human – couldn't figure out. Although in the end, it had been her who'd crafted a plan.

A not-too-gentle knock at the balcony door startles her and she whips her head round to see who the culprit is. She sighs. Chailai is standing on the other side of the glass, hands on her narrow hips, a look of surprise laced with disapproval on her beautiful face.

'Yes, yes, I'm coming,' Coco mumbles, leaning forward. There's a glass ashtray on the table, helpfully provided for fallen women like her, and she twists the remnants of her cigarette into it. Then she pushes off the chair, wonders how her 22-year-old body can feel like it's packing up already, and smiles at her maternity nurse. Then she takes one last look at the busy river, tries to suck some energy from it, and steps back inside her room.

'Sorry to disturb you, miss, but I think your baby needs feeding.'

Coco looks towards the bed and the rectangular cot attached to its side. She shifts her gaze to the creature inside, eyes closed, snuffling and gnawing on one minuscule fist. Like some mad biological sorcery, her bloated breasts tense and pull at the sight. She's both appalled and intrigued by the primitive behaviour her body has demonstrated over the last two days. To Coco, woman-hood is about relentless hair removal and finding a bra that gives you cleavage. Not staring at a tiny baby and feeling like its mother.

Chailai must sense her reluctance because she glides over to the cot – that's how she moves, like a ballerina performing adagio – and lifts the baby out. 'You can sit in the chair, miss. I can pass her to you.'

She could refuse. Chailai wouldn't question her decision – that's not what happens when you tip someone a month's salary. The nurse would make up a bottle with one of those powdered milks, a blend of nutrients scientifically proven to keep your baby healthy, or so the adverts say. Coco suspects her own provision isn't as impressive. A diet of Pad Thai, bananas and Singha beer (just one per night, she's not completely irresponsible) isn't likely to produce gold-standard breast milk. But weirdly, even with the pain of her nipples being sucked by a Dyson in disguise, she's quite enjoying feeding her daughter.

Coco sinks into the armchair and reaches her hands up. Chailai has wrapped the infant in a soft yellow blanket and Coco feels her warmth as she positions the baby in the crook of one arm. Then she leans back against the plump cushions and lets her child forage for what she needs. Out of the two of them, it's the little one who seems to know what she's doing the most.

'So today you go home?' Chailai asks, smoothing down the ruffled sheets, then perching on the side of the bed.

'This afternoon.' Coco turns towards the balcony again. She'll be glad to be out of here; however many pictures of flowers you hang up, you can't mask the smell of a hospital room. But going back to her guesthouse means she'll be on her own with a baby. And not a clue what to do, either now or later.

Except that's not true, of course. She knows exactly what she's going to do, what she needs to do to make everything all right again. It's a plan she came up with in one of the temples, under the watchful eye of a golden Buddha statue. A plan she set in motion when she booked her all-inclusive childbirth package at Thonburi Hospital.

It's a good plan.

'Well, I'm going to miss you. You have made me smile a lot these past days. You know, I don't think it matters that this baby doesn't have a daddy when she has a mummy like you, Miss Grace.' Then Chailai beams her widest smile, and slips out of the room.

Chapter 24

Coco peels another banana and shifts her position on the bed. The sun is blazing outside, but she's got the air con just right and the half-pulled curtains are keeping the glare off the TV screen. The baby is fed, changed and now asleep beside her. Harry Potter is doing his bit to fight dark magic on the screen in front of her, even if the *Deathly Hallows Part Two* DVD that she picked up at the Khaosan Road market the day before is proving to be dodgy, the swaying heads of cinemagoers along the bottom of the picture giving a clue to its circumspect provenance. Coco isn't drunk, high, or sizzling with excitement about how her night might unfold. And yet – quite incredibly – she feels content.

As the soft fruit melts in her mouth, she watches Harry head towards the Forbidden Forest for his showdown with Voldermort. He'll come out on top though, Coco decides, unsure why that matters. Except he doesn't. The ugly bald guy casts some killing curse and Harry is out for the count. As Coco watches Harry's still body, tears well in her eyes. She shakes her head and blinks. Why is she crying over a movie? Why does she care about a fictional character? The baby lets out a whimper, as though reminding her why. *You're a mother now; you're not sane anymore.* Coco smiles and strokes her daughter's belly, smoothing away any dream monsters or, more likely, rumbling wind. Then she rests her head back against the pillow and, with a sense of satisfaction, watches Harry leap out of Hagrid's arms, very much alive.

Coco always assumed she'd be a shit mother. She's read enough women's magazines to know about that cycle. Abused child becomes abuser, detached parents raise emotionally defunct kids. On that score, Coco was destined to be a reluctant mother at best. So it's been a surprise, really. Perhaps David and Martina did Coco a favour by dumping her on another family, lining up a much better role model in parenting skills. Maybe it's Faith's influence that has made Coco fall head over heels in love with her daughter.

Which is why she's been putting off the next stage of her plan.

In that hotel room in Phuket at New Year, she had no idea about the curve ball that life would throw at her this year, so she's not quite sure why she stole Grace's passport, while Marcus was still in the bathroom washing sand off her rum-addled best friend. Perhaps Coco's parents' letter had spooked her enough to want the comfort blanket of a second identity, the powerful currency that a British passport brings in a fledgling economy like Thailand's. Or maybe, after five and a half years apart, Coco just wanted a memento of her best friend to carry with her for a while.

She hadn't thought for a moment that Grace's passport would be the solution to her pregnancy problem. But that's how things turned out.

With an extra twenty thousand Thai baht in her pocket, Chailai had been happy to overlook the clumsy overlay of Coco's head-shot into the passport – doctored by a Canadian drug dealer Coco had charmed. Chailai had faxed it through to the local *Tessaban* for them to issue the baby's birth certificate, with the logo of Bangkok's finest hospital adding much-needed cachet. Coco knew that Grace would have reported her passport stolen, so she spent the next couple of hours worrying that the cancelled passport number would set off some alert. But luckily that detail hadn't made its way to the local Thai authorities, and Coco was presented with her *Jang Gert* later that day. Mother's name, Grace Windsor. Father's name, unknown.

She called the baby Kaia. The most popular girl's name in New Zealand, according to Google. It was all part of her well-thought-through plan.

The problem is, she's not sure it's such a good plan anymore.

The movie is reaching its crescendo, Harry's final showdown with his nemesis, but it's making her tired now. All that surviving against the odds. She wants to survive without the hardship, to live in a warm cocoon with everything she needs to keep her and Kaia happy. She closes her eyes and lets her mind wander to him, Kaia's father, imagines him crawling inside their cocoon too. Does she want that? Could they be together again after everything that's happened? Not that her opinion matters. She's only ever been good enough for a secret fuck, and he's got his own life now. And dreams much bigger than hers. There's no way he'd want any part of it.

Of course, she could just continue floating around the world with Kaia by her side. The two of them, hanging out, having fun. It sounds perfect. Except for one thing.

There's no money left.

After her eventful New Year's Eve on Patong Beach, Coco decided to stay in Phuket for a while longer, to get her head around what had happened. She emailed her parents, made up a story about having a few weeks' modelling work lined up, and promised to be home by March. The idea was to party every night until all of her airfare money was spent. When she was broke, and ready to go home, she would plead for some more. Even if her parents refused to give her any cash, she knew they'd buy her a plane ticket. They wouldn't leave her stranded. But in the end, she'd found that she wasn't interested in partying. After a day on the beach, all she wanted was banana pancakes and her bed. So the money lasted longer, and the weeks rolled away.

When her period didn't come and then she was sick three mornings in a row, she bought a pregnancy test. The positive result wasn't a total surprise by then. It's not like she doesn't understand how important contraception is, but things can get a bit sketchy when the drugs are in charge. And they were most definitely in charge that night.

Telling her parents that she needed money for medical help was a stroke of genius, especially when she added that her illness was an infectious disease, just to make sure they didn't do something wildly out of character like visit her. They'd transferred more money to cover her medical bills and even sent a *get well soon* card in the post. It had been waiting for her when she waddled into the hospital on that humid afternoon in late September.

But then, in some weird fit of efficiency, her parents had remembered that they'd taken out medical insurance for Coco. All she needed to do, her mother enthused over one crackly phone call, was email over the invoices and she could claim all the money back.

So now Coco is stuck with a few hundred pounds, no medical invoices (excluding her childbirth package, and she's not showing them that) and no air ticket out of Bangkok.

And a three-week-old baby, of course.

Kaia begins to stir again, and Coco knows that this time she will wail. She quickly picks her up, hoping to pre-empt the high-volume cry. Hathai – the owner of the guesthouse – has been kinder than she needs to have been since Coco got back from the hospital, but she has gently reminded her that most guests are young couples on holiday. And high-pitched newborns down the hallway aren't exactly ideal. As Coco lies back against the headboard, she catches sight of the two photos she's stuck to the mirror on the wall opposite. One taken nine months ago, of her and Grace on Patong Beach, the other when she was 16. The older photo has got an extra shine on one side where she's held it over the years, stared at it, willed it to mean something more than it does. She rises off the bed, peels it off the mirror and slips it inside her bag.

Then she turns her attention to the newer photo. Her own pupils are dilated in the picture, her green eyes almost totally obscured by black holes, and Grace's stare is fuzzy and off centre. But their smiles are beautiful. Wide, eager. Excited to see in the new year together. With their arms wrapped around each other, their closeness looks easy, and it reminds Coco of school, when they shared a room. The two of them would lie in the darkness and whisper to each other, reveal their most secret of secrets. Or almost. Coco never admitted how much she wished Henry and Faith were her parents, how she dreamed of being a natural Windsor rather than the fraud who infiltrated their family every school holiday. That was a revelation too far. But she talked about her loneliness at home, the heavy weight of being an only, and unwanted, child.

They were 15 when Grace told Coco her own secret. How she'd sneaked into a local farmer's barn with a friend from her primary school one afternoon when she was 8. And how they'd climbed the stack of haybales inside. Except her friend had got scared and clambered back down to the ground. Not Grace though – she'd embraced the challenge of climbing to the top. When she fell, she landed on a seed drill. Coco asked her to describe the pain, but she said she couldn't, that it was too crushing for words to make sense of it. Grace's friend had run full pelt to get Faith, who'd called an ambulance and then bounced across the fields in her Volvo Estate to reach her daughter as quickly as possible. But Grace still spent nearly half an hour on her own, blood seeping out of her, thinking she was going to die.

The doctors saved her life. The night that she told Coco about her accident, Grace had slipped out of bed to show her the scars. In the moonlight, Coco could just make out a tiny cobweb of faint white marks high up on her thighs, and a slightly deeper vertical one on her belly. It hadn't looked like life or death scarring, but

Grace had explained that most of the stitches were on the inside. And that there had been so much damage that the doctors had been forced to remove her womb. It was that part of the story that was Grace's most secret of secrets.

Coco positions Kaia over one shoulder and rubs her back. This plan isn't just about solving her own problems, extracting herself from the mess of being a single mother with no money, no job, and zero sense of responsibility.

Kaia is also a gift.

The most precious gift she could ever give her best friend.

Then her thoughts turn to New Year's Eve and what happened after Grace fell asleep. She's never believed in regrets – what's the point when you can't change anything? – but she can't stop a sense of shame dropping on her like a shroud. Perhaps Marcus owes her this too, she realises.

She closes her eyes, rubs her cheek against the soft fuzz of her daughter's head, and lets the tears roll down her cheeks.

It wasn't supposed to be this hard. But she knows it's time.

Coco leans over, picks up her phone, and with shaking fingers, scrolls down until she sees Grace's thumbnail image in her contacts. The mobile number originated in the UK, and she can only hope that it's still active on the other side of the world.

It is.

'Hello?'

'Grace,' she whispers, her voice unsteady. Sounding desperate is in the plan, but she doesn't need to act.

'Coco? Is that you?'

She doesn't know which part of Auckland Grace and Marcus moved to, the conversation never reached that level of detail at New Year. But she imagines them near a harbour, with pristine white sailing boats shimmering in the distance. And a pool in the backyard filled with rippling blue water. 'I need you. Your help.'

'What's happened? Where are you?'

It will be spring in New Zealand, Coco calculates. There'll be blossom on the tree. It will be a vivid pink; pollution doesn't rub away at nature there like it does in Bangkok. It's the perfect place to raise a child. 'I can't do this.'

'Can't do what? Coco, slow down. Help me understand.'

In that moment, Coco knows that her friend will come. That Grace will book an air ticket, leave Marcus in Auckland chasing his dream, fly to Thailand. That she will arrive at Coco's guest-house, ask Hathai where she can find room 5, and the owner cum receptionist cum concierge will point at her door. 'I need you to come to Bangkok.'

'What? Why?' Now it's Grace whispering, her voice cracking.

'Because you're the only one who can save me.'

Coco will act the exhausted single mum on the brink of collapse. She will beg Grace to stay for a few days, to help out with the baby. Then that first night, when Grace is knocked out by jet lag, she'll just slip away. The rest will happen naturally. The woman who can't have children of her own will fall in love with Kaia, take her five thousand miles east to New Zealand, and won't try too hard to find her birth mother. Coco will remember why life is more fun without children. She'll use her last few hundred pounds for a flight home, and then she'll start over. Get a job, a boyfriend.

It will all be fine.

Grace is silent for a moment and Coco holds her breath, her vision swimming with imaginary blossom petals floating into an imaginary pool. And then Grace speaks. 'I'm coming. How can I find you?'

Chapter 25

GRACE

2019

'Kaia seems brighter today.' Faith pushes back an errant bramble and walks deeper into the woods, forcing Grace to drop in behind her on the narrow path. 'But I suppose chocolate can do that.'

Grace smiles to herself, a rare event these days. Perhaps chocolate can do that too. 'I think it's more the contest that excites her than the spoils, to be honest.' Henry sets an egg hunt for Kaia in their garden every Easter Sunday and it's become a hallowed tradition now, something the two of them do together. It was a relief this morning, a bona fide excuse for Kaia to miss rugby, and an opportunity for Marcus to have a couple of hours pitch side by himself. And it means Grace can enjoy a walk with her mum without worrying about Kaia's safety.

'Yes, it's funny how she's inherited Marcus's competitive streak, and his talent on the rugby pitch, despite everything.' Faith's voice trails off and silence fills the air for a while. *Despite their lack of shared genetics*, Grace knows her mum means. Despite him having no paternal rights over Kaia whatsoever. But with that thought, another more toxic one begins to scratch at Grace's temples. She rubs it away with her fingertips.

As they continue westwards through the Common, the pathway between the trees widens, and it allows Grace to move up next to Faith. She takes a deep breath. 'Parenting is hard,' she observes.

'Of course it is. But it's also an honour.'

'Perhaps it's harder for us because there's no biology to glue us together?'

'Harder for Marcus, is that what you're asking? Hard enough for him to lash out?'

'Maybe.' As Grace thinks about her husband, multiple images come up, like a frenzied slide show behind her eyes. She's witnessed a thousand different emotions on his face, in his body language, over the years. How can she ever know for sure which one represents him most accurately?

Faith pauses for a moment and Grace follows suit. They've reached Caesar's Well, a centuries-old spring in the middle of Wimbledon Common. It's not as impressive as it once was, twelve simple stone slabs radiating out from its lip, the hole half filled with murky black sludge. But it used to gurgle with water from deep underground, and it's reputed to have served the Iron-Age hillfort that sits a few hundred metres southwards, so it deserves a moment of reflection.

'Kaia is my grandchild,' Faith says, a new gravitas in her tone. 'And the unorthodox way that she came into our family makes no difference to me. I will always love her completely, do you understand?'

Grace is taken aback by the intensity of her mother's words, but she nods her head, and feels a resurgence of gratitude. 'You never judged me, for doing what I did.' Grace remembers that morning like it was yesterday, being dragged out of her deep, jet-lagged sleep by a crying baby. Finding Coco's note on the pillow next to her, along with Kaia's Thai birth certificate, its English translation and Grace's old passport. The two friends had slept in the same king-sized bed, but she still hadn't heard Coco get up, get dressed, pack her bag, and disappear out of that guesthouse in Bangkok.

'But I think it's worth recognising,' her mum continues, 'that it's Kaia who's unknown to us, not Marcus. Genetically, she's the mystery.'

'How can you say that? Biologically, she's Coco's daughter. The girl you practically raised from the age of 11.'

'And I know that Coco had her issues. Smoking drugs at 15. Multiple addictions. Fragile mental health.'

'Caused by her phenomenally shit parents,' Grace counters. 'Not her genes.'

'And we don't know anything about Kaia's biological father. The lifestyle Coco was leading at the time, it could be someone even more unstable than her.'

Faith slips her arm through Grace's and they continue to walk in tandem. The toxic thought is back, tapping at Grace's temples, but it's spreading across her skin now, slipping through her pores. It first appeared when she turned up in Bangkok that autumn afternoon and discovered that Coco had a newborn baby. Nine months after they last saw her. But it became lighter and flimsier over the years, almost to the point that it floated away completely. But it's back now, fuelled by the other questions racing around her head.

They reach Wimbledon Common's western edge, which is marked by Beverley Brook, a narrow river that was once the official boundary of south-west London. The shallow water meanders down towards Richmond Park, and Grace watches a young black Labrador splash into it, chasing a stick. A heron, perched nearby, flaps its huge wings in disgust and flies off downstream.

'I didn't tell you how drunk I got the new year that we spent with Coco in Phuket,' Grace starts, still not sure how far she's willing to let this conversation progress.

'It must have been exciting, bumping into her like that.'

'It was. It made me realise how much I missed her.'

'Your friendship was special. You were always thick as thieves.'

Grace lets the familiar expression roll over her. Who is the biggest thief out of the two of them? Coco for stealing Grace's identity, or Grace for stealing Coco's baby? And where does Marcus fit in? Is he part of this illicit exchange?

'Marcus and Coco had to carry me back to the hotel room. I was out of it.'

'It was a good job they were there.'

'Mum, I sometimes wonder—'

'Well, don't,' Faith interrupts, her voice sharp. 'Marcus is a decent man who loves you. And you were the one good thing in Coco's life; she would never betray you.'

'But the dates fit so perfectly – Kaia was born in late September. And they could have done anything that night, I would never have woken up.'

'Just because they could, doesn't mean they did.'

'And I've been thinking about it,' Grace continues. 'If Marcus is hurting Kaia, perhaps it's because they *are* genetically linked. All the guilt he must feel, seeing the consequence of his cheating every day.'

'He's not hurting her. Kaia is recovering from concussion and, for some reason, is taking her frustration out on Marcus. The psychologist is fixing her. Don't do this to yourself, Grace. Marcus isn't her biological father.'

'Then why did Coco put my name on the birth certificate? Maybe it was her way of making Marcus shoulder his responsibilities?'

'Don't be silly, Grace. Coco used your name because she wanted to give Kaia the best mum possible.' A pause. 'And because she knew that you wouldn't refuse her.'

Grace finds an old tissue in her coat pocket and wipes her eyes. The scar on her lower abdomen is so faint now that it's hardly visible. But the damaged tissue is still tight, and it pulls at her at moments like this. She's only ever told two people that she can't have children naturally: Coco when they were at school, and Marcus when he asked her to go to New Zealand with him. He had looked crestfallen when she confessed her body's limitations. The man who isn't satisfied until he's summited every life challenge, thwarted at base camp by the infertility of the woman he loves. But he'd bounced back, like he always does, talked about adopting an army of children like Brad and Angelina when the time was right. And they'd left for Auckland, a little bruised perhaps, but still strong.

At least, she'd thought so at the time.

Chapter 26

'Here, this will cheer you up.' Faith pulls two small Lindt bunny rabbits out of her pocket and hands one to Grace. 'I pilfered them from Henry's stash.'

Grace smiles as she unwraps the gold foil and takes a bite of smooth chocolate. They've reached the end of the wooded area, and to avoid the playing fields where a football game is in full swing, they cut away from the brook and back up towards the old well and home. As they get closer to her parents' house, Grace imagines Kaia avidly searching for eggs. Henry and Faith's garden isn't vast, but it's generous for London and full of hiding places in the many herbaceous borders. Her thoughts wander to last Easter, a memory of how Kaia had claimed not to have eaten a single egg even though her face was smeared with chocolate. They'd all happily accepted that she was lying then.

'I wonder if Coco would regret her choice now, if she knew what Kaia was saying.'

'Of course she wouldn't.' Faith takes Grace's hand in hers. 'Kaia just needs some help working out what's real, and she's getting that now. Life will be back to normal soon, I promise.'

Grace sighs. Over the last few days, having to lie to Harriet, seeing Marcus's temper flare at the aquarium, she'd been almost sure that Marcus was the one telling lies, the abuser that Kaia needed protecting from. She's watched him like a hawk since Friday, and not let him get close to Kaia. But her mum's words make sense too. Does she owe him more loyalty? She rolls the foil into a tiny gold jewel and drops it into her pocket. 'Except our whole life stems from a lie, Mum, the one I told, over and over, to different officials in Thailand.'

Grace wouldn't have been able to tell that lie without Marcus by her side. As soon as she'd read her own name on Kaia's birth certificate that morning, and realised, with her heart thumping so hard she thought it might explode, that Coco had no intention of coming back, she'd phoned him. Hysterical. Her panicky explanation hadn't made any sense, but he still dropped everything, squared some time off with his coach, and flew to Bangkok to be with her. She was calmer by the time he arrived, and they sat on the bed, Kaia between them, and talked about what to do next. They knew they couldn't stay in Thailand for long, not with Marcus's commitments. So they decided to take Kaia back to New Zealand and search for Coco from there.

Except it wasn't that simple. Kaia needed a passport to travel, and that meant registering her with the British Embassy in Bangkok. But they couldn't do that with Grace's old passport number on the birth certificate. They knew a red light would flash on some computer, and the whole act would be over. So their lies had started at Bangkok's district office, or the *Tessaban* as it was called locally. When they were finally called to the front desk, Grace had presented both of her passports (removing Coco's photo had been easier than she feared), and apologised for making a stupid mistake in the hospital. The officer had stared at the different bits of paperwork for a while, but eventually stamped a new *Jang Gert* with only a slight tut of suspicion.

The British Embassy had been their next stop. Grace hadn't been able to disguise her shaking limbs when she walked inside the white colonial-style building, no language barrier to protect her this time. But luckily Kaia had chosen that moment to bring up some milk on Grace's shoulder. It had created enough distraction, and soon Grace was sat by a small desk opposite a tanned blonde woman with crow's feet that deepened and softened as she talked. Grace filled in the application form, handed over the documents that had been listed on the website, and paid the £50 fee to turn her new daughter into a British citizen. Once she had that paperwork, getting a passport was easy enough.

They reach the small car park and pick up the narrow road back towards Wimbledon Village. A group of golfers in bright red jerseys and white gloves nod and smile as they walk past, their bags rumbling along the tarmac behind them. 'I should have tried harder to find Coco at the time.'

'You did what you could; she didn't want to be found.'

'I'm not sure I did.'

Grace wonders, if she could turn back the clock, put more effort into searching for Coco back in 2011, would she do it? At the start, she emailed and phoned her friend every day, left long messages telling Coco that she wasn't angry, that they could work it out together, but that she must come back. That Kaia was her child, not Grace's. But Coco didn't respond. And with every day that passed, every night pacifying the tiny baby with her own warmth and love, things gradually changed. Kaia became Grace's baby, not Coco's. The emails became weekly, the phone calls stopped altogether. And then one day, with a cool south-westerly wind swirling around the Auckland Blue's rugby stadium Eden Park, the two of them watched Marcus get stretchered off the rugby pitch.

And finding Coco was no longer a priority.

'What more could you have done? You had a five-month-old baby, and Marcus in hospital, not knowing whether he would ever get his sight back, his whole life's dream shattered. You were a rock for both of them.'

Grace walks on in silence. It had been tough, juggling the needs of a small baby with trying to be there for Marcus. She'd

147

listened to him question his purpose while her mind was elsewhere, calculating feeding times and whether Kaia's nappy rash warranted a visit to the paediatrician. When Marcus's doctor had explained how fragile his retina was following the operation to reattach it, and that he would never be able to play professional rugby again, moving back to England was the obvious choice. But it also gave them the perfect opportunity to present Kaia as their child.

In New Zealand, Kaia had been explained as Marcus's sister's baby who they were looking after for a while. But they hadn't had time to make any proper friends while they were there, so it was easy to cut ties when they returned to the UK, and then introduce Kaia as their own. A happy accident. Friends had asked why there were no big announcements before the birth, pictures of Grace with a protruding belly on Facebook. And of course, Marcus's parents had been particularly upset to have a granddaughter sprung on them months after she was born, Josh too to some extent.

But Grace and Marcus had concocted a story about a complicated pregnancy, premature birth, and some time on the neonatal ward. And explained how they didn't want to tempt fate by publicising their news. They weren't forgiven straight away, but luckily Kaia's smile did a good job of helping everyone move on. And then, just this Christmas gone, Grace had finally spilled the truth to her brother over a bottle of Californian red. It had felt good, confiding in him, absorbing his words of understanding. And she wonders how it must be for Marcus, with none of his family invited into their inner circle.

'I've started looking for Coco again,' Grace admits, curious to know whether her mother will approve.

'Do you think that's a good idea? It's been a long time.'

'I need her here, to explain things to the authorities, if it comes to that.'

'And what if she wants Kaia back?'

'What choice do I have? I've already ignored two calls from Kaia's head teacher. If the school decide to tell social services about Kaia's accusations, they'll quickly find out that Marcus has no legal rights over Kaia. How do you think that will affect their judgement? And if they dig any deeper, how long do you think it will take for them to learn that the child we described as our niece in Auckland miraculously became our daughter during a thirty-hour British Airways flight to Heathrow?'

Faith is quiet for a while. They're nearly home now, and they both slow their pace. 'Perhaps you're right,' she finally says. 'And did you find her?'

A frown creases into Grace's forehead. 'No, nothing. She didn't come up on any social media searches.'

'And have you tried Coco's parents?'

Grace sighs. 'I've been putting it off. The way they treated Coco, how upset she'd get talking about them. And I know Coco kept her pregnancy a secret from them. After everything that's happened, I'm not sure I could look them in the eye.'

'If you're serious about finding Coco, they're your best bet.'

'I know you're right. And I suppose they'll be easy enough to track down. The amount of businesses David is involved in.'

'Well, you don't even need to do that.'

'Sorry?'

'I have their address.'

'You've kept in touch with them?' Grace spurts out, reaching for the wrought-iron gate that leads to Faith and Henry's front door, but leaning on it rather than pushing it open. 'How could you take that risk?'

'We don't keep in touch,' Faith corrects her. 'We exchange Christmas cards, that's all. I decided it would be more of a risk if I stopped, in case they wondered why.'

Grace sucks in some air. She can hear Kaia bouncing a ball in the garden behind the house. 'And do they ever mention Coco in their cards?'

'We started exchanging them when you girls were still at school. So it would always be signed from Martina, David and Coco, written in that sloping way that left-handers write. And that continued, even when Coco was off travelling the world. And then one Christmas, the card just said Martina and David.'

Tears prick at Grace's eyes and her chest constricts. 'When was this?' she whispers.

Faith takes her hand, looks into her eyes. 'Christmas 2011.'

Chapter 27

Grace peers at the digital screen sunk flush into the car's dashboard and swears. The satnav had told her to take the next right-hand turn, signposted Great Rollright, the name of Coco's parents' village, and she'd still missed it. Her mind is elsewhere, wondering how the hell she's going to keep her huge secret from showing on her face.

She carries on towards Little Rollright and the Rollright Stones, and can't help picturing Mick Jagger atop some stone megalith, topless and sweaty, as she waits for the satnav to reconfigure her journey. Luckily the in-built map reader finds an alternative route and guides her down the next right-hand turn. The road cuts across a gentle hill and a series of fields sinks away to Grace's left. Against the spring blue sky, they look like a patchwork quilt of green and cream squares, stitched together by hedgerows. She'd felt frustrated when Coco's father insisted they talk in person when they spoke on the phone yesterday, but now she's here, amidst this genteel landscape, she's grateful for an excuse to escape London.

With the Byrnes' address written on a slip of paper in Faith's neat handwriting, all it had taken was a basic Google search to track down their number. Martina had answered the phone, her voice quiet and raspy. On the few occasions when she'd visited

Grace and Coco's school, she wouldn't say much. Just stand next to David looking beautiful and bored. And she'd been the same on the phone. Grace quickly gave up trying to make small talk and just asked if they were in touch with their daughter. The older woman had become even more aloof then, just passing the phone to her husband, and then David had asked if they could talk face to face.

As she slows down for the final leg of her journey, Grace hopes that Kaia is behaving herself for Faith. She'd wondered whether her mother might refuse to look after her, after the way Kaia acted on Easter Sunday. Her behaviour had nosedived as soon as Marcus arrived, refusing to sit next to him, pushing Faith's roast lamb around the plate with a scowl. But when Grace called her mum last night to ask the favour, Faith had played down Kaia's behaviour and – as London has suddenly hit twenty-five degrees – offered to take her to Tooting Lido for the day. That had been a relief for Grace because there was no way she could leave Kaia in Marcus's care.

But she did decide to tell him about her visit. Partly because she couldn't bear the thought of any more secrets, but she was also interested to see how he would react. Would he look guilty? Fearful of her getting one step closer to finding Coco? She watched his expression carefully but couldn't decipher what was going through his mind. He just looked conflicted. Like he couldn't decide whether finding Coco was a good idea or not. But he hadn't asked her not to go.

She passes a sprawling garden centre with its own farm shop and homemade ice cream. The car park is busy, plenty of customers eager to add some colour to their gardens now that winter has finally disappeared. Then she turns into Great Rollright. It's officially a village, but it's not much more than a collection of houses built in Cotswold stone, some close to the road, others set back behind iron gates and winding driveways. She's not surprised when she arrives at the entrance to Onslow House and finds heavy timber gates guarding the property and a shiny chrome intercom system attached to the newel post. She feels a sudden urge to turn round, to drive back to London and dive into the pool alongside Kaia. But the video camera on the gate has picked up her image, and she knows there's no turning back when the sturdy gates silently fold inwards.

The Byrnes' home is a typical Cotswold manor house. The window and doorframes are painted in sage green, complementing the clotted cream local stone, and the garden sweeps around the whole property. But the entranceway is surprisingly unimpressive, a simple farmhouse-style front door with a latch. Just as she's about to knock, the door edges open and David is standing there. He's still tall and lean, but his red hair has receded and the freckles on his face have spread and merged.

'Good morning, Grace. Do come in. Thank you for driving all this way.' He looks beyond her to the Range Rover parked on the wide driveway and a wave of sadness, gilded with envy, crosses his face.

The hallway is wide and high, and the sitting room next door is even more dramatic, exposed brickwork on one wall, oak rafters zigzagged across the steepled ceiling. David gestures to a dusty pink sofa dressed with duck-egg-blue cushions, then sinks into a tan leather armchair opposite.

'Martina is making tea. We only drink green these days. I hope that's okay?'

Grace smiles and nods. Even though she hates green tea.

'It was quite a shock for her, you calling out of the blue.'

'I'm sorry, I didn't mean to upset you. I've just been thinking about Coco lately,' Grace says, trying to sound casual. 'I thought you might know where she is.'

David smiles, but it's not warm. He opens his arms, stretches them out across the top of the armchair. 'I didn't realise you were still friends. You at Oxford, Coco pissing about in Asia, or South America, or wherever the hell she ended up.'

Grace pauses. Should she tell him about bumping into Coco

in Phuket? Or is that a risk she doesn't need to take? Before she has a chance to decide, there's a rustling sound in the doorway and she turns to look. Martina is wearing tight white jeans and an asymmetric fawn-coloured jumper. Her skin is tanned and oiled, but her shoulder bone juts out and the sinews in her neck strain as she smiles.

'Grace darling, you look so grown up.'

It's a strange thing to say to a 30-year-old woman, Grace thinks. 'It's been a long time, I guess. Thank you for inviting me here.'

'It feels like yesterday.' Martina sighs, then lowers a drinks tray onto the low wooden coffee table and perches next to Grace on the sofa. The centrepiece of the tray is a deep blue cast-iron teapot with a large handle that arcs over the top. Martina pours steaming liquid into three glass cups and passes one to Grace. 'I sometimes think that Coco is still travelling, that she'll turn up one day with a new tattoo and a bag full of washing.'

Martina's tone is sombre, wistful, and tension prickles on Grace's neck. 'You don't know where she is then?'

David takes his arms off the back of the chair, leans forward on his knees. 'Grace, we haven't heard from Coco for a long time. It'll be eight years this autumn.'

Grace's smile freezes; her heart slows. That was the last time she saw Coco.

'So no, we've no idea where she is now.' David's eyes flit over to Martina, their unspoken fears obvious in their shared look. 'She was supposed to come home ages ago; we sent her a letter soon after she turned 22.'

Grace knows about the letter. Coco showed it to her on that beach in Phuket, her summons back home.

'But then she caught some horrible disease,' David continues. 'And was stuck in Thailand for months.'

'At least that's what she said,' Martina adds. 'We sent her thousands of pounds, but when we asked her for the medical bills so that we could claim on insurance, she went quiet on us.'

Grace's heart hammers against her chest. It wasn't a disease, it was giving birth to Kaia. No wonder Coco went quiet. 'You haven't heard from her since then?' she manages.

They exchange another look.

'There was a letter,' David finally says, leaning back once more and turning to face the window. 'Saying that she was coming home, for definite this time. That she was at the airport, waiting for her flight.'

'In the autumn of 2011?' Grace asks.

'October. But she didn't get on the aeroplane out of Bangkok. We checked, when she didn't show up here. She hadn't taken the flight.'

'David, for God's sake! She wasn't booked on the flight, Grace. We checked that too. Coco told us countless times that she was on her way home over the years; she never was. I don't know why David believed her that time.'

'The letter – it seemed different. Authentic. Usually she just sent postcards, sometimes with nothing more than her name scrawled across it. Or the odd text. To go to the effort of writing to us, opening up to us, I think she genuinely wanted to come home.'

'She was just drunk, that's why the letter sounded so heartfelt. She admitted as much. Rambling on about Mother Teresa and the devil, how much she hated the love of her life, it didn't make any sense.'

Grace tries to keep the emotion off her face, but it rears and bucks inside her. 'Do you still have it, the letter?'

Martina gives her a disparaging stare. 'Of course we do. What kind of parents wouldn't keep the last thing their only child ever gave them?'

Chapter 28

'I suppose you can read it,' Martina says with a sigh. 'It's in a box upstairs, with her postcards. We kept them all,' she adds pointedly. Then she pushes off the sofa, her head hung low, and slips out of the room. Grace wants to scream after her, how dare she act the heartbroken mother? For years the two of them treated Coco like an accessory, not bothering to see her in the school holidays, happy to let her be loved by another family. And now that she's not here, they pretend to care?

'You think we're terrible parents,' David observes.

'Every family is different – it's not for me to judge.'

'You'll have children one day, then you'll understand that parenting is …' He pauses. 'Complicated. You have this perfect ideal. But they rarely turn out the way you want.'

Grace sets her jaw and tries to give nothing away as she smiles at him. This is no longer just about protecting her secret; she doesn't want to share Kaia with this man and his vile expectations.

'We did try to find her, you know. Even hired a private investigator for a time. But there wasn't any record of her in the Bangkok hospitals, or on any flights to the UK. And where do you stop? It's a big world out there. If someone doesn't want to be found, it's easy enough to stay hidden.'

Grace thinks about her own name on Kaia's birth certificate. And wonders how often Coco used her passport over those nine months.

'We thought she'd turn up eventually,' Martina says as she walks back into the room carrying a shoe box, Christian Louboutin scrawled on the outside. 'For years we gave her a monthly allowance. Other than during the year she waitressed in Montmartre, she relied on that money. We thought that by stopping it, we'd smoke her out.'

'It didn't happen though,' David interjects. 'Months became years, and here we are. None the wiser.'

Martina holds the shoe box out to Grace, and with shaking hands, she rests it on her knees. It's heavier than she was expecting, and when she opens the lid, she sees a handful of digital camera memory cards alongside the postcards. Coco always loved to take photos, saying it was for when she was old and senile – a way to remember all the fun she had. Grace can't help wondering if she'll live long enough to enjoy that moment.

The solitary letter lies on top. Grace picks it up and slides the flimsy piece of paper out of the envelope, the then king of Thailand staring back at her through the pink and green hues of Thai postage stamps. She looks up for a moment, feeling David and Martina's eyes on her, but they immediately avert their gaze, and with a deep breath, she starts to read.

Dear both of you,

I don't know why I'm writing this really. My flight leaves soon so I could just tell you when I see you. We can put on Hunter wellies and Barbours and romp through the Cotswold countryside, catching up on all our news. There's a pub in your village, right? I couldn't do a walk without a pub at the end, but I imagine neither could you.

I probably won't send this letter anyway. I bought an envelope and stamps in the airport shop, and there's a post box somewhere here, so there's nothing to stop me. I'll just lose interest though – that's what I do, isn't it? Except when I should lose interest, then I don't.

I've just done something. Something big. And I can't decide if I'm Mother Teresa or fucking Lucifer. A selfish bitch or the best friend ever. Who knows? I would say who cares, but it turns out I do. I do care.

Anyway, it's done now. So I'm coming home. And do you know what? I actually want to come home this time. I'm going to get a job, earn some decent money for once. I'm going to make you proud of me. (Shit, ignore that, we're not Modern fucking Family.)

Sorry for all the swearing. I'm drunk. There's not much else to do in an airport lounge, is there? Go shopping I suppose. But I only had enough money left for my air ticket. A Dutch guy bought me some drinks, I forget his name, Luke or Lucas or Liam or something. He was fucking dull to be honest.

If you're worried that they won't let me on to the plane, don't be. I can hide my drunkenness. I'm good at hiding things.

Like him. I hide how I feel about him. And I fucking hate myself for being under his spell, even now, after everything. I thought we were just two teenagers in love. But that was pure fantasy. I was his dirty little secret, and then he became mine.

And now I'm here, drinking myself to oblivion. Destroying myself because of him. And still, I'd probably go running back, if he asked.

I won't though. You'll help me, won't you? Invite young suitors round for champagne and canapés. We can quaff and laugh and get married in a field full of primroses. See? It's all going to be fine.

Okay so my flight has just flashed up. It's boarding. It's still fifty-fifty whether I'll post this letter to be honest. But you'll see me, in the flesh, really soon, so stick the Dom Perignon on ice. The prodigal daughter is coming home.

Love, Coco

Grace pushes her lips together. *We were two teenagers in love.* The sentence reverberates around her head. The man Coco was in love with is someone she knew as a teenager. *Destroying myself because of him.* Is leaving her three-week-old baby the destruction she's referring to? Is this man she's in love with Kaia's real father, not just a random guy she picked up in Phuket?

Coco left England when she was 16, so she had three years of teenage life as a traveller to meet and fall in love with someone. There was the boy she met in Saint-Tropez, the one who convinced her to go travelling in the first place. Grace remembers how excited Coco sounded when she texted about him. How long did they stay together? Could he be Kaia's real father? Grace looks up from the letter. 'Do you know who she's referring to? The man she calls the love of her life?'

Martina purses her lips. 'No idea, I'm afraid.'

'Could it be the boy she hooked up with when she stayed with you in Saint-Tropez? When she first went travelling?' Grace tries to hide the hope in her tone.

'Perhaps,' Martina muses. 'She was certainly acting like a love-sick puppy those few weeks, and she took her time getting down to us. We guessed there was some French boy involved, but she didn't introduce him.'

Grace tries not to let the frustration show on her face. She wants conclusive proof that Marcus isn't Kaia's father, that Coco fell in love with someone else that summer, and he's the man who's haunted her ever since. But she's not surprised that her best friend kept her new boyfriend from her parents. They always had a way of ruining things for her.

David is right about one thing though – the letter does suggest Coco was serious about returning home. So what happened between Bangkok airport and leafy middle England that changed her mind? Grace's thoughts wander to Marcus, and him arriving in Bangkok the day after Coco walked out on her and Kaia. But it's ridiculous of course, the chances of them bumping into each other in that busy airport must have been close to zero. She shakes the thought away.

'When did it arrive, the letter?'

'On the 31st October,' Martina says. 'It was Halloween – we were hosting a little party that evening. I remember putting an extra bottle of champagne on ice.' Her voice cracks at the memory, and tears form in her eyes. 'I was never a good mother. The truth is, I didn't like children. Still don't. But I was looking forward to having an adult daughter – going for spa days together, shopping trips. But I never got that chance.'

Martina is still thinking about herself, Grace notices, not Coco's happiness or safety. 'It sounds like you've written her off. She could still come back.'

David stands up, rubs his palms together. 'We can't spend our lives hoping for something that will likely never happen. As far as we're concerned, Coco is gone for good.'

'Do you think she's dead?' Grace asks quietly.

'Perhaps,' David says, his voice almost business-like. 'One risk too many, maybe. But the private investigator looked into that possibility too and came up blank. The truth is, I don't know where Coco is. Our door is always open, but other than that, we're getting on with our lives.' He sighs, and his voice softens a notch. 'Listen, thank you for coming all this way, Grace. It's been good to see you. But you need to let Coco go – we all do.' He walks to the door of the living room, and looks at her expectantly.

Grace doesn't feel ready to leave yet, too many questions still hang in the air, but she knows her time is running out. She looks back towards the open box. 'The memory cards, have you looked at those?'

'No clues there. All the photos are from her first few years of travelling, before we got her an iPhone for her twentieth birthday and the camera became surplus to requirements.'

We were two teenagers in love. 'Can I take them?' Grace asks. There might not be any clues about Coco's whereabouts now, but these are her teenage years. Kaia's biological father might be on there. She thinks of her final years of study, A levels in Cheltenham, degree in Oxford, the weeks that would go past without her seeing Marcus. His international rugby tours.

But Coco met someone in Saint-Tropez, she reminds herself. Someone she fell for so deeply that he convinced her to leave her life behind.

David shrugs. 'We'd like them back. They're all we've got left of her.'

'I'll take good care of them,' Grace promises, and drops them into her bag.

Chapter 29

MARCUS

2005

Marcus looks at the heavy oak gates and swears loudly. Best-laid plans shot to fuck. He leans his head back against the warm wood, wipes the dripping sweat off his forehead and wonders what to do next.

When they left Lyme Regis yesterday, Marcus had quickly accepted Josh's offer to drop him at the B&B; he was knackered after mixing vodka with his colossal effort on the water. But he'd forgotten that his bike was leaning up against the garage door at Northcross House. When he'd woken up with an image of it sitting there, it had seemed like the perfect plan to combine his morning run with picking the bike up. He'd assumed someone would be home – the Windsors are that kind of family – so hadn't bothered calling Josh first. But now, as he stares at the pair of locked main gates, a clear sign that nobody is in, he realises that was a mistake.

He eyes the intercom and, with a sigh and heavy sense of futility, prods it.

'Hello?' Coco's voice chimes through the speaker.

Marcus straightens up. 'Uh, it's Marcus,' he says, sniffing under each armpit and wondering why he'd hadn't foreseen this problem before setting out on a run in twenty-five-degree heat. 'I came for my bike.'

'Well, I'm in the summer house. It's the perfect spot for morning yoga. Or so Faith tells me anyway. Everyone else is out, I think. Why don't you come down?' Coco's invite is followed by a small click, and then the soft drone of the gates opening.

Marcus stares at the vast drive, and the rolling garden beyond the border of rose bushes. He can see his bike in his peripheral vision, exactly where he left it, but he ignores it. Instead, he imagines Coco lying on a thin mat in the summer house, wearing Lycra yoga pants and a tiny vest top with *Namaste* scrawled across it. Stretching out in the sunshine with feline hedonism. He remembers her comment: *everyone else is out*. Was that code for something?

Trying to keep his pace to a languid stroll, and the bubble of possibility in his belly to a gentle fizz, Marcus walks through the garden, and towards the small timber-framed structure next to the tennis courts. He sees Coco before he reaches her, sitting sideways on a double swing seat, her legs sunk into the plump cushions and crossed at the ankles. No tight yoga gear, but she looks hot enough in a short white sundress covered in tiny lilac flowers. 'All right?' he says, awkwardness taking over now he's reached her side.

'Good to see you, Marcus. Take a seat.' Coco swings her feet onto the floor and pats the now empty cushion.

Marcus eyes the space, but feels himself hesitate, a danger sign flashing somewhere in his subconscious. He flicks his head back up towards the house. 'None of the Windsors around then?' he asks.

'Eurgh, Grace has gone completely mad and decided to try wild swimming in the River Axe,' Coco starts, pulling her legs under her and scrunching her nose up. 'Faith is meeting a friend in Exeter, and Josh and Henry have gone for a run.'

'They'll be back soon then, I guess.' Despite his efforts, Marcus's comment sounds loaded.

'Josh and Henry? No way. They won't be satisfied unless they're crawling back with at least half a marathon under their belt, Henry red-faced and wondering if this is the day he meets his maker.' She pats the cushion again. 'Come on, we've got the place to ourselves for at least a couple of hours.'

Marcus grins and feels his shoulders relax. But as he drops down beside her, his weight causes the seat to lurch backwards. Coco squeals and tips forward. Marcus acts on instinct, thrusting his arm out to block her from falling, but his hand connects with her chest, the curve of her breast. 'Shit, sorry!' He whips it back.

But Coco doesn't look offended. Her eyes dance, somewhere between a jive and an Argentine tango. 'What for?' She giggles. 'Maybe I liked it.' Then she flashes a suggestive smile and laughs again, but it sounds false to Marcus.

He leans back against the soft cushion and tilts his head towards her. 'You don't have to do this, you know.'

'Do what?' She scrapes her bottom lip with her teeth.

'Put on a performance for me.'

'Who says it's a performance?' She starts to raise her eyebrows, but then looks away.

With her red hair and green eyes, it's easy to see Coco as a chameleon, but it's more than her colouring that creates that image. Sometimes she looks sassy and intimidating, other times playful and fun. And right now, she looks unsure of herself. He feels a sudden urge to reassure her. 'I just recognise it, I guess. Because I spent two years doing something similar at school.'

'What, flirting with rugby players?' she asks, but the tease sounds strained now.

'Pretending to be confident when I felt the opposite,' he explains. 'I was the state-school kid when I arrived at Chilford.

My rugby helped a bit, but that was a niche crowd. To most people, I was the poverty case on a scholarship.' He shrugs. 'So I acted. Did a pretty good job to be honest.'

'A very good job, I'd say, if Josh is a measure of your reputation. He talks about you like you're some kind of man god.'

'He does?' Marcus asks, surprise overriding any sense of pride. Josh has always been so confident in his own (extensive) abilities; it's hard to imagine him revering anyone else, especially someone like Marcus.

'Totally looks up to you.'

'I doubt it,' Marcus scoffs, kicking his worn trainers against the cedarwood decking.

'But you're right that the Windsors are perfect,' Coco continues. 'Grace too. What do you think makes them that way?'

Marcus has never considered the 'why' behind Josh's brilliance before. 'Money, I guess, and good genes. Brains, athleticism, looks. They did pretty well out of the man upstairs.'

'And a stable family, no insecurities to fuck them up.'

Marcus thinks about his own mum and dad, his twin sisters. What a tight unit they've always been over the years. 'Everyone has insecurities, if you dig deep enough.'

'Not the Windsors. They're in a league of their own.'

'And you? How deep are your insecurities?'

She laughs, a deep, dirty cackle. 'Oh, mine are pretty unruly. They turn up whenever the fuck they like, usually when they can do the most damage. They're high-achieving that way.'

Marcus smiles at the image, but he feels sad for her too. She's only 16, but already talks like she finds life exhausting. 'And does anything make them go away?' He wants to know what he can do to make her feel more secure, but her answer is way off romantic.

'Of course.' She smiles, then starts counting her fingers. 'Vodka, skunk, speed, wine if I drink enough, a shag with a stranger can sometimes do it. I have plenty of options.'

A wave of repulsion sweeps over him suddenly. Is he really

165

contemplating getting close to this girl? Him, a future rugby international, and her, a messed-up 16-year-old tramp? What the fuck is he thinking? Maybe he should just grab his bike and get the hell away from her.

'I'm joking about shagging strangers by the way.'

'It's hard to work out the lies from the truth,' he says, his voice hard.

'I'm sorry. I do that, I think. Try to shock people, push them away.'

Marcus turns to look at her; she's blinking back tears, trying to look brave. He softens a bit.

'As a rule, I don't get close to people,' she continues. 'Just Grace. And Faith, I suppose.'

'Why not?' Marcus stares at the dense trees beyond the tennis court. Even in the sunshine there's something ominous about them.

'Too much of a risk.'

'What about the risk-reward continuum? You sounded like a fan when it was about Henry's parenting strategy yesterday. Lending Josh the car to test his sense of responsibility.'

Coco's hand is resting on the cushion between them and he picks it up, lets her fingers run loosely through his. The voice telling him to get away is still there, nagging at him inside his head. But it's just noise now. The truth is, he loves the enigma of Coco. She's not driven like he is, but she's also not horizontal like his family. She's a free spirit, but one flying at breakneck speed.

'I am a fan,' she says, her forehead creasing slightly in thought. 'But it's easier with a sports car that's been proven to make your belly flip. It's different with people. No guarantee the reward will be worth it.'

He looks at her hand entwined in his. Fuck it. If he's going to do this, it may as well be now.

'Maybe you just need to do your research well?' He leans towards her and brushes her hair away from her face. She looks unguarded now, more genuine, and he feels a new surge of desire. But it's too open out on the deck, the grand house and sparkling lake in the distance, the dark woodland muttering in the breeze. He takes her hand in his, and gently pulls her up. Then he leads her inside the summer house. He pulls her down next to him on the sofa and leans in. At first, he just brushes her lips with his, testing the water, but she doesn't resist and millimetre by millimetre, he pushes further, deeper, lingering but insistent.

Gently, he guides her onto her back. As he hovers over her, she smiles, but there's a childlike apprehension spreading across her face. He kisses her, to reassure her. Then he runs his hand down her body until he reaches a hem. Should he do it? Push her dress up, snap open her bra? He's done it before, both his ex-girlfriends wanted sex as much as he did. And Coco is bound to be at least as experienced as them. He pushes her dress up a little, runs his hands along her thighs. She doesn't protest, so he keeps going, cupping the mound of her bottom and fighting the urge to squeeze it. A little further and now he can explore the curve of her hipbone, the silky skin of her flat stomach.

'Marcus?'

His breathing is getting heavier; she's beautiful and he's hard now. He nudges her dress a little higher and slips his hand underneath. She's not wearing a bra. He closes his eyes and squeezes her nipple between his finger and thumb. It hardens and rises and *oh my God this is fucking amazing.*

'Marcus, I'm not sure …'

'It's okay,' he rasps, not opening his eyes. 'Just relax and enjoy it.' He finds the edge of her knickers, just a tiny triangle of lilac silk.

'I just feel a bit …'

Stop fucking talking – you're ruining the mood! That's what he wants to scream at her. *You flirted like a minx and now you owe me!* Her flesh down there is soft and warm. It's so tempting.

But then a talk at school starts rubbing at his memory. And his dad's voice reminding him about consent, respect. An image

167

of his feminist mum pops up, then his two little sisters, their blue eyes staring at him in horror. He pulls back. 'What is it?' he asks.

'I don't think I'm quite ready for this yet.'

He removes his hand from her knickers. His heart is battering his chest so hard that he's struggling to breathe. He came so close to ignoring her. 'Of course,' he manages.

Coco smooths down the soft cotton of her dress and smiles at him. 'I'm really sorry, Marcus. I thought I wanted to, but I feel a bit exposed here, kind of tense. Maybe I just need a few drinks inside me?'

'Maybe,' he agrees. And a new fantasy starts forming in his mind.

Chapter 30

GRACE

2019

Grace slips her key in the door and enjoys the silence that follows. Faith will be dropping Kaia off soon, and then Marcus will be back from work, but for now she has the house to herself.

After leaving Coco's parents' house she stopped at the garden centre just outside the village and ordered a pot of tea in their café. There were so many thoughts swirling around her head that she didn't feel safe to drive any distance without having some time to process them all. Who was Coco referring to in her letter, and was he Kaia's biological father? Was it the guy she met in Saint-Tropez? Or someone else? Could that person be Marcus? Coco did flirt with him that summer they all met, but Coco flirts with everyone. Did Marcus reciprocate? There were moments maybe, when he seemed drawn to her, but nothing tangible that Grace can remember. And why would he have asked her on a date if he was interested in Coco?

And she'd have known. If her best friend and boyfriend had a thing all that time. She'd have known.

After a second pot of tea and a chicken salad, Grace had left Great Rollright feeling better. During those five years when she and Marcus lived apart, he was focused on his rugby career, on winning matches when he was in Europe, not sneaking away to feed some illicit passion. And if he wasn't Coco's secret lover, then her letter implies he isn't Kaia's biological father either. With that new certainty, she'd suddenly felt impatient to check the camera memory cards that David let her take with her. Because they might hold some clues about who is. If Grace could somehow track Kaia's real father down, then he might know where Coco is now. Perhaps they're even still together. Grace knows it's a long shot, but at least it gives her something to focus on, another avenue to find her friend.

With the house empty, Grace heads straight upstairs to her small office overlooking the street. When they bought the house, the estate agent had described the space as a single bedroom, which was stretching the truth. But Grace doesn't mind its bijou size. A desk, ergonomic chair and enough shelves for her books. That's all she needs.

The room feels stuffy after the one-day heat wave and Grace turns on the fan to create a breeze. Then she picks one of the memory cards out of her bag at random – there are no dates written on any of them – sinks into her chair, and slips it into the card reader on the side of her laptop.

As she waits for the pictures to load, her phone rings from inside her bag. She assumes it will be Marcus or her mum, but there's a phone number rather than a name on the display, and it's one she doesn't recognise. 'Hello?'

'Ah, I'm so glad I've finally caught you, Ms Windsor. I thought I would try after working hours, see if I had more success.'

Grace grips the phone a bit tighter. Kaia's head teacher. 'Mrs Armstrong, I'm sorry I haven't returned your calls.' Her voice trails off – she can't think of a good excuse.

'I imagine you're very busy with your book writing. But I wanted to talk to you about Kaia.'

'We took your advice,' Grace says quickly, trying to keep the panic out of her voice. 'Kaia saw a psychologist last week; she opened up a little. I think, with time, it will resolve things.'

The line goes quiet for a moment, Kaia's head teacher assessing this new information. 'That is good to hear,' she starts carefully. 'But we've had a meeting at school to discuss things.'

An image appears. Knitted cardigans and chipped china cups. An open packet of custard creams, plastic wrapping spiralling outwards. Grace sucks in some air and keeps talking. 'She's worked with children suffering from post-concussion syndrome before. Apparently changes in behaviour aren't uncommon.'

'I'm glad Kaia's getting professional help,' Mrs Armstrong interrupts. 'But my problem is that I have a duty of care towards Kaia. Her suggesting that her father, Mr Stuart, pushed her from the tree wasn't cause for concern on its own, especially as we knew she'd been seen at the hospital. But Ms Reynolds, the PE teacher, noticed bruises on her wrist too. And when she asked about them, Kaia attributed those to Mr Stuart as well. It's an unusual injury to sustain by accident, Ms Windsor.'

Grace closes her eyes, imagines the older lady in her own home office, a cat purring beside her. Worry marks creased across her forehead.

'I can't ignore the possibility that Kaia's telling the truth about her father. It would be a dereliction of my duty if I did nothing, do you see?'

'What are you going to do?' Grace asks, her voice a whisper now.

'I want to give social services a call, ideally with your blessing.'

'No!' Grace coughs, adjusts her voice. 'I mean, I don't think that's necessary. The psychologist is helping her. And Marcus would never hurt Kaia,' she adds.

'From what Kaia says, you weren't there on either of the occasions in question. How can you be so sure?'

This again. People demanding proof from her. Grace stands up out of her chair and leans against the bookcase, its wooden shelves digging into her back. Adrenalin races through her, but she's got nowhere to run. She has to make a choice, take a side. 'I've considered the possibility, but I know Marcus. He's not capable of it.'

Mrs Armstrong sighs. 'Well, I commend your loyalty, Ms Windsor. And I hope you're right. But unfortunately, I don't know him like you do, or what he's capable of. So I'm afraid I will have to call social services tomorrow, let them get to the bottom of things. And try not to worry. If what you say is true, he's got nothing to hide.'

Grace taps her phone to end the call and tries not to cry. Of course they've got something to hide. A lie so big that exposing it will destroy them all.

But not abuse.

What they did for Kaia, for Coco, came from love, sacrifice, duty. And now they're being punished for it.

Because Marcus is not hurting Kaia.

She's almost sure of that.

Grace sinks down into the chair and sees that the pictures on Coco's memory card have loaded on her screen. She stares at a huge mountain, regal against a deep blue sky. It looks familiar. Coco is stood in the foreground, arms making a V shape in the air, red hair flowing out from a black beanie. How simple life can be if you have zero responsibilities. The next photo is a panoramic shot. The same mountain sits tallest in a long range of white peaks and Grace realises why she recognises it. It's Mount Everest. Coco must have been to Nepal. She clicks through a few more photos, all of them equally eye-catching, and they soothe her. Beautiful vistas, many of them with groups of young hikers in the foreground, small backpacks flung over their shoulders. And there are photos taken at night. The inside of Nepalese tea houses, red faces and blurry smiles, traditional blankets draped over wooden furniture.

Grace right-clicks on one of the images and discovers that the photo was taken in July 2006, a year after Coco left Devon, and normal life, behind. As she skims through dozens more photos, she begins to realise one boy is in more of the shots than anyone else. Dark hair, one ear pierced, brown eyes that crinkle when he smiles. And then she clicks onto the next photo and it's them together. Coco sat on his knee, arms wrapped around him, lips connected. Grace stares for a moment.

Is this the man Coco fell in love with in the south of France? She peers at the screen trying to work out if his eyes are almonds with tails, like Kaia's. But it's impossible to tell. And even if he is Kaia's father, how could she track him down from a picture taken over ten years ago?

Chapter 31

Grace stares at Kaia across the living room as she watches *Horrible Histories* on TV. Her long wet hair, freshly washed after a day spent in chlorinated water, hangs down each side of her pale face and her dark eyes track the medieval characters bobbing across the screen. They were lucky that Kaia didn't inherit Coco's green eyes or red hair. With both her and Marcus a similar shade of dark auburn, that would have been hard to explain. She did get Coco's Irish skin, porcelain white, but that can be attributed to Faith or Tania's fair colouring easily enough. She peers harder. Can she see a hint of Marcus in Kaia's eyes? Ironically those look more like her own. There are other things though, like her sports skills and competitive nature. But is that down to her genes or, as her mum claims, just Marcus's relentless encouragement?

'Why are you staring at me like that?' Kaia asks without looking away from the television.

Grace shakes herself back to the present. 'Sorry. I was just wondering if you had fun at the pool with Granny?'

'Not really.'

Grace sighs. Where has her easy-going daughter gone? 'Sorry to hear that,' she manages. She's too tired for a fight.

Kaia shrugs. 'I'm used to it now. No one believing me.'

Her words sting. 'What did you tell Granny?'

'That Daddy pretends to be nice but he's not. That he hurts you as well as me. But she just shushed me and bought me an ice cream.' Kaia pulls away from the historical images on the TV. Her eyes look black and empty. 'She's a bitch for not believing me.'

'Kaia!' Grace leaps up. It's been a long day, and she's had enough. 'How dare you talk about Granny like that!'

'I hate her,' she spits out.

Anger rises up in Grace. It's all rubbish; Marcus doesn't hurt her, so he can't be hurting Kaia either. She's not letting Kaia criticise her mum, disrupt her marriage, any longer. She pushes up and grabs her around the wrist. Let the bruises form, she thinks, let Kaia make her wild accusations of abuse. Let social services investigate and see what she's really like. Faith is right. Coco was fucked up, and now she's passed those faulty genes on to her child. The baby she gave away. The daughter she forced on Grace. She pulls Kaia out of the living room and up the stairs, Kaia's little feet stumbling step by step behind her. They reach Kaia's room and Grace shoves her inside.

'Get to bed. I've had enough of you today.'

'I want my iPad,' she growls.

'You lost your privileges when you swore.'

Kaia's eyes drill into her own, but Grace won't be intimidated by her daughter. But as she holds Kaia's stare, she becomes aware of the rise and fall of her daughter's narrow chest. Short and shallow under her purple pyjama top like the peck, peck, peck of a garden bird. Is fear powering Kaia's racing heart? Grace thinks about her words. *I'm used to it now. No one believing me.* She reaches out and gently pulls Kaia towards her. The moment floats between reality and nostalgia.

'I'm sorry, Mummy.'

'Me too.'

'Granny isn't a bitch.'

'Kaia, where did you learn that word?' Grace listens to the

silence and counts Kaia's heartbeat against her chest. One, two, three, four.

'It's what Daddy calls me,' she finally answers.

Grace closes her eyes and feels her face twist inwards. Is that true? Or is Kaia's long pause proof that she's making up a response to fit her story? 'We're going to Harriet's again tomorrow.' She can't think what else to say. 'She'll help us work things out.'

'Do you promise?'

'I do,' Grace whispers. They stay wrapped together for a few more moments, both their heartbeats getting lazier. Then Grace hears Marcus's key in the door.

'Mummy, can I play Wizard Street, just for a bit?'

Grace hesitates. Marcus's sister Izzy introduced Kaia to Wizard Street when they went to Devon last summer, but it's only over the last few months that she's fallen in love with the computer game. It's like Minecraft with magic. Kaia makes potions and flies around on dragons or witches' broomsticks. She chats with other kids on there too, little Harry Potter fans who want to build their own magic school. With everything that's going on, Grace has been grateful that Kaia's had a virtual world to hang out in.

But she has already refused to let her play tonight.

'Please, Mummy?'

It feels so long since Grace has seen Kaia like this. She knows she should be resolute, but perhaps Kaia needs this journey into fantasy. So she nods and watches her daughter unplug her tablet from the socket in the corner of the room.

*

Grace leans back against the sofa and rubs her eyes. It's been a long day.

'Top-up?' Marcus asks, holding out a half-full bottle of red wine, his arm swaying slightly.

'No thanks.' Grace watches Marcus fill his own glass almost

to the rim. He was always careful about how much he drank when he was playing rugby, worried about how it might affect his performance on the pitch. But gradually those standards have slipped to non-existent.

'Social fucking services. This is a fucking nightmare.'

His drunken swearing reminds Grace of Coco's letter. Written in an airport bar in Bangkok, perhaps on the same day Marcus arrived in the city. She has told him most of what David and Martina revealed: that Coco was due to return to the UK in the autumn of 2011 but didn't show up, and that they hadn't seen her since, despite hiring a private detective. But she didn't tell him about the letter, or the stack of camera memory cards now stowed away in her desk drawer.

She didn't tell him about Kaia's outburst either.

'We can do this without Coco,' she says. 'We just need to stick to our story. It's my name on Kaia's birth certificate.'

'Written in some illegible Thai scrawl,' Marcus moans. 'And no mention of me.' He takes a long gulp and drops his head into his hands. 'Oh why didn't I adopt her?'

'You know why,' Grace reminds him. 'We agreed that the adoption assessment was too intrusive, that a social worker tasked with finding Kaia's biological father was a risk we didn't need to take.'

'And what about the risk now? That people accuse us of kidnapping her in Thailand?'

'No one would ever claim that.'

'Really? With the biological mother missing from exactly the same time?'

Grace sighs, rests her hand on Marcus's shoulder. 'We're scared because we know the truth. But look at us, we're a middle-class family with good jobs and structured lives. Why would anyone suspect that Kaia's not legally ours?' Grace gently pulls Marcus back against the sofa cushions, focuses on his expression. 'She even looks like you.'

'No, she doesn't.' His eyes dart away. 'Only on a superficial level anyway. Brown eyes, auburn hair. Same as you.' His tone sounds defensive and a new tension prickles on Grace's skin.

'The most important thing is understanding why Kaia is saying these things about you.' She pauses. Marcus is drunk and angry; this is not the right time to question him. But Kaia's bedtime whispers are still there in her mind. *He did push me, Mummy.* 'Are you sure you haven't hurt her? Got angry, lashed out in the moment?'

Marcus slams his glass down, red liquid splattering over the coffee table. 'For fuck's sake, Grace! How many times do I have to plead my innocence with you?'

As he stares, his eyes full of fire, his wide shoulders leaning over her, Grace realises she feels scared. But is that fair? Once, he's hit her. And in fourteen years he's never raised a hand to her since, not even a flinch. But still. 'She's going through a difficult phase,' she whispers. 'I would understand.'

'Fuck you, Grace,' Marcus growls. He stands up, runs his hand through his hair. 'It was you who wanted to keep her. Your friend who caused this mess. I went along with it all for you, Grace. And now, what? I'm the bad guy?' He snaps his fingers, like he's just thought of something. 'Maybe you want me to leave. It's your money that makes us a middle-class family after all, you who creates this wonderful, structured life. Maybe I'm surplus to requirements now? The failed rugby player who beats his child?'

Marcus walks over to the fireplace and slams his fist against the mantelpiece. It trembles under the impact and a glass vase, bright with red tulips, rocks. Any moment it will fall, Grace thinks. Shatter against the hard wooden floors. She watches, mesmerised, waiting for the crash.

But it's a different noise that makes her jump. She stares at her phone, the screen lit up and handset buzzing. Who could be phoning her this late at night? She reaches for it and the answer is provided by the US dialling code lit up on her screen. 'Josh?'

'Hi, sis, how's things?' His voice is relaxed, cheerful. It sounds so out of place.

'Okay,' she whispers, looking over to Marcus who is now slumped in the armchair opposite her. 'It's late though. Can I call you back tomorrow?'

'Shit yes, of course. The time difference. Listen, I won't keep you. I just wondered if I could come and stay for a few nights. Pre-orders on my book have gone wild apparently, seems it's not just academics who love a good nose in people's private lives. My publisher has organised a launch event in London, last minute.'

Grace's heart thuds against her ribcage. She knows how much Marcus hates having Josh to stay; she can't do it to him now, not with everything that's going on. 'What about staying at Mum and Dad's? They're much better hosts than me, and Mum would love the chance to spoil you.'

'I'm sure you're right, Gracie.' He pauses and Grace imagines his thoughts ricocheting west to east off Atlantic waves. 'The thing is, it's not just about having a roof over my head. I haven't been able to stop thinking about our last call, about Kaia. I suppose I'd like to help you work out what's going on.'

'It's not your problem to solve,' she whispers, her cheek burning against the cool glass of her phone. She doesn't want Marcus to hear this conversation, but equally she can't walk out, show him that she shares secrets with her brother.

'I know that. But perhaps if I spent some time with Kaia, she'd open up. I know I don't see her often, but we're close in a way. And I've got all these letters after my bloody name. If I can't use them to help my niece, my sister, then what's the point of them?'

Grace closes her eyes. Perhaps this is what she needs. Help from someone who knows Kaia, knows the truth of her birth, but also understands how the mind works, and what might make a girl tell lies about her father.

Or a father hurt a child he's raising as his own.

Who might be his own.

179

Fuck, this is a mess.

'Of course you can stay.'

'Thanks, Gracie. My flight gets in Friday lunchtime, so I'll be with you mid-afternoon. And maybe don't mention it to Mum and Dad just yet, the last thing I need is them feeling offended – especially if I don't get time to see them.' He pauses. 'We'll get it sorted, I promise.'

The line goes dead and Grace lifts her eyeline to face Marcus.

'Your brother's coming to stay.'

'He wants to help.'

'You told him what Kaia's saying about me.'

'He's a professor of psychology.'

'He's a fucking cunt,' Marcus spits out, his features gnarled with bitterness.

Grace gasps. They used to be best friends. Josh idolised Marcus, the rugby hero, when they were at school together. One mystery falling-out, a fight that split Grace's lip. Of course their friendship was finished after that.

How dare Marcus be so rude? 'He's my brother, and he's staying,' she hisses. 'And as it's my money that pays the mortgage, you'd better get used to it.' Then she walks out of the living room, slamming the door behind her.

Chapter 32

COCO

2011

Coco stumbles down the pavement until she reaches the place she's been heading since arriving at Charles De Gaulle airport. The reason why she took a train and then walked all the way from Gard du Nord station. Then she closes her eyes, thrusts her arms above her head in a V-shape, and lets the red light wash over her. She's home.

Not actual home, of course. That would be a twee country house in the middle of a damp field.

But somewhere that feels like home. The huge letters, glowing crimson against the night sky. And the iconic red windmill on the roof.

The fucking Moulin Rouge, baby. Paris.

She lowers her arms until they're shoulder height, then reaches them out to the sides. She kicks her legs, high as she can, one at a time, and wishes she was wearing a corset. Fishnet stockings and high heels. Not some Thai wraparound dress and dirty

Converse trainers. That's not what cabaret girls wear when they're performing the can-can.

People are staring at her. The air is still warm, some strange Indian summer they're having in Paris, and the streets are busy. Tourists who think they're edgy because they've come to the red-light district. Locals who know if they really want edgy, they should head east to the 19th arrondissement.

Let them stare, she thinks. Let them judge her.

The devil woman who abandoned her child.

But it's not long before her lack of fitness forces her to stop anyway, to lean against one of the giant red plant pots and catch her breath. As she looks out across the wide Boulevard de Clichy, listening to the thrust of motorbikes rumbling up and down, she spots somewhere even more familiar, the real reason she's come to Montmartre. Without checking for traffic, she saunters across the road, through the ornate central reservation with its tall trees and old-fashioned lamp posts, and across to the bistro on the other side.

It's been three years since she was last here, but it hasn't changed. Powerful downlighters send swathes of fire across the red canopy; young people drink, and smoke, around the small outside tables; and the same upbeat jazz music sprinkles out of hidden speakers. She hesitates for a moment, then pushes on the door handle and walks inside.

'Can I help you, madam? Do you have a reservation?' The heavy French accent of the maître d' doesn't hide his reproachful tone. But he's professional enough to keep smiling, and not grimace at the smell of someone who's been on a plane for twelve hours, and in an airport bar for an indeterminate amount of time before that.

'Is Julien here?' At least she doesn't sound drunk; she can act professional too sometimes.

'Of course,' he says, as though it would be preposterous to imagine his manager ever having a night off. 'And whom shall I say is asking?' His English is better than hers.

'Tell him it's Coco. I was just passing, wanted to say hello.'

That's not really true. She was planning on booking a flight to London, even told her parents that she had, but when she saw there was one to Paris just an hour later, she'd decided it must be fate. That she was destined to come here one final time, just for a night, back to where it all started. A memory sweet enough to keep drawing her back to this city. 'I used to work here,' she adds, hoping that information will warm up the maître d's face.

It seems to work, his eyes crinkle. 'Ah, yes!' He snaps his fingers. 'I thought I recognised your face.'

Coco squints slightly and stares at him. High cheekbones, bald head, dark skin. None of these features are familiar to her. 'Did we work together?' she asks, more disbelieving than embarrassed. It's hard to humiliate Coco these days.

He smiles, and she adds perfect white teeth to his list of features. 'There are lots of photos on the wall in Julien's office. You are in one or two of them, I think.'

Coco's mind wanders back to her year working in the bistro, the friends she made. Julien would get them all to huddle up after closing time, shout *ouistiti* at his camera. For weeks she thought it was a rude word, it had that kind of ring about it. But Julien finally explained that it's a South American monkey, so no more offensive than shouting cheese. There were some group photos she missed. Those times when he came to Paris, Kaia's father. Then she would go AWOL from work, suspend her life, submit herself to him. Of course, he never stayed long. She would feel abandoned when he left, but then Julien would throw a party, and she'd remembered who she really was: discarded daughter, toxic wild child, everyone's favourite party girl. She'd get wasted, shag a stranger, and normal life would resume for a while.

'You can wait at the bar, order a drink *du patron*. I'll let Julien know.'

A drink on the house. With no more money left, that's exactly what she needs. She walks over to the bar, climbs onto a stool, and orders a large cognac on ice. The barman nods at the maître d's quick instructions in French, and then free-pours from a bottle of Courvoisier over a glass of ice and slides it in front of her. 'Merci,' she offers, wondering, as she always does, how she managed to work in Paris for a year and only pick up the very basics of their language.

As she sips the drink, enjoying the sensation of it both burning and cooling her throat, she thinks about her cash flow problem, and tries to focus on how the hell to solve it. When she checked the flight prices from Bangkok to Heathrow, she'd been relieved to see that there was enough money in her account to cover it, and hadn't worried that it left her flat broke. She knew that when she was back under her parents' control, they'd look at the dark circles under her eyes, her post-pregnancy sagging skin, and forgive her for the misplaced hospital invoices. An allowance of sorts would kick back in for a while, long enough for her to get her life on track at least.

But then she'd seen the flight to Paris on the departures board, a few drinks in by then and with fourteen missed calls from Grace flashing on her phone, and it had felt so right that she hadn't stopped to think about how she was going to pay for her Eurostar ticket back to England. Or any accommodation in Paris. She drains her glass and when the barman asks if she would like another, she just nods. Julien won't mind stretching his hospitality.

'Coco! I can't believe it, why didn't you tell me you were coming?' A man with thick black hair, slicked back off his forehead, kisses her cheek, once, twice, three times. 'I could have arranged for some of the others to be here. Sandrine is working in a restaurant on the Champs-Elysées now, very posh, but you know, the shirt she has to wear is so stiff, and Christophe has become a tour guide, can you believe it? Dealing with dumb questions every day – urgh. They will be so sad to miss you.'

Coco laughs at Julien's enthusiasm and raises her glass. '*En santé*,' she says, but the words merge as they slide out her mouth.

'So that's not your first drink then,' he observes with a grin.

'I'm commiserating.'

'Well in that case, I'm offended.'

She laughs again but it's louder, and then she snorts, which makes her giggle even more. Julien was always funny. 'It's over,' she explains when she calms down enough to speak. 'I've been summoned back to England, and this time I'm going.'

'Ah, then I shall not disapprove of you getting wildly drunk.'

'I knew I could count on you, Julien.' Coco raises her glass to the barman and after a glance towards his manager, he pours another double measure into her glass. 'But I need someone to drink with,' she pleads. 'When do you finish here? You always know where the parties are.'

'Not anymore, I'm afraid.'

'Don't be silly, you're a bad boy, Julien. I remember that.' She reaches out, runs her fingernail down the edge of his shirt until she finds a button. She tries to twirl it in her fingers, but he pulls away.

'A lot can change in three years.'

Coco wants to cry suddenly. To fucking drown in her own salty tears.

'Amie is expecting a baby, any day now, the doctor said. I need to get home as soon as I finish here.'

The words swirl around Coco's head and she thinks she might be sick. She grabs onto the bar and swallows the acid forming in her mouth. 'That's wonderful,' someone says. Maybe her.

'Thank you. I'm a little nervous, but also excited. It's time, I think. For me to grow up and take responsibility for someone else.'

Coco raises her glass to hide her watery eyes, and gulps at the amber liquid to burn away the acid. 'Congratulations, Julien, I'm so happy for you.'

He beams, then checks the clock on the wall behind her. 'Sorry, I need to get back to work now.'

She flicks her hand in the air, plastering on a smile. 'Of course,

I just wanted to stop by, say au revoir one last time.' She wishes he would just fuck off now. She can't keep the act going forever.

He hesitates for a moment, concern creeping onto his face. But then he shakes it away, kisses her twice more, and disappears between the tables. She watches him go, and it's like a slice of her is dying.

'Excuse me, miss. Is this seat taken?'

As another slice is born.

Coco slowly pivots on the bar stool and tries to focus on the man with the American accent. He's older than her, thirty at least, and has got that golden boy look about him. Blonde hair, blue eyes. Face too round to be handsome, but good enough for cute. Not her type. But she's not feeling fussy tonight. 'Go ahead, it's yours.'

He smiles, like he's won a prize, and she has a sudden urge to punch him. But that might be a missed opportunity, so she raises an eyebrow instead and lets the corner of her mouth turn upwards. Then she winds a strand of hair around her finger and giggles. Even this drunk, she can play him like a fucking puppet.

'You know, I'm in the mood for champagne. But I can't drink a whole bottle by myself.'

Wimp, Coco thinks. She could drink a whole bottle of champagne while she puts her make-up on. 'I'm always up for sharing,' she purrs. 'I'm Coco, by the way.'

'Todd,' he says, holding his hand out. She takes it in her own and gently squeezes. His skin is softer, warmer than she was expecting, and she's surprised to feel a touch of fondness for him. As she watches him get the barman's attention, then order a bottle of Veuve Clicquot and two glasses, a quiver of excitement trembles in her belly after all.

Chapter 33

Coco loves Todd. The idea is so crazy that she adores him even more for making it true. She leans back against the soft leather of the taxi's back seat and looks out of the window. Cars and bikes rush past; lights flash and glare. Le Marais, she thinks he said. That new trendy part of Paris where the expats live, following each other like sheep to eat falafel in the Jewish district or kale crisps in one of the new vegan cafés. She turns to look at the man sitting next to her, his hand on her knee. He smiles suggestively, and she laughs. She really does love Todd now.

After they finished the champagne, he'd whispered in her ear. His hot breath both disgusting and enthralling. Then they'd disappeared into the ladies' toilets and he'd got to work, pulling a small wallet from inside his jacket, shaking a baby mound of powder from a plastic bag onto a pocket-sized mirror, then cutting four white lines with an Amex card. It was all so fucking clichéd; he'd even produced a rolled-up fifty-dollar note. Coco had still snorted two lines though, and then decided the scene was perfect.

That's when Todd told her about the party at his boss's place in Le Marais. He works for some American bank, and his manager has an amazing apartment overlooking Place des Voges. It's his wife's birthday today and he's throwing her a party. They're wild,

Todd had promised. Free champagne 'til dawn. It was just what she needed, somewhere to hang out overnight. She might even convince Todd to give her the money for a Eurostar ticket back to England tomorrow. So they'd left the bistro, Coco dancing between the tables and ignoring the look on Julien's face. Fuck him, she'd thought. If he really cared, it would be him taking her dancing, not some yank from New Jersey. As soon as they were outside, Todd had hailed a taxi, a black Mercedes Estate that was too good for a coked-up tramp like her really, although the driver hadn't seemed to care.

'*Monsieur et madam, nous sommes arrivés*,' the driver says, bringing the car to a stop and nodding his head towards a striking apartment block on their left. At ground level, stone archways obscure cafés and boutiques, and above there are tall glass doors with Juliet balconies. One set of doors is open. As Coco slides out of the taxi, she can hear Lady Gaga spilling out into the night. Laughter too, and the clink of glasses. An American party – she hasn't been to one of those for a while. She thinks for a moment, scrunches up her face. Actually, she's never been to an American party before.

'Shall we go up?' Todd appears behind her and slips his arms around her waist. He's hard and she can feel him against the small of her back. She doesn't love him anymore.

She twists away, looks at him for a moment, then runs towards the entranceway. 'Come on, quick. I need to dance.'

He runs to catch up, then presses the intercom. A female voice crackles a greeting through the box, then buzzes them up before Todd has a chance to speak. Coco pushes open the door and takes the stairs two at a time.

'Todd, man. Nice of you to show up.' A tall man with dark blonde hair and a lazy smile saunters over.

'Sorry, Jack, I got a bit distracted, you know.' Todd's face breaks into a cheesy grin, and he tries to look conspiratorial, but his boss doesn't play ball, and suddenly Coco loves Jack way more than Todd.

'Nice to meet you?' He holds out his right hand. The Americans love a handshake.

'Coco,' she says, taking his hand and then pulling him in for a kiss on the cheek, then two more. They're in France now. 'Thank you for inviting me to your party, Jack.' The cocaine has done its job and she sounds almost eloquent now.

'There's drink, food …' He floats his hand around the huge double-aspect living space. 'Please, help yourself to whatever you need.' He winks and smiles again. 'Todd man, could I borrow you a minute?'

Todd throws her an apologetic smile, then follows his boss further into the room. Coco sighs with relief – she hadn't realised quite how claustrophobic Todd was making her feel – and prowls around the edges of the room. She finds a stretch of wall that isn't bejewelled with expressionist paintings, or objets d'art teetering on slim shelves, and leans back.

The party isn't as exciting as she'd hoped. Yes, there are ice buckets perched in every corner, bottles of champagne slouching in each one. Guests chat in twos, or threes, and some sway to the beat thudding out of the speakers. But it's too fucking calm. No hunger for the unplanned, unusual, unspeakable. She picks a canapé off an abandoned silver tray and shoves it into her mouth, bits of pastry flaking on her lips. She can't remember the last time she ate, but she doesn't feel hungry. It sticks in her throat, so she gulps at a glass of champagne discarded on the side table. It's flat now, but she's past caring about that. She closes her eyes and feels the music vibrate against her skin.

'So, Todd seems to have abandoned you.'

Her eyelids fling open; her vision blurs, then settles. It's the host, Jack. He smells of expensive aftershave. She edges closer and breathes it in. 'I'm good,' she promises. 'I like people watching, especially beautiful Americans like your guests.'

He smiles. 'That is a compliment, especially coming from an English princess.'

189

He's handsome. Not cute, or clichéd like Todd, but fucking gorgeous like Leonardo DiCaprio. She imagines kissing him, running her fingers over his stubble, wrapping her legs around his taut body. 'Well, this particular princess is looking for a prince,' she says, her voice low and deep.

'I guess it's your lucky night then.'

This party is getting exciting after all. Their shoulders are touching, but she wants more. She twists on her rubber soles and suddenly he's leaning against the wall and she's pushing up against him. This is exactly what she needs. She takes his face in her hand and rams her lips against his, burrowing her tongue inside his mouth.

But something's wrong. He's shaking his head, shoving her off him. She stumbles and reaches out; her hand connects with something solid, the sound of glass crashing against the hard floor stings her ears.

'Jesus, I meant Todd, not me! And now look what you've done.' Jack pushes his hands through his hair, staring at the shards of glass sparkling in the semi-light.

'It was an accident,' Coco says lamely, still smarting from his rejection. He'd been flirting with her, definitely.

'That cost thousands of dollars!'

'Jack? What the hell are you doing?' A skinny woman in a tight black cocktail dress shimmies over. 'I just watched you kiss that girl!'

'Honey, she kissed me, it's not what it looks like.' Jack reaches for the woman, but she slaps him away. Then her face darkens even more.

'Oh no, not the Lalique. Please tell me she didn't smash the Lalique.' Her voice rises, in volume and octave. Slowly she turns to face Coco. 'Who the fuck are you anyway? This is my birthday and I sure as hell didn't invite you.'

'Listen, I'm sorry about the vase, but it was just an accident, okay? You need to chill out.' Coco looks at the floor and twists on her toes, a tic she picked up on those few occasions when Martina bothered to tell her off.

'Chill out?' the woman roars, strands of bottle blonde hair sticking to her cheeks with sweat and foundation. 'A stranger walks into my party, kisses my husband, and then destroys my ten-thousand-dollar ornament. And I'm supposed to be okay with that?'

Someone has turned the music off and the room is silent, except for Jack's heavy breathing and the squeak of Coco's toes against the floorboard. She looks over for Todd, but he's disappeared. Maybe he's hiding in the toilet, or managed to escape somehow. She knows Jack is his boss, but still. Fucking wimp.

'I should go,' she declares, with as much dignity as she can dredge up.

'Lady, you're not going anywhere. Jack, phone the police.'

'Do you really think?'

'Phone the fucking police, Jack,' the woman growls.

Coco sighs and slides to the floor.

She's the only guest left when two police officers turn up twenty minutes later, looking surprisingly casual in navy bomber jackets zipped up to their chins. They don't seem happy to be there, caught up in an argument between capitalist pigs from countries other than their own, and Coco wonders if they might direct their annoyance towards the hosts, for wasting police time over a fucking accident. Maybe even force them to apologise to her. But it's wishful thinking. They stick her in handcuffs, tell Jack someone will be back in the morning to take a statement, and escort her out to their Peugeot 308.

It only takes them five minutes to get to the station, not even long enough for a power nap. Which is a shame, because Coco is hell tired now. It's been a long day, or week, or whatever it's been since she last had a full night's sleep. With her daughter in a basket at the foot of her bed. As the car door opens, a moan escapes from her lips and her face collapses inwards. But no one cares. She shuffles along the seat and twists herself out onto the road. The short policeman, the one that looks like a bulldog, ushers her towards the building, but behind the fog of tears, she can't see where she's going. She stumbles on a loose paving slab and falls to her knees. Pain shoots through her thigh bone, then nausea rises up from her gut. She spews champagne and brandy all over the pavement. The policeman shouts at her in French, then drags her up, and pulls her into the station.

Strip lighting glares at her and she thinks she might be sick again. She sways from foot to foot, staring at the floor, and listening to the bulldog bark French to the man behind the desk. At some point, a woman helps her to a seat, then later, she's led into another room, a cell maybe. Thankfully it's darker, and she slips into some space between awake and asleep. There's talking in the distance, and a few familiar words waft into her consciousness.

Elle n'a rien. She has nothing, or maybe she is nothing.

Pas de sac, pas de passporte. But that's not true. She does have a bag, at least she did. Where the fuck is her bag?

Elle n'a personne. She has no one.

And with that, Coco finally slips into oblivion.

*

She's woken by the cell door opening, sunlight streaming through the narrow window. Her head screams at the brightness and she squeezes her eyes closed. Her brain feels swollen, and her heart hammers against her chest. Acid bubbles in her belly.

'You have an *avocat*, a lawyer?' An older man with salt-and-pepper hair leans on the door handle and stares at her, his eyes questioning.

'What?' She slowly lifts her aching body until she's upright on the bench. 'No, I don't have a lawyer.'

'Someone you can call then?'

'Why? Can't you just let me go?' She rubs her eyes and tries to focus on his face, the bridge of his hooked nose.

He shrugs, in that dramatic French way, and puffs air through his lips. 'You go to the court soon. For drunk behaviour. If you pay the fine, you can go. If you cannot pay the fine …' He shrugs again. 'You come back here.'

'I haven't got any money.'

'I know. That's why you need to call someone.' He walks further into the room and gives her a phone. Not a mobile phone, but a fat cordless one that feels heavy in her hand. She thinks about phoning Julien, but how could she possibly face him now? She could contact her parents. She pictures them answering her call, the pursed lips and rolling eyes. The tuts of disappointment, even though this whole fucking mess started with them.

Then she thinks about him. Should she call him? He owes her. And if he doesn't realise that yet, she'll enjoy telling him. Then he'll transfer the money for her fine, without criticism or judgement.

She stares at the matrix of digits in front of her, and then slowly taps his number in.

Chapter 34

GRACE

2019

Grace stares at the blank sheet of paper and tries to concentrate. Usually sharpening a pencil, clearing her mind with a few doodles, is enough to get her started with a new story for her Quin Adventures series. But it's not working today. Every time she tries to imagine Quin, with his magic scooter and uniform of navy shorts and pink wellies, she sees Kaia instead.

Being led away by social services.

She puts down her pencil and gets up from the kitchen table, her makeshift desk during the school holidays so that she can keep an eye on her daughter. The good weather has held for another day, and Kaia is in the garden. Grace filled the paddling pool first thing, imagining Kaia splashing in and out, trying to create some tableau of happy family life. But the water has remained still all morning and Kaia is lying on the trampoline again, chewing her hair and kicking her heels against the netting.

Grace walks outside and tries to get her daughter's attention.

'Uncle Josh will be here soon,' she calls out. 'Why don't you come inside?'

Kaia rolls onto her side. A rare smile spreads across her face and she slides along the taut fabric and jumps off the trampoline. Grace wishes she could feel the same enthusiasm about her brother's impending arrival. In some ways, she can't wait to see Josh. A friendly face in all this mess, and someone whose opinion she trusts. Social services haven't been in contact yet, but it's only a matter of time. Grace knows she's got another fight on her hands, and that's fine. She's fought before. But not without knowing whose side she's on. And Josh can help her figure that out. All the same, there's a knot sitting in her stomach at the thought of him coming. Marcus is still furious about his visit, and she's nervous what conclusions her brother might draw about her angry, inhospitable husband.

As Grace watches Kaia slip inside, she wonders again what happened behind the psychologist's closed door yesterday, as she sat in the clinic's reception area staring at it. Harriet had asked whether there'd been any developments, by which she meant further accusations, and Grace had said no, nothing, choosing to keep Kaia's outburst the previous night to herself. The therapist had nodded, with a look that suggested she didn't quite believe Grace, and then gestured for Kaia to go with her, and the two of them had walked inside her room.

After fifty minutes of staring at the traffic breezing past the window on the Upper Richmond Road – she couldn't face checking her Instagram feed – the door to Harriet's room had finally opened. But while Kaia emerged, her expression blank, Harriet had stayed in her office. The receptionist explained that there'd been an urgent phone call, but that Harriet would contact Grace as soon as possible with an update on Kaia's session. That was over twenty-four hours ago and she hasn't heard from her yet.

Grace walks back into the kitchen and sinks into a chair. The notepad is still there, next to her laptop, and one of Coco's camera memory cards sits beside it. It was a spontaneous decision that she made when she was collecting some paperwork from her office earlier. Just in case the itch to continue looking at Coco's photos gets too strong. And it's an itch she feels intensely now. She looks over to Kaia, who has taken up position by the front door, and then slides the slim plastic square into her laptop.

There are so many amazing pictures that Grace almost gets carried away by the culture fix. Coco riding an elephant in Chang Mai, white-water rafting on the River Kwai. She must have travelled to Malaysia and Vietnam too because there are buildings Grace recognises from Kuala Lumpur and Ho Chi Minh City. Unfamiliar places that take her breath away too, like a patchwork of multicoloured stairs, and beaches with white sand and sparkling aquamarine sea. While Grace was travelling between cold lecture halls and stuffy seminar rooms at university, Coco was exploring the most exciting places in the world. How ridiculous to feel jealous though, knowing the loss that Coco has suffered since.

There are plenty of other people in the photos. Fellow travellers looking suitably excited, nervous or drunk depending on the occasion. Some locals too, full of smiles for Coco. She has that effect on people. But the boy who starred in her Nepal photos doesn't make an appearance, and no other men feature heavily enough to be a candidate for Kaia's father. She thinks about the periods when she didn't see Marcus during the early years of their relationship, the weeks he spent away with his rugby team. She can't help feeling relieved that he isn't on Coco's memory card either.

She flicks through to the final photo, ejects the card from her laptop and cranes her neck to check on Kaia. She's found a half-full plastic water bottle on the windowsill and is now flipping it on the floor. Over and over. Grace sighs and sticks a new memory card in her laptop. The photos are immediately different. Like a filter has washed away the Asian spice and replaced it with a blander European civility. Paris.

Like a virtual tourist, she scrolls through pictures of the Eiffel Tower, Arc de Triomphe and Notre Dame cathedral. She pauses at that one. It was less than two weeks ago that a fire ripped through the iconic French church, and Grace finds it poignant to see it looking so beautiful in the photo. How things that seem eternal, can be destroyed without warning. Then the photos become less touristy. A few friends sat in roadside cafés, tables busy with espresso coffee cups and ashtrays spilling with cigarette butts.

There are also photos inside a traditional Parisian bistro, most taken next to a polished walnut bar. Young people dressed in black and white, the accepted uniform of restaurant staff the world over. Coco is among them in some photos, her long red hair tied neatly behind her shoulders. She must have worked there, Grace realises. She scans the other faces with interest, checks to see if any of the photos imply something more than friendship. The man Coco met in Saint-Tropez was French. Was he Parisian? Did she follow him back home? Is that why she lived there for a while?

She clicks through a few more photos, but her concentration is broken by the sound of the doorbell. Josh has arrived. She flips down the lid of her laptop, blows out a breath and walks into the hallway. Kaia has already flung the door open. She watches her daughter melt into her uncle's arms, and tears well in Grace's eyes. Eventually he disentangles himself and looks up at his sister.

'Hey, Gracie.' He walks closer and places his cabin suitcase on the tiled hallway floor. 'How are you holding up?'

The sympathy in his voice is too much. The dam breaks and she frantically rubs tears off her cheeks so that Kaia won't see her crying.

Josh gently pulls her towards him and Grace sinks against his solid chest. 'Oh, sis, what a nightmare this must be for you,' he whispers. His frame is more slender than Marcus's, and his muscles less obvious, but she can feel his athleticism beneath the coarse material of his sage-green sports jacket.

'I should know what to do, who to believe. Isn't that what a mother's instinct is supposed to be for?' she whispers in Josh's ear.

Josh takes a step back but keeps his eyeline focused on Grace. 'Listen, the one certain thing is that none of this is your fault.'

Grace's smiles weakly. She wants to say more. *Even if Marcus is hurting Kaia? And I'm letting it happen? Am I innocent then?* But she can't express these thoughts with Kaia stood beside them. So the words sit in her throat, choking her.

Josh seems to pick up on her growing claustrophobia. 'You know, if you wanted some space to figure it all out,' he says in a low voice. 'I could help you. Find you somewhere to stay for a while.'

She looks down at Kaia, who seems unwilling to meet her eye. Is this her fault? Her lies threatening to break up Grace's marriage? Or is Marcus the rotten one? Getting some space is a good idea of Josh's, but the thought of leaving Marcus after all this time feels overwhelming.

Her phone is on silent, but it buzzes suddenly on the kitchen table. She watches it until it double jolts – voicemail left – and finally falls still. She looks back towards her brother who's teetering on the edge of their kitchen. 'You must be thirsty,' she reflects. 'Would you like a drink? Water, tea, juice?' She checks her watch; it's almost 5 p.m. 'Or a beer, glass of wine?'

He doesn't seem offended that she's ignored his offer of help. 'A cup of quintessential British tea would be amazing. It's a bloody sad thing to admit, but I think it might be the thing I miss the most from my native country.' He looks at Kaia. 'Present company excepted, of course.'

Kaia smiles and reaches for his hand. While Grace makes the tea, Kaia leads her uncle into the garden. They're chatting like old friends and a wave of relief washes over Grace. This break from the norm is good for Kaia, and Josh will have some good advice for her. As the kettle reaches its crescendo, Grace hears the scrape of a key turning. This was inevitable, Marcus coming back from work, but it still causes her heart to race. She turns on her heel and goes to meet him.

Chapter 35

Marcus prowls around the kitchen table looking like death. It hadn't taken him long to disappear last night. A curt acknowledgement of Josh's arrival was as much as he could manage before telling Grace that he was heading to the rugby club for a few beers. And that she shouldn't wait up. Grace wishes she'd found out why Marcus still dislikes her brother so much, after all this time. They used to be such good mates. But with Josh living so far away, and his visits limited, it's been easier to just let the animosity fester.

But now Marcus is making his hatred glaringly obvious.

'So when's the big book launch?' he growls, reaching down and grabbing the carton of orange juice off the table.

'Tomorrow morning.' Josh makes a point of sounding friendly, pretending not to notice his ex-best friend's belligerent tone. 'At the London Review in Bloomsbury Square.'

'Wow.' Grace can't help feeling a niggle of jealousy herself. She's written over fifty books and has never had a book launch. And if she did, it would probably be held in a soft play centre or farm park. Not a highly respected literary bookshop. 'Can we come?'

'I'd love that, Gracie, but apparently the invite list is rigid. Academics and book bloggers only, although it will be fun watching them trying to find some common ground. Science versus scandal.'

'Revealing people's private personas,' Grace muses. 'It's strange that we're so intrigued by what people do behind closed doors.' She looks over towards her husband, his dark expression and fist squeezing the carton of juice.

'But I'm free today, so I wondered if I could take Kaia to the park? Give you both some time off?' Josh looks knowingly at Grace; he wants the chance to talk to Kaia alone. There wasn't much opportunity the night before. Kaia had quickly become tired after the initial excitement of Josh's arrival. So much so that she hadn't even wanted to play Wizard Street, usually a must-do element of her bedtime routine. Grace had put her to bed, and then ordered a Deliveroo for her and Josh to share. He'd asked if she wanted to talk about Kaia and her accusations, but Grace had pleaded for a night off, and instead listened to Josh's stories about life in San Francisco, the house he's been single-handedly renovating next to the rugged expanse of parkland, Edgewood Park.

'Don't worry, mate,' Marcus answers, accentuating the last word to show how far away from friends they are now. 'I'm taking Kaia to the park this morning.'

Kaia gives him a dark look. 'I want Uncle Josh to take me.'

Marcus puts the juice carton back in the fridge and slams the door closed. 'He doesn't know the park like I do.'

'I don't want to go with you.'

Marcus closes his eyes, then whips them back open. 'It's not up for negotiation, Kaia. You're coming with me.'

'I won't!'

Marcus slams his fist against the work surface. 'You'll do as you're fucking told!'

Grace gasps in horror. Josh stands up on instinct, as though he might need to protect Kaia from Marcus's temper. Kaia's lip drops.

'Marcus, apologise,' Grace hisses.

'Stop treating me like a child,' he hisses back. But he looks around him, at Josh, as though he'd forgotten he was there, and then to his daughter. 'I'm sorry, Kaia.'

'You scare me.'

Marcus drops his head into his hands. 'I shouldn't have sworn at you,' he says, without looking up. 'But you shouldn't be scared.'

She pauses, takes a breath. 'Stop hurting me then.'

Marcus lifts his head, rubs at his cheeks. His eyes are bloodshot, and he stinks of stale booze and fags. Grace feels a sudden wave of disgust for the man she's supposed to love. Maybe that's just it, the person she fell in love with doesn't exist anymore. But when did he disappear? On a rugby pitch in New Zealand? Or before, in a hotel room in Phuket?

'I think Josh should take her,' Grace says, trying to sound measured, in control.

But Marcus keeps going. 'She's my daughter.'

'My daughter too.' Grace wants to add that it's her name on Grace's birth certificate, not Marcus's. And that he has no legal claim to her. But she would never say that. At least, not in front of Kaia.

'I don't want to cause a fuss.'

Grace turns to look at Josh. His voice is the calmest in the room.

'I thought it would help, but I seem to be making things worse.' He turns to Kaia. 'We can do something together this afternoon instead.'

Kaia looks from Josh to Marcus and her eyes droop a little. She pauses for a moment more, then nods her head. 'Okay, fine.'

But Marcus's eyes are still burning with the injustice of having to haggle for Kaia's company. Grace can't allow this hungover, angry man to be alone with her daughter. 'I'll come too,' she says. She's supposed to be Kaia's protector, and has been letting her down for weeks.

'No! I'm taking my daughter to the park,' Marcus shouts. 'On my own. You can stay with your precious brother! Come on,

201

Kaia.' Marcus grabs her hand and she yields to his grip, trotting on her toes to keep up with his strides.

Grace races after them. 'You're not taking her, Marcus! You asked me to trust you, but I don't. Not anymore.'

'I'm brave, Mummy, I'll be okay.'

'Brave? What the hell are you talking about?' Marcus erupts again. 'I'm not the flipping enemy!' He grabs his jacket off the line of coat hooks in the hallway, throwing his arm back. A half-empty packet of cigarettes falls on the floor. He quickly retrieves it and shoves it back in his pocket, swearing under his breath.

'Please don't take her, Marcus,' Grace warns, but the words don't penetrate the dense air.

'Come on,' he says through gritted teeth. Then he swings open the front door, half drags Kaia through it, and slams it closed behind them. Grace stares at the shuddering doorframe, rooted to the spot. Why didn't she stop him? What's he going to do to Kaia?

'Don't worry, he won't hurt her now.' Josh's voice is deep and smooth. She looks at her older brother, now standing behind her in the hallway. There are still signs of his youthful charm, the chestnut eyes that shone with high spirit, but they're now overlaid by a maturity, a sense of worldly wisdom.

'Because they're in the park?' she asks. 'You'd be amazed, what people choose not to see. I need to find them.'

'Listen,' Josh goes on, reaching for Grace's arm. 'I get that a man of Marcus's stature would be intimidating to call out. But anger comes in waves, building to a crescendo and then receding. Marcus has hit that peak already, in here, when he swore at her. He'll only be feeling remorse now.'

Grace shakes her head scornfully. 'You think his anger is only verbal? Did you see how fired up he looked?' She pulls away from him then yanks her trainers from the shoe rack and sinks onto the floorboards. 'Have I been letting it happen?' she asks, pulling at the laces. 'Under my own roof, and doing nothing?'

'Listen, Gracie, I've seen for myself that Marcus can be

aggressive, but show me a rugby player who doesn't have that fire. Abusing his own child is completely different.'

'But Kaia's not his own child, is she?' Grace says, looking up at her brother. 'He's raising Coco's child. Could that be causing this? The weight of it?'

Josh stays silent for a moment. 'Who did Coco put as Kaia's father on her birth certificate?' he eventually asks.

'No one, father unknown.' Grace pushes off the floor and reaches for her jacket. She needs to find her daughter, protect her, but the comfort of being here, with Josh, is slowing her down.

'That must be difficult for Marcus to look at.'

'Even Kaia's passport causes tension, their different surnames. I keep it in my desk drawer in my office so that Marcus doesn't come across it by accident.'

'Lack of legitimacy is difficult, especially as children get older and push boundaries more generally. That's why the adoption process is so lengthy, because it can be harder for non-biological parents.'

'Unless she is his biologically,' Grace spurts out. It's too hard, keeping her fears to herself.

'What do you mean?'

Grace leans her forehead against the front door and closes her eyes. 'I never told you this, but Marcus and I bumped into Coco in Phuket on our way to New Zealand. It was New Year's Eve, and I got blind drunk. Coco and Marcus carried me back to the hotel room; I blacked out, and nine months later Coco has a baby.'

'You think Marcus is Kaia's real father?' Incredulity sparks off Josh.

'I know it sounds crazy.'

'And that he's been keeping the truth from you all this time? Do you think he's capable of that?'

'Perhaps not, but isn't that the point?' She whirls around to face her brother. 'He drinks too much, smokes even though I beg him not to. It used to take a huge amount to make him angry;

now it seems the smallest thing can set him off. Maybe he can't cope with all the lies, and that's why he's hurting Kaia?'

Josh blinks and scratches at his neck. Then he locks eyes with Grace, and his expression says it all. A chill skitters down her spine as she pushes open the front door.

Chapter 36

MARCUS

2005

Marcus stretches up as far as he can, then twists his racket and thumps the ball over the net, his eye tracking it to the inside corner of the opposite service box. But he's overdone it. The ball bounces just beyond the white line.

'Just out, mate,' Josh calls, spinning his racket as he waits for Marcus to set up his second serve.

'Fuck you, arsehole,' Marcus murmurs as he bounces another ball, knowing Josh is well out of earshot. He should have suggested they do some weight training. Or sprint sessions. But Josh challenged him to a game of tennis and, like a mug, he accepted. Now he's three games down and serving to stay in the set.

He uses less force on his second serve, and Josh returns it with ease. They trade a few shots, back and forth over the net, but as Josh's hits go deeper, Marcus knows it's only a matter of time before he fucks one up. And with that thought, he slams a backhand into the net.

'That's my game, I think?' Josh calls from across the court.

'Of course it's your fucking game, and set,' Marcus responds under his breath. He needs to stop talking to himself. He raises, and lightens, his voice. 'I think that gives you the win, mate.' He watches Josh walk towards the net and steels himself for the inevitable handshake. This happens in rugby too, congratulating the other side at the end of a match, and Marcus still struggles to stomach the fake sportsmanship. At least, when he loses.

'Man, it's hot.' Josh wipes his Wimbledon wristbands across his forehead. 'Shall we get a drink?'

Marcus takes in his friend's open expression. Josh has moved on already, not bragging about his win. So why the hell can't he? He closes his eyes for a second, brings up the image of his glory try that sealed Chilford's place at the top of the schools rugby league last season, and smiles. 'Yeah, a drink would be good.'

Faith is in the kitchen when they walk inside. 'Hi, Marcus, good game?'

'Oh, you know, got annihilated by your son.'

Faith laughs nervously, but looks at Josh. 'That's not the way to make friends.'

'Marcus doesn't mind, do you?' Josh jostles him playfully, then hands over a cold can of Coke.

Marcus forces another smile as he takes the drink, and the two of them wander into the adjacent sitting room.

'What are the girls up to today?' Marcus asks, trying to sound casual. The truth is, he's been dying to see Coco again and is going nuts about their lack of contact. After their time together in the summer house, their unfinished business, he'd hoped she'd want to see him again, like he did her. But as he'd said goodbye, she'd asked him to keep their liaison a secret. She didn't want Grace to know, which meant keeping it from Josh too. Marcus had gone into defensive mode, shrugging like he wasn't bothered either way. But on his cycle home, he'd realised that they hadn't even agreed a time to meet up again in secret.

It hadn't helped that Josh then went to London for the weekend to see Dom. Not only was Marcus peeved to not get an invite – his fight with Johnnie had evidently lost him a place on Dom's appropriate friend list – he also hasn't had an excuse to visit the Windsors' house for five whole days.

'Dunno. They're upstairs, I think,' Josh answers, disinterested. 'Shall we play FIFA?' He drops to his knees in front of the TV and scrabbles among the wires. There's a load of expensive gaming kit in front of him, Marcus notes, and he's treating it like cheap spaghetti.

Marcus twists in his seat. 'Nah, I don't really fancy it. Maybe we should see if the girls want to do something?'

Josh looks up. 'You want to hang out with Grace and Coco?'

Marcus shrugs. 'It's just a thought.'

'You fucking paedo. They're only 16,' Josh says, smirking.

'Legal,' Marcus can't help pointing out. Coco is only two years younger than him for God's sake.

Josh sits up straighter. 'That's my fucking sister!'

Marcus realises that the conversation has taken a wrong turn, but he can't explain that he's referring to Coco; he promised to keep his mouth shut. 'I was just making a point,' he says, lifting his hands, palm side up. 'I don't want to shag your sister. I'm just saying that legally I could.' Shit, that's not what he meant to say either.

Josh stands up, walks over to the sofa, and hovers over him. For a moment, Marcus thinks his friend is going to punch him. Maybe he wishes he would. Marcus is much stronger, more powerful. And he's had enough playground scuffles to know how to fight. Not like Josh with his soft public schooling. This is one challenge he knows he can win. He curls his hands into fists and stands up slowly. Nose to nose, Marcus struggles not to land the first punch, to wipe the smug smile off Josh's face.

Josh takes a step backwards. 'I've just remembered, the girls went into Exeter. Shopping.'

Marcus shakes his head in confusion. Weren't they supposed to be brawling by now?

'They told me to invite you over later. Mum and Dad are going out, so we'll have the place to ourselves.'

'I thought you didn't want us mixing with them,' Marcus grumbles. He should be over the moon to be seeing Coco again, but Josh has messed with his head. Maybe she is too young for him, perhaps he is taking advantage of an unstable little kid.

Josh shrugs. 'I didn't think you'd want to, but clearly I'm wrong.'

'I'm not a …'

'Whatever, Marcus. I'm not going to judge you. Come back around eight tonight?'

Marcus is clearly being dismissed, and anyway, he's keen to leave himself. Fucking Josh. That's exactly what he's doing, judging him. For what? Falling in love?

Not that he's in love. He just wants to have sex with Coco.

And she wants it too, just needs a couple of drinks to loosen her up.

He brushes his shoulder against Josh, gives him a slight nudge to remind him who would have won if they had ended up fighting. Then he ambles back through the kitchen, gives Faith a wide smile – Josh isn't the only one who can turn on the charm when he wants – and leaves through the back door.

His bike is leaning against the garage, and he wheels it across the gravel driveway, the ground cracking and crunching under its weight. Of course he's excited at the prospect of seeing Coco later, touching her luscious body again. But he's also vaguely disgusted with himself for being caught under her spell. How can it be that he feels both disappointed with himself for taking advantage of someone so young, and worried that he's falling for a slut?

As he climbs onto the bike, his mind moves to Josh, and how close they came to fighting. How much he wanted it to happen. They're supposed to be best mates. What was he thinking? Have his feelings for Coco warped his view of his best friend?

Josh's house is on a hill and Marcus freewheels most of the way home. When he gets back to the B&B he can hear his sisters giggling in the front room, the Pussycat Dolls playing at high volume. He's not in the mood for their buoyancy today so he heads for the stairs. But it's too late, they've spotted him.

'Marcus!' Izzy squeals. 'Come on, we've got a cameo role for you in our dance.' She grabs one arm, and Karin clutches the other. Together, they drag him towards the front room.

'I'm not being in your dance,' Marcus warns. 'You know that, right?'

'Please, Marcus, you just need to do a couple of press-ups with Izzy sitting on your back,' Karin explains.

'Yeah, show off your big muscles!' Izzy squeezes Marcus's arm but she catches a nerve or something because a jolt of pain fizzes through his bicep.

'Jesus, Izzy, lay off will you. I'm not your bloody dance prop.'

'Oooh, someone's in a bad mood.' Karin giggles, and then her sister joins in.

Marcus usually likes the sound of their laughter, but today it grates on him. He's fed up with people thinking they can push his buttons without any fear of reprisal. 'Just let go of me,' he whispers angrily. The two of them are still holding an arm each.

'Make me,' Izzy says, her eyes twinkling. Daring him.

That's when Marcus sees red.

He circles his right arm, and the sudden movement knocks Karin to the floor. Then he grabs Izzy around the neck with his free hand and wrenches her off him. It's not hard – she's got no strength against his – but he doesn't let go straight away.

He wants her to feel scared.

Then she starts crying, and he drops his hand. And walks out of the room.

Feeling better.

Chapter 37

GRACE

2019

At first, Grace just walks fast. It's Saturday morning; the park will be busy. What harm could Marcus do to Kaia there? But her feet don't trust that logic. They lift, and lurch forwards, and soon she's running down her street and then zigzagging through the heavy traffic on Garratt Lane. She races past St Andrew's Church with its newly planted garden. She can see the park up ahead, a small grassy area on one side and the typical range of swings, slides, bars and climbing frames on the other. But it's not as busy as she'd hoped, just one family in the toddler area and a couple of kids kicking a football on the grass. And she can't see Kaia.

A few dozen steps more and then she swings open the heavy gate and scans the playground. A jet of endorphins races through her as she sees Kaia in the far corner, hanging on the monkey bars. She's halfway along, with only her fingers curled around the smooth metal, her face twisted with the effort of holding on. Marcus is sunk down on a park bench, arms crossed, eyes closed, oblivious.

A memory of that ambulance ride, Kaia's little head strapped down, flashes in Grace's mind. 'Kaia!' she shouts, and surges towards her.

Marcus looks up from the bench he's sprawled on, sees Grace first, then Kaia. But he doesn't move, just watches the drama unfold, a smirk playing at the edges of his mouth. 'It's the monkey bars, Grace. It's designed for kids to fall from.'

Grace can't stand his mocking tone. She puts her arms around Kaia's torso and lowers her down, then crouches to find eye contact. 'Are you okay?'

Kaia pushes her lips together. It reminds Grace of those times when she tells Kaia a secret. A present she's bought for Marcus's birthday, or a surprise dinner she's cooking. 'Can we go home now?' Kaia finally asks.

'Of course we can. Go wait by the gate.' She watches Kaia traipse over to the entrance, one hand disappearing up her opposite sleeve and rubbing at her forearm. Then Grace straightens up and looks at Marcus. 'You shouldn't have left without me.'

Marcus stares back, lets out a deep sigh. 'What? In case I pushed her off the climbing frame? Kicked her down the slide, maybe?'

'She was about to fall when I got here; and you were ignoring her!'

Marcus pushes off the bench and walks towards her, his acidic breath polluting the air. 'Do you know what, Grace? I'm getting a bit bored of having to justify myself to you.'

She wants to be mad with him for turning this on her, but as his wide frame looms over her, it's fear she feels, not fury, and she stays mute.

'You and your smarmy brother, making out like I'm some sort of thug. I suppose I've always been your bit of rough, haven't I? Posh Oxbridge graduate dates thick rugby player. So I'm bound to be hitting my daughter, aren't I? Someone like me could never control their temper.'

'You don't seem to be controlling it now.' But it's a whisper, not an accusation with any strength.

'Kaia is my daughter, Grace. And I have no regrets about the way I bring her up. So let the social worker come snooping, let the school pass their judgement, and that psychotherapist look down her nose at me. Kaia is mine. I'm not giving her up.' He pauses. 'And you're not taking her from me.'

Grace is only half listening to Marcus's words. She's staring at his clenched fists, the tendons in his neck straining as he speaks, his eyes still bloodshot and his mouth gnarled as he spits out his warning. Was it his strength that she fell in love with? She remembers how much his physical power enthralled her 16-year-old self, even when he turned it on her. But there was a vulnerability too, a chink of fragility that she wanted to fill in and smooth over. Did the way Kaia came into their life dig away at that crevice, crack him open and let the poison seep out?

'She's not legally yours though, is she?' Grace hisses, her heart thudding with such ferocity that she grabs hold of the metal frame to steady herself. But Marcus doesn't react as she expected. He just copies Kaia's expression from a few minutes before, pushing his lips together. In that moment, Grace sees Kaia so profoundly in his features, that she gasps and takes a step backwards. It's all so fucking obvious, and she's been refusing to see it.

'I'm fighting for her, Grace, and you're not going to stop me,' Marcus snarls, then he drops back onto the bench. He pulls his cigarettes out from his jacket pocket and leans forward, lighting one up and inhaling slowly.

Grace stares at him and blinks away her tears. She's certain now, doesn't need any photos to prove it or to find Coco so that she'll admit the truth. Marcus is Kaia's biological father. Whether she's the product of one drunken fuck, or a secret tryst that's been going on for years, she doesn't know. Doesn't care.

But she knows one thing. It's Kaia, not Marcus, who she trusts now.

She walks away from her husband and reaches for her daughter's hand.

*

Grace walks into her bedroom and looks down onto the street below. A group of kids wander past carrying a basketball, heading for the nets in Garratt Park probably, and their laughter floats through the open window. She can hear Josh and Kaia in her bedroom too, his low voice murmuring, her higher one interrupting from time to time, the odd peal of laughter. Normal, everyday sounds, and she tries to let them soothe her. But she can also hear Marcus beneath her, shouting angrily at the TV. He arrived back half an hour after her and Kaia, with a carrier bag full of lager and dark fury etched into his features, and now he's watching some rugby game behind the closed door.

As Grace turns back towards the bed, she spots her phone on her bedside table. A memory from the day before jerks into her head. The missed call, and voicemail. It will be from Harriet. How could she have forgotten something so important? She grabs the phone and checks the number. She's right: it's the clinic in Putney. She clicks play on the voicemail and pushes the phone against her ear.

'Hi, Grace, I was hoping to catch you in person, but I still think it's best if I explain how Kaia's session went yesterday. I think it's important you know as soon as possible.'

There's a gravity in Harriet's tone and Grace perches on the bed to ready herself for what's coming next.

'I decided to do a little assessment on Kaia. Nothing intrusive, but something that might explain why she's being dishonest, if that is what's going on. I asked her to look at pictures of different expressions to ascertain her ability to empathise. For a child as young as Kaia to lie in a premeditated way, I would expect to see a low score, a lack of awareness about how her actions could affect others. But the opposite happened. Kaia scored very highly.'

Grace squeezes her eyes shut but the tears still seep out. All this time, Kaia's been telling the truth. And Grace hasn't believed her.

'Based on these results, I think it would be very unlikely that Kaia's making false accusations about her father. Not impossible,

213

but unlikely.' A pause. *'I'm sure you understand the ramifications of that.'*

Grace nods her head to no one, then hangs it in shame. Harriet's voice drops an octave and becomes lighter, less certain.

'But Kaia said one other thing that I think you should be aware of. She still refused to talk about her father's involvement in her injuries, but she seemed convinced that Marcus was going to attack you. She told me it was her job to save you.' Another pause. *'There's lots of help out there, Grace, some excellent charities. Call me, please.'*

The voice message clicks to end and the phone slips out of Grace's hand. While she's been labelling her daughter confused, or a liar, Kaia has been trying to protect her. It's not surprising that a child with high levels of empathy would make that leap: if her daddy is hurting her, then it stands to reason that he must be abusing her mother too.

How could she have failed Kaia so badly? Perhaps because they don't share blood. Because she's not a proper mother, just a stand-in, a fake. Incapable of truly loving her child. They call it unconditional love, but where was hers when Kaia put it to the test?

Chapter 38

A rap sounds on her bedroom door, lifting Grace out of her quagmire of guilt. 'Hello?'

The door swings open. Josh is stood there, his hands on Kaia's shoulders. He gently pushes her inside. 'Gracie, there's something you need to see.' He's not smiling and Grace swallows down the lump of vomit that's collected in her throat. She can't speak, so she just watches him guide Kaia to sit on her bed and roll up the sleeve of her sweatshirt.

Grace doesn't understand at first, the slow release of Kaia's naked arm, Josh's downcast expression. The silence that hangs heavy in the air.

But then she sees it.

The perfect red circle on Kaia's forearm.

A needlepoint of fire.

Rage boils in Grace's gut and she gasps. Kaia's arm retracts back inside her sweater like a startled tortoise. 'I'm sorry, Mummy.'

'Did Daddy burn you with his cigarette?' Grace demands, her tone harsher than Kaia deserves. She remembers seeing Kaia nursing her arm earlier. 'Before I found you in the park?'

Kaia's eyes flick between her and Josh and then she drops her head. 'Yes,' she whispers to the floor.

'Why didn't you tell me?' Grace pleads in a strangled voice. 'When I found you?'

Kaia looks at her like the answer is obvious. 'You never believe me.'

Grace just stares. Because what can she possibly say to make things better? She wants to wail, perform some act of self-flagellation. But how would that help her daughter? And she owes her so much.

Josh breaks the silence. 'We need to get her out of here, Gracie. Both of you. It's sick, burning a child like that. We need to go to the police.'

A vision careers into Grace's head. Marcus being led away in handcuffs. The slam of a cell door, the special treatment reserved for child abusers. The man she's loved since she was 16. She can't think about that now; she just needs to get Kaia to safety. 'I'm so sorry I didn't believe you, honey. I should have listened better. But I believe you now, I promise.'

'I'm scared of him.'

Grace's chest constricts and her heart feels like it's crushing under the weight of her guilt. She needs to get out of here. 'Come with me.' She takes Kaia's hand and carefully guides her back to her own bedroom, aware that Josh is a few steps behind them. She doesn't know why she's bothering to be quiet; Marcus is engrossed in the rugby match on TV, swerving with rising drunkenness between cheering and swearing. He won't have a clue what's going on upstairs. But she still feels an urge to hide from him.

Josh disappears into the guestroom, and then Grace closes the door of Kaia's bedroom behind them. She opens the wardrobe and pulls out Kaia's overnight bag. 'We'll go to Granny and Grandpa's for a few nights. Can you put a couple of your favourite toys in here?' She's too rattled to pack her own bag, but Kaia needs as much comfort as she can carry.

'But Granny's on his side. She'll let him in.'

'No, Kaia.' Grace shakes her head. 'Granny got it wrong too, like me, but I promise she won't let Daddy hurt you anymore. You're safe now.'

Kaia still looks uncertain. What have they done to her? She and her mum discussing Kaia's accusations like some soap opera plot twist. After a pause, Kaia takes the bag out of Grace's hands and starts filling it with the toys from her bed; her favourite green tree, the unofficial Stanford University mascot, goes in first. Grace stares at the mop of mahogany waves framing Kaia's face for a moment, then she kisses the top of her head, says another silent apology, and heads out of the room.

The guestroom door is closed now so she knocks quietly.

'Come in,' Josh's low voice seeps out. She pushes on the door and walks inside. They were never close growing up, their lives too separate for that, but Grace always looked up to him. The older brother for whom life seemed so easy. He was a good role model. Even when he was given awards, achieved top grades, won tennis trophies, he never lauded his superiority over her. And in turn, she never felt jealous of him. Only proud. Even her mother's obvious awe for Josh doesn't rankle Grace for long. She smiles at him.

'Ready?' he asks.

She nods. 'We can stay with Mum and Dad for a few days. Kaia will be safe, and it'll give me some time to figure out what to do next.'

'Mum adores Marcus,' Josh warns, echoing Kaia's words. 'She'll convince you to forgive him.'

'Not this time,' Grace promises, her voice gravelly. It's true that Faith has a soft spot for her husband; defending him is her default position, excusing his hangovers, wafting away the money he's wasted on risky investments over the years. But even Faith can't defend a cigarette burn.

*

217

'Remember, we must stay really quiet,' Grace whispers, as she tiptoes down the stairs. She can sense Kaia behind her and then Josh at the back. Her soft-soled trainers hardly make a sound against the thick carpet, and even on the wooden floorboards her footsteps are muted. Grace carefully removes the car key from its home on the windowsill, a Japanese-inspired ceramic bowl picked up in a gift store in Auckland's Ponsonby district. As she feels the cold plastic against her fingers, she sighs with relief. The TV is still blaring and the living-room door is firmly shut. Marcus won't know a thing until they're safely out of his reach. She takes Kaia's hand, then turns towards the front door.

BANG! THUD, THUD, THUD.

Grace gasps and whips her head around. Josh is lying at the bottom of the stairs.

'Shit! I tripped,' he half whispers, half hisses, his eyes wide with apology.

'Come on, we need to go,' she pleads as quietly as her thumping heart will allow.

But it's too late. The TV goes silent. The living-room door flies open.

'What the hell is going on?'

Marcus's eyes are bloodshot, and his speech slurred. Grace didn't want this conversation if he was sober, and she definitely doesn't want to have it now. 'We're just going out for a bit,' she says lamely.

Marcus looks at the bags on the floor, then at Josh, who is gingerly pulling himself up. Without speaking, he grabs Grace's arm and yanks her into the living room, slamming the door shut behind them.

She stares at the closed door, then at the rage on Marcus's face, and feels her bladder loosen.

'Going out, bullshit. Tell me the truth,' he snarls.

His face is so close that Grace can smell alcohol fumes on his breath. Instinctively she wants to take a step back, to run away,

218

but why should she? How dare he intimidate her? She's not 16 anymore, frozen under his furious glare, willing to accept his closed fist in her face because she loves him. She takes a deep breath and curls her lips into a scowl. 'How dare you pull me in here, like I'm your property.' She pushes at his chest, not hard, but he stumbles backwards and grabs the sofa.

'He's poison, your brother. And now he's poisoning you against me.' His words slip into each other, and spittle flies out of his mouth.

'You're pathetic, you know that? This is about Kaia, not Josh.'

'You can't take her away from me.'

Grace laughs, more like a cackle, and takes a step closer to him. 'That's why I'm leaving, to protect her from you. I saw her arm, what you did. You're a monster, Marcus. Not a father.'

'How fucking dare you?!' he screams back at her. 'Do you think I wanted a kid at 24? You made me do it.' He jabs at Grace's shoulder with his open fist, but she stands her ground.

'And when she pisses you off, you burn her,' she hisses back.

'For fuck's sake, SHE'S LYING!' Marcus's arms flail up towards the ceiling, then crash down, whipping against Grace's cheeks on their descent. It's like a switch has clicked to red in his eyes. Danger. He lunges for her, anger carved into every crevice of his screwed-up face. Grace screams and ducks, loses her balance, and falls to the floor.

'Get your hands off me!' she tries to scream, but as she stares up at his looming torso, his knuckle-white fists curled and ready, her voice splinters and breaks. She closes her eyes and waits for the punch to land.

The door flies open. 'What the hell are you doing to her?!'

Josh grabs Grace's arm, pulls her to her feet, puts a protective arm around her shoulders. 'You're a fucking liability, mate,' he shouts at Marcus. 'Come on, Gracie.'

Then Josh pushes her out of the room, out of the house, and into the car, where Kaia is sat, thankfully oblivious to it all.

Chapter 39

COCO

2011

Coco blinks in the bright morning sunlight. After two nights in a cell, she knows she stinks. Of course, her antics during the thirty-six hours before being arrested played their part too. Her day's drinking in Bangkok airport followed by an overnight flight to Paris. Then her disastrous evening with all-American Todd and his wanker banker friends. She's still wearing the wraparound dress that she slipped on in the dark in that Thai guesthouse as her baby daughter and best friend slept, a lifetime ago now. But the pale yellow has turned a tired shade of grey and the hem has frayed where she's pulled at it. She looks how she feels.

Coco increases her pace to a scurry. It's the only way she can keep up with the determined stride of the police officer who swung open the cell door a minute ago and beckoned for Coco to follow her, a short woman with spiky hair that shines under cheap gel. She climbs the stairs and quickly arrives in the main reception area. There's a man dressed in navy jeans and a tight white T-shirt at the front desk, signing some paperwork. A pair of Vuarnet sunglasses hang down his chest.

As she gets closer, he looks up. Then down. Like a farmer appraising a new cow. 'You're Coco Byrne?' he asks, with a strong French accent and a hint of disappointment that she's not used to. 'Quickly, my car is on a meter.'

She looks at the police officer stood next to her, who seems unmoved by the fact the man escorting her out of the station appears to be a stranger. Should she point this out? That the man with flash sunglasses and an obvious God complex could be a serial killer searching for vulnerable prey under her nose?

However, the woman in uniform clearly mistakes Coco's hesitation for confusion because she gestures to the front door and gives her a reassuring smile. 'You have your liberty back, Mademoiselle.' The French accent makes her English sound more eloquent, not less. 'You can go now.' She nods at Mr Flashy Pants. 'This man cleared your fine at the courthouse. And also,' she continues, reaching her arm around the desk, 'your bag. The American woman, from the apartment you entered illegally, dropped it off for you.'

'Jesus, I thought she'd burn it. Just with her fucking eyes.'

Coco is pleased to hear the man laugh, but the police officer's expression hardens. 'She said that on reflection she felt sorry for you. That your life was clearly very sad.'

Coco blinks and pushes her lips together, her swagger gone. 'Thank you,' she manages, and takes her bag from the police officer's outstretched hand. It's sticky and smells like sweet vinegar but she doesn't allow her face to grimace. Then she twists on her rubber toes and lets herself be guided out of the sliding glass exit.

'I'm Matteo, by the way,' he says, pointing at a white Renault Megane parked across the street.

'My knight in shining armour,' Coco murmurs.

'What? Oh yes, I see.' But Coco isn't sure he really understands the English idiom. He clicks his key fob and the car responds with a low clunk. Coco pulls open the passenger door and climbs inside.

'I'm just helping out a friend. He called me. Explained what happened, where you were. Asked if I would help. Of course I agreed. He's a good friend.'

'Oh?' Coco asks. Kaia's father doesn't have many proper friends. He's too driven for that. It's one of the things that excited her in the beginning. But Matteo doesn't seem to want to elaborate much.

'I've known him a long time. I've only ever left France once, so his life is, you know, more interesting than mine.' He pauses. 'I knew about you right from the start, when you first met. He told me you were special.'

Coco leans back against the headrest and closes her eyes. It had all seemed so simple back then. A beautiful French love story. Well, maybe more *Fifty Shades* than Mills & Boon, but it was perfect for them. Long days in bed, nights spent in bars drinking cognac and smoking Gitanes. Croissants for midnight feasts and champagne for breakfast. She'd thought it would go on forever.

How stupid she was.

'I wondered if he might come himself,' she says vaguely, staring out of the window as the high white buildings of the 4th arrondissement roll by. 'Rescue me like a superhero, put me on his back and fly me through space to some tropical island.'

Matteo spits out air, the French symbol for derision. 'From what I hear, I think you've made that very difficult for him. Maybe you should be grateful that he is willing to help at all.'

Coco turns her head slightly and stares at the man driving her. She still doesn't know where they're going; she's too tired to ask. But she does wonder how much he knows. How much her secret lover was prepared to tell him. Not the whole truth; she's almost sure of that.

Like how their romance started. It should have put her off him for good. If she was a different kind of girl, it would have done. If she was a feminist like those hairy girls at school, or

222

had principles like Grace. Or some level of fucking self-respect maybe. But she didn't say anything, just let it all happen to her. And she even let herself fall in love with him. Because she liked his strong arms around her, the feeling of surrendering to him. She liked being his property.

And that was when he dropped her.

For the first time.

They've reached the outer part of Paris now and the vista has changed a lot. The buildings appear almost fake, tired white walls that look thin enough to collapse if you blow hard enough. Small concrete parks with soccer goals at each end. A man in a Puffa jacket and black beanie leans against a doorway and stares as they drive past. She doesn't know this part of Paris and a taste of fear washes up into her mouth. 'Where are we going, anyway?' she asks, trying to sound casual.

'Does it matter?' he responds. 'Surely anywhere is better than jail?' He laughs again, but the noise isn't pleasant anymore. It revolves around the small car and makes Coco feel claustrophobic. She eyes the passenger door. But even if it was unlocked, that would be a crazy idea. They're on an A road now and Matteo must be doing at least 70 kilometres per hour. She's trapped in here. Just like she was by those strong arms all those years ago.

'Look, I'm grateful that you've paid my fine and everything,' she starts. 'But I can sort myself out now. If you could just drop me here …'

'He doesn't want you to go back to England.' His voice is commanding now, his French accent arrogant.

'What? Well, that's where I'm going,' Coco blusters, but a ribbon of fear twists in her belly. 'Listen, just stop the car, okay?'

That mocking snort again. 'You owe him. For the fine, the mess that he's cleared up for you, for telling lies. You don't get to make demands.'

Coco's heart is racing. Her earlier exhaustion has disappeared and she feels a desperate urge to throw the car door open anyway, take her chances against the oncoming traffic. She wraps her hand around the door handle. 'This is kidnapping – you can't just take me wherever the fuck you want.'

He laughs again and she wants to rip the ugly Vuarnets off his face and stab his eyes with the arm. 'I'm not kidnapping you, you stupid girl. What would I do with a slut like you?'

She can't stop the tears then. She can't even be bothered to try. They roll down her face and she stares at the grey tarmac and wonders where the hell she'll end up.

Chapter 40

GRACE

2019

Grace looks out of the car window but doesn't see any of the familiar landmarks rolling past her in the Saturday evening traffic. Her head is too full. Wondering how the hell she's managed to screw up her life so much. She was given the huge head start that privilege brings, and yet here she is, running away from an abusive husband, soon to be a single mother. She turns to look at Kaia in the back seat and is relieved to see that her daughter's eyes are closed. Grace hopes that she's asleep, dreaming about flying around the magical Wizard Street, not the pain her dad has inflicted on her.

'Are you okay?'

Grace turns to look at Josh. He seems so at ease behind the wheel of her car. He's always been like this, she realises, able to adapt to unforeseen situations with the coolness of someone who predicted them all along. What would have happened if he wasn't there? Would Marcus have hit her or pulled back just in time?

She's glad that she didn't need to find out. 'Yeah, I'm fine,' she mutters in response and turns back to the window. As her mind settles, she starts to take in the view. Opulent homeware stores and darkly lit restaurants edge the road as it snakes right, then left. 'This is the King's Road,' she says matter-of-factly.

'I'm just following the satnav.' Josh gestures to the small screen set into the dashboard. 'I've no clue where I am.'

'Shit, Josh. The satnav can't be working. This isn't the way to Mum and Dad's. Surely you know not to cross the Thames?' Grace doesn't want to sound ungrateful, but it's only a ten-minute drive to Wimbledon Village from her house, and Josh has taken them fifteen minutes in the opposite direction.

'I'm not driving to Mum and Dad's,' he says quietly.

'Why not?'

'I told you, Mum adores Marcus. She'll either try to change your mind about him or be devastated herself. You don't need either of those scenarios right now.'

Grace continues looking out of the window as she processes Josh's explanation. He takes a left just past Bluebird restaurant with its glass awning and neat hedgerow. The sky is still cloudy and Grace watches people huddle and shiver around the outside tables, al fresco dinner plans made earlier in the week when the sun shone and the temperature reached twenty-five degrees. It's amazing how quickly promise can turn into disappointment.

'Maybe,' she finally says. 'But I don't want to stay in a hotel; it's not fair on Kaia.' Or herself, Grace doesn't add. She loves her daughter, and she knows she needs to make things up to her. But she's also desperate for some space, a chance to work out what to do next. And a hotel room isn't going to give her that.

'A friend from Stanford has a mews house in Chelsea. He only uses it when he comes over, said I could borrow it while I was here.' Josh takes his left hand off the steering wheel for a moment, squeezes Grace's arm, then drops it down by his side, as if he needs to keep it ready to comfort her again at a moment's notice.

226

'I told him that I wanted to stay with you, but he gave me the key anyway, just in case. Seems like too good an option to ignore.'

Perhaps a night away from everyone is a good idea, Grace thinks. A chance to get her head straight before she tells her parents. Leaving Marcus solves one problem, taking Kaia out of immediate danger. But what happens next? When social services find out that she's left him, they'll ramp up their investigation, discover that Marcus isn't Kaia's legal father. And who knows where that road will lead? All the way to Thailand perhaps, and Kaia's fake birth certificate. 'You're right,' she says. 'I'm not sure I could face Mum and Dad at the moment.'

Josh smiles and crosses over the Fulham Road, heading northwards. 'It's just up here, I think,' he says, peering at the satnav. A minute later, he pulls onto a narrow, cobbled street. Grace's shiny Land Rover should feel incongruous here, among the modest row of houses built originally as stable blocks for the grander homes close by. But nowadays London mews houses are worth millions, and the cobbles are lined with a mix of Chelsea tractors and flashy sports cars.

'You have rich friends at Stanford,' Grace observes, unclicking her seatbelt and opening the car door. Despite the situation, she's quite curious about staying here. Living in Devon and schooling in Gloucestershire meant that London was always a distant, exotic place, full of celebrities and beautiful people. While her dad's ex-council flat in Pimlico never appealed, a few of her school friends' families had more glamorous London pads, and they would discuss how they were going to spend weekends there when they were old enough. It never happened though. Coco left, and Grace fell in love, and all their plans just faded away. Of course, Grace has been living in London for almost seven years now. But the identical red-brick terraces of SW18 aren't exactly the London she pictured as a teenager.

With Kaia still fast asleep in her arms, Grace follows Josh into the flat-fronted two-storey building. Some of the houses have kept the original stable door, but this one has been replaced with a six-panel window. Josh pushes open the shutters and the last of the evening light filters into the living room. Grace looks at the array of pastel-coloured cushions on the sofa and feels an urge to sink into them. It must show on her face because Josh comes over and takes Kaia from her.

'You look exhausted. I'll put Kaia to bed upstairs, then pour us a glass of wine. Charles promised there would be a bottle in the fridge.'

'Thank you,' she mumbles, lowering herself onto the sofa. The cushions are as soft as pillows and she loves how they collapse and re-form around her shoulders. As she waits in the silence for Josh to return, she takes in her surroundings. She can tell the house isn't lived in much – there's no mess, none of the home stuff that builds up over time. But it still looks loved. Thoughtfully chosen ornaments on the mantelpiece. Four beautiful landscape paintings on the back wall. In fact, it's hard to imagine that it's owned by an American academic, although Grace realises how prejudiced that sounds.

'She didn't even wake up,' Josh says proudly, walking into the room and handing Grace a glass of white wine. He sits in the armchair opposite and raises his glass. The wine is very chilled – perhaps a hint of its American owner after all – and she loves the feel of it trickling down her throat.

'That tastes good,' she says with feeling, letting her head fall back against the sofa. 'Don't let me drink too much of it though.'

'You deserve a drink, Gracie. After what you've been through today.'

Perhaps he's right. Grace takes another large sip and snuggles down further. This does feel good. Although she doesn't know why she considers alcohol a friend. She sees how bad it is for Marcus, how it strips him of self-control, blinds him to the cares of those around him. It's made her life harder too, she thinks. Like that New Year's Eve in Phuket. Being too drunk to know whether Marcus and Coco slept together, too out of it to stop them making a baby together.

If that is what happened of course. She still has no proof. Maybe she isn't thinking straight. Coco met someone in Saint-Tropez. Perhaps he's got auburn hair and brown eyes. He could be a natural sportsman too.

As she drains the last drops from her glass, she allows her mind to wander to the first time she suspected there might be something between Marcus and Coco. During the summer of 2005. A fleeting moment, quickly pushed away, but never quite forgotten. As the memories start rippling back into her mind – her smarting eyes, Marcus's fury, the taste of blood – she wonders if she does need another drink after all. Just one more, she promises herself, to help her sleep. She holds out her glass for a refill.

Josh leans forward and pours.

Grace runs her finger around the rim of the glass. 'Do you think I'm a terrible mother, Josh?'

'Of course not,' he answers quickly. 'How could you possibly have known that Marcus would turn into such a monster?'

'There were clues though, weren't there? His temper.'

'Everyone has a temper, Gracie.'

'His violence.'

Josh sighs and looks into his own glass, the wine refracting in the artificial light. 'You mean the night we had a scuffle, I suppose. That summer in Devon.'

'He beat you up, Josh! How can you be so cool about it?'

'Not just me,' Josh reminds her. 'And I didn't forgive him as quickly as you did.'

Grace closes her eyes. Why did she forgive him so easily? Where was her self-respect? She'd been frightened that night, angry the next day. But by the time he came by a week later, hiding his shame behind a huge bunch of flowers and a newly tanned face, she'd been ready to forgive him. Coco was in Saint-Tropez by then and Grace was feeling lonely, so when he suggested a date, it had been all too easy to accept. 'Why was he so angry, Josh?'

'I've thought about it over the years. He was jealous of our lifestyle for sure, and I'd beaten him at tennis earlier that day, so maybe it was a competitive thing. But honestly? I don't know. He just attacked me, out of the blue.'

'And you promise you're not hiding anything from me?' she whispers. 'I know I wasn't away for long, but when I got back, Coco looked, I don't know … guilty, I suppose. And she never told me why.' Looking back, Grace knows that she suspected something happened between Coco and Marcus that night. She'd asked Coco the next day and her friend had denied it so vehemently that she'd managed to push it out of her mind for a while. It had come back later that summer when she realised she'd fallen in love with Marcus. It nagged at her until she eventually broached the subject with him. He'd looked into her eyes and promised that nothing had happened between them. She believed him too, and had buried her suspicion in the graveyard of her mind.

But were they both lying to her?

She never got to ask Josh at the time, the third person in the room. He left for Île de Ré soon after that night, a holiday with his county tennis partner's family, and was only back in Devon for a few nights before he headed to the United States and Stanford University.

She looks over at him, sitting on the opposite sofa, gently rotating the glass in his hand. Perhaps she should ask him now.

'That night, when I wasn't there, did anything happen between Marcus and Coco?'

'What? No,' he says quickly.

'And you're absolutely sure?'

He drops his head, then lifts it and looks directly into her eyes. 'I'm absolutely sure, Grace.'

That should be enough. Coco, Marcus and Josh have all denied it now.

Except Grace can read her brother's face.

And she knows he's lying.

She holds out her glass and watches Josh refill it.

Chapter 41

MARCUS

2005

Marcus smiles stiffly. He's already necked a couple of vodka and Cokes and doesn't want Faith to notice. For some reason, her approval is important to him. She's that kind of mother.

He wouldn't usually drink by himself before a night out, but he needed something to take the edge off after that run-in with his sisters. He probably went a bit far, throttling Izzy like that. He just couldn't help himself. Yeah, he does struggle to contain his anger sometimes, but they did provoke him.

'Good evening, Marcus. Henry and I are just on our way out. The others are in the garden room. Are you okay to make your own way down there?'

'Of course, Mrs Windsor. Thanks for letting me come over,' he says, carefully enunciating each word.

His efforts pay off. 'Oh please, call me Faith,' she says, wafting her hand in the air. 'And you're welcome any time. I imagine it's quite hectic at the B&B this time of year.'

Marcus is vaguely aware that she means well, but it's still fucking patronising. 'That's really kind of you, Faith.' Another wide smile. Then he slips out of the French doors and walks down the garden, a light shining from inside the summer house to guide him down. Josh is standing just inside, attaching an iPod to a docking station. He looks up as Marcus walks inside, and the speakers above the sliding doors come to life.

'Hey, mate. Looking pretty hot tonight.' Josh leans in, takes a deep sniff. 'My God, you smell gorgeous. I assume all this effort is for me?' Josh winks, then laughs to himself. 'I've made a punch. Want some?'

Marcus looks at the bowl of bright blue liquid sitting on the dresser at the side of the room. He half expects to see it bubbling, a toxic waste sign stuck to the side. But he nods his head anyway. When Josh hands him a glass, he discovers that the mystery drink tastes pretty good. 'Drinking alone?' he asks, the most subtle way he can think of to find out where Coco is.

'Girls were here a minute ago. Coco dragged Grace down to the woods, girl talk or something.'

Marcus feels his back stiffen. He wonders what Coco is telling Grace. About him maybe? And if so, what is she saying? That she had an amazing time on that very sofa and can't wait for the next instalment, or that Marcus went too far, that he's a predator who doesn't know when to stop? He bloody hopes it's the first, because he's been fantasising about having sex with her ever since that morning. Fuck it, maybe he should just come clean with Josh too. Tell his mate that he and Coco are having a thing.

A bubble of laughter permeates through the open doorway of the summer house. Coco and Grace appear, walking arm in arm. Coco spots him, releases her friend, and sashays over with a wide grin on her face. She looks gorgeous, as always. Her red hair meanders down her back, and she's wearing a strappy sea-blue dress, the material thin enough to reveal the contours of her body. 'Well, hello, lover boy.' She reaches up and kisses his cheek.

He smiles back. Maybe this is the moment to announce it; she clearly doesn't mind making it public.

'And hello to you too, gorgeous,' she adds with a giggle, before planting a kiss on Josh's cheek as well.

'You're such a minx, Coco,' Josh breezes, raising his eyebrows and shaking his head in a fake fatherly way. 'Anyone for punch?'

Marcus grinds his teeth and holds out his empty glass. Jesus, she's such a tease. And why is Josh immune to her tricks, when Marcus falls for every one?

'Me too.' Grace picks a glass off the table and holds it out. Her smile is wide and her eyes dance with a mischief Marcus hasn't seen before. He feels another wave of attraction for the more sensible, more predictable Grace Windsor.

'I'll only consume that poison if I can drink it through a straw,' Coco declares. 'A pink one.'

Josh raises his eyebrows again. 'I think there are some straws somewhere. Hold on a minute.'

Marcus watches Josh walk over to the dresser and yank open a couple of drawers until he finds a box of straws. He clearly decides she's worth the effort after all, because he then spends ages making Coco's drink look like an exotic cocktail. Marcus bristles and throws Grace a smile. Why should Coco get all the special attention? Then he watches the chameleon sink down onto the sofa and curl up her legs. Her dress is so flimsy that he can make out the darker flesh of her nipples underneath the fine material. Despite his annoyance, he feels himself harden at the memory of her body.

Why does she have this power over him?

He snatches the full glass of punch from Josh and necks it.

'Let's play truth or dare,' Coco suggests. 'Come here, Marcus. Sit next to me.'

'I'm up for it.' Grace drops onto the sofa, leaving a space for Marcus, and returns his smile with a wider one.

Dropping down between the girls, he realises that his head

feels nicely woozy. The girls must be wearing the same perfume because a spiced, citrusy scent is spreading from both sides of the sofa. He leans back a bit further and lets it float over him.

'I'll go first,' Coco offers, snapping her fingers for no obvious reason.

'So, Coco,' Josh says in an interviewer-style voice, designating himself the playmaker. 'You have to either answer my question truthfully, or accept the dare I give you.'

'I can't guarantee I won't do both.' Coco unfolds her legs and stretches them out in front of her. Her flip-flops drop onto the floor, and red-painted toes flicker in the dimmed spotlights as she points and flexes her feet.

'Would you sleep with a man for a dare?'

'Wait.' Coco's brow furrows. 'Is that my question, or my dare?'

'That depends on whether you're willing to tell the truth.'

Coco drops her head to one side. 'I might sleep with a man for a dare,' she says eventually. 'But only if I want to sleep with them.'

'So your answer is no,' Grace says. 'You would be sleeping with them because you fancied them, not to fulfil a dare.'

'I might fancy them because of the dare though. The thrill of it, you know?' Coco picks at the hem of her dress, and Marcus watches it ride up her thighs.

'That's not a proper answer,' Josh decides. 'Too confusing. Which means you have to do a dare.'

Coco fake sighs, like a balloon deflating. 'Fine. What's my dare then?'

Josh slides her glass of punch to the edge of the table in front of her. 'Down it.'

She scrunches her nose up. 'All of it?'

'Come on, Coco. I thought you were the ultimate party girl?'

Coco raises her eyebrows and lifts the glass to her lips, the challenge clearly more important than her palette. As Marcus watches her gulp it down, he makes a silent wish that she's not throwing up before he gets a chance to rekindle their romance.

'Who's next?' Josh asks, his eyes moving between Grace and Marcus.

'I think it's your turn, big brother.' Grace slams her empty glass on the table and Marcus notices that the mischief in her eyes is now spiralling. 'Truth or dare?'

'Oh, it's a dare for me, every time.' Josh knits his fingers behind his head and stretches back. A lazy grin spreads across his face and Marcus fights the urge to slap it off him. Josh doesn't do insecurity. Fear of failure is a language he will never understand. Of course he would choose dare; it's just another chance for him to show how fucking good he is at something.

'You have to kiss Coco,' Grace announces with a giggle. 'Tongues included.'

'Eurgh,' Coco squeals, but Marcus can tell she doesn't mean it. He can almost see the excitement fizzing on her skin. 'Is that legal?' she giggles.

'You're not actually related, you idiot. Anyway, it's just a bit of fun.'

Marcus turns to Josh. He looks blindsided, and Marcus feels a moment of joy. There's finally a situation that Josh doesn't know how to handle. But then realisation hits him again. His best friend kissing his girl. No, sorry, that will not fucking do.

'That's a shit dare, Grace.'

'Huh?'

She sounds hurt, which isn't his intention, but he can't let the kiss go ahead. He keeps going. 'Well clearly neither of them want to kiss each other. To be honest, it's a bit weird that you even suggested it.' He's on a roll now. 'Like sexual harassment or something.'

'It was just a dare, a bit of fun,' she repeats. She looks down at her hands, her fingers knotted together in her lap.

Marcus fidgets on the sofa. She looks so dejected. 'I'm sure you could think of something else, one hundred press-ups maybe?' he suggests, trying to sound conciliatory. But it doesn't work. He watches her push off the sofa, her eyeline directed firmly away from him.

'Yeah, whatever. You decide.' She takes a few steps towards the door.

Shit, she looks like she's going to cry. 'Grace, I didn't mean to offend you,' he starts, rising up to her level. 'I just don't think …'

'No, it's fine. My stupid idea. Forget it. I'm just going to get some air.' Then she slides the door open and walks out into the night.

Chapter 42

GRACE

2019

Grace wakes up in a panic. She pushes up onto her elbows and looks around the room. As the unfamiliar furniture comes slowly into focus, the events of the previous day start to replay in her mind. The cigarette burn on Kaia's arm. Marcus's clenched fists. Josh walking into the living room before anything worse happened, then driving them to his friend's mews house in Chelsea.

And last night. How awkward Josh looked when she asked him about Marcus and Coco.

Grace lies back against the silk-covered pillow and stares at the ceiling. Her head is like a cement mixer starved of water, heavy and unyielding. And her mouth tastes sour. This is not the state she wanted to be in this morning. Surely she didn't drink enough wine to feel this bad? She sighs and reaches for her phone. The room has a large window overlooking the cobblestones. Heavy curtains block out most of the light, but sunshine is leaking around the edges and its brightness tells her that it's later than she normally wakes up. In fact, she's surprised Kaia hasn't sneaked in next to her already.

Grace prods her phone a few times but the screen stays blank. Shit. She didn't plug it in when she went to bed, and it must have run out of battery overnight. Still feeling groggy, she pushes herself up to sitting, then twists her legs over the side of the king-size bed and yawns. She's wearing the T-shirt she had on yesterday, but luckily she managed to get her jeans off. At least, she assumes it was her doing. She can't actually remember going upstairs.

She wrestles inside her bag until she finds her charger, then pushes it into a socket by the side of the bed. She waits impatiently for the faint outline of an empty battery to disappear, and finally her home screen springs into life. As she smiles at the photo of Kaia taken last summer before any of this mess started, messages start ding-ding-dinging through the tiny speaker. Voicemails, texts, WhatsApp messages. But all from Marcus, and she's not ready to engage with him yet. Belatedly, she checks the time.

'Jesus.' She pulls on her jeans, shoves her phone in her back pocket, and whips open the door. 'Kaia?' she calls out. It's 10.05 a.m. She never sleeps this long, and neither does her daughter. With panic resurfacing, she trots down the landing to the next door along and pushes it open. A bathroom. She tries the next one. This room is empty, but the duvet on the bed is ruffled and Kaia's bag is on the floor, a mix of her clothes and toys spilling out. Grace feels her heart rate settle. Kaia's already up, she realises. She'll be in the garden probably; she might even have found a ball. Smiling at the thought, Grace uses the bathroom and then heads downstairs.

The living room at the front of the house is empty. There's an eerie quiet about the place too, and Grace feels an irrational sense of being abandoned. Usually she loves it when the house is quiet, Kaia immersed in a task, Marcus at work or the rugby club (he's never managed to master the art of being quiet at home). But this morning she feels like she's floating in uncertainty and needs the familiarity of Kaia's voice to anchor her back down. She opens the door to the kitchen, hoping to find life. Josh at the coffee machine showing off his Californian-learned barista skills, Kaia throwing an old tennis ball against the glass door from the garden. But the room is empty too. And the Crittall doors across the back, with their individual panes of glass shining between heavy charcoal bars, show that no one's in the garden either.

Where are they?

Grace's mind starts whirring. The sun is shining and it's past ten o'clock. The garden is small and Josh is a great uncle. He will have taken Kaia to the park, of course. Or perhaps for a milkshake in one of the many cafés around here. She pulls her phone out of her back pocket and taps on his number. She could have a quick shower and then join them. It will be good to do something fun. Forget about all the mess and just enjoy their company for a while. But after eight or so rings, the phone clicks into voicemail. She leaves a message, then sends a text. Her phone still has less than 10 per cent battery life, so she plugs it in to the Apple charger snaking out of the wall.

The throbbing in her head is subsiding, but her mouth is still parched. She takes a glass from the cupboard and runs the tap until it's icy cold. As she gulps at the water she looks back at her phone. There are twenty-one WhatsApp messages from Marcus. She sighs, then clicks on his name. She can track his gradual sobering up from the tone of his messages. They start angry. *How dare you take Kaia from me! I LOVE HER! IM INNOCENT!!!* Then they get maudlin. *You and Kaia are the only good things in my life. Please come back. I need you.* And finally remorseful. *I'm sorry, Grace. I acted like a complete dick. Can we talk?*

Grace lifts her head and rubs her eyes. Marcus has been her soulmate, her best friend, for fourteen years. How is she going to be able to do it all without him by her side? She forces herself to remember the anger on his face yesterday, the burn on Kaia's arm. And then she takes her mind much further back. To that summer of 2005 when his anger toppled over into violence. And how it started. Her suggesting that Coco and Josh share a stupid, innocent kiss. Is that what he couldn't handle? Was he so obsessed with Coco that he couldn't bear to see her kiss someone else?

Grace pushes off the work surface and walks to the back of the room, opening the back doors. The garden might be small, but it's bright and vibrant. Flowerbeds run down each side and a collection of different-sized pots on the patio burst with colour. The owner must have a gardener, she surmises as she twists round and rests the back of her head against the glass.

And then she forces herself to continue joining the dots.

If something happened between Marcus and Coco on their last night together in 2005, it makes sense that they would rekindle that romance when fate brought them together six years later. And of course dates don't lie. Kaia was born on the 27th of September 2011, almost exactly nine months after their night together in Thailand.

But in her letter to her parents, Coco had suggested that Kaia's father was a man she'd been in love with for years. An ongoing affair, albeit secret, not a faraway memory re-enacted when the opportunity presented itself. Coco and Marcus's lives ran so separately in the intervening years that it's hard to believe it's him. And she still remembers how excited Coco sounded when she texted Grace that summer about the man she'd met in France, a romance powerful enough to lift her off her feet so high that she never really came back down to earth.

Grace had hoped that the fresh morning air would clear her head, but the more she tries to work things out, the foggier it gets. She knows there's an obvious way to find the answer. A simple DNA test. But is she ready for the truth? Perhaps it's time. But right now, she has a more urgent question that needs answering.

Where the hell has Josh taken Kaia?

Grace walks back to her phone and tries her brother again. When the call clicks into voicemail, she swears under her breath.

His lack of contact is starting to irritate her. Surely he knows that she'll be wondering where they both are? He could have left a note or texted her explaining his plans. Perhaps this is normal behaviour for him. A bachelor, living alone, only ever answering to himself. But still, he should have been more thoughtful.

Suddenly a thought pops into her head. It's Josh's book launch today. He was due at the London Review at 10 a.m. in preparation for the mid-morning event. Kaia wasn't on the invite list, but he must have decided to take her, let Grace sleep off the wine she drank last night. No wonder he's not answering his phone – he'll be busy signing books and nodding politely at a long line of psychology enthusiasts. She feels bad for forgetting, and for her earlier annoyance, but she's still desperate to hear Kaia's voice. At least she knows where her daughter is now.

She clicks into her Google app to find the phone number she needs.

'Good morning, London Review bookshop,' an efficient female voice answers.

'Um, good morning, I'm Josh Windsor's sister.'

'That's nice,' the voice continues, and Grace thinks she can detect a slight impatience.

'I think my daughter is with him in the store?'

'Are you hoping to speak with your daughter, Ms Windsor?'

A wave of relief washes over Grace. She hadn't realised quite how desperate she was to track Kaia down until the prospect became imminent. 'Yes please.'

'Well, I'm awfully sorry but we're very busy this morning and we don't have one of those loudspeaker things. I can't really ask every male customer with a child if their name is Josh Windsor.'

'No, you don't understand,' Grace tries to explain, but her head is feeling woolly again and her mouth has dried up. 'He's not a customer. He's an author. He's doing a book launch event in your store this morning. Surely you know that?'

'I'm sorry, madam, but there's no book launch here today.'

241

'You're wrong.' Grace shakes her head, pushing away the woman's statement that makes no sense. 'There must be.'

'I'm sorry, madam.' The voice is softer now, slower. 'But your brother and daughter aren't here.'

Chapter 43

GRACE

2019

Grace stares at her phone. There must be some mistake. Did she get the wrong venue? But no, it can't be that. She remembers how envious she felt, Josh launching his book at one of London's most prestigious bookshops. She drums her fingernails against the work surface and then tries his number again. As his voicemail clicks in for a third time, she slams the phone down and listens to it slide across the granite until the cable pulls tight. There's an energy racing through her now and she needs to release it, so she starts pacing the room, trying to work out what to do next.

Why would Josh lie about his book launch?

And where has he taken Kaia?

A thought jumps into her mind and she lunges for her phone again. She's not certain of anything anymore but maybe he took her to their parents' house. And if not, Faith might have some idea where he is. She clicks on her mother's number and thankfully Faith picks up on the second ring.

'Morning, darling, how are you?'

'Is Josh with you?'

'Josh? No. I presume he's in San Francisco.'

Grace's skin starts to tingle and the muscles in her neck tighten as she remembers Josh's request not to tell their parents about his visit. She grinds her teeth and blinks back tears. 'Josh is here in London, Mum. He stayed with us. He said he had a book launch at the London Review, but I called them and she didn't know anything about it. And now I've no idea where Kaia is!' The words spurt out, stinging her throat like a whisky chaser.

'What has Kaia got to do with this?' Alarm is building in Faith's voice too.

Grace forces herself to take a deep breath. 'I found out yesterday that Marcus has definitely been hurting Kaia, no question, and he almost hit me when I confronted him about it. Josh pulled me away. God knows what Marcus would have done if he didn't. Then Josh took us to his friend's house in Chelsea. I thought he was saving us, but he's gone and so is Kaia and now I don't know what to think.' Grace's voice cracks and she bites her lip.

'Oh no.' It's a whisper but slow and ominous. 'Please no.'

'Mum? What is it?'

'Why didn't you tell me Josh was coming, Grace?' Faith spits the words into the phone. 'He only ever comes at Christmas.'

Grace's heart hammers and her ears ring with the effort. Why is her mum so angry about her firstborn coming to stay? 'I don't know, he thought you might be put out, him staying with us and not you. And I've had so much on my mind. Why does it matter?' Grace shakes her head in confusion. Faith is usually so reverential when she talks about Josh.

'You need to track him down, Grace, get Kaia back.' Her tone has changed to urgent.

'I know! But why are you being so weird? You're scaring me.'

Faith stays silent for a while and Grace listens to her shallow breaths propel down the phone like tiny helicopter seeds. She imagines her mother pacing their hallway where the phone lives, her fingernails scratching her neck as she thinks.

'I've always kept you safe from him,' Faith says eventually, her voice just a wisp of sound. 'Made sure there was a distance between you. Different schools, different countries as soon as we could.'

'What are you saying?' Grace asks, tension rising in her voice.

'I suspected something when Josh started nursery school. Your father wouldn't listen.' Faith sounds plaintive now. 'He said all young boys are like that, selfish, immune to how other people feel. But Josh got older, and nothing changed. I watched him once, at Sports Day, tripping up another child so that he could win the race. Kids do that, I know. But, Grace, he didn't care. Not a speck of remorse when the child was wheeled into the ambulance with a broken wrist. I wanted to tell the teacher, but how could I? He was my son.'

Grace listens to the words but struggles to comprehend their meaning. The older brother she always looked up to. The boy with so many friends, accolades, academic achievements. And now her mother is describing him as a sadist.

Not Marcus, Josh.

A sadist who has Kaia.

Grace looks at her feet but they won't move.

'We took him to a therapist. Your father didn't want him to go at first, but I convinced him that it was our duty as parents.'

'When we took Kaia to see a therapist,' Grace whispers, remembering a conversation from a different lifetime, 'you warned me that I might hear things I didn't like.'

'I heard things I didn't like,' Faith murmurs, lost in her memories. 'But I had no choice but to face the truth. I had to know *you* were safe.'

'And was I?' Grace whispers, pleading that the answer is yes. And that Kaia is safe with him too.

'The therapist did an empathy assessment with Josh.'

Grace thinks back to Harriet's voicemail. 'Kaia took the same

245

test,' she whispers. 'She has very high empathy.' The words sting, because how will that depth of feeling be affecting her now?

'High empathy?' Faith repeats. 'That's wonderful, darling.' The relief in her voice is palpable. Then she sighs. 'Well, Josh got the opposite result. More than that, his therapist agreed that Josh displayed all the classic symptoms associated with psychopathy. But he still refused to diagnose Josh a psychopath, said a child should never be labelled.'

'You think Josh is a psychopath?' Grace cries out, shaking her head in disbelief. It can't be true. He's a professor of psychology for God's sake. 'So what did you do?'

Faith scoffs, bitterness creeping in. 'It became my responsibility, didn't it? To protect you from him. It's always the mother's job.'

'It worked,' Grace offers. 'You kept me safe.'

'Maybe.' Then Faith starts crying and the telephone line crackles with her sobs. 'The hay bales,' she starts. 'Josh had an exeat from boarding school the weekend before, and he'd been playing in that barn. When I came to get him for dinner, he got cross. Told me he was going to punish me. I ignored his threats, but two days later you were lying in the exact same place in a pool of blood.'

Grace can't bear it. She closes her eyes to push the thought away. But then the images come, the memory of that excruciating pain. Believing she was going to die. She thinks about the uneven hay bales, not stacked with the farmer's usual care. Could Josh have sabotaged it? He knew she liked to play in the barn. Was he trying to hurt her? And if he was capable of that, what might he do to Kaia?

'Mum, we need to find him,' she spits out. Her feet have come back to life and she's pacing the room again.

'Grace, you need Marcus. Does he know Kaia's missing?'

'Do you think I would contact him after what he's done?'

'You still don't know—'

'Yes I do!' Grace interrupts. 'He stubbed a cigarette out on her arm for Chrissakes!'

246

'When?'

'Yesterday. You should see the burn mark, Mum.' Grace's voice cracks.

'Was this after Josh arrived?' It's a rhetorical question, and her meaning is clear.

Grace pulls a sharp breath in. None of this makes sense. Josh has taken Kaia without any note or explanation. And he did spend lots of time alone with her yesterday. He would have had plenty of opportunity to harm her. But why would Kaia blame the injury on her own father if it was Josh who burned her? And this problem has been going on for weeks. How could Josh be to blame when he was in San Francisco until Friday?

'You need to tell Marcus, Grace. He's her father. He might not be perfect, but he loves her. And you.'

'Do you think he's innocent, Mum? Have I got this all wrong?' Grace isn't sure what she wants the answer to be. Her legs feel weak suddenly, and she drops to the floor, resting her back against the cool wood of the bespoke kitchen units.

'Do you remember that summer, before Josh left for America?' Faith asks.

'Of course, it's when Marcus and I got together.'

'Marcus came over a lot, didn't he? To hang out with you all. But Josh hated him – I could see it in his eyes. I watched him play with Marcus like a cat with a mouse. Lifting him up, swatting him back down. I hated it happening in my house, but all I could do was prop Marcus up with a smile and a compliment. I was worried for him. Even when he gave you that split lip, I was sure it was somehow Josh's doing.' She pauses. 'That's partly why I sent Josh to France early, to stop him causing even more damage.'

'And you think he's taking Kaia to get at Marcus? Why would he do that?'

Faith lets out a deep sigh. 'Because he's jealous of Marcus, I suppose. His rugby talent first and foremost. When Marcus joined Chilford, all the sports coaches adored him. Josh got sidelined and lost his place in the First XV rugby team. He never got over that, being the camera boy making a film instead of performing the starring role. And then because Marcus has you and Kaia too, I imagine. Josh isn't capable of loving anyone except himself, but that doesn't stop him wanting what other people have.'

'Have you always known he feels this way?'

'I suppose I have,' Faith says with a sigh. 'And for the last seven years, all of Kaia's life, I've never let Josh spend time alone with her.'

'But I have! Why didn't you warn me?'

'You haven't, Grace. Not until this weekend. I've made sure of it.'

Grace thinks of Josh's annual visits, his trips to Wimbledon Common with Kaia. It's true that either Faith or Henry have always tagged along. Until now, when they didn't know he was in the country. 'Do you think he would hurt her?'

Grace listens to her mum breathing down the phone. The weight of her confession compressing her lungs.

'I hope not. But … perhaps,' Faith finally admits. 'Josh is capable of anything.'

Nausea rises in Grace. She's going to be sick. She grabs hold of the sink, retches as she pulls herself up, and vomits a pathetic stream of toxic liquid into the basin. She ends the call with her mum. Then with her eyes half closed and sick still dribbling down her chin, she presses on Marcus's number.

She needs him.

Chapter 44

GRACE

2019

Marcus picks up midway through the first ring.

'Grace? Thank God you called. I'm so sorry for yesterday. I acted like such a prick. But I promise I didn't give Kaia a cigarette burn. I don't know what the hell is going on but I love her. I would never—'

'He's taken her,' Grace interrupts, not willing to let Marcus finish. Finding Kaia is all that matters now.

Stopped mid-flow, Marcus takes a moment to process her words. 'What?'

'Josh. He's taken Kaia somewhere and he's not answering my calls.'

Marcus doesn't sound as surprised as Grace wishes he would, as surprised as she was when Faith opened up about her son. 'How long ago?' he asks, in a business-like tone that doesn't disguise his unease.

'I don't know.' Grace starts crying again as she realises how bad that sounds. What a failed mother she's turned out to be. 'I drank too much wine last night. I overslept.'

Marcus's voice hardens. 'Did Josh pour the wine?'

'Yes,' Grace whispers.

'Out of sight?'

Grace nods, forgetting that Marcus can't see her. But her silence tells him all he needs to know.

'It's not your fault you overslept, Grace,' he says grimly. 'I bet the bastard planned it, put sleeping pills in your wine.' Grace thinks about how groggy she felt this morning, and how she doesn't remember going to bed. She only drank two or three glasses of wine last night – not enough to have such an extreme effect on her.

'But what does he want with her?' Grace whispers, finally admitting to herself that she doesn't know her brother at all. That the person she has looked up to all her life is a dangerous liar. She wishes that she was at home, with Marcus's strong frame to hold her up. Not here, in some stranger's house. She takes a few steps out of the kitchen and stares at the front door.

'To punish me,' Marcus says. 'To take what's mine.'

Grace thinks she can hear him crying. Tension squeezes between her shoulder blades. Marcus never cries. She thinks about her mother's words. And how similar Marcus sounds. She shakes her head. How do they both know what Josh is really like when she's been completely in the dark? Why have they kept the truth from her? 'Why didn't you tell me?' she asks, anger beginning to seep in. 'Warn me about him, what he's capable of?'

'I tried to keep you away from him. But he's your brother, your idol on some level. I couldn't destroy that.' Marcus pauses. 'And I never thought he'd sink low enough to take my daughter.'

My daughter. The words fly into Grace's head like a lightning bolt, lighting up a memory with vivid intensity. The confession she made to her brother last Christmas. That Marcus isn't Kaia's natural father, and that his name isn't even on her birth

250

certificate. Did Josh spot an opportunity to hurt Marcus? To take his most precious thing, knowing how difficult it will be for him to demand her back?

And if it is just a game, what will he do with Kaia now he's won?

'Oh God, Marcus. I did something terrible.'

'This isn't your fault, Grace. That's what he does, twists things, makes you feel like you're to blame.'

'Listen!' she screams into the phone. It works, the line goes silent. She takes a breath. 'He knows. I told him about Kaia. At Christmas.'

'What?' The line crackles with new tension. 'That we're not her biological parents? How could you?'

Tears roll down Grace's face. 'I'm sorry, but, Marcus, you can't be innocent in all of this. Kaia is petrified of you. It can't have been Josh who did those things to her. Even an evil bastard can't reach across the Atlantic to pinch her skin, or push her out of the tree.'

'I don't know how he's managed it. But it's him, Grace. He's twisted her mind somehow. Turned her against me. Convinced her to do those things to herself.'

'Surely he's not that cruel, or that clever?' But even as the words slip out of her mouth, Grace grasps that he is both those things. There's a muffled thud and she imagines Marcus sinking to the floor, dropping his head into his hands.

'She trusts him completely.' His voice cracks with the realisation. 'She'll do anything he asks.'

'We need to find her,' Grace shouts. 'They could be anywhere. We need to call the police.'

'Hang on, wait a minute.'

'Mum called him a psychopath. She even thinks he might have caused my accident. He's dangerous, Marcus.'

'I know he is! But we can't call the police, not now he knows our secret. He's so manipulative. He'd persuade them that I'm the one who needs arresting; I know he would.'

'Well, what then?' How can she push back against Marcus's

warning? She's been under her brother's spell for thirty years. And it's her fault that Josh has this power over them.

'Has he taken the car?'

Of course. The car. If it's still outside, maybe he hasn't gone too far. Grace whips open the front door and looks out, hoping to see their Range Rover parked on the cobbled street. But the space where Josh left it last night is empty. And she doesn't remember him giving her back the keys. 'He's taken it.' She sighs.

'I'll call you back,' Marcus suddenly barks at her. And then the line goes dead. Grace stares at her phone, now just an inert black screen. Why did he cut her off like that? She closes the door and slips into the living room, sinking down onto the sofa. She thinks about Josh. The years they spent living in Devon together. Except they weren't together very much, she realises now. She was only 6 when Josh left for boarding school. And his holidays were always jampacked with sports camps, ski trips and exchanges to France or Switzerland. She remembers feeling envious of his adventures, but also proud of her worldly wise, accomplished older brother. She never considered that it was because he was too dangerous to have at home.

She pushes off the seat and prowls around the small living room, tapping her phone as though she's sending Morse code through to Marcus. *Call me back.* There are four identically sized pictures lined up on the back wall and something about them draws her gaze. It is the same scene painted four times, showing the different seasons. She looks closely at the spring picture. The colour palette is mainly pastels: blue, yellow, green and pink. The fresh-faced innocence of new life. Grace remembers when Kaia was new, holding the tiny baby in her arms for the first time. She had no idea then that Coco's child would become her own daughter, but still, looking into those big eyes, feeling her tiny fingers curl around Grace's thumb, she'd fallen in love anyway. And now her daughter is gone. Taken away by a psychopath while Grace slept.

Even though she's been waiting with every muscle taut, Grace jumps when her phone starts ringing. She swipes at it and relaxes a notch as she hears Marcus's voice.

'I've found them.'

'What? Where are they?' Grace's heart hammers against her chest.

'Hillingdon.'

Grace's mind clatters through its internal filing cabinet to work out what she knows about the outer west London borough. Exactly nothing, she realises. 'Are you sure?'

'I subscribe to this app. Secure Tracker it's called. I can use the vehicle tracking system to find out where the Range Rover is.'

Grace's face stretches into a smile for the first time today. 'And it's in Hillingdon?'

'Yeah exactly. Not moving, so it must be parked.'

'But why would he take her there?'

'I've just got the postcode, I'm looking it up now.'

A few seconds pass and Grace finds herself staring at the pictures on the wall again. The bright colours of summer, the tired warmth of autumn and the sparkle of winter frost. All with a countryside view that she seems to recognise. Rolling hills and patchwork fields. But it's not Devon.

'Oh fuck. Shit. No.'

Grace whips her eyes away from the artwork. Marcus's words sting her ears. 'What is it?'

'Grace, the Range Rover is in a car park.'

'And?' Grace asks, wondering why that revelation is so terrible when he'd already worked out that the car is parked.

'It's the short stay car park at Heathrow.'

Grace gasps. Heathrow is the UK's biggest airport. Every minute of the day a plane takes off, escaping this country and flying somewhere new. It's where she and Marcus began their new life in New Zealand, and where they returned fifteen months later with Kaia in tow. Grace thinks about the South-East Asian country they visited on that trip, twice, almost exactly nine months apart. But she can't let herself be drawn into that now. Who Kaia's biological father is isn't as important as finding her. And quickly.

Because Heathrow is also the airport that Josh flew into only two days ago.

From San Francisco. Five thousand miles away.

Is he leaving? Is he trying to take Kaia with him? Grace sways at the thought; she can almost feel the blood draining from her face. She pictures Kaia's passport in her mind. And the surname she shares with her uncle. Kaia Windsor. Another thing that distances her from Marcus. A conversation comes into focus too, telling Josh where she keeps Kaia's passport.

'Marcus,' she says, her voice low and strained. 'Check my desk, right-hand drawer.'

'What for?'

'I need to know if Kaia's passport is in there.'

'I'll call you back.'

As she listens to the silence on her phone, and the dull thump of her heart banging against her chest, she looks again at the four pictures on the wall.

Chapter 45

MARCUS

2019

Marcus takes the stairs two at a time. Adrenalin surges through his veins, fear and anger screaming at him. *Kill the bastard who has taken your child.* Marcus knows he needs to stem the flow, to control his thoughts and actions, but it's hard. Especially as his head pounds with the memory of too many beers drunk the day before as he watched his family leave him. Then sitting in the dark until the early hours staring at his phone, willing Grace to respond to one of his messages. Sleeping fitfully until she finally got in touch. But with news that he could never have predicted.

He whips open the right-hand drawer of Grace's desk and dives in with both hands, pulling everything out and scattering it across the floor. Notepads and pens. Hair ties and loyalty cards. Rubber bands and paperclips.

But no passport.

Josh must have taken it.

He should act, Marcus thinks. Call an Uber. Tell the driver to put his foot down and race to Heathrow. Run along the concourse and scream for his daughter.

Except she's not his daughter. At least, not legally.

And now Josh knows that too.

Marcus sinks onto the floor. Perhaps it's not surprising that Josh would take Kaia away once he knew the truth. A scalding-hot lie to prod Marcus with. He's known since that summer how much Josh hated him. And how far the bastard was willing to go to prove it. Before that night, he'd really thought that Josh was his best mate. How could he have been so gullible? Looking back, it was obvious that Josh spent the whole time toying with him, undermining everything Marcus valued. But that was fourteen years ago. Does he still hold a grudge strong enough to steal Marcus's only child?

With his eyes tightly closed, a pointless attempt to shut out the guilt and shame, Marcus thinks back to that New Year's Eve in Thailand. To what happened between him and Coco after Grace fell asleep from too much booze. Could Coco have seen Josh again after that night? And told him what passed between the two of them? Did that resurrect his anger?

But even if Josh wanted to punish Marcus for a second time, why would he choose to take Kaia to San Francisco with him? It's one thing to want to scare Marcus, to teach him a lesson, but to be lumbered with a 7-year-old child? That's not Josh's style. And there's the practical stuff too. Wouldn't Kaia need a visa to get into America? Or is it only adults that need the extra paperwork? Marcus rubs his temples, as though it will release the answer. But nothing happens. He shakes his head in frustration. How can he not know these things?

He takes a deep breath and tries to make sense of the thoughts whirling around inside his head. Kaia loves her uncle; the smarmy bastard has made sure of that with his flashy gifts and fake interest in her life. But she wouldn't get on a plane to San Francisco with him. Not without Grace or Marcus there.

256

Would she?

Marcus forces himself to think about the last few weeks. The stories Kaia has made up about him. The terrible lies she's told Grace and her teacher about him hurting her. Perhaps that psychotherapist too. Why would she do that? What has he done to provoke such hate in the child he loves? He thinks about the timing. How they noticed her starting to become distant in the winter, only a few weeks after Josh's Christmas visit. Then things getting much worse after her fall on Mother's Day. It must be Josh's doing. But how? Did he tell her that Marcus isn't her real father? Would that inflame enough hate for her to try and ruin his life?

Marcus crawls back four dark months in his head to Josh's last visit – an annual tradition that he barely copes with. Josh always heads back to the States on the 27th December, so if Grace told Josh the truth about Kaia on Christmas night, he only had Boxing Day to blab to Kaia. Marcus thinks back to that day. It had snowed overnight and Josh took Kaia up to the Common to go sledging. But they weren't alone. Faith went with them, and Marcus knows she would have watched her son like a hawk. Faith has never confided in Marcus about Josh – not directly. But over the years he's seen how tense she gets when her son visits. The fear and mistrust in her eyes. Grace thinks it's awe, but she's wrong. She's always been wrong about Josh. Just like he was before his supposed best mate showed his true colours that night.

Marcus remembers that they spent the rest of Boxing Day together as a family. A long walk followed by a late lunch. They were thick as thieves, but he's sure Josh didn't spend any time alone with Kaia. And then he left the next day. It was an evening flight out of Heathrow, but he spent most of the daytime shopping. Stocking up on Britishness, Marcus remembers him saying. He was only back long enough to pick up his bags and distribute a couple of extra gifts. Thank-you presents, he'd called them. The arrogant motherfucker had even bought Kaia an iPad.

A fistful of comprehension explodes in his belly.

'Oh fuck, no. It can't be that.'

He pushes off the floor and runs out of the room, along the landing and into Kaia's bedroom. He knows he needs to get to the airport, to find Kaia before she disappears out of the country. But he can't go without understanding what's going on. To know what he's up against. Stan – the Stanford University mascot, another gift from Josh – isn't sitting on her pillow, and a few toys are gone. But otherwise, Kaia's room looks normal. She must have packed light when they fled the house yesterday. He checks under her bed and then inside her matching IKEA chest of drawers and wardrobe. Glittery star stickers brighten up the white laminate panels and their simple optimism threaten to overwhelm him. He blinks and continues searching.

But it's not anywhere. He runs his fingers through his hair in frustration. Where is it? Did she take it with her after all? He twists round and sinks onto the bed. Then, despite the gnawing fear and the pulsing anger inside him, Marcus laughs.

In the opposite corner of the room, by the plug socket, Kaia's iPad winks at him.

'Hiding in plain sight,' he whispers to himself as he snatches it away from the charger and brings the screen to life with a tap. There's no password so he's straight onto Kaia's home screen. But what is he looking for? She doesn't have an email address or a phone number. Or any of the messaging apps that kids use. She's 7 years old. She reads stories and plays games. Her favourite game is Wizard Street, a fantasy world full of magic. Marcus has always liked her playing in such an innocent space, but it doesn't help him now. Kaia can only interact with other kids on there, and he or Grace must approve any new connection she makes.

Colour drains from Marcus's face as he realises how stupid he's being. Of course Grace would agree to Kaia connecting with Josh. He's the generous uncle who gave her the tablet in the first place. And Kaia plays on that game every evening. Marcus and Grace treat those precious twenty minutes of guaranteed peace as a godsend after a long day of childcare, but what has it done to their daughter?

Or more accurately, what has Josh done to her?

Marcus taps on the game and an enticing world opens up. Stars sparkle in the sky as different creatures fly by. There are fireworks in the distance too, or perhaps a spell gone wrong. It's hard to believe that a child could be groomed in a place like this. Except that's what happens, of course. Perverted old men pretending to be little girls, luring in their prey with fake interests and innocence. You read about these stories all the time.

Except Josh wouldn't have to pretend to be someone else. He's Kaia's favourite uncle; she would love to chat with him. Every night if he wanted to. With a swell of impatience, Marcus clicks on every link he can find until the tab he's looking for opens up. The message history. And sure enough, there they are. Hundreds of messages from Joshwiz279 from February to April. He stares at the handle and lets the wave of nausea engulf him for a moment – 27th September. Kaia's birthday. He clicks into one, then another, then another. Sweat beads on his forehead and tears roll down his cheeks. Message after message, wheedling and manipulative. Turning Kaia against the man who has loved her most in the world, from the first day he held her.

And then something even worse.

On Saturday 30th March, the evening before Mother's Day, instructions to visit a website with an account name and password. Nothing dark, or dangerous. A wholesome website address: familyphotos.com. But Marcus knows about Josh's skills with a camera, his ability to turn a picture from telling a thousand words to a thousand lies. And he knows what content Josh has to work with.

Ten minutes later, Marcus has seen enough. He knows why Kaia hates him, why she went to the lengths she did to banish him. He needs to get to Heathrow before Josh takes her away. He needs the chance to explain, to give her some context, to tell her he's sorry. He prods frantically at the Uber app on his phone until it opens, then books the first car available. It's just around the corner. He flies out of Kaia's bedroom, runs into his own, rips open his bedside drawer and grabs his passport. Then he clatters down the stairs, picks up his coat and wallet, and slams the front door behind him as the Toyota Prius pulls up outside the house.

Chapter 46

MARCUS

2005

'Bit harsh, mate.' Josh looks at him with disapproval. 'Grace was only suggesting the kiss for a laugh. You didn't need to put her down like that.'

'Yeah, Marcus. You fucking prude,' Coco adds, her words slurring, the effects of her own dare to down a drink coming out. God knows what Josh put in that punch.

He turns to face her. 'I thought I was helping you out,' he counters, his voice needling. 'It's you that keeps going on about Josh being like a brother. I thought snogging him would make you feel awkward.' He tries to add some hidden meaning to his last sentence, but she's too drunk for that to register.

'He's Grace's brother, not mine, stupid,' she says, giggling. 'And look, he's gorgeous.' Then she leans over towards Josh and runs the back of her fingers down his face. He flinches slightly, but doesn't stop her. He clearly enjoys her proving his point.

'Look, I think you should go after Grace,' Josh says after a pause. 'Apologise for being an arse.'

Marcus looks out of the large glass panes of the summer house's sliding door. The patio outside is lit up, but nothing more. He can just make out the tennis court in the distance, the crisscross of the fence surrounding it, and the light and shade of the lines on the court. But Grace isn't there. She must have walked further away, into the woodland beyond their garden. It will be pitch-black in there, easy to get freaked out even if you do know it well. And she's been drinking Josh's punch too. If she's in as bad a state as Coco, she really shouldn't be out there on her own.

He should go and find her. Say sorry. He knows it was his own jealousy that made him call her out, so not Grace's fault at all. She deserves an apology.

But that means leaving Coco and Josh together. He turns back to look at them. Josh's playlist has moved from some chilled-out Usher song to a full-on Missy Elliott dance track and Coco is flinging herself around. He remembers that it's called 'Lose Control'. It seems that Coco is doing a pretty good job of that. Josh is still on the sofa, staring back at him, waiting for Marcus to follow his advice. Instruction maybe.

Marcus sighs and stands up. 'You're right. I'll go and find her.'

The temperature has dropped and Marcus enjoys the fresh air against his skin as he walks past the tennis court and through the little gate at the end of the garden. He assumes the Windsors own this bit of land too, but it looks like public woodland. A load of trees and uneven ground. The clear night means there's some moonlight to walk by, but it's still bloody dark. He wishes he'd thought to bring a torch.

'Grace?' he calls out into the blackness. 'Are you there?'

He hears a rustle in the trees and a shiver of fear runs through him. What is he scared of? A killer squirrel maybe? A pissed-off girl?

'Yeah, I'm here,' a voice responds, luckily sounding more

despondent than angry. Marcus walks towards the sound and finds Grace leaning against a huge oak tree.

'Are you okay all alone out here?'

'Why, do you think this is weird too then?' she asks, the whites of her eyes sparkling in the darkness. 'Deviant dares and a strange tree fetish?'

'No of course not. I just mean, it's quite scary, isn't it? On your own, in the dark.'

Grace laughs. 'If you told me to climb this thing, then yes, I'd be freaking out. But what's there to be scared of in here? It's just a wood.'

Marcus leans next to her. 'You're braver than me then,' he admits with a smile.

'Not sure you'd say that if you saw me on a rugby pitch.'

'You've got other talents.'

'Oh?' Grace pushes off the tree and turns to face him. 'Like ruining drinking games?'

'Listen, I'm sorry about that. I was an idiot. It was a good dare. Awkward snogging is the very backbone of truth or dare.'

She giggles again and Marcus feels his shoulders relax. 'Am I forgiven?' he asks, dropping his head to one side with a look that's supposed to say sad but lovable puppy.

She gives him a gentle shoulder barge, knocking his features back into place, then smiles. 'I suppose so.'

He grins properly and gestures towards the gate. 'Shall we go back inside then?'

'You go; I'm just going to hang here for a few more minutes.' She leans back against the tree again. He wonders if he should try once more to convince her to go with him, but she seems so sure of herself. He remembers Coco's description of her best friend, how comfortable Grace is in her own skin. He can sense that now, and it calms him. He gives her a simple nod and walks away.

He follows the light emanating from the summer house. The music is still loud and he can feel the beat thudding inside his chest by the time he reaches the tennis court. He thinks about Coco dancing, how drunk she was. It's strange that Grace seemed so much more sober. Hadn't they drunk about the same amount? Perhaps Coco had been tucking into her private vodka stash before he arrived.

Josh had brought a cheap disco light back from London with him, and its glittery colours are now bouncing off the glass doors. It creates a sense of chaos, something dangerous and unappealing after the subdued tranquillity of the woods. But that's what he wants, isn't it? Marcus reminds himself. Thrills and excitement. So why does he feel a sudden urge to stop, to turn around and lean against that tree with Grace again? He sighs and keeps walking. Perhaps the booze is catching up with him too.

He slides the door open.

What the fuck?

He freezes on the spot. The music's deafening; it pulses through his veins, wraps around his heart like a vine and squeezes it.

Josh is leaning against the wall opposite. His eyes stare at Marcus, shining with arrogance. The conqueror, the master, the winner. They laugh too. And taunt him. *You fucking loser*, they say.

Coco's got her back to him. The pale cheeks of her naked bottom dimple and stretch in Josh's hands. Her legs splay out either side of him. Marcus watches her red toes rise and fall. Her head has dropped into Josh's neck and her body curls loosely around his torso like a damp lettuce leaf.

She's got no idea what's going on.

The music pounds at his head. 'Josh, what the hell are you doing?' he hisses, finding his voice at last.

'She loves it,' Josh mouths, his lips contorting into a snarl. There's not a hint of embarrassment on his shiny features; it's almost like he wants Marcus to see it. Of course he fucking does. Then his face drops in concentration, his eyes close, and the thrusts come faster. Marcus stares in horror as Coco's body bucks and tremors, until finally, with a low grunt, Josh reaches his climax.

Coco doesn't react at all, and Marcus realises she's hardly conscious. Josh lets go of her and she slips to floor. The movement must trigger something though because she jolts suddenly and looks around her. The confusion on her face makes Marcus want to weep. What the hell has Josh done to her? He watches her laugh, dribble, and then sleepily pull down her dress. Then she stares into the night and her eyelids droop down.

'I was only gone ten minutes,' Marcus growls.

'She was all over me like a rash.'

Marcus looks at Coco. She's almost asleep. 'No she wasn't. She was pissed, and you took advantage of that.'

'Oh really? Like you took advantage of her last week?' He nods towards the sofa, his whole face smirking.

Marcus scratches at his neck. 'No I didn't ...'

'Coco asking you to stop; you ignoring her.'

'I did stop!'

'Eventually,' Josh says smugly. 'Third time of asking, wasn't it?'

No. That wasn't what happened. Marcus shakes the image away. 'How do you know about it anyway? Were you watching us?'

'More than watching, my friend. A little summer project I've been working on, recording people's movements in here; I wasn't expecting anything quite as juicy, of course.'

Josh looks so triumphant, and Marcus feels his hands ball into fists. 'What?' he screeches. 'You filmed us?' Blood surges around his body; he thinks he might be sick. He looks at Coco. How can she act so calm after what he's done to her? 'Did you give her something?' he demands, pointing at Coco. 'Punch doesn't do that to someone.'

'Well, I couldn't let you have all the fun, could I?' He laughs. 'You know, maybe I should tell you my secrets. Rohypnol is probably the only way a scumbag like you is going to get a shag. Remember that they put blue dye in it nowadays, my friend. The killjoys. But a bit of Blue Curacao in the punch solves that problem.'

Marcus launches at him, his fist flying, but Josh manages to slap it away, then ducks and twists out of his way.

'Oooh, the big rugby star's angry. Be careful, Marcus, or your thuggish ways are going to get caught on camera.' He snorts with laughter and nods towards the smaller speaker positioned high up on the wall. But Marcus can see more than a speaker now. There's a small black-and-chrome box nestled in above it, angled down, with a red dot shining on its top.

'You're still filming?' he asks incredulously.

'Absolutely. Why do you think I suggested this little gathering? And now I can watch our little fracas whenever I want,' he says, giggling. He's so fucking proud of himself.

Marcus's mind whirrs. 'So you filmed what you did to Coco too?'

'You want a copy?'

Oh God, the guy's a monster. Marcus lets out a strangled cry and surges forward. He slams with his right fist but Josh flicks his head round just in time and it connects with his shoulder. Marcus tries again with his left, does better this time, hitting Josh under the chin. How could the bastard do those things? Film them all? Put Rohypnol in Coco's drink and rape her, just to prove a point? He's an evil bastard who needs to learn a fucking lesson.

Rage swirls in Marcus's eyes, stealing his focus, and he doesn't know where to punch anymore. So he screws his eyes shut and lunges, swinging his heavy arms, smashing his fists again and again. Into soft flesh. 'You fucking bastard!' he screams.

And Grace screams back.

Marcus stops. Blinks.

Then he watches Josh put a protective arm around his sister's shoulder and guide her to the sofa. There's blood running down her chin. Marcus looks down at his own hands, still curled into angry fists. The same blood stains his knuckles.

Then he looks at Coco. Her eyes stare at him, confused, and

266

there's a faint smile on her face. Like she has no idea what's happened.

Josh has transformed too. There's no hint of the arrogant rapist anymore; he's just a concerned brother now. And Marcus is the villain.

He pelts out of the door.

Chapter 47

KAIA

2019

'Uncle Josh, can we go home now?' Kaia looks around her. This isn't the trampoline park her uncle promised her when he woke her up this morning. He'd whispered that they were going to do something fun together and give Mummy a lie-in. He'd said Kaia deserved a reward after following his instructions so well, and she'd felt proud and excited when they tiptoed out of that house together.

But she doesn't feel like that anymore.

Partly because Uncle Josh is acting so different. Mean. Even his face has changed. His eyes look like little black beetles and his lips are thin and twisted.

And partly because she's here. She should be jumping on a trampoline by now, but instead she's dodging big bags on wheels because there's so many people and no one is looking where they're going. They're looking up instead, at massive signs that flash with lines of writing.

She misses her mummy. She just wants to go home.

But Uncle Josh doesn't answer her question. He just digs his fingers deeper into her arm. It hurts.

Although not as much as the burn that he gave her yesterday with the cigarette.

He promised that it would only sting for a moment. And that Kaia had to be brave because it was her fault that no one had believed her so far. Not Mummy, or Granny, or Dr Gupta or Miss West. (She'd been too scared to tell that lady Harriet in case she could see inside Kaia's head.) So she let him do it. Because she knows how dangerous her daddy is, how many times he's hit her mummy. And if Mummy is too scared to tell anyone, then Kaia must do it for her. Pretend Daddy hits her so that Mummy leaves him, and she's safe again. That's what Uncle Josh told her to do when they were playing Wizard Street together, and of course Kaia wanted to save her mummy.

The video was the worst. Daddy looked so angry and then he punched Mummy in the face. Over and over. Every punch exactly the same. His big fist smashing into her mouth, then blood spurting out. Again and again. Mummy's lip must have hurt so bad.

Mummy and Daddy looked different in the video. Fully grown but still like children somehow. But then Uncle Josh put some photos on that website as well as the video. Familyphotos.com. And they showed Mummy getting older. In one of them she's even wearing a dress that Kaia recognises, a silvery one that she wore last Christmas. But there's blood on it in the photo, and her eye is a mix of horrible dark colours. She doesn't remember Mummy ever looking like that, but when she told Uncle Josh that, he explained that make-up can hide a black eye. Poor Mummy. Having to hide how much Daddy was hurting her because she was so scared.

Suddenly Uncle Josh stops and she almost trips over his feet as he swivels to face her. He looks taller than usual and looms over her. 'Listen, Kaia.' His voice is different too, like a witch reciting a spell over her cauldron. 'There's been a change of plan. Your father has threatened to kill you, and so I need to get you away from him for a while, okay?'

Kill her? But what about Mummy? Her tummy squeezes shut. She wants to ask Josh where they're going. And if Mummy is coming too. Or if she's still all alone in that house. And whether Daddy could find her there. But the words just bunch in her throat.

'You see that lady over there?' He points at a high counter with a woman in a blue uniform standing behind it. 'I need to talk to her now. I might stay stuff that's a bit confusing, but you just need to keep your mouth shut. Do you understand, Kaia?'

His beetle eyes stare into hers and her skin starts to tingle. She thinks she might cry. Daddy never makes her feel like this. He's supposed to be the dangerous one, the bad man who hits her mummy, but she's starting to wish he was here all the same.

'Say yes, Kaia,' Uncle Josh growls.

She still can't speak but she nods and that seems to be enough. He grabs her arm again and leads her over to the woman. She looks a bit like a butterfly. Her yellow hair is twisted up on top of her head and her face is shimmering with bright colours. Blue on her eyes. Pink on her cheeks. Red on her lips. And orange everywhere else.

'Good morning, sir.'

Uncle Josh's face looks different again, more like the one she's used to. But she can still see the beetles, their tiny claws clamping down her tongue. Kaia watches him hand over two identical little books and recognises one as her passport.

'Hi, Kaia, how are you today?' The butterfly is talking to her. What should she say? She wants to tell her that she's not feeling good. That Uncle Josh is scaring her, and that she wants her mummy. And maybe to see her daddy again, to explain why she made up those stories about him hurting her. But before she has a chance to say anything, the butterfly starts talking again. 'I bet you're excited, going on holiday with your daddy.'

Why is she calling Uncle Josh her daddy? Kaia turns to look at him. The beetles are rearing up, their claws snap at her. *Keep your mouth shut.* She turns back to the butterfly and tries to smile.

'Sorry, she's a little shy.' Uncle Josh smiles at the butterfly; his eyes are shining like blackcurrant fruit pastilles now. The butterfly smiles back.

'Gosh don't apologise. I was just the same at her age.'

Kaia pushes her lips together. She's not shy. She's brave and strong. She scores more tries on the rugby pitch than anyone else, her daddy taught her to do that. And she's clever. She loves reading out loud at school and shouting out the answers when they play the times tables game. She used to love school. Playing with her friends, impressing her teachers. But lately she's been so worried about Mummy, so desperate to save her, that she hasn't wanted to be there. And that's made her angry with just about everyone.

Like that time when Miss West was talking about stranger danger online. It was as though she was talking directly to her. *Stop messaging with your uncle on Wizard Street, Kaia.* But how was she supposed to help Mummy if she didn't read Uncle Josh's messages? If she didn't look at the website address he gave her and see the terrible things that Daddy does to Mummy? She needed to shut Miss West up that afternoon, so she pulled Lily's chair back. It worked exactly as she hoped.

But she feels bad about that now. Lily used to be her best friend. She misses her.

Should she ignore Uncle Josh's warning and tell the lady who looks like a butterfly that he's not her daddy? That he's scaring her now and she want to go home? Would she believe Kaia? They're still smiling at each other.

'Right, that's all done for you. I'm afraid there's a bit of a delay, but keep an eye on the board.'

'A delay? Really?' A tiny bit of the new Uncle Josh is creeping out.

'Have you got someone meeting you on the other side?' She looks down at Kaia. 'Your wife, perhaps?'

He nods his head a little and the smile comes back. 'Yes, exactly. Kaia has been staying with my sister while I've been working. We're meeting my wife over there. We're all excited about being together as a family again.' Uncle Josh's smooth voice floats down over Kaia, like the gossamer of a hundred baby spiders.

But he's still lying. They're not going to meet Mummy; they're leaving her, asleep in a strange house in London. She needs to tell the butterfly lady. Her throat still feels full of words but she manages to squeeze two out. 'Excuse me …'

Butterfly lady looks down at her. 'Yes, honey?'

'Um, I …'

But the grip on her arm gets tighter. His fingernails slice into her skin. The beetles crawl all over her screeching, *I told you to keep your mouth shut.*

'I think she just wanted to tell you how much she's looking forward to seeing her mummy, isn't that right, Kaia?' He nods and she copies, petrified by the angry black beetles.

Then he pulls her away, and they're marching across the shiny floor. She tries to look back, to find the butterfly's eyes, to scream and cry and beg for her help.

Their eyes connect.

I'm scared. Help me. Stop him taking me away.

Does it work? Does the message get through?

Will the butterfly save her?

272

Chapter 48

MARCUS

2019

'Good luck, man. I hope you find her.'

Marcus looks at the cab driver, the genuine care in his expression, and feels his eyes smart with tears. As soon as the cab had left Earlsfield, he'd phoned Grace and given her a garbled explanation of how Josh has manipulated their daughter, the video he hashed together to make one accidental punch look like a frenzied attack, and the fake photos that turn Grace into a battered wife. He vaguely knows there's software for that. Deepfake, he thinks it's called. A way to ruin people's lives by pure fantasy. Of course camera-mad Josh would have worked out how to do that.

He ended the call by telling Grace he'd get to the airport in time to find Kaia. But his voice had cracked with the promise, and he'd caught the driver staring at him through the rear-view mirror. A simple *Are you all right, man?* had been like a dam exploding, and then the whole story had tumbled out. Muhammed, a father of four himself, had set his jaw and lane-swapped so expertly that he got Marcus to Heathrow Airport in less than twenty-five minutes.

'Thanks, mate.' Marcus slams the car door closed and races towards the modern glass structure of Terminal 3, side-stepping the shiny anti-terrorism bollards and running across the smooth paved entrance area. The doorway is wide, but it's also busy, and Marcus gets stuck behind a family of four, the dad struggling to manoeuvre the trolley piled high with suitcases as his kids make things worse by trying to clamber on top. Marcus swears under his breath, each wasted second feels excruciating now, but then he arrives in the main concourse and the family evaporate as he stops to stare at the huge departures board above his head.

There are only two direct flights to San Francisco today. American Airlines in the morning and Virgin Atlantic in the afternoon. Marcus had considered it a eureka moment when he remembered in the cab that the luggage tag attached to Josh's holdall was for American Airlines. He'd closed his eyes and seen it there, in the hallway, hanging by its elastic string to the side of the bag. It makes sense that Josh will be flying back with the same airline. He scans the board, searching for the information he needs. Fifth row down, his eyes lock on.

The American Airlines flight was due to leave half an hour ago, he reads, but it's been delayed. Tears prick at his eyes again as he silently thanks fate for giving him another chance. But then the board flashes with new life and a *Go to Gate* sign suddenly appears next to the San Francisco flight. Shit. Marcus quickly scans the row of check-in desks and then races to Zone C.

'Hello, sir, bag drop or check-in?'

Marcus tries to smile at the woman in the navy American Airlines uniform standing the other side of the desk. She's beautiful in that distinct air stewardess way, perfectly turned out, a mask of perfection. 'Neither actually.' He smiles. He needs to sound friendly, relaxed, but it's so hard. His heart is hammering against his ribcage like a cuckoo on speed. 'I wonder if you could help me.'

'Oh?' The muscles in her glistening pink cheeks flex slightly.

'Your flight to San Francisco. AA 6998. My daughter is booked to travel.' Marcus drops his eyeline. He takes in the woman's red, white and blue silk cravat, and then the gold pin etched with her name. Tammy. It's an all-American name, like Madison or Mary Lou, and it spurs him on. 'Her name is Kaia Windsor; I'd like to know if she's checked in?'

Tammy purses her lips and lets a small frown crease her forehead. 'I'm afraid I can't share details of the flight manifest.'

'She's only 7,' Marcus explains. He was expecting this spiel about confidentiality and has already prepared his comeback. 'She's with her uncle. She knows him of course, but he doesn't have parental responsibility for her. So I wondered whether you'd checked that? You know, asked where her parents were? Or for a letter confirming his right to take her out of the country?'

Tammy's eyes dart to her computer screen and her neck reddens under the smooth layer of foundation. 'We have strict processes. Everyone is rigorously checked.'

Marcus's face aches from forced nonchalance. He's walking a tightrope between pushing her to open up and not alienating her. 'Look, I know you're not supposed to tell me who's travelling. I get it. I'm putting you in an awkward situation.' He senses that she's teetering and flashes the most persuasive smile he can dredge up. 'But it's important that I find them. There's a chance he might hurt her.'

Tammy bites her lip, looks left and right. 'Look, I can't tell you who's checked in.' She pauses, flicks back to her computer screen, then takes a deep breath. 'But I can tell you that there are sixteen minors in total on the flight but just two of them are travelling with a single adult.' She pauses. 'And only one of them is a girl.'

'And she's travelling with her uncle?'

Tammy sighs again and pulls at her cravat. Her neck looks an even brighter shade of red now. 'A man checked in here, with me, about an hour ago. I don't remember the name, but he was travelling with a little girl who I imagine was about 7, although I don't have kids so, you know, she could have been older. Or younger.' Her voice trails off, but Marcus glares at her and it's enough to get her talking again. 'But she can't be your daughter.'

'Of course she can be!' Marcus shouts, exasperated now. 'Surely there's at least a chance that it's her? You need to stop them boarding. Please. Can you get a colleague to find them? I need to see my daughter!'

'You're not listening, sir.' The all-American friendliness is gone, replaced with a professional steeliness. 'The man accompanying her was her father, which means you can't be.'

The words drill into Marcus's temples like sharp, poisonous needles. Because of course Josh would claim to be Kaia's father. Their surnames match up after all, and who would think to ask any awkward questions that would reveal the truth?

Marcus whips out his passport from his jacket pocket and eyes the departure board. It's still flashing *Go to Gate*, gate number 24, but it won't be long before that changes. And then Josh will fly his daughter five thousand miles away. Then what? Will he pretend that she's his, just like Marcus and Grace did when they came back to the UK? Is that the game? Or will he get bored of his niece when he decides that he's won and do something even more terrible? He needs to stop them.

'I want a ticket.'

'Sir, she's not the girl you're looking for.'

'There are spaces on the flight, right? You can still sell me a ticket?' Marcus pulls out his wallet and slides his Amex card out. Then he leans forward and drums his fingernails against the cool ceramic counter.

Tammy stares at his impatient fingers. 'What if you cause a scene? Attack the man?'

For fuck's sake! The bastard deserves far worse than that!

Marcus closes his eyes for a moment and pleads with himself to control his temper. This is why everything goes to shit. Because

276

he can't stem the anger that rages inside him. But he mustn't let that happen today; getting Kaia back is too important. He sucks in some air and holds it inside his chest for one, two, three. Then he exhales. 'I won't cause a scene. I just need to get airside, to see for myself if she's my daughter. Just a ticket, please?' He looks at the departure's board and watches it change from *Go to Gate* to *Boarding*. He moves from foot to foot waiting for her answer, then almost cries with relief when she picks up his passport and credit card and then pushes a ticket over the desk.

Marcus sprints up the stairs towards passport control like he's heading for the try line with the whole of his opponent's back line on his tail. Miraculously, there's no queue and as he's travelling light, he doesn't have to slow down too much to get through immigration and out into the departure lounge. Usually he likes airports, people watching the eclectic mix of stag-do ravers, serious-faced businessmen, sleepy-eyed travellers and the jet-setting international elite. But today he's blind to everything except the airport signage. He spots Gate 24 to his right and runs in that direction. *Ten minutes*, it warns on the overhead sign; he'll do it in two he promises himself.

As he runs down the moving walkway, side-stepping the standers and spinning past the walkers with a hand raised in apology, he feels his phone buzz in his pocket. It stills after six rings, but almost immediately starts again. He knows it will be Grace, calling for an update. But he hasn't got time to talk to her now. He will find Kaia, explain things, and then he'll call Grace. With good news.

Marcus can see Gate 24 now. He sprints a few more metres then stops and takes a breath. He doesn't want to make a scene as soon as he walks inside. The small lounge is separated from the walkway by a glass wall, and Marcus can see that the room is still full of people. Most are sat down, reading books or staring out of the window with big headphones on. A handful of passengers are lining up against the desk, passports and boarding passes in hand. But the mix of boredom and frustration in their expressions suggests that no one has been able to board yet and Marcus almost yelps with relief.

He's made it.

He pushes open the door and scans the room wildly. Sixteen children, she said. He counts them off, one by one.

Chapter 49

GRACE

2019

Grace finishes her call with Marcus and slips down onto the sofa. She's feels useless, just waiting to hear if Marcus finds Kaia in time. But what else can she do?

She thinks about what he told her. The fictional tale of domestic abuse that Josh has spun. No wonder Kaia has been so badly behaved lately, carrying this terrible secret around for weeks. Grace feels the twist in her heart, the clawing of pain in her belly. She drops her head into her hands and presses her palms into her eye sockets.

How could one punch from fourteen years ago have led to all this? A moment of violence that she forgave within a week. She'd been shocked the night it happened, and it bloody hurt, so she'd been glad that Marcus left when he did. But then the pain subsided, and the swelling went down, and Grace took it for what it was. Not an attack on her, but a fight between Marcus and Josh that she accidentally got in the middle of. She was desperate to

279

find out what had caused the violence, but she had no one to ask by then. Josh was with his mate on Île de Ré and Coco had left for Saint-Tropez. And she couldn't face asking Marcus.

Then exactly a week later, he'd knocked on their front door, tanned and refreshed, carrying a huge bunch of flowers and a spiel that he'd clearly been practising. How devastated he felt, how he'd never hit a woman on purpose. He'd asked after Coco too, if she was okay after getting so drunk. Grace had wondered for a moment why he cared so much. But then he'd sighed with such relief when he'd found out she was fine, and she'd gone to her parents' villa in France, that any tendrils of jealousy had withered away. For a while.

Marcus had asked what he could do to make it up to Grace. First she tried to get him to explain what the fight was about, but he'd looked sheepish and begged for her to choose something else. So she'd picked a water skiing date. It seemed to be the right level of penance, and she was confident that he'd reveal his motives for attacking Josh in time. But she was wrong.

Just like she got her brother wrong, believing he was someone to look up to.

And she got things so radically wrong with Kaia, dismissing her accusations as lies rather than trying to unravel them. Putting her own fear of exposure ahead of her daughter's.

And she got Marcus wrong in the end too. Thinking him capable of hurting his daughter.

With a surge of energy, Grace pushes off the sofa and starts pacing the room. She looks at her watch. How long has it been since he called? Has he found her? Is he too late? She can't stand not knowing, so she jabs at the most recent number on her phone to call him. It rings for a while, but then just clicks into voicemail. No point leaving a message. She tries again but gets the same result; she needs to be more patient.

To distract herself, she looks at the four pictures hanging on the wall. They still look familiar.

Hang on.

Suddenly her heart starts thudding faster.

Could it just be a coincidence? The Cotswolds is a beautiful part of the country, and popular with international tourists. Victoria Beckham and Soho House made sure of that. But that view, painted over four seasons, isn't just a generic picture of the Cotswolds. She recognises the Rollright Stones in the distance, and the gentle hills and patchwork fields sloping down from the road. The image is exactly what she remembers from her visit there earlier in the week.

Her visit to Coco's parents' house.

Who also own somewhere in London.

She shakes her head, trying to bring back memories from fifteen years ago, when she and Coco were at school. Coco's parents had lots of properties. The villa in the south of France, a ski chalet somewhere, an apartment in New York. And they had a place in the capital too. Grace and Coco used to talk about staying there for the weekend, going shopping in the West End. But Coco left before they ever got the chance. And now Grace can't remember anything about the property, even whether it was a house or a flat.

She runs into the kitchen and pulls open the drawers. It must just be a crazy coincidence, she tells herself. Americans love British history. They're so enthralled by Stonehenge that it features in their Marvel movies, so of course they'd be excited about some Neolithic stones in Kate Moss countryside. And why would Josh have keys to Coco's parents' house?

But still, Grace can't stop herself from searching. She's been shocked too many times today to think that one more surprise couldn't be possible. And right now, she'll try anything to get Kaia back. The blandly expensive kitchen drawers don't give anything away. There's satin-finish cutlery in one, a set of wooden chopping boards and a roll of clingfilm in another. Just the usual kitchen equipment. Excluding crockery, the cupboards are all empty except a box of Fortnum and Mason green tea in one. She runs her hand along the cool metal tin and thinks back to the last time she drank green tea. In Martina's living room. But millions of people drink the stuff nowadays, she reminds herself with a frown.

With a gasp of frustration, Grace turns to the dark grey painted dresser pushed up against the side wall. The top section has three shelves, all sparsely dotted with a few colourless ornaments. They're no help to her. Lower down, there are cupboards on each side but when she checks inside, they're just shimmering with glassware. Champagne, red wine, white wine, water. A different glass for every occasion. She slams both doors closed in unison and wrenches open the drawers running down the middle.

She finds her answer in the bottom one. Framed photographs piled on top of each other, as though they've been stripped off the shelves and hurriedly tidied away. With shaking hands, Grace pulls them out one by one. The first shows Martina looking glamorous at some red-carpet event. The next is of David in cargo shorts and a baseball cap proudly holding out a shining silver-blue fish. There are three pictures of the couple together, and a group shot of a ski holiday somewhere. Only the final photo is of Coco, at maybe 6 or 7 years old. As Grace stares, she feels her eyes grow heavy with tears. Coco looks so happy in the photo, her smile wide and green eyes dancing with curiosity. What happened to that little girl? Where did she end up?

And why the hell has Josh got keys to her parents' house?

Grace grabs her phone and scrolls through her recent calls. The landline number jumps out straight away and she stabs at it with her finger. After a few painful seconds, David picks up.

'Good morning.'

'David, it's Grace.'

'Oh. I didn't expect to hear from you again so soon.' He pauses, his brain ticking over. 'Have you found something in the photos? A clue for where Coco might be?'

Was it only Friday that Grace last looked at Coco's photos? It seems a lifetime ago now. She hadn't finished scrolling through the last memory card she'd downloaded – those pictures are still on her laptop – but nothing she'd seen so far had thrown up any clues about who Kaia's father is, or Coco's whereabouts. 'David, do you have a mews house in London?'

'Well, yes,' he says, flustered by the unexpected question. 'In Chelsea. Is this about the fibre optic cables?'

'What?' Grace shakes her head. 'No. No, it's not. Do you rent it? Airbnb maybe?'

'Of course not. Why would we do that?'

Grace scrunches her eyelids together. People like David could never understand how normal people live. 'Who has a key then?' she asks, trying not to sound rude.

'Grace, I've humoured you. But you really need to tell me why you're asking all these questions.'

Grace blows out some air in an effort to stay calm. Of course she's not making sense to him, but she doesn't have time to explain. Marcus might be trying to call her right now, Kaia in his arms, reaching for the phone. 'It's a long story, too long. I just need to know if Coco has ever had a key,' she pleads.

David sighs. 'Well, the answer is yes. Coco had a key. And she never gave it back, so I suppose she still does. But why do you need to know? Do you think Coco is there?'

Shit. David might be a terrible father, but she doesn't want to give him false hope. 'No, nothing like that. I'm sorry, I have to go.' Ignoring his protestations, she taps to end the call, her head still spinning with it all. Why does Josh have Coco's key? Have they been in touch all this time? Then another thought hits her. *We were two teenagers in love.* Her mind flips back fourteen years until she's there in the summer house. Marcus furious with Josh, Coco spaced out on the floor. Grace has always suspected that the fight was over Marcus liking Coco. But it was Josh who'd been alone with her when Marcus had come looking for Grace in the wood. Did something happen between them?

Is it possible that Josh is the man Coco's been in love with all this time? Not Marcus, not the French guy she went travelling with. But Grace's own brother.

Nausea rises in Grace's chest. Could Josh be Kaia's real father?

Vomit threatens again, but she needs to know the truth. Her laptop. She hasn't finished checking the photos and the truth might still be on them. Her laptop is in her bag. She lunges forward then rotates around to grab it. As she twists back, her foot gets caught on the rug. Momentum carries her torso forward, but her foot is stuck, jammed against something solid. She teeters, then falls to her knees, the contents of her bag spilling out across the oak flooring.

'Shit!' she screams into the empty room. There's so much to do, and yet here she is, sprawled on the floor. She looks back towards her feet, and to the mound underneath the rug that caused her fall. She lifts up the heavy piece of material and discovers a small bronze handle underneath.

Attached to a trapdoor.

Chapter 50

COCO

2019

He smiles at her across the room. It's a sheepish smile, both grateful and contrite, but she's not really paying attention because he's also nodding towards the small fridge and saying, 'One for the road?' And she's thinking, yes, she'd like that.

Then she watches him pour from a bottle of Singha beer into two glasses and gesture towards the patio doors. She looks back for a moment, at the sleeping body of her best friend, and a waft of guilt floats over her. But then it's gone, and she's smiling, and following Marcus out onto the little terrace attached to their hotel room.

The night is a mix of bright lights and dark patches. Fireworks exploding above them, revellers still seeing in the new year, and the swimming pool fifty or so metres away glowing bright aquamarine. But his face is in the shadows, not looking at her, thinking backwards to a different time, maybe. She sinks down into the white plastic chair, knowing he'll talk about that night, needing to be ready. She takes a long gulp of beer.

'I owe you an apology.'

Here we go, she's thinking, he's started. 'No, you don't.'

'I should have done something, told someone.'

'I'm not your responsibility.'

'But then you went to your parents' place in Saint-Tropez, and I convinced myself that it wasn't too bad. Just one of those things. What a fucking coward. If I could just go back, make different choices. If I could make it up to you …' His voice trails off.

'It wasn't your fault. I just fucked up, got too drunk. It happens.'

'Is that what you think? That Josh raping you was your fault?'

'It wasn't rape; I didn't push him away. I was up for it, I think.'

'Jesus, Coco, you weren't up for it, you were out of it. The bastard spiked your drink! I should have phoned the police, told them what I saw. But he'd filmed us too, and then I lost my temper, and hit Grace by accident. Her lip all fat and bloody, Josh so fucking smarmy, what would the police think of that scene? Who would they blame?'

'He spiked my drink? He filmed us?'

'Rohypnol. That's why the drink was blue, to hide the dye. And he hid a camera above the door too.'

'He actually raped me?'

'Jesus, Coco. What did you think it was?'

WHAT DID YOU FUCKING THINK IT WAS, COCO?

LOVE? DESIRE? YOUR STARS ALIGNING?

DID YOU SLEEP WITH HIM AGAIN? AND AGAIN? DID YOU RUN TO HIM EVERY TIME HE CLICKED HIS FINGERS? DID YOU FALL FOR HIS BULLSHIT? DID YOU THINK HE LOVED YOU?

EVEN AFTER YOU KNEW THE TRUTH?

YOU'RE SO FUCKING STUPID, COCO!

HE'LL DESTROY YOU AND YOU FUCKING DESERVE IT!

Coco gasps, flicks open her eyes, listens to the thud of her heart beating. That dream again. Not just a dream though, a memory of her conversation with Marcus from that New Year's Eve in Phuket, finding out that the first time she had sex with

Josh was actually a violent crime, not her being an easy lay. And that everything that came after was built on a lie.

A memory that turns into a nightmare as sour as her breath when she thinks about what has happened since.

Coco reaches for the thin blister pack on her bedside table and splits the foil with her nail. She should swallow it. Go back to sleep, deeper this time, into oblivion. She rolls the blue pill between her finger and thumb and feels her mouth go moist with anticipation. She wonders what would happen if she didn't. If she went through the agony of withdrawal and out the other side. But what would be the point?

She stares towards the window, the thin blind doing just enough to keep the brightness away. Her T-shirt is sweaty against her chest and she wonders when she last changed it. Her knickers too. She considers making the short journey to her bathroom, stepping inside the shower and letting his dirt wash off her. But there's no redemption in showering. However hard she scrubs, she knows the stain of him can't be washed away. It needs effort, and courage to be rid of him. And she has neither. Not anymore.

How did it get to this? The boy who persuaded her to go to Paris with him all those years ago. Who convinced her to love him during those three perfect days in Montmartre. They weren't two drunk teenagers against a summer house wall anymore. They became the couple who drank champagne for breakfast and had sex between Egyptian silk sheets.

Except it was just a fantasy. All of it built on a lie.

And she never learned. Every time he left her, she promised herself that it was over. Then she would go somewhere new, party for days, sleep with random men. Convince herself that she didn't need him. But then he would turn up again somewhere, with that smile, and his charm. And those promises would be forgotten.

Like that Christmas when she was supposed to go home but ended up in Mexico.

Drinking margaritas and getting high.

Getting pregnant.

And then finding out a week later that Josh wasn't just a rogue; he was a rapist.

But why did she accuse him from that police cell in Paris? She thought it gave her power over him, a way of compelling him to pay her fine. Buy her a ticket back home. How stupid she was, not considering how a man like him would respond to being accused of a crime. Of a threat to his carefully built reputation.

Of course he would never let her take that accusation back to England.

She looks back towards the window. Josh's house is close to Edgewood Park, a slice of California that's not spewing with tech towns or sprawling university compounds. The house is cut into the hillside and her room sits underneath the garage, hidden from the road. When she first arrived, he would lock her inside. But containment wasn't necessary for long, not once the pills kicked in. Then when he was out at work, she'd roam the house in her drug-induced haze, and daydream about walking out of the front door. Barefoot of course, because he'd taken her shoes. But then his voice would boom in her head: *If you left me, I would find you and fucking kill you*, and the CCTV cameras would click at her, and the front door stayed closed. These days, she can hardly be bothered to walk upstairs.

Once a year he drives them to a restaurant. A posh French one, an hour's drive away. He orders champagne and scallops and calls it their anniversary celebration, the date of their first fuck in his summer house in Devon. No mention of Rohypnol or rape. The first time he suggested the night out, she made plans. She would stand on her chair in the restaurant and shout that she was being held captive. *'Save me!'* she would scream. But Josh forced her to take three Valium before they went out and she spent the whole evening just staring into space.

She didn't bother planning anything when their anniversary supper came round a year later.

With a sigh, she drops the pill onto her tongue and dry-swallows. She closes her eyes and waits for it to take effect.

Coco's muscles start to relax and her head gets heavy against the pillow. But just as sleep starts to pull her under, she sees his face. Superior and smiling. Her body jerks in frustration and she flips onto her belly. Why the fuck did she get into that French man's car – Matteo, a friend Josh made on a French exchange trip when he was 15 she later found out – and then onto that flight to San Francisco? Did she really believe he wanted to explain, to apologise, for them to be a proper couple at last, as Matteo suggested? Was she that stupid? Maybe she was so desperate by then that she didn't care. Or perhaps, in her exhausted state, mourning the loss of her child, she wanted someone to love her so badly that it was worth the risk.

*

A hand grabs her hair and pulls her onto the floor. Her scalp screams in pain, and she wriggles to create her own momentum, to lessen the impact. She lies on her side and pulls her knees into her chest. This is how her baby lay inside her, she thinks vaguely, safe and warm in her little cocoon.

'You are such a fucking liar.' His voice sounds strangled. This isn't like him – he's usually so controlled. Coco shifts her head slightly and opens her eyes. Sweat beads on his forehead, wisps of anger flick out from each eye.

'A fucking evil piece-of-shit liar!' His foot, encased in a camel suede brogue, flies out, scrapes under her folded legs and connects with her ribcage. Pain shoots through her and she cries out. What has she done? Why is he so angry? But her brain is like a flock of birds escaping a farmer's shotgun, flapping and squawking in fear and confusion.

'I will never forgive you for this,' he growls. 'All these years, keeping her from me.' He kicks Coco again but she doesn't react. The physical pain is nothing compared to the sting of his words.

The only part of her that she kept away from him.

The only truth she managed to keep safe.

He knows.

'I had to hear it from my fucking sister! A Christmas night confession. That her daughter isn't hers. That she's yours. And that you left her to rot in a Thai shithole!' He kicks her onto her back, then drops to his knees onto her chest.

It wasn't a shithole. It was clean, and calm. A perfect haven. The best days of Coco's life.

'And born nine months after our little trip to Playa del Carmen,' he continues, adding scorn to his fury. 'She's my fucking child, Coco!'

'She's not yours,' Coco whispers. She needs to keep him away from Kaia. 'I met someone in Thailand. He's Kaia's father.' The effort of talking leaves her desperate for breath and she pants like a frightened dog.

Josh's hands fly forward and grab her neck. Fingers and thumbs cross at her throat. 'Stop lying, Coco! Don't you think I considered that? How a slut like you sleeps with anyone who buys you a drink? That's why I nicked the kid's hairbrush. Had it tested.' One hand leaves Coco's throat and disappears behind his back, but the other hand squeezes harder. She can hear the rustle of paper, then Josh flicks open a letter and shoves it into her face.

'The results arrived today. It's there in black and white. She's mine, Coco.'

'No, please,' she manages to squeeze through his grip.

'Yes, Coco. And I'm taking her back.'

She rails against him, writhes under the weight of his knees, tugs at his hand throttling her neck. 'She's just a child,' Coco rasps. 'You can't take her from her parents!'

Suddenly Josh's hands release her. Eerily gentle, he strokes her cheek. 'Of course you're right, Coco. That would be cruel. That's why you're coming with me.'

'What?'

'We're her parents, you and me. She deserves to live with us. Somewhere special.'

'Where are you taking her?' Coco's voice warbles.

'To paradise, Coco. And you're coming too.'

Chapter 51

GRACE

2019

Grace stares at the trapdoor. She feels the blood drain from her face as she wonders what's down there. Perhaps it's a wine cellar, she thinks with a waft of hope. David's pride and joy, Martina would call it as he disappeared down the steps, already red-faced and puffy, to collect a bottle from his '98 stash to impress dinner party guests with. Or it could be a storeroom, or a laundry area. Even a darkroom or a music studio.

There are lots of innocent explanations. She should put the rug back. Forget she ever saw it and call Marcus again. What could possibly be down there that could help her find Kaia? A caterpillar of dread crawls across the back of Grace's neck.

Kaia.

With a sharp intake of breath, she pulls at the brass handle. Her body's shaking, so it takes a huge effort to push the door back onto its hinges. Could Josh have left Kaia in this basement, tied up and gagged while he escaped to America? Staged the whole thing so that Grace would be frantically searching for her daughter when she's only a few metres away? Would he find that funny?

The open door exposes a wooden staircase, but it's the smell that Grace notices most. Rancid and sour. A dead rat, maybe, left to rot in this empty house. Or a broken freezer, the meat inside, green and putrid. 'Kaia?' she calls out above the sound of her feet hitting the bare steps. She dips her head to avoid knocking it against the frame of the opening but misjudges the distance. The rough wooden edge scuffs her crown, and hair rips away from her scalp. She blinks hard to banish the pain. 'Are you there?' she calls into the darkness.

'Grace?'

Grace tumbles down the last step. She knows that voice, of course, but she can't process it. She runs her hand along the wall searching blindly for a light switch. For proof. But when her fingers stumble across one, the dull click achieves nothing. She shuffles forward into the shadows, scrunching her eyes, then releasing them. She can't focus properly. 'Coco, is that you?'

'Over here.' The small voice crawls along the ground.

Grace slips behind the staircase and drops onto her knees. Coco is lying on a thin mattress in the corner, a dirty white sheet pulled up to her chin. Her green eyes have lost their sparkle, but her wavy red hair is still vibrant, spilling over the edges. There are packets of pills, at least half a dozen, piled on the concrete floor beside her, like the finale of a narcotic-themed Jenga game. Tears well in Grace's eyes. 'Oh, Coco, what has he done to you?'

Coco slowly pushes against the mattress. Her back curls, exposing the round beads of her spine through her thin T-shirt. Then she twists to sitting and pulls her knees into her chest. 'I'm so sorry, Grace.'

Fear tap-taps at Grace's skin. 'Why? What for?'

'I never wanted to take her, I promise. But he told me that we had to, that she was ours, that Kaia needed her true parents.'

As her green eyes fill with water, the meaning behind Coco's words filters into Grace's brain. She lunges forward, grabbing her friend's bony shoulders. 'You've taken Kaia? Where is she?'

'But he was lying to me; I was never part of his plan.'

Grace softens her grip but doesn't let go. 'What plan? Please, Coco.'

'I thought he was going to kill me.' Coco looks down at the floor. 'The day he found out that he was Kaia's father. I'd been there so long, there was nothing left of me … I was happy enough for my life to be over. But then he flipped again. He let go of my throat and announced we were going to take Kaia somewhere special, together. I knew it was wrong, and I told him. But the thought of seeing her again, just once.' She looks up at Grace, searching for forgiveness. 'I'm not sure I believed anything he said, but the chance of it, that was enough to get me on the plane. I was full of pills of course, Josh made sure of that, but I still dreamed of her during the flight. At least my version of her. Red hair and lilac toenails. But she doesn't look like that, does she? He showed me a photo on his phone. She looks like him, not me.' Coco pauses for a moment, searches Grace's eyes. 'And like you,' she whispers. 'I hope she has your heart.'

'Where is she, Coco? Where's he taken her?'

Coco sighs. 'I wish I knew. He locked me down here as soon as we arrived, reminded me that I'm too much of a slut to be Kaia's mother. He'd already made sure my parents wouldn't be here, phoning them pretending to be BT, telling my dad that they would be laying cables on the street for a fortnight. No way David and Martina would visit during that disruption. I don't know why he brought me here, maybe to get me out of his house in San Francisco, or just for kicks; fucking with me one last time. But he came to see me this morning, told me he was leaving, that I'd never see him again. I begged him to take me with him. Can you believe that after everything he's done? But he just laughed.'

Tears sprout again, grow heavy, and roll down Grace's cheeks. She lowers her hands, stroking some warmth into Coco's arms.

'It wasn't always this way, you know,' Coco whispers. 'He loved me once, I think. In his own way.'

Grace wants to scoff at her friend's stupidity, but then she thinks about her own childhood, and how Josh managed to con her too. 'When did it start between you?'

'That summer, that night. I should have walked away; if I'd known the truth then, perhaps I would. But suddenly he was going to Paris, and he convinced me to go with him, in secret. And my dumb 16-year-old self thought that meant we were in love. But three days in, he dropped me like a bomb and I exploded into a thousand pieces. I couldn't come back here after that; I couldn't face you.'

'That's why you went travelling? What about the boy you met in Saint-Tropez?'

Coco sighs. 'There was no boy. That was Josh's idea, putting you off the scent. Just in case you suspected us. He couldn't have his little sister think he was fucking her best friend.'

'I had no clue.' Grace thinks back to that time, how lost she was in her mixed feelings for Marcus. 'So Josh was the boy you wrote about in that letter to your parents?'

'You've read it? How are they? Do they hate me?'

Grace remembers Martina's wistful look when she described their Halloween party, her special guest not showing up. 'I think they've missed you.'

'I was planning to go back.' Coco raises her head again. 'But I ended up in Paris. I got in trouble, and I called Josh. At the time, I didn't think I deserved anyone better. He sent me a plane ticket to San Francisco. Even knowing what he'd done to me, drugging me, I still got on that plane; I didn't have anywhere else to go. I spent eleven hours hoping, dreaming, that we could be a proper couple. I didn't imagine an underground bedroom and a locked door. I dreamed about leaving him, walking away when he was at work.' Her forehead crinkles with the memory. 'But it seemed impossible. It was easier to do what he wanted. Except I never gave her up. I protected her from him.'

'Kaia?' Grace whispers.

'But he found out that she was mine anyway. He said you told him, and then he put the rest of it together. He took her hairbrush, brought it back with him, so he's got DNA evidence now too.' She pulls at her neck. 'He couldn't stand that I'd asked Marcus to raise his child. He hates him so much.'

'I was scared that Marcus was Kaia's real father,' Grace admits. 'Now I wish he was.'

Coco looks confused. 'Marcus?'

'That New Year's Eve. It was nine months before Kaia was born, before I got that phone call from you. I have this memory of you from that night, your heads so close together. But maybe it was my imagination.'

'Not your imagination,' Coco murmurs. 'He was saying sorry. For being a dumb teenager. For not doing enough to stop Josh that night. For hiding away instead of convincing me that what Josh had done was rape. I told him he had nothing to apologise for, but he said that he owed me. I remembered that when I found out I was pregnant.'

Grace thinks back to that guesthouse in Bangkok. Marcus racing there from the airport, the alarm on his face when she told him what had happened. 'He said yes straight away. He was 24, following the biggest, most impossible dream. But he still took Kaia on, no hesitation.' And now he's searching Heathrow Airport for her. Grace picks up Coco's hands, tries not to squeeze too hard. 'Where's Josh taken her, Coco?'

'I really don't know. Taking her back, somewhere special, that's all he said.'

Grace drops her head into her open palms and sucks at the air. Back where? To San Francisco? All she can hope is that Marcus gets to them in time. Because if Josh takes Kaia to the United

States, and shows a judge his paternity test results, will they ever be able to get her back?

Her body jerks and she gasps. Her phone is ringing. She grabs it. 'Have you found her?' she pleads into the tiny microphone. 'Please tell me you have. I know why he's taken …'

'She's not here, Grace.' Marcus cuts her off. 'That bastard fucking played us!'

Chapter 52

GRACE

2019

'Nowhere? Are you sure?' Grace's voice cracks.

'She wasn't on the American Airlines flight, so I checked with Virgin Atlantic. I think the bloke there could see how desperate I was because he checked the manifest for me. Neither Kaia nor Josh are booked on that flight either.'

'Maybe they're not flying direct? There are dozens of flights to the States. They could be on any of them! You need to search the airport, Marcus, all of it.'

'I thought that too. And I did it; raced up and down the whole terminal.'

'And?'

'And then it hit me. The one thing that I knew for sure was at the airport.'

'The car!' Grace slams her palm against the cold concrete floor. It makes a loud slap and Coco jumps.

'I tracked it to the exact spot it was parked in,' Josh explains. 'In the short stay car park.'

'You found the car?' Grace whispers, unable to ask anything more. Like whether their daughter was inside. Strapped into her car seat. Or locked in the boot.

'There was a note. Under the windscreen.'

'From Josh?'

'From someone called Paul. An apology, for his part in the prank. For taking two hundred quid off my supposed mate to drive my Range Rover to Heathrow and leave it there, keys on the wheel arch.'

'You mean …'

'They're not here, Grace. They never were. We have no idea where our daughter is.' His voice cracks and Grace listens to her husband cry. She can't stand it.

'This is all my fault,' she whispers. 'I was the one who told him Coco was Kaia's birth mother. I let Kaia connect with him on that stupid game. I invited him into our home.'

'You couldn't have known.'

'Where was my mother's instinct, Marcus? Is this because she's not really mine?'

'Of course she's yours. That's why she's strong, and brave. Why she stands up for what she thinks is right and protects the people she loves. Coco would never do that. She's probably on some party island, not giving a fuck about anything, right now.'

'She's here.' Grace's words bounce off the cold basement walls. 'What?'

Grace imagines him shaking his head, stood in the middle of Heathrow short stay car park all alone. 'She's not been partying since she left Thailand. Josh lured her to San Francisco, locked her up in his house. Then he brought her to London, drugged up, and left her here, in the basement.'

'What?' he stutters again. 'Coco's with you?' Disbelief has slowed his thoughts.

'And, Marcus …' She lowers her voice, says it as gently as she can. 'Josh is Kaia's real father.'

'No! He can't be. He raped Coco; I saw him do it!'

Grace looks at Coco, the dark circles under her eyes, and small scars where Josh's temper has flared up over the years. 'It's not always that simple,' she whispers. 'He made her believe it was something else.'

'Love? Is she that blind?'

'Not as blind as me,' Grace's voice cracks. 'She managed to keep Kaia a secret from him.'

'Hang on.' Hope edges in to his voice. 'Does she know where he's taken Kaia?'

Grace looks at Coco, sees defeat in her eyes and imagines hers look the same. 'No, he didn't tell her.'

'She must know something. Talk to her again. I'm heading back to London now, to you. Text me the address of where you are.' The line goes dead. Grace looks back at Coco.

'I would tell you if I knew, Grace. I promise.' Coco drops her head into her knees. Her body rises and falls with racking sobs. 'I'm so useless.'

'No, you're not,' Grace says firmly. 'You're clever, and funny, and can read people's innermost thoughts like a book. Think harder, Coco.'

She lifts her head, stares at the wall beyond Grace. 'He spent a lot of time on the phone before we left. Bank. Utilities. Freight company. I don't think he's going back there.'

'That's good, Coco. Not San Francisco then. But where?' Grace asks. 'Come on, please think.'

'Oh God, I don't know! Somewhere special, he said. Paradise. That's all.'

'But that could be anywhere!'

Coco throws her hands up. 'I know!' She rears back from Grace and pushes up to standing. But she stumbles and staggers, then teeters and falls backwards.

Grace grabs Coco just in time to stop her head smashing against the hard floor. She looks down at the smorgasbord of drugs beside the dank mattress. Of course her friend is struggling to remember. There are so many chemicals raging through her bloodstream, blocking her brain cells from working properly.

Suddenly Grace remembers what she was doing before she fell and discovered the trapdoor. Looking for clues about Kaia's father on those camera memory cards. Coco's photos. Special moments captured; special places too? 'Coco, did you ever take a photo of Josh when you met up?'

'I wanted to, but he wouldn't. Only if he was in control of the camera, he'd say.'

'Nothing at all? Not one picture?' Grace pushes her.

Coco scrunches her eyes closed and sighs. 'There was one photo,' she whispers finally. 'In a tiny vineyard on a hill in Montmartre, those few days when I thought everything was perfect. An old man took it on my camera. He'd been sitting in a café watching us kiss, young people in love, he'd called us. Then he said we should have a keepsake to reminisce over when we grew old, like him. I remember Josh trying to refuse, but even his phoney charm didn't work that day. I kept that photo with me for years. I remember hiding it from you in Bangkok, and I took it all the way to San Francisco with me. He stole it from me then of course. And I haven't seen it for years.'

'Was it special, that day?'

'The whole trip was perfect.'

'Was it paradise, Coco?'

Coco's eyelids flick open. 'Paradise. That's what the old man said. That you'll always find Paris in paradise.'

Grace's eyes blur with tears. *You'll always find Paris in paradise.* This is just a fucking word game to Josh.

Chapter 53

GRACE

2019

Grace sprints down the King's Road. Of course he'd choose Paris! He speaks fluent French and he went there so many times during his university summer breaks.

Grace knows she'll never find him there without help from the police, but that would mean unravelling all the lies. Can she get to him before he leaves? The only good news of the morning came when she checked the train schedule out of St Pancras International. Over-running engineering works delaying all trains to Paris. Maybe there's a chance.

Public transport will be quicker than a cab, the journey from west to north London always heavy with traffic, but the pavement provides its own challenges. By the time she arrives at Sloane Square Tube station, she's given up on being polite and barges her way past a group of giggling teenage girls without an apology. She whips through the turnstile and clatters down the escalator. She needs to go one stop on the District line, then change lines at Victoria. She arrives on the eastbound platform, and mercifully a train pulls up. She jumps on. Her heart thuds, but she doesn't know whether that's the physical exertion or her desperation to get to Kaia before it's too late.

She doesn't know for sure that Josh will choose the Eurostar to get to Paris, but her instinct tells her he will. It was how he and Coco travelled there back in 2005, and she imagines he'll see it as an easier target than an airport. Fewer eagle-eyed staff at passport control. She hopes he's wrong.

The train pulls into its first stop and Grace pushes against the door. Why won't they open? Then they do, and her foot almost disappears down the gap between the train and the platform. She whips it free and swears at her stupidity. Then she's running again, ignoring the curious stares from other Tube riders, and following the signs to the Victoria line. It's a much deeper Tube line and she tap-dances down some stairs and then an escalator, before finally arriving on the northbound platform. She checks the electronic sign overhead and almost bursts into tears. Four minutes until the next train. She can't stand still, so she prowls up and down, staring at advertising boards for dating apps and multivitamins. Both promising her a better life. If only it was that simple.

She feels a soft whoosh of warm air against her face and a train emerges from the tunnel. It's four stops from here, but she doesn't sit down. She waits by the door, ticking each station off in her head. Green Park. Oxford Circus. Warren Street. Euston. Then finally the doors whip open for her stop and she races off the train and out of the Tube station. Brick archways welcome her to St Pancras International. She's so close now. There's a piano in the middle of the station and a young guy in a tracksuit and baseball cap is banging out Billy Joel's 'Piano Man'. He's drawn quite a crowd, including two police officers in white shirts and stab vests. Then Grace spots the escalator to departures and takes it two stairs at a time.

The top floor of the station is an architectural masterpiece.

Dozens of red-brick arches with flower petal windows and mosaic tile detailing. Grace has been here a few times before, a meeting with her French publisher, picking up Marcus after a rugby game at the Stade de France. Usually it feels peaceful up here, but today is different. It's thronging with people, all late for something, and the atmosphere is heavy with irritation. She pushes her way through the crowd to reach the departure gate.

'Excuse me.' Grace reaches out to a petite woman in uniform, hair in a perfectly ironed bob. Her hand touches the woman's jacket who recoils with a frisson of distaste. 'I'm looking for my daughter,' she continues.

The woman's eyes immediately soften. Perhaps she's a mother too. 'Is she lost?'

'He's taking her to Paris,' Grace garbles. She knows she's not making sense, but fear has frozen the mechanics of her brain.

The woman's perfectly shaped eyebrows narrow. 'Who's taking her? What do you mean?'

Grace shuts her eyes, takes a deep breath and starts again. 'Have any trains left yet? For Paris?'

'It's been a nightmare; they promised the work would be finished. I've been on shift since 7 a.m. and I've had nothing but abuse.' She checks her watch. 'For five hours.'

'So everyone's still here? All the passengers?' Something good starts to tingle on Grace's skin. Hope.

'Luckily we got the trains running half an hour ago, thank God. The 9.20, 10.20 and 10.50 have all left. We're almost back on track.'

Grace stumbles backwards.

They were gone by ten when she woke up, and Josh could have taken her hours before that. Kaia is always awake by 6.30 a.m. There's no way they'll still be at the station now if three trains have already left.

Her phone buzzes in her hand. She stares at his name on the screen but lets it ring out. She can't talk to Marcus now, doesn't have the strength to say the words out loud.

'Are you okay, madam? Can I get someone for you?'

Tears sting in Grace's eyes. She gives a quick shake of her head and turns to go, away from disappointment, the hope that she might have arrived in time. With each step, she tries to think rationally. Now that she's found Coco, they can stop hiding from the authorities. Coco can explain to social services why she and Marcus lied about Kaia, and tell the police how dangerous Josh is. All Grace needs to do is find a police officer.

She stares at the mass of people around her. Another departure call crackles over the tannoy system and dozens of passengers push or skim past her on their way to the train. Hurried, purposeful. Like they have somewhere to be.

She turns away from them. Her eyes can't focus and her head continues spinning even though her feet have stopped moving. She wonders if she's going to faint.

Buckle and collapse onto the shiny floor.

She needs some air.

She pushes against the current of would-be travellers until the crowd finally starts to thin out. She sucks in some oxygen. The Meeting Place Statue is just ahead of her now, a nine-metre bronze sculpture of entwined lovers at the opposite end of the mezzanine. She walks towards it. It reminds Grace of the photo Coco described, the one she kept with her for all those years despite everything Josh did to her.

Is that why Coco gave Kaia up? So that he wouldn't get his tentacles on her too?

Grace feels exhausted. She needs to call Marcus, talk to a police officer, book a ticket to Paris, search for Kaia. She will do it all. She's Grace Windsor after all. But she just needs a minute to breathe, to think. To miss her daughter and the life she has so painstakingly built. She sinks to the floor, rests her back against the plinth of the statue and closes her eyes.

'Mummy!'

Her eyelids burst open. 'Kaia?' But she can't say anything more because she's engulfed. Kaia's arms around her neck, her legs clambering over her midriff. She can't breathe, can't speak, but she doesn't care. The miracle of having her daughter back is enough.

So much more than enough.

'I'm sorry, Mummy. Daddy never hurt me.'

'It's okay, baby.'

'Uncle Josh told me he hits you, and that I had to lie to save you. But Uncle Josh, he lied to me. He showed me some pictures, a horrible film. But they weren't real, Mummy. Granny told me they were fake.'

'What? Granny?'

'Hello, darling.'

Chapter 54

GRACE

2019

Grace turns to face her mother, gasps in surprise. 'Mum? What are you doing here?'

'The same as you.'

'But how did you know Kaia would be here? And if you knew, why didn't you tell me?' A surge of anger rises through Grace's chest and she pushes to stand up, careful not to let go of Kaia for a second. 'First you don't tell me how dangerous Josh is, then you come here without me! How could you? How dare you?' She's hissing rather than shouting but the venom in her tone travels. Passing strangers glance in her direction, then look away in embarrassment. They're curious, but don't want to be caught in someone else's row.

Faith reaches out, tries to touch her arm. 'I didn't know for certain, Grace. But when you told me that he'd taken Kaia, I guessed he'd choose Paris.'

'Because he loves the city?' There's hope in Grace's voice. She wants her old mum back. The one who bakes banana loaves and listens to her deepest secrets. Not the one who keeps her own.

'Because I suspected he took Coco with him when I sent him to Paris in 2005,' Faith admits, looking down at the floor. 'I could see the poison he was spreading, with Marcus, and Coco, so I sent him away; I didn't think that she would follow him there, until it was too late.'

'You knew about Josh and Coco?' Grace spits out, her voice incredulous. But she can't say her thoughts out loud, not in front of Kaia. She pushes her hand into her pocket and finds her AirPods. Then she kneels down in front of her daughter. 'Will you put these in your ears for me, honey? Listen to a story?'

Kaia's eyes well up and Grace wonders if she's going to hesitate, ask questions Grace can't answer. But then her face grows into a cautious smile. She takes the little white plugs and twists them into her ears. Grace connects them to her phone, clicks open her Audible app and feels a sense of relief as one of Jacqueline Wilson's book takes over her daughter's world for a while. Then she sets her jaw and turns back to face her mother. 'Josh is Kaia's biological father. Did you know that?'

'No, I didn't know.' But Faith doesn't sound shocked. She looks at her granddaughter and sighs. 'But maybe I suspected.' She turns towards the statue, the entwined couple staring into each other's eyes. 'That summer after your GCSEs, Coco came to me one morning, distraught. She and Josh had had sex the night before, she told me. It was her first time, and she wished it had been more special than a drunken encounter she could barely remember. Looking at her, all confused and ashamed, I knew that he'd manipulated her into it somehow.'

'And you punished him with a trip to Paris?'

'He was going to France a few days later anyway, to stay with his tennis buddy Matt on Île de Ré. But I wanted him out of the house sooner than that. To protect you all.'

'You just wanted to send the problem away, like you always do.'

'When Coco told me she was leaving too, I assumed she was going straight to her parents' villa. But when I called them, to check she'd arrived safely, they told me she was having a few days in Paris. Martina suspected there was a boy involved, she seemed almost excited that her daughter was falling in love in the world's most romantic city. I just prayed it wasn't Josh.'

'Psychopaths aren't capable of love.'

'Don't you think I know that?!' Faith screams. Then she gasps, shocked by her own outburst. The volume lowers but the sound of her heartache is still deafening. 'Do you know what that feels like? Having a child who will never love you?'

Grace pulls Kaia a bit tighter, strokes her hair.

'A child who will only ever take from you. With an insatiable appetite and not an ounce of remorse. Can you imagine what that's like?'

'Why do you do it then?' Grace whispers. 'Keep protecting him?'

'It's not him I'm protecting; it's you.'

'That's bullshit!'

Faith grabs hold of Grace's arm, and this time she lets her. 'He's so clever, Grace. He can fool anyone into believing him. I just wanted Kaia back, and him gone.'

Grace looks down at her daughter's head, the mix of Josh and Coco's colouring in her hair. 'A teenage crush doesn't make a baby.'

'What?'

'You said that you suspected Josh was Kaia's father, so you must have known about the rest. The two of them meeting up when Coco was travelling.'

'I didn't, I promise,' Faith pleads, but then she looks away, and Grace can see the guilt tugging down the corners of her eyes. 'Josh comes to stay every Christmas,' she finally says. 'But he changed his plans in 2010, called last-minute and told me he wasn't coming after all. I didn't think much of it at the time – you were in Thailand that year, so it wasn't going to be a traditional Windsor affair anyway. But when he called on Christmas

Day, I could hear a woman's voice in the background, drunk, calling "Merry Christmas, Faith!" before he told her to shut up. I recognised her straight away. And then you flew back from New Zealand fifteen months later, and told us about Kaia, that our granddaughter was Coco's baby. Perhaps deep down I knew straight away, but I wouldn't accept it. But then she grew up so like him, sporty and competitive. Those persuasive brown eyes.'

'And you kept it from me? All this time? Let me believe Marcus was Kaia's father?'

'I'm not proud of myself, the lies I've told.'

Grace searches Faith's face for the mum she knows, the one who bounced across fields to rescue her, refused to leave the hospital for days, comforted Grace during those long months of recovery after her fall without showing any of the trauma and grief she must have been feeling. Is it the same steely determination that has enabled her to also protect a psychopath for decades?

'I couldn't risk Josh finding out,' Faith continues, desperate for Grace to understand. 'Coco clearly hadn't told him, and I didn't want him having any hold over Kaia.' She falls quiet for a moment. 'Although I was scared that it had happened anyway.' She sighs. 'When you told me that Kaia threw a netball at a girl in her class. It was just like Josh tripping up that boy on Sports Day. That's why I could never believe Kaia over Marcus after that.' Her voice breaks and she looks down at Kaia, a wide smile of relief still frozen on her granddaughter's face. 'But I was wrong. Kaia is nothing like him.'

'Josh should be arrested for what he's done,' Grace says, her voice low and angry.

'For taking his daughter on holiday?'

'Don't say that!'

'I hate it too, Grace, but that's what he'd say, isn't it? And he's the only one out of the three of you who can prove any biological link.'

'But I found Coco!' Grace spurts out. 'He'd locked her in her parents' basement. That's kidnap, false imprisonment.' Grace flicks her thumb, then her forefinger at her mum, counting his crimes.

Faith doesn't even look surprised. 'You're sure it was locked? No handle on the inside?'

Grace blinks, pulls forward the image of the trapdoor, of lifting it when she was scared of what could be down there, then shoving it back open again when she realised Josh was taking Kaia to Paris. There wasn't a lock. So why hadn't Coco escaped? Walked up the stairs and simply pushed her way to freedom? She knows why, of course; because Josh had built a prison for Coco inside her head.

But it would be the first question a police officer asked.

'You see? He's too clever for all of us,' Faith says. 'It's better this way.'

'Him getting away with it?'

'Him not taking Kaia away from you.'

Grace reaches out for her daughter, gently pulls her little body towards her. The action dislodges one of Kaia's earphones and Grace watches her try to nestle it back in. 'How did you convince him to give her back, anyway?' she whispers to her mum. 'After all the effort he went to, grooming her for months, why would he raise the white flag just because you showed up?'

Kaia taps Grace on the arm, then takes both the AirPods out of her ears. 'It was the lady who stopped Uncle Josh, Mummy, not Granny.'

'What's that, honey?' Grace looks down at Kaia.

'I was scared. I didn't want to go on the train with Uncle Josh. I tried to tell the butterfly lady at the desk but he was so angry with me, and I couldn't say it properly. I think she guessed though because a man came to talk to us. He was wearing a really thick waistcoat.'

A thick waistcoat. A stab vest. Josh was stopped by the police.

'Then suddenly Granny was there!' Kaia exclaims, offering her palms to the ceiling as though she's describing a magic trick. It's amazing how children can find joy in the darkest of places. 'She talked to the man, explained that we were all family and there'd been a misunderstanding. She said Uncle Josh was a famous author and needed to get to Paris urgently.'

He was caught, questioned by police. And her mum helped him get away.

His mum too, of course.

What would Grace have done if it was her at that departure gate? Give Josh his freedom in exchange for preserving her own neatly constructed life? Or take the risk that Coco would help them prove that her brother is a criminal, and ensure he has no access to Kaia, paternity test or not. She hopes she would have been brave enough. Faith claims to be protecting Grace and her family from him. But that's not true. She didn't care about the students Josh teaches, or poor Coco, kept on his toxic leash for years. It's Josh she's been protecting all this time, knowing what he's capable of, and letting him do it regardless.

'His trail of destruction is on your hands,' she whispers over Kaia's head.

'He's my son.'

'He's a dangerous psychopath who should be locked up.'

Faith looks hard into Grace's eyes. 'I made my peace with that a long time ago. I brought him into the world; I owe him something.'

'What could you possibly owe him?'

Faith looks at Grace, then down towards Kaia. 'Unconditional love, Grace. That's what a mother owes her child. Unconditional love.' Then she turns towards the grand exit, her shoulders hunched, but her head held high, and slowly disappears under the arches.

Grace looks down at Kaia. Her legs feel heavy and she has a sudden urge to sit down. 'Shall we get a hot chocolate before we go home?'

Kaia's smile widens. She slips her hand inside Grace's and nods her head. They walk to the café beyond the statue and choose a

312

small round table close to the door. As Grace watches Kaia look for familiar words on the menu, she thinks about the messages that her daughter's been reading every night for months, the story of domestic violence that Josh has been weaving. She's been through so much. 'I'm sorry Uncle Josh told you those lies.'

'I'm glad they're lies,' Kaia whispers. Tears sprout in her eyes. 'Will Daddy ever forgive me?'

Grace inhales sharply. 'Of course he will!' She reaches across the table and takes Kaia's hands in hers. She thinks about the accusations Kaia's made over the last few weeks, the lies she's told for the noblest of reasons. Does the fact they're not true absolve Grace for not believing Kaia for so long? Or should it be her asking for Kaia's forgiveness? 'No one's perfect, Kaia,' she decides on. 'We just have to do what we think is best at the time. You thought you were protecting me. I thought I was preserving our family. It doesn't matter that neither of us were right.'

Kaia squeezes Grace's hands and drops her head to one side. 'Can I ask you a question, Mummy?'

Grace squares her shoulders and takes a deep breath. 'Of course you can, honey.'

'Do you think they have marshmallows here?'

Chapter 55

COCO

2019

It's noisy in the crowded room and Coco strains to hear what the man standing next to her is saying. But she takes the drink he's proffering – its fizz bubbling with excitement – and raises her glass to him. He smiles, winks, and matches her wordless toast. She watches him take a long gulp of champagne and then takes a sip of her own.

Kombucha isn't exactly vintage, but it's growing on her.

When the doctors first told Coco that she'd never be able to drink alcohol again, that even though her liver had healed incredibly well, it still suffered too much damage from seven years of over-the-counter drug abuse to cope with the toxicity of alcohol or drugs, she'd been horrified. She'd started drinking when she was 14 years old. Crazy-drunk party girl is her label. How could she ever have fun again if she was always sober? How would she meet a man or get a job without a dose of Dutch courage to help her?

But five months on, she still hasn't touched a drop. And she's discovered that she actually quite likes being sober. Waking up in the morning with a clear head. Making decisions that she's still proud of the next day.

Liking herself.

And she's managed to get a job. A good one, for a charity. Helping victims of domestic abuse. She loves the generosity of her colleagues, their praise for what she's already achieved. She even likes her Monday-to-Friday routine. Showered and dressed by 7.30 a.m., ten minutes to the station, oat milk flat white from Oscar's en route, then six stops on the District line to her office. But what she loves best are the women she supports. Their determination to build a better life for themselves and their kids, but also their dark jokes and hilarious dirty stories. Real women. Tarnished by life, but not destroyed.

They have that in common.

Coco wonders whether Josh thought she'd die in that basement, if it was his way of hammering the final nail in the coffin that he'd been crafting for seven years. A drug addict and sex slave, hidden away. If Grace hadn't found her, would she have had the courage to look for help? She remembers lying there, thinking of all the terrible choices she'd made over the years, falling for him at the top of her list, wondering whether she'd ever get the chance to make better ones. But not moving. Not until Grace appeared.

When her friend came tumbling down those stairs into the basement, Coco was groggy with chemicals, but she could see the love on her friend's face. Tears of relief that she was alive. Why would Grace cry for her? A supposed best friend who'd deserted her, dumped a baby on her, chosen a psychopath over her. Coco decided then that if she survived, she would do anything to make it up to her friend.

As it turned out, there was something Grace asked for.

'It's a bit loud here, isn't it?' Henry's gruff voice rises above the din of twenty-five children kicking balloons around Grace and Marcus's terraced house, wearing a mix of Disney costumes, football strips and party dresses.

'Maybe I shouldn't have brought the iced gems?' Coco suggests to Grace's dad, smiling at the memory of distributing packets of the retro snack to outstretched hand after hand when she first arrived, and watching the pure sugar gem work its way into each of their bloodstreams.

'If you can't eat vast amounts of sugar on your eighth birthday, then I'm not sure when you can,' Henry remarks, his eyes twinkling. Then he softens his voice. 'And you, how are you feeling about everything?'

Coco looks at Kaia. She's wearing a black rugby strip with a white fern in the corner of her shirt. Marcus bought it for her on their recent trip to New Zealand in the summer holidays, and apparently she's refusing to wear anything else at the moment. While her tenacity is causing Grace a few practical problems, Coco is quietly impressed. But she kept that view to herself. Kaia is Grace's daughter after all.

She turns to Henry. 'I'm good, happy that everything's sorted. Grace and Marcus have always been Kaia's parents really.' She smiles. 'And now they have an adoption certificate to prove it.' It had been her father who'd dealt with the Thai authorities. She'd offered to do it herself – it was time she shouldered some responsibility for her own fuck-ups – but he'd been adamant that she needed to focus on her health. And then he pulled every string he could to keep them all out of trouble, and new documents produced without too many questions. It might have taken a fourteen-year absence, but David and Martina seem to have finally realised that they do love their only daughter after all.

Once Kaia had a birth certificate with Coco named as her birth mother, it had been a relatively simple process for Marcus and Grace to adopt her. Coco had assured the courts that the birth father wanted no part in Kaia's life, and expressed how much she wanted Kaia to stay with the only mother and father she'd ever known. That was more than enough to persuade the courts. Of course things quickly improved for Kaia at school too without those vile messages from Josh filling her head, and with her accusations retracted, it had been easy enough for Harriet to assure social services that Kaia was safe.

And a birthday party for the whole class is clearly Grace's way of putting it all behind them. The host looks slightly harassed as she appears at the living-room door. She spots Coco and scampers over. 'Oh my God, I need a drink.' She looks at her friend, pulls a face of apology. 'Oops sorry.'

'Forget it. I've had more than my fair share of hangovers. You're welcome to them.'

'That's very generous of you.' Grace finds a clean paper cup on the table and holds it out towards Henry. 'Load her up, Dad. I've got another hour of this mayhem.'

Coco laughs as she watches Henry acquiesce, then widens her gaze. There are quite a few parents here, and they all seem to be enjoying the adults-only fizzy drink. She feels a little uncomfortable all of a sudden. The non-drinking, mystery spinster aunt. 'I might head off now.'

'Are you sure? You can stay as long as you want – you know that right?'

Coco's heart swells. It was Grace's idea to tell Kaia about her. They could have kept pretending, introduced Coco as an old friend, but Grace said that their daughter deserved the whole truth, that they all did. So she, Grace and Marcus had taken Kaia to the aquarium together just before their big trip. They'd talked about the stopover they'd booked in Thailand, en route to New Zealand, and the tropical fish Kaia would see there. And when the moment felt right, they'd told her. Explained the story of two best friends doing what they felt was the right thing for a perfect, innocent baby. Then they explained how lucky she was to have two women who would love her forever. Unconditionally.

'I know, Grace. But there are twenty-five kids here. I'm not Mary bloody Poppins.'

Grace giggles and takes another couple of gulps of champagne.

With honesty on the agenda, Coco and Marcus had had some explaining to do too. A bit of flirting that summer they met. A fumble in the summer house. But nothing more than that. Marcus had also admitted to having a problem with his temper, and for never coming to terms with the cruel way his rugby career ended so abruptly. He'd asked Harriet to recommend a good therapist and according to Grace, the sessions are really helping. And work is improving for him too. He's even picked up a small contract with Twickenham Stadium apparently, wherever the hell that is.

'Marcus!' Grace calls across the room. 'Coco's going in a sec.'

Marcus nods in acknowledgement, says a few words to the group of parents he's standing with, and wanders over. 'It's musical bumps in a minute. Are you sure you don't want to hang around?'

Coco raises her eyebrows and slips on the Prada jacket that she's been holding protectively to her midriff, and away from sticky fingers. If she's going to be teetotal and work for a charity, she definitely needs one vice. 'I don't think that's a good idea – you know how much I like to win.'

Marcus grins. 'Maybe you're right. Come on, I'll show you out.' He plants a kiss on Grace's cheek, and Coco can't help feeling a tremor of envy. Not for Marcus, but for what Grace and Marcus have together. Something Coco still doesn't know whether she'll ever experience for herself.

Marcus guides her through the fray and into the hallway. A green-and-black trail bike is resting against the wall with a big bow tied around the frame.

'Wow, that's quite a bike.'

Marcus lifts his hands. 'We're picking a spaniel up on Saturday and she's Kaia's birthday present from us. The bike is from Faith and Henry.' He gives Coco a knowing look. 'Faith takes the whole family thing very seriously.'

'Yes, she does,' Coco whispers. She turns to look at Faith in the kitchen, filling cups of water for the thirsty revellers. When Grace told her that Josh had disappeared again, she knew that Faith would have helped him get away. That's what she did in 2005 after all. In truth, Coco had felt grateful at first. It would only be her word against his, in a strange court across the Atlantic, and she didn't have the strength to fight him at the time. But she's physically better now. And through her job, she's meeting women every day who are willing to fight for their justice. She's starting to regret not having that opportunity.

Marcus opens the door. 'Are you sure you'll be okay getting home?'

'Yes, of course.' She peers into the house one more time. 'And you'll say goodbye to Kaia for me?' She grazes his cheek with hers.

'Come over next Sunday, meet the puppy.'

Coco raises her eyebrows – she'll definitely leave her Prada jacket at home for that introduction – and then lifts her hand in a wave. It's a twenty-minute trek to the Tube station from Grace and Marcus's house, but the late-September weather is still warm enough for it not to be a chore. She knows the route well and moves on autopilot, cutting through the modern housing estate and into the walled park. It's quiet for a Sunday afternoon, and she breathes in the fresh pre-autumnal air.

She does still think about Josh, she can't help it. Whether he's still in Paris. If he ever goes to the places they visited together. It's not love that drives these thoughts anymore though. It's hatred and fear. He's still out there somewhere, and who knows when he might reappear? Because one day he will, Coco is certain of that.

She reaches the end of the park and pushes on the heavy iron gate. She listens for it to clang shut behind her, but there's only the rustle of someone catching it before it closes.

Acknowledgements

I wrote *Every Little Secret* in the run-up to my debut novel *A Mother Never Lies* being published. The mix of apprehension and excitement that both these endeavours caused meant that they are indelibly linked in my mind, and so my thankyou's spread across both.

I have been amazed by the support I've been given from fellow authors. Thank you, Sophie Flynn, Emma Murray, Clare Pooley, Victoria Dowd and Catherine Cooper, for your advice and inspiration. Thank you, Lauren Simpson, for your guidance and expertise. And a big thank you to my Faber Academy crew – Tilly, Malwa, Sarah and Olivia – for your amazing support. Thank you also to the wonderful array of social media groups that have welcomed me – I have learned so much (although TikTok is still a mystery …)

Thank you also to my family. To Adam for reading every review and Nicky, Max and Lily for letting him do this out loud. Both my mum and my husband have shouted about *A Mother Never Lies* much louder than I could, thank you so much. Thank you, Hannah – how lucky I am to have a sister-in-law like you – and

Sue, James, Milly and Max. And thank you to all my friends who have championed my debut, and to Jules for organising and hosting my first live book club.

And there are lots of thankyou's for *Every Little Secret* too. Firstly, a huge thankyou to everyone at HQ Digital, particularly Dushiyanthi Horti for your thoughtful and perceptive editing, and Cicely Aspinall for approaching my book with such enthusiasm and support.

For the medical aspects of the book, thank you, Dr Jayne Wood, for finding me a concussion expert and a big thankyou to Dr Mike Forsythe for your detailed and informative answers to my many questions (any inaccuracies are all mine). Thank you also Dr Amy Partridge for your help with Grace's childhood injury and Louise Simpson for your A&E insight. Thank you, Victoria Stuart, for helping with my New Zealand research (I'll come back one day!), Gwen Boles for being my go-to French expert and Dr Julia Yates for your psychology advice. And for the hours I spent virtually walking the streets in Thailand, I must also acknowledge Google Earth – you filled the twenty-five-year gap since I was there.

Thank you, Jo Anderson, for reading my first few chapters when I panicked, and to my dad for reading the manuscript so quickly when I needed a little reassurance. Thank you to my friends for listening to me angst over second book syndrome, and of course to my family. To Scarlett for managing to understand every garbled plot issue, and Finn for your invaluable advice on being a teenage boy. And thank you, Chris – our Friday morning dog walks on Wimbledon Common have made this book so much better.

Dear Reader,

Thank you for reading *Every Little Secret*. I hope you enjoyed unravelling all the secrets that Grace and her family were keeping.

I love creating characters that sit in the grey area between good and bad. Marcus had a temper, but do you think he was ultimately a good husband and father? Or was his behaviour unacceptable? And could you empathise with Grace struggling to choose who to believe, or should her default have been protecting Kaia even if she had doubts? And could you ever forgive Faith for protecting her son? Or did you see psychopathic characteristics in her too? I'd love to hear what you think!

You can reach me by email at sarah@sarahclarkeauthor.com or via social media. I am on Twitter as @SCWwriter, and on Facebook and Instagram as @sarahclarkewriter.

I was blown away by the amazing feedback I received for my debut novel *A Mother Never Lies*. If you enjoyed *Every Little Secret*, I would be hugely grateful if you could spare a few moments to review it too.

You can also follow my publisher @HQstories for lots of book news and great giveaways.

Happy reading,

Sarah

Don't miss *A Mother Never Lies*, another
unputdownable novel from Sarah Clarke.
Keep reading for an excerpt.

SARAH CLARKE

A MOTHER NEVER LIES

...unless the truth is her worst nightmare.

Prologue

She pushes hard against the wound. Her hands slip and slide in the blood as it seeps out across his chest. They start to shake uncontrollably. There's too much blood. But she can't let him die. She made a promise; the two of them against the world. She lets the tears flow but won't allow herself any more weakness. The panic needs to be kept at bay.

She has never done a first aid course or paid much attention to those public service adverts on TV. She doesn't really have a clue what to do. But her instinct tells her to stop the blood. To plug the hole. She rips off her jacket – ignoring her own injuries – and screws it into a ball. She pushes deeper into the wound. Does he flinch? She thinks so. That's a good sign, she decides. He's not dead yet.

Today was supposed to be special. How could it have ended up like this, a scene of such horror? But as she pushes and prays and whispers, 'C'mon, c'mon, c'mon,' over and over, the faint sound of an emergency siren reaches her. 'Thank you,' she gasps through the tears. Seconds count with a wound like this; that's something else her instinct tells her.

Dark green uniforms start running in her direction. Relief floods through her. Someone will save him. Not her, but someone.

She has to believe it.

Because how could she possibly survive without him?

Chapter 1

NOVEMBER 2019

Phoebe

He's asking if I'm okay. I want to answer him. He's got kind eyes. But I can't speak. I can only breathe. At least, I can only breathe in.

'Do you need a paper bag? Shall I get you a paper bag, love?'

My chest is huge now. It can't expand any more. What happens next? Will my lungs explode? Why the hell can't I just breathe out?

'Here you go. Do you want to take it? Can you do it yourself, love?'

Shit. I've dropped the bag. My hands are shaking. My fingers are numb.

'Ah, she's dropped it. Should I do it for her? Should we get someone? Jen, you do it. She won't want my fat thumbs all over her face.'

I can't breathe in now either. I might faint. I want to faint.

'Give it here then, you big oaf. Her lips are going blue. Hurry up!'

Paper crinkles around my lips. I know how this works. But I need to blow out first. Pollute the air with glorious carbon dioxide.

'Do it, Phoebe, do it!' my brain screams. Suddenly, my breath rushes out into the bag. I suck it back desperately. Again. I'm hooked now. In and out. In and out. My mind clears. I want to cry. God, I am crying.

'There, there. Nothin' to be embarrassed about. No one even noticed 'cept Dave and me. All them young 'uns rushing around, heads stuck in their phones. Would have left you for dead – wouldn't surprise me.'

Left me for dead. I sometimes wish things had turned out that way.

I've been back in London for two weeks now. The city has moved on over the last fourteen years, but I haven't been here to move with it. And now the smallest thing can knock me off track. I used to love the noise, the frenetic energy of too many people vying for the same space, but not anymore. Of course, I know this fear is not really about being away from the city; it's about what happened before I left.

This evening I thought I'd be okay. Completely exhausted after a day on my feet, I was impatient to get home. Eyes down, I ignored the jostling commuters, and the slouchy teenagers, and made it onto the platform without a problem. But then I saw them, huddled together in their dark coats, and they looked so similar that it took me right back to that night. And that's when Jen and Dave found me.

'This is our train now. You going to be all right? You keep the bag, it's fine. Dave has stuffed his sherbet lemons in his pocket now; they'll be gone in a flash anyway.' I nod at Jen, wiping away my tears and smiling widely to show her just how all right I am.

'You take care of yourself,' Dave adds, heaving himself onto the train. He looks a bit embarrassed now. I'm not sure whether that's down to him hesitating with the paper bag or Jen exposing his sugar habit, but I like him more for it either way.

'Thanks,' I say. 'Thanks for saving me.' I know I sound dramatic. But however many panic attacks I've had, they still make me think I might die – like faulty adrenaline levels really can override vital organs.

'It was nothing, love,' Dave mumbles, and then the doors close and his sloped shoulders gradually disappear inside the busy train.

Now I'm worried about Dave and Jen. I don't even know where they're heading, so it's hard to know when I can relax. When I can be certain they've arrived safely. I feel the panic start to bubble again in my stomach; new tears prick at my eyes. I need to stop feeling like this. I need to get off this platform.

I turn back towards the exit and focus on my breathing as the tide of commuter traffic carries me along. Down the stairs, back through the turnstiles – my new Oyster card registering my failed attempt with a disappointed beep – and out onto Old York Road. I half expect to see ambulances, police cars. Flashing lights and paramedics rushing past. But it's just a regular Wednesday evening. City workers filter out along the various residential streets, heads down, collars up against the November wind. A few don't make it further than the Anchor pub where the big screen is on, ready for some football game or other.

The fresh air calms my nerves but I'm tired. I would be home by now, if I could just have made it onto that train. Not really home, of course. But at the moment, it's the best I can do. Instead, I have nearly an hour's walk ahead of me. There was a time when I would have hailed a black cab without even thinking about the cost. Not anymore.

I know the underpass will get me there quicker, but its dark shadows and hidden threats put me off. So instead, I wait impatiently for three different green men to flash me across the multiple lanes of Wandsworth Bridge roundabout and on to York Road. Then I begin the long walk eastwards, the traffic droning past relentlessly. I watch a skinny cyclist with a flashing head-cam hurl abuse at a white van driver, who just gives him the finger and swaps lanes. And at one point I'm forced to step off the pavement by a homeless man curled up against a bus stop, causing some cyclist-type road rage myself. But I suck in the smell of Middle Eastern food drifting out from the grubby cafés and share a half smile with a young mum herding her kids and it feels good to be back. I've missed this.

When I get to the Volkswagen dealership, I can't help pausing, remembering a visit from a lifetime ago. How good it would be to waltz into that showroom now, actually buy a car, instead of yielding to some misplaced loyalty and leaving empty-handed like last time. Although I waddled more than waltzed back then. I need a car now more than ever, but I can't see my Universal Credit stretching that far. As I continue staring, I notice the salesman looking at me suspiciously through the giant glass panes. Clearly I don't look like a prospective customer anymore either. I drop my gaze to the pavement and keep walking.

Eventually I peel off York Road and head south into Battersea. I know plenty of people who don't like this area – its perfect skin of Edwardian townhouses hiding an underbelly of council-flat blocks – but I do. I'm sure it's partly the familiarity of growing up here. But more than that, I like that everyone – the wealthy and the struggling – walks down the same street, grabs last-minute shopping from the same corner shop. I've never managed to work out where I sit in the British class system, so it's a relief to be somewhere where everyone fits in.

It's not even seven o'clock when I arrive at my old childhood home, but the sky is black and I feel ready for bed. I dream of sinking into a hot bath and then crawling underneath my duvet, giving my aching body as much rest as possible before I go out again tomorrow. My father will be in his study by now, pretending to read an old script while chain-smoking his way through a packet of Marlboro Reds. I feel a momentary pang for a nicotine hit of my own, but I know I'd be crazy to start down that road again.

I assume my mother will be asleep, or more accurately comatose, after gradually working her way through her daily dose of
gin. Unfortunately, I'm proved wrong.

'Is that you, darling? Your father's in a foul mood so I'm in
search of a drinking partner. Come have a G&T with me?'

I stifle a sigh. 'Actually, I was going to run a bath ...'

'Can't do that, I'm afraid, darling. No hot water. Boiler's on
the blink again. Luckily the fridge is in full working order so the
tonic's lovely and cold. It's Sicilian lemon, darling. Divine.'

Her shrill voice and heroic attempt at enunciation can't hide
the fact that she's probably been drinking these divine gin and
tonics since lunchtime. But I can't refuse her. She's given me
somewhere to stay after all.

'Sounds great, Flora,' I reply. My parents have never been fond
of traditional titles, so it's been Flora and Paul for as long as I
can remember. They've never been fond of traditional parenting
either. There was a time when I couldn't wait to get away from
them; now I'm grateful for their charity.

As I make my way into the front room, I can't help noticing
the decay. This was a splendid house once, although it had already
started its downward spiral when we moved in forty years ago.
There is still evidence of its former glory, the beautiful ceiling roses
in both living spaces and the sturdy oak newel post guarding the
staircase. But now the neglect is more obvious. What's left of the
carpet is stained with red wine spills, and the windows are spotted
with fluffy green mould. Everything is covered in a layer of dust
and nothing seems to work properly. Except the fridge, of course.

'Any luck, darling? With the job hunting?' Flora asks, while
handing me the perfect gin and tonic, weirdly out of place in
this shabby setting.

I look closely at her face to see if I can spot any trace of suspicion. I've told her that I spend my days looking for work; she
wouldn't approve of my real purpose, so I've kept it to myself for
now. I'm relying on her not knowing that job hunting is mainly

331

carried out at home in front of a computer screen these days. 'Nothing today. Maybe tomorrow.'

'And ahh, did you cope okay?' At least she has the good grace to appear concerned. I know she doesn't understand really. She's had her fair share of trauma in life too, but she has always found solace in a bottle, letting the numbing effects of alcohol carry her pain away.

'Yes, all good. It was a sunny day so I decided to walk.' I hope she won't grill me further. Even in her drunken state I worry that she can see right through me. For all her hands-off parenting, she always had a way of knowing when I was keeping something from her.

But she just throws me a quizzical look and – miraculously – chooses discretion. 'Well, you don't need to rush things. And walking is wonderful exercise, of course. You'll be fifty before you know it, and you can't take that slim body of yours for granted forever.'

I look at her slight frame and silently question her logic, but I'm glad she's moved on.

'Perhaps you should take the day off from job hunting tomorrow, darling? Give those legs a rest. You've got your dole money after all. We could do something maybe? Just you and me?'

She's looking for forgiveness, I realise. For my childhood, perhaps. For not doing more to save me when she had the chance. I stare at her. She was a young mum, and beautiful too, but time doesn't stand still, and she's looking her sixty-eight years now. Age spots poke through her cheap cover-up and her once signature chestnut mane has reduced to a slender tangle of home-dyed strands. Her wide smile looks almost ghoulish, lips painted with an unsteady hand and teeth discoloured by years of neglect. But her eyes still sparkle, the depth of their blue undiminished.

'Thanks, Flora, but I should probably keep looking. I can't imagine it's going to be easy to find something and I want to pay my way.' I feel guilty about lying, but not enough to stop. I've been so patient, I can't wait any longer.

'Don't be silly, darling, we don't need more money. We're fine!'

I look around me. Everything is falling apart. The boiler needs replacing, and I'm not convinced the creaking central heating system is going to last the winter. Fine is not a word I would use, but for now, there's not much I can do to help.

At least they own the house without any mortgage to worry about. They bought it with the proceeds from Paul's sole film role when I was eight. We all had such high hopes back then. First Hollywood, then the world. But the film got slated by the critics, so it was soon back to scraping a living in regional theatres and the like. I remember it was around that time that Flora went on a health drive – doing Jane Fonda workouts in front of the TV, leaving bowls of cemented All-Bran everywhere – and I sometimes wondered whether she secretly enjoyed his failure, saw it as a chance to rekindle her own acting career after it was brought to a crashing halt by my unwelcome arrival. It didn't last long though – the contentment or the healthy living. And she never made it back onto the stage either.

'Maybe Saturday,' I suggest as a way of bringing the conversation to an end. But I realise I mean it too. Suddenly I feel a surge of love for this old woman with a twinkle in her eye. I need to forgive her. We've all made some bad choices, none more so than me.

And what am I back in London for, if not to find forgiveness?

Chapter 2

There's noise but it's muffled. Sneering. Crying. I'm trapped, weighted down. He walks towards me. He's smiling. He's coming for me. No, he's coming for Charlie ...

I jolt upright in bed, breathing heavily. I'm drenched in sweat and my body immediately starts to shiver. I throw my sodden T-shirt on the floor and reach for my hoodie, still there from the night before, after I finally managed to extract myself from Flora's company. I'll definitely need a shower this morning. I curse the broken boiler and the falling temperatures and my drunken parents, and how the hell I managed to let my lovely three-bed terrace on the other side of the borough slip away.

It's still pitch-black outside but I know I won't get back to sleep now. So I lie back against the lumpy pillow, close my eyes and allow myself to think about him. It's purgatory of course. But addictive purgatory.

Time has taken its toll and I can't remember Charlie as a living, moving human being anymore. I can't remember his smell or the feel of his touch against my skin. But I have preserved images of him, like a pack of camera stills. I see him in his highchair with mashed banana sticking to his rosy cheeks. I see him experimenting with sand and water, all mucky fingers and serious expression. I see him horizontal on the sofa with one thumb in his mouth and the other clutching his chewed cloth rabbit, spellbound by *Teletubbies* or *Peppa Pig*.

But suddenly I see him petrified. And I want to be sick all over again.

I get out of bed and head for the shower. I am almost glad for the freezing cold water now, hitting me like sharp needles. But as my body temperature drops, my mind calms. He's my son, whatever mistakes I've made. My flesh and blood. They say time heals, but not for me.

I start getting dressed, while mentally running through my plans for the day. I'll try Hollybrook Academy, I decide. I know it's not exactly a scientific approach – eyeballing every 17-year-old in the borough – but I have to do something. In a few months' time he'll turn 18, and I hope he will come looking for me. But I refuse to rely on that. I can't just sit by and leave it to fate.

Most importantly, I hope that he's still in Wandsworth. I learned a lot about adoption during those dark days. Not through my own research – I wasn't capable of concentrating on anything much back then – but through the solicitor that the family court assigned me. She was young and earnest and desperate to please. Looking back, I should have been more grateful, but I was too lost in my own grief for that.

However, she did explain – slowly, kindly – that the local authority always tries to help its own list of prospective adoptive parents first, so they would place Charlie locally if they could. Remembering his crinkly nose and solemn, innocent eyes, I can't believe any childless couple could turn down such an adorable 3-year-old, so he must have stayed in Wandsworth.

I have had letters from his adoptive parents, twice a year, ever since it became official – always exactly six months apart, as fixed by the Family Court. Knowing that I would keep that connection with Charlie was the only thing that got me through the adoption process. Of course, I didn't realise then how distancing the letters would be. How unrevealing a page of writing about a boy doing well at school, having friends, enjoying sport could be. All I've really got are the memories.

Discounting the all-girl schools, there are eleven secondary schools in Wandsworth that Charlie could be a student at, and I've been to five so far. He'll be in upper sixth, or Year 13 as they call it nowadays, and I've come to realise what a relief that is. It's almost impossible to distinguish one teenager from another when they're all wearing the same uniform and moving around in packs, but sixth formers wear their own clothes, which makes things easier. There are moments when I question whether I'd recognise him after all this time, but it doesn't take long to silence those doubts.

For the last couple of days I've stood outside Rushton School in Putney with no luck. But today could be different. I have to believe that.

I'm working out which of my jumpers is the thickest – the cold shower has left me desperate for warmth – when I hear a knock on the front door. There's a frustration to their rap, which I realise is probably the result of them trying the broken doorbell first, so I towel-dry my mess of curls into a half-civilised style and race down the stairs. There's no way either of my parents will be raising themselves this early in the morning.

I open the door to a middle-aged woman in ill-fitting jeans and an anorak, standing on my parents' broken paving slabs.

'Can I help you?' I ask.

'Hello, Phoebe.'

Her directness knocks me off guard and I take an involuntary step backwards, which unfortunately she treats as an invite. Before I can do anything to stop her, she pushes open the door and steps inside.

'I wonder if we can have a chat?'

The patronising tone, the tilt of her head; I can almost smell social work on her. I want to refuse, to just slam the door in her face and pretend this never happened. But I know that kind of behaviour will bring its own repercussions, so I surrender to the inevitable and stand aside.

For a woman who wears no make-up and keeps her mousy hair sensibly short, she has a surprising air of authority, and I feel more like the visitor than the host as she walks purposefully down the hallway.

'In here?' she asks, inclining her head towards the living room.

I nod and watch as she scans the room before choosing to perch on the edge of Paul's prized leather Chesterfield, which is cracked and dulled now of course.

'We never met back in 2005,' she starts. 'I know that Taisha was your social worker through it all.'

My heart starts thudding faster as she pauses; I know what she's about to say.

'I'm Clare Morris. I was Charlie's social worker.'

The woman who took my son away. A massive shot of adrenaline surges through me, and I struggle not to act on it. My hands ball into tight fists and my breathing gets shallower. Shit. I can't do this. I think about why I'm back, how I will find him, and it gives me the strength to find my voice. 'What are you doing here?'

'I heard that you were back.'

'From who?'

She ignores my question. 'I thought it would be a good idea to drop by, see how you're settling in, now you're living locally again.'

'From who?' I repeat. My tone is more assertive now and it works because, after a moment of indecision, her shoulders droop a little. She leans forward, resting her elbows on her knees.

'I was chatting to your mum; she mentioned that you'd moved in.'

'Flora?' I ask, surprise knocking me off guard.

'We've kept in touch over the years.' She says it as though it's obvious they would be friends. Perhaps it is. In many ways they were on the same side back then. 'I give her a ring every now and again; she didn't have the professional support that you got, remember.'

I stare at the social worker expectantly; I still don't know why she's come.

'She says you spend every day out of the house.'

'I've been job hunting,' I whisper.

'Yes, she said that too.' Her words hang heavy with disbelief. She's clearly less naive than Flora; less drunk too, of course. 'Look, I just want to make sure …' she pauses for a moment and I enjoy her discomfort as she struggles for the right words '… that you're not being distracted by the past.'

I shift my weight from one foot to the other. 'So this is a threat, is it?' I ask. 'Forget about Charlie, or else?'

'It's not like that.' She speeds up her words as though suddenly desperate to get it over with. 'Look, I'm not here to run you out of town or dredge up the past. I know that you've suffered. But my responsibility isn't to you.'

'He'll be 18 soon,' I throw back. 'He won't be your responsibility then.' I don't add that I'm counting the days until his birthday, spending every minute wondering if he'll come looking for me. Dreaming about that knock on the door.

'Officially, Charlie hasn't been my responsibility since 2007. His care was signed over when he was adopted. But that doesn't mean I stopped thinking about him. He was a lovely kid, *is* a lovely kid,' she corrects herself. 'And I don't want to see him hurt again.'

'And you think I'll hurt him?' I'm spitting my words out now.

'I know how much you loved him, and I'm sure you still do. But the Charlie you remember doesn't exist anymore. He's got a new name and a new family.' She pauses again, and I realise I'm holding my breath. 'Phoebe, he doesn't know anything about you.'

Her words burn into me, scalding my eyes. They also don't make sense. 'But I wrote to him twice a year,' I remind her. 'Via the council. They *encouraged* it, for his Life Story project.'

'Look, Charlie was very quiet when he was first adopted, withdrawn. He was clearly very traumatised—'

'And?' I interrupt, even though I don't want to hear the rest.

'Normally we suggest adopted children should know about their past, keep that connection to their birth parents, but Charlie's wasn't a normal case. His adoptive parents decided it would be best to make a clean break. Give him a completely fresh start.'

'My letters?' I repeat, like a broken toy. 'And the photos I gave Taisha?' I can sense her trying to make eye contact with me, so I turn to face the window.

Eventually she sighs. 'Phoebe, you know that his parents aren't legally obliged to give Charlie those items until he's 18.'

Perhaps I do know that. It registers somewhere in the back of my mind. But that's not what I've been dreaming about all these years. I've imagined Charlie waiting by the front door, eagerly ripping open the envelope, devouring my words. Not my letters being shoved to the back of some unused drawer by his new parents. Maybe they didn't even keep them. Now I see them ripped in half, thrown into the bin alongside cracked eggshells and soggy teabags. I shake that thought away. It's their legal duty to keep them until he's an adult; I only have another three months to wait.

'Do you have children?' I ask, sensing the answer will be no.

'I work with children every day. And I've been trained to always put their needs first. As a social worker, the paramountcy principle rules everything. But isn't that also the job of parents? To put the needs of their child before their own?'

'To you, needs are surface-deep.' My voice rises in anger. 'A warm bed, clean clothes, GCSEs and family camping trips. But needs run deeper than that. My own mother has let me down countless times – is still letting me down,' I add pointedly. 'But we have a bond. You can't play God just because a parent doesn't fit your idea of what makes the perfect family.'

I watch Clare dip her head towards the floor, before raising her eyes up, shining with a new resolve. 'You were angry back then, broken; I know that. You'd lost someone very special. But just think about how much Charlie suffered. Doesn't he deserve some distance from that?'

My eyes smart with tears; acid forms in my mouth. How dare she say these things? I'm his mother. But I can't speak, I can't even move. The silence hangs between us for a moment before she continues.

'Leave him alone, Phoebe. You lost your maternal rights to him a long time ago.' She stands up but doesn't move any further; she's not finished. 'And don't forget, it's against the law to approach him. He may be turning 18 soon, but his right to anonymity from you is permanent.'

I watch her zip up her anorak, hover over me. Hairs prickle on my neck.

'And, Phoebe, you need to prepare yourself for him never coming to look for you.'

I want to shout and scream at her, to slap that patronising expression off her face. 'Why are you so sure?'

'I've spoken to his adoptive parents. Phoebe, he has absolutely no memory of you.' And with that, she disappears into the hallway, and out of my parents' front door with a thud and a clatter.

*

I sit perfectly still and process her parting words. I think about my memories of Charlie. How I've nurtured and preserved them over the years. The effort it has taken to carry him with me. Perhaps it is too much to ask for him to have done the same. He hadn't even turned four when I was forced to give him up.

The Life Story project had been my glimmer of hope. I remember that earnest young woman explaining it to me, how Charlie would be given some mementos – like family photos – to remember Dan and me by. How I could write to him twice a year. I didn't mention Dan's death in my letters, or everything that came after. Those details I wanted to explain softly, gently, in person. But I told him how much better I was feeling, and how much I hoped that we'd see each other again one day. I never thought he might not read them. Or that his adoptive parents would make sure I was wiped from his memory.

Suddenly desperate for fresh air, I grab my jacket off the broken peg in the hallway and head outside, into the park opposite my parents' house. Park is an exaggeration, more a postage stamp of green space plus two swings, a slide and a rusty roundabout. But it has a kind of urban peace about it that I like. I sink onto the metal bench, its unforgiving bars digging into my back.

I replay the social worker's words. *Doesn't he deserve some distance from that?* A speck of doubt starts to worm its way into my thoughts. Could she be right? Is our relationship beyond repair? But I shake the feeling away. No, I've waited so long for this chance; I'm his mother, and I'm not walking away now. And if his adoptive parents have kept me from him, severed our bond, then it's even more important that I find him. I take a deep breath and stand up. I'm fed up of being controlled by other people. It's my turn now.

After nothing but gin, tonic and a grab bag of McCoy's crinkle cut crisps for dinner, I realise I'm starving. I should go back to the house, make myself something nutritious, but I can't face going back inside. My mission feels more urgent now. So instead, I stop at the first café on my route and order a fried egg bap and takeaway tea. At the last minute I ask her to add bacon, and the taste of that sizzling fat is worth every extra penny.

It takes me an hour to reach Hollybrook Academy, a small school on the edge of Wandsworth Common. Everything is quiet when I arrive, so I find a wall to lean against and try to blend into the background. I feel a quiver of excitement in my belly. Like I've found Charlie's school. Like today is going to be when

341

I see my son for the first time in fourteen years. I check myself. This is exactly how I felt yesterday morning and look how that day turned out.

The waiting gives me time to think about what Charlie might look like now. The last time I saw him his hair was a deep brown colour, the same shade as my own before the speckles of grey appeared. He has my eyes too – mid-blue with indigo flecks. But he's Dan from the nose down. Slight hook, with a solid square jawline. Handsome. Height-wise, I imagine him to be about six foot. He was three foot exactly when I measured him at 2 years old, and I remember the old wives' tale about your full height being double that. And with parents the shape of Dan and me, he's unlikely to be picked for the rugby forward pack any time soon.

Suddenly the bell goes and a few seconds later the noise hits me. A few hundred children emerge from a maze of different doorways, chatting and barging their way into the playground, seemingly undaunted by the wall of blazers obstructing their path. It must be break time. Somehow the sea of blue uniform shifts and settles. Some younger students start kicking a football in one corner; others cluster around illicit phones.

That's when I notice a group of taller, lankier boys materialising from a separate building. This is good. They're definitely sixth formers and they're loping so slowly I can easily make out their faces. I look at each boy, searching for some familiar features. Nothing jumps out. Is it the wrong school? The wrong crowd? Or is there a chance I don't recognise him anymore?

'Can I help you?' a voice asks, local accent.

'No thanks,' I respond without turning around. The boys will be back inside soon and I can't miss this opportunity.

'A parent?' it continues, still friendly, but with a slight edge this time. I realise I need to tread carefully.

'Prospective parent.' I turn to face the man in uniform and force a smile.

'That so?' The security guard doesn't believe me. Perhaps I look too old.

'Sixth form,' I respond, in a higher pitch than I planned. 'My son is at Rushton School at the moment. I'm thinking of moving him.'

'Right, well Hollybrook is a great school. Takes security very seriously too,' he adds with meaning. 'See that sign over there?' He points at a large banner attached to the school fence, advertising a sixth form open evening in a couple of weeks' time. 'Why don't you come back then?'

I pause for a moment. I so want to stay, but I know he's moving me on. 'Great. I'll do that,' I answer through gritted teeth and slowly turn away. I can't risk being on some school watchlist, so I know I have to play along. I walk away from the school and deeper into Wandsworth Common, sensing his eyes following me until I reach the cover of the trees.

Dear Reader,

We hope you enjoyed reading this book. If you did, we'd be so appreciative if you left a review. It really helps us and the author to bring more books like this to you.

Here at HQ Digital we are dedicated to publishing fiction that will keep you turning the pages into the early hours. Don't want to miss a thing? To find out more about our books, promotions, discover exclusive content and enter competitions you can keep in touch in the following ways:

JOIN OUR COMMUNITY:

Sign up to our new email newsletter:
http://smarturl.it/SignUpHQ

Read our new blog www.hqstories.co.uk

🐦 https://twitter.com/HQStories

f www.facebook.com/HQStories

BUDDING WRITER?

We're also looking for authors to join the HQ Digital family!
Find out more here:

https://www.hqstories.co.uk/want-to-write-for-us/

Thanks for reading, from the HQ Digital team

If you enjoyed *Every Little Secret*, then why not try another gripping thriller from HQ Digital?

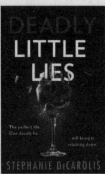

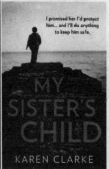

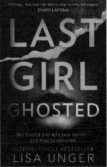